What We Thought We Knew

About the Author

Claire Dyer is the author of five novels and one novella and her fourth collection of poetry with Two Rivers Press is due for publication in 2024. She co-curates Reading's Poets' Café Online, teaches creative writing and runs Fresh Eyes, an editorial and critiquing service. She has an MA in creative writing from Royal Holloway University of London and is a regular contributor on BBC Radio Berkshire. Her website is www.clairedyer.com.

Claire Dyer

What We Thought We Knew

Vanguard Press

A CIP catalogue record for this title is
available from the British Library.

ISBN 978 1 80016 779 7

Vanguard Press is an imprint of
Pegasus Elliot Mackenzie Publishers Ltd.
www.pegasuspublishers.com

First Published in 2024

Vanguard Press
Sheraton House Castle Park
Cambridge England

Printed & Bound in Great Britain

By the Same Author

Fiction:
The Moment
The Perfect Affair
Falling for Gatsby
The Last Day
The Significant Others of Odie May

Poetry:
Eleven Rooms
Interference Effects
Yield
The Adjustments

Acknowledgements

This book began life ten years ago and has therefore had a long gestation, finally finding its current form during the difficult days of lockdown and my parents' last illnesses.

As a memento of this time, the book and I are very grateful to Pegasus Elliot Mackenzie Publishers for giving us the chance to have a place in the world. And thanks must go, once again, to my brilliant agent, Boo Doherty of DHH Literary Agency, for her unswerving belief and forensic editorial eye.

Additionally, I would like to thank my writing, poetry and other friends, especially Sam Smith, and my family, without whom I would be utterly rudderless.

So little do we people who spend our days together know each other!
- Charlotte Mew, 1869-1928

I can look and look my fill inside – never catch you
blinking. I can never have enough of you.
Now I have you in the palm of my hand,
the warm and the cold you.
Or here on the desk where you hold my life in place,
stop all my surfaces from sliding loose,
keep the best bits of me from blowing away.
Robert Seatter, *Paperweight*

Prologue

"How could you?"

We're standing facing one another on the path. The rain is falling in rods around us, and the wind is howling.

Just three small words, that's all she's said and yet they contain a lifetime of betrayal and regret.

I'd followed her out of the house when she'd run from the room and, as I reached the front door and stepped out into the storm, I called her name.

She turned then, eyes wide, her mouth open like an O and that's when she'd said it. "How could you?"

And I have no answer, not here, not now.

I thought I was prepared for this. I'd feared it for years, feared that I would let it happen, and now it's here, I don't know what to say.

And there's more. There's the other secret, the one only my mother knows. Another betrayal, more regret. How could I have done that too?

She's still looking at me, hair plastered to her head, and then she starts walking backwards, away from me.

Say something, I tell myself. *Do something.*

At the end of the path, she turns to face her own house, one of the three, numbers two, four and six, in this quiet cul-de-sac off the spur road of Penwood Heights.

Three marriages, three families, bound irrevocably by the present and the past.

The moment is slipping away. *Say something*, I tell myself again.

And that's when I call out to her. "Hey," I say, lifting my voice above the noise of the weather. "What would you have done had it been the other way around? Would you have told me?"

She shrugs and I can't tell from this distance and in this darkness whether they're tears or it's rain on her face, and then she's gone, running again, this time up the path to her front door which opens and closes behind her – an oblong of yellow light – and there's nothing more for me to do than go back into my own house and face the wreckage of the friendships and marriages that awaits me there.

Part 1 – Before

The sun was bouncing off the concrete path as I rang the bell at number four.

"Hi there, all ready to go?" I asked.

"Hello Faith," Ben said from the shadow of their hallway. "We're almost ready. Sara and Anthony around yet?"

He seemed a little out of sorts. *Never mind,* I thought. *The picnic will soon put that right.*

I cocked my head to one side, listening. "Sounds like them now," I said, as I heard the doors of Anthony's Mercedes close on the drive of number six.

I waved to Sara and said, "Right then, looks like we're almost off." And I skipped back to our car, basking in the familiarity of it all – days like these helped to paper over the cracks I felt in my life, diffuse the bomb I held in my hands. I climbed in and rested my palm on Harvey's knee, but his skin was too hot, and I took it back off again, looking over my shoulder at the boys. They were both reading their comics and Ashley had obviously put his hand through his hair as a tuft of it remained standing. I tried to reach out to flatten it.

"What you doing?" he said, scowling.

"Just trying to straighten out your hair, my boy," I said, laughing. "Looks like you're trying to communicate with the mother ship."

"Maybe I am," he said and jerked his head away from me, pulling the comic up in front of his face.

I didn't dare look at Harvey; I knew what he would be thinking. Yes, I fussed over them too much; I worried about them too much.

"You OK?" I asked my elder son.

"Mmm," he replied. "Suppose so."

Blake was almost eight, almost always angry, and I had no idea how to treat him either. He'd made it clear he didn't want to be nagged, his usual refrain being, 'Just leave me alone', and then after a pause, he'd add, 'please Mum'.

Harvey started the engine as Ben reversed his Honda out of his and Lizzie's drive and the three cars drove off in convoy, Harvey tapping the steering wheel to some imagined soundtrack. I wished he'd stop doing so and I rested my head on my hand and looked out the window at the hot countryside streaming by.

"Glad I packed the sunscreen," I said as Harvey parked up in our usual layby. The road was strangely quiet for a Saturday; it was as though the heat was keeping everyone at home.

"Yeh," he replied, looking over his shoulder at the children. "Bet the guys are going to love that!"

As he stepped out of the car, I noticed a small patch of sweat had darkened the shirt on his back. It reminded me of the day we met but, for some reason, I didn't like it so much now.

"Do we really have to go?" Ben had asked earlier, leaning on the breakfast bar. It was ten o'clock on Saturday morning and he had a hundred better things to do than to spend the day sitting on a prickly blanket in this heat while the kids rampaged through the countryside, and the women spoke of inconsequential things. Harvey and Anthony would, he knew, be dreading it as much as he, and he especially didn't want to see Sara, not today, not with everyone else around. He couldn't put his finger on it, but some days were just more difficult than others, that was all.

He'd had a crap week at work, his figures for the new build on the A4 at Hungerford had been blocked at every turn by client and contractor alike; he'd never felt so unnecessary and so powerless and Nigel, his stupid fucking boss wasn't helping matters either, just saying, "Oh, it'll work out in the end, I'm sure of it. Just remember who's the client Ben, that's all, just remember that." As if Ben could forget!

All he wanted was to spend the day by himself, pottering around the house and garden, activities he could lose himself in, so he didn't have time in which to think about all the other stuff.

"Of course, we have to go," Lizzie said, nipping the stalk out of another strawberry and putting the strawberry in the Tupperware box next to her elbow. "It's our turn to take the dessert. You know that. I told you earlier in the week and anyway, everyone will be there. They'll be ready in about five minutes. It's too late to change our plans now. We have to go."

Ben ran his fingers through his hair and sighed. There were times these days when he wondered whether the choices, he'd made had been the right ones. Life with Lizzie was…

However, he didn't have time to think about what life with Lizzie was because, at that moment, Clemmie burst into the room.

"Daddy," she said, beaming up at him. "Can I take my bicycle to the picnic, please Daddy, please? Mummy said I had to ask you."

Ben looked appealingly at Lizzie's back, but she stayed resolutely turned away from him, busying herself with the stupid fucking strawberries, leaving him to be the one to disappoint their daughter yet again.

"Look, sorry love," he said. "I just don't think we'll have room, what with the picnic stuff and the cool box. The boot's not really big enough and anyway, we're going down by the river and there's really nowhere there where you can ride your bike, the ground's too bumpy."

Ben knew he was fibbing. There would be room in the car, especially if he could be bothered to put the bike rack on the back of it but, to tell the truth, he couldn't. He wanted today over with; it was too hot, and this was the gazillionth picnic they'd had this summer – he was bored with them, bored with the others. He wanted…

Again, he didn't have the opportunity to formulate the thoughts of what he really wanted because, in front of him, his daughter's face was like thunder.

"It's not fair," she whined. "I don't like playing with the boys. They never let me win anything. I want to take my bike."

"Lizzie," Ben said to his wife's back. "Help me out here."

Lizzie turned round; her shoulders tense, worry lines etched on her face. "I think Daddy's right, Clemmie love," she said. "It's just not a good idea to take your bike today. How about Daddy takes you for a ride in the park when we get home?"

Oh great, thanks Lizzie, Ben thought. *That's really great. A long day in the sun, being bored out of my mind and then I have to make the effort to go to the park later when all I'll want to do is have a beer and watch TV.*

But he couldn't say this, could he? So instead, he said, "Yes, now there's an idea, let's do that shall we, Clemmie?"

Clemmie's bottom lip was still quivering but she looked up at him with large liquid eyes and said, "OK then, Daddy. If you promise."

"I promise," he said.

Before they left, Douggie had asked Sara, "Can I finish my Lego castle?" He'd picked up a large red piece and slotted it into place on what he'd told her earlier was a turret.

"Yes, if you're quick. We don't want to keep the others waiting," Sara said, walking across his bedroom to the wardrobe and getting out a pair of shorts.

"Won't it be fun to run in the fields with Blake, Ashley and Clemmie?" she asked. "But you have to promise that you won't go too far and always be able to see Mummy and Daddy, OK?" Douggie didn't answer, he was too busy playing so, holding up the shorts, she said, "Hey, why don't you wear these instead of your trousers?"

At that moment Anthony popped his head round the door and said, "How are you two getting on?"

Sara looked up at him and smiled. "Just coming, aren't we, Douggie? He's just finishing the turret and changing into some shorts and then we'll be ready."

"Well, the car's all packed," Anthony said lightly, looking at Sara just a fraction too long so that she started to feel uneasy. *Could he see what she was really thinking,* she wondered? *Would he ever guess?*

Sometimes she wished he would and that this could all be over, but at other times the need to preserve what she had was so intense that it almost burned her. After all, she'd made herself a promise, hadn't she?

Douggie was still squatting on the floor in amongst the Lego, but somehow, he'd managed to change into his shorts, leaving the trousers crumpled on the floor.

"Don't worry," Sara said. "We can put them away when we get home. There'll be plenty of time before bedtime to tidy up."

She laughed and picked up her son; he smelled so good, a mixture of Corn Flakes and toothpaste and the faintest trace of left-over sleep. Last night she'd sat with him for ages, just watching him breathing, seeing his small arms and legs twitch to the rhythm of his dreams; she'd watched him until Anthony came padding along the landing and tapped her on the arm and asked, "You coming to bed soon?" Then she'd followed him back to their bedroom and got into her side of the bed. It had been cold, and Anthony had kissed her fondly, turned away and said, "Goodnight" so quietly she almost hadn't heard it and she'd lain awake for a long time staring into the dark.

"Come on, soldier," she said, picking up and carrying Douggie across the room. "Let's go. Daddy'll be waiting."

She didn't look back as she closed the door. Instead, she rested her cheek against Douggie's head, felt the warmth of him, felt how right everything was, just now, just like this.

"We're coming," she called from the top of the stairs and, putting Douggie down, let him scamper down the stairs to where Anthony was waiting in the hallway looking up at them both and smiling.

Clemmie was still scowling when Lizzie got out of the car, and they started walking through the trees to the fields and the river. This was a quiet spot and they all loved it, no crowds, no visitors' centre or signposted paths. Just a public right of way through the woods, which no one else seemed to have thought of visiting today.

The men were carrying the hampers and Lizzie had hold of Clemmie with one hand and had a rug tucked under her other arm. She was thinking about last night again.

They had a bottle of wine with dinner, and she'd felt nicely woozy as she slipped into her nightgown and into bed. Ben was still in the main bathroom and, listening carefully, she thought she could hear him shaving; he said the light was better in there.

"That's a good sign," she told herself. She heard him flush the chain, turn out the bathroom light and then pause as he reached Clemmie's door. She knew he'd look in and he did. The door creaked ever so slightly and, in the silence, she could imagine her husband's eyes growing accustomed to the dark, picking out the faint outline of his daughter under her Barbie duvet cover and she knew that there was some part of him that was wondering how he would ever live up to being her father.

He'd said it to her often enough. She sometimes thought he thought too deeply about these things, but then, as she turned off her bedside light, she was a fine one to talk. There was, she knew, still a gap between her instinctive theoretical love for her daughter and the everyday love she ought to have, and which she found it very difficult to feel, for her contrary and sometimes very unlovable child.

"She's sound asleep," Ben said as he came into the room.

He was wearing pyjama trousers; his chest was bare, and his skin shone in the low light from the landing. She loved the way he walked, how the trousers rested gently on his hips.

"Good," she said, turning onto her side to watch him get into bed. Between her legs was singing, she wanted him to touch her there. It had been so long. She moistened her lips and rested her head on his chest as he lay with his hands behind his head staring at the ceiling.

"Ben?" she asked. "You tired?"

"Yes, I am a bit," he said. "It's been a long week. Best get some shut eye ourselves, I guess."

"Oh, OK then," she said in an even voice as he turned away from her but inside, disappointment was coiling like a spring. Why wouldn't he make love to her? What had she done wrong?

The back of Ben's head was facing her, and she watched it, the way his dark hair curled, and she willed for his skull to open up so that she could crawl inside and understand why he was so unhappy and what she could do to help.

"Mummy?" she heard Clemmie say now.

"Yes," she replied, shaken from her thoughts and, looking down, saw that she still had hold of her daughter's hand.

"You're hurting me."

"Sorry, angel. Look we're nearly there. The others are putting out the blankets and setting up camp. Are you and the boys going to have an explore before lunch?"

Clemmie didn't answer.

"Well, if you do, make sure you stay with Blake and don't go out of sight of the grown-ups. Make sure you can always see us. OK? Clemmie? Promise me."

"I promise," she said and slid her hot hand out of Lizzie's and ran off to join Blake and Ashley who were standing just to the side of the picnic area. Both of them were kicking up dust with their shoes.

"Come *on*!" Blake cried, running ahead.

"Wait up," his brother bleated, panting; the long grasses scratching at his legs.

Summer again, another picnic, the grown-ups busy laying out blankets and emptying hampers.

"Go and play, you lot," Anthony had said.

"Let's play war," Blake said. "I'll be the general. Ash and Douggie, you two can be my soldiers. Clem'll have to be a nurse. Girls can't be soldiers."

"They can too," Clemmie said, glowering at Blake. "I'm going to be a gunner; look it's pointing at you!" She held up a stick and thrust it at Blake. "There, see. I *can* be a soldier."

Her face was dark and broody, and her hair stuck to her forehead with sweat. It was already really hot although it wasn't even lunchtime yet. They would have hours to kill before the grown-ups had had enough, she reckoned. God, how she hated these picnics. How she hated all these boys.

Blake ran on, and the others followed; like they always did.

The sun was at the midpoint of the sky by the time the children reached the field.

Blake, being tallest could, if he stood on tiptoes, just see over to where the adults were sitting on the blanket near the cars. He could also just about hear their voices, his dad's mostly. There was quite a bit of laughter. The heat was buzzing around his head.

"Come *on*!" he shouted again to the others. "I don't want to play war anymore; I want to play races. We can pretend we're Olympic runners. Eh? Bet I can beat you to the river. Come on, Douggie, Clem, Ash. Let's run. Come on!"

The others didn't want to race because Blake always won, and it wasn't fair, so they didn't answer him straight away. Instead, a lone blackbird shouted from a treetop nearby and faraway, in amongst the high skeins of the heat-hazed clouds, a red kite cried as it threaded the air searching for carrion.

The air was soupy with heat. Flies buzzed lazily, hovering just above the surface of the water and the horses in the next field hung their heads low.

Next to the stream, the long grasses were still, dust suspended in between their blades and the children stood with their hands on their knees, panting. The stream itself was not much more than a trickle between two banks about three feet high. On each bank, the earth was dry and crumbly. The sun made diamonds in what water there was. These diamonds danced in front of the children's eyes.

"Told you I could beat you," Blake said in between gasps.

"You're older so it's not really fair," his brother retorted, swiping angrily at the sweat running down his face. "We should have had a head start, shouldn't we Clemmie? Douggie?"

The other two lifted their heads and Clemmie scowled at Blake, "Yeh," she said. "It's not fair."

"OK then," Blake said straightening up and dusting down his shorts. "Let's see if you can jump from one side of the stream to the other. I'll go up a bit where it's wider so that it's fair." His voice was snidey and unkind. "You three do it here where it's narrower. OK?"

Blake walked backwards away from the bank; then he ran, leaping across the gap, his left foot trailing down, but he scrambled up, grabbing onto the grass on the other side and stood triumphant, looking back at them, the sun glinting in his eyes and making him look much older and wiser than he really was.

"Come on you two," Ashley said, staring across at his brother with dislike. "He's not going to shut up until we try. Douggie, you go first?"

Douggie nodded and then, copying Blake, walked backwards from the bank and ran. But, reaching the edge his foot slipped on the dry earth and, as he flew, his legs windmilled through the air. It took a second, but it seemed to last forever.

There was a cry and a splash which echoed through the field. Blake, Ashley and Clemmie stood mesmerized as Douggie plummeted down, his head cracking on a stone. Blood trickled into the water in ribbons as he lay motionless, face down in the inch or two of water, his right arm extended at an obscene angle and his deep brown eyes staring unseeing into the stream.

"Go and get help," Blake cried from the far bank. "Go on you two. Run!"

Harvey closed his eyes. He could hear the children in the field. They'd been told to stay within shouting distance and to keep away from the water even though, in this heat, the stream would have dried to nothing more than a shallow trickle.

Blake will look after the others, he said to himself as he let the sun seep into his skin.

There was no one else about, just the six of them; he preferred it this way.

Around him the women were chatting; they'd already made quite a dent in the wine before lunch and were putting the world to rights again. He heard loose strains of their conversations:

"Well, then she said he'd come back with his washing and asked her if she'd do it and then he left again to go back to *her*; I can't believe that, can you?"

"I would have told him where to go, that's for sure!"

"Stupid woman, but I suppose I feel sorry for her. He's just such a complete bastard."

The talk ebbed and flowed, sometimes he could hear Faith, and other times it was Sara or Lizzie, the voices becoming interchangeable after a while.

Anthony was reading the sports section of the paper propped up against a tree trunk and Ben had his headphones on listening to music. It was, Harvey thought, a perfect moment; the six of them, their children, like one unit, seamless.

He shifted, trying to get more comfortable; the ground under the blanket was knobbly and drought-hard but perhaps, he thought, here he could forget what his father had told him during the week; perhaps it wasn't really true, and he wouldn't have to tell Faith and the boys that his mother was going to die, soon and quickly by the sound of it. How the fuck was he going to cope with that? She was his mother; she was supposed to be invincible.

He screwed up his eyes even tighter and breathed out long and low. It had to be a mistake surely. He heard the buzz of Ben's music and the rustle of Anthony's paper as he turned the pages and he willed himself back to sleep and, overhead, a lone blackbird shouted from a treetop nearby and far-away, up high, the thin cry of a red kite.

The kids will run back soon, hot and hungry, he thought.

By the time Anthony got to the article he'd wanted to read on the latest transfer news, he had started to feel uneasy. There was nothing he could put his finger on, just a pulse in the air around him. An eddy of hot wind tugged at the paper in his hands, and he looked up, gazing over the long grass of the field in the direction he'd last heard the children's voices. He listened but couldn't hear them, perhaps they were playing hide and seek he thought and, reluctantly, trained his eyes back on the newsprint. He'd go and check on them in a minute when he'd read this bit.

The others were all dozing in the high heat; they should have lunch soon. He turned the page, and it was then that it happened.

Ashley and Clemmie burst out of the long grass, and he knew, he knew something awful had happened. It was their faces, the pinched, hurt looks in their eyes, the way they looked at one another not knowing what to say.

"What is it?" he barked. "What's wrong?"

At the sound of his voice, the others started to rouse themselves, all except Ben who still had his headphones on.

Ashley swallowed. His t-shirt was torn, and his shorts were dirty. He must have lost a shoe in the frantic run across the field.

"An accident," Ashley said, the words tripping unwillingly out of his mouth. "You have to come. Blake says you have to come *now*."

"Who is it?" Anthony asked, grabbing hold of Ashley by the shoulders, but already he knew it was Douggie and that it was something irreparable.

"Hey," Faith shouted. Her voice sounded muffled, but still, it forced Anthony to let go of Ashley.

The other four scrambled to their feet and stood, chilled now despite the heat, in a too-still circle. Movement would mean reality; they all knew that, and they all knew that they should be running by now, Anthony most of all.

He thumped Ben on the leg. Ben sat up, snatching his headphones off. "What?" he stammered. "What is it?"

Anthony knelt down in front of the children, trying to steady his breathing and spoke quietly so, he hoped, he wouldn't scare them further. "Do we need an ambulance?" he asked.

Both children nodded. *How could they know?* he thought. They're only babies. Oh my God, they're only babies, all of them. We should never have let them go off on their own. They were fine before, each time we came here, they were fine. Why now, why this, why now?

"Ben? Call an ambulance. Do it. Do it now!"

As Ben did this, the rest of them ran; all of them. And, as they ran, Anthony's head was filled with the thought that the kids should have stayed behind. Someone should have stayed with them to look after them, to shield them from whatever it was that they were running towards.

They slowed as they got near the riverbank and Anthony reached out for Sara's hand. He could see the top of Blake's head as he crouched next to something.

Blake looked up at them, his eyes were huge. "I got him out," he said. "I got him out."

Then Anthony saw his boy, lying crooked on the parched riverbank, his arm flung out to one side, his eyes open and staring.

"Oh my God." He tried to modulate his voice, but he guessed he must be shouting. Beside him, he could hear Sara sobbing.

No one told Blake he should not have moved Douggie's body. No one had the heart to.

The sky was full of the sound of the sirens and there was running and paramedics and police everywhere. They seemed to be asked a hundred questions that none of them could answer.

Harvey and Faith gathered their boys to them and both boys turned, pressing their faces into their parents' bodies.

Lizzie picked up Clemmie who sobbed against her mother's shoulder, her small body shaking, her small feet twitching.

"Why won't he wake up, Mummy?" she asked. "Why won't Douggie wake up?"

Anthony held onto the stretcher as it was lifted into the ambulance, afraid to touch any part of his son's body for fear he would hurt him and, as she climbed in after him, Sara looked back at Ben who was standing to the side, his arms hanging down, his face white and stricken.

Among the tiny fragments left of her, there was one thing which stayed intact. Sara wanted Ben to understand, to know the truth now, at this moment, right now, but all he was thinking was how would he keep his promise to Clemmie now. How could he take her to the park now?

Anthony threw up on the morning of the funeral. He'd risked eating a small bowl of cereal and immediately wished he'd hadn't. The bile rose up in his throat as he opened the dishwasher door and he'd had to abandon the crockery on the draining board as he'd run to the cloakroom, bent his head over the toilet and vomited. It felt like his insides were being ripped open and that it wasn't cereal and milk but grief that was pooling in the water below him.

The days after Douggie's death had been a blur of official paperwork and calls with well-meaning people whose job it was to make the necessary arrangements, the postmortem, the police reports, and the funeral.

The children had been interviewed by the appropriate people too, in brightly coloured rooms, with toys and books on painted shelves and squash and biscuits and men in open-necked shirts and women who squatted down in front of them and said, "Can you tell us what you remember about the day of the accident? Would you like to draw a picture of it for us?" And Faith and Harvey and Lizzie and Ben had borne it all and taken their ashen kids home via a McDonald's for a Happy Meal. But even the toys had remained in their plastic wrappers, and they'd thrown them away when they'd got in.

Then there'd been that bloody journalist and the article in the paper which had only told a fraction of the story; it was all just words, inadequate words and a picture of Douggie which he had no idea how the paper had got hold of. Anthony hated the thought of strangers touching the newsprint, accidentally brushing their fingers across his son's face, then putting the paper into the bin at the end of the day, or worst still, letting it drop so that it flapped uselessly against a set of railings somewhere in town.

The six of them spoke little, just mechanical stuff about practicalities: transport, food, who had/hadn't been told; none of them could bear to look each other in the eyes and say, "Fuck, this hurts." And he wished they could. Inside, Anthony was raw and screaming. Outside, though he had to stay strong for Sara who had crumpled into her bed like a discarded tissue the morning after they'd returned from the hospital and hadn't moved since.

"Please try some soup, or maybe some scrambled eggs. I could make you some toast too, if you'd like," he'd said hopefully, sitting on the edge of the bed and looking at her small curled-up body, her hair spread on the pillow like spilt oil.

"No thank you," she'd replied, in a tiny voice, muffled by the bedding. "I'm not hungry." And Anthony would creep out, leaving Sara and the room to their darkness and he would pass Douggie's room on his way downstairs, but he wouldn't dare go in.

The postmortem told them Douggie had suffered a blunt force trauma, hard enough to render him unconscious and then, basically, simply, irrevocably, in the tiny minutes between Ashley and Clemmie running for help and Blake pulling him out of the water, his lungs had filled with an obscenely small amount of water that, although also tiny, had been enough to drown him.

Drown. Such a simple word, Anthony thought, as he heard it said to him down the phone, but if you listen carefully to the word it takes you down with it. It is a gaping word, of dark spaces and silences and Anthony hated it, hated it so much he wanted to take a cleaver to it and split it apart, smash each letter and scatter the pieces in all the corners of the world, and he wanted to run and run and run and never come back, never have to hear the word spoken again. There were times during the black, sleepless nights when he sat in his chair in the lounge and listened to Sara's exhausted sobs from their bedroom above him that he hated her, wanted never to have to see her again either, never have to speak to her because he knew that whatever he said couldn't make this nightmare go away.

"Hello? It's me."

The handset was cold against his mouth. It was four o'clock in the morning.

"Hi," Faith said. Her voice was quiet and sleepy.

Outside the birds were just starting to stir; although he'd lived a thousand years since that Saturday, summer was still here and he wanted to tell them to shut the fuck up, they had no right to sing, not today, not ever really.

"Sorry, it's late, or early. I don't really know which, but I couldn't sleep."

"Don't worry. I was only dozing."

"It's going to be awful tomorrow, today, I mean."

"I know. It is."

He could hear her rustling the bedclothes.

"Hang on," she said. "Let me put my dressing gown on and take you downstairs."

Her footsteps padded on the carpet, and he could hear the brush of her hand against the wooden bannisters. "You still there?" she asked after a minute or two.

"Yes."

"Do you want me to come over?"

"No, it's OK. I just need to talk, to hear my own voice."

"How is she?"

"Not good. Not good at all."

"Eaten anything?"

"I did manage to get her to have a cup of tea earlier. I really do wonder though whether she's going to be strong enough to come."

"She will. She'll have to."

"You and Lizzie thought any more about the kids coming?"

"We've talked of little else, but no, we've decided they're still not going to. It'll be too hard for them. It wouldn't be fair to let them see us so sad."

"Your call. I just hope it doesn't rebound on you later. When they're older, that sort of thing."

"Have *you* eaten anything today?" she asked. In the background, he could hear her filling the kettle.

"Yes, I had a sandwich earlier. Just not hungry, that's all. The funeral's taken so much organizing. It's surprising."

"Oh, Anthony, I wish there was something more I could do."

"You've done plenty, just by being there. We wouldn't have got through this without you, all of you."

He drew in a deep breath to stop himself from saying it out loud. He couldn't blame the children; it had been an accident and it had been as much his fault as anyone's. He should have gone to check on them earlier, seen what they were doing, and stopped them. He shouldn't have carried on reading that fucking paper and he hated himself too, all of himself, because of it. He'd replayed every second in his mind ever since, over and over and over again.

In his mind, he'd got up ten minutes before, walked through the long grass, rounded up the kids and brought them back for a cold drink and a rest.

"It's hot," he would have said. "Here, sit down, have a drink, something to eat. We'll go home in a bit, it's too hot for this today."

But he hadn't said that, he hadn't got to them in time and there was absolutely nothing he could do to change it, and that was what was impossible to bear.

"You'd better try and get some rest," Faith said.

Anthony snorted gently, "Yeh," he said. "Suppose I should."

"I'll see you later."

"OK and," he paused, looked around the dark room and at the shapes the furniture made, at the small red standby light on the TV. "Thanks, Faith," he said. "Thanks."

There was a second's pause and then, "It's what I'm here for," Faith replied.

He hung up the phone and sat holding it for a moment before standing and stretching his long bony legs and walking wearily to the bottom of the stairs.

He lay on top of the covers on the spare bed fully clothed and stared at the ceiling, willing dawn to come so that tomorrow, today, could be over, willing it to stay dark forever.

"It was Anthony," I whispered as I clambered back into bed beside Harvey. I'd left the kettle switched off. I didn't have the energy to make a hot drink.

"How is he?" Harvey's voice was still clogged with sleep.

"Not good."

"Did you check on the boys on your way back to bed?"

"Of course."

"Guess we'd better try and get back to sleep."

"Yes, I guess we should."

But I didn't sleep, and I couldn't cry; like Anthony, I relived a hundred different lives and in all of them, as I waited for the dawn, Douggie didn't die and I didn't know what I knew, didn't have the weight of it lodged beneath my ribs.

The church was only half full, the coffin far too tiny. Sara and Anthony sat at the front, heads bowed, like puppets with no strings. There were too many flowers; the air was heavy with the scent of them. I sat at the end of a pew next to Harvey two rows from the front. Lizzie and Ben were the other side of Harvey. There was a scattering of others, but not many. Douggie hadn't had the chance to make any friends, and neither of Sara's nor Anthony's family was there. Sara had once said there'd been a falling out between her and her parents, and Anthony's parents, who I'd obviously known when we were at school, were travelling in Vietnam and couldn't be contacted. They'd be devastated when they found out.

No one spoke and, when the organ ground into sound for the first hymn I wanted to shout out for everyone to shut up, to be silent; it was the only way I could think to mourn him properly.

The service was lovely of course. The minister said wonderfully comforting things which made absolutely no difference at all. It was all shit, and as the pallbearers picked up the tiny box and carried it back down the aisle, I reached out my hand and touched it, wanting to pull it onto my lap. The men carrying Douggie looked down at me in surprise and, glancing up, I caught sight of Anthony's face staring at me over his shoulder. He looked no older than the boy I'd known at school, not nearly old enough to be doing this, not old enough at all.

The procession started up again and my hand slipped off the cool smooth wood. Harvey pulled me towards him, so my head rested on his shoulder. I didn't see Sara and Anthony walk out of the church because, at last, I was crying.

Lizzie plucked another bottle of milk from Sara's fridge. Faith had done the shopping for the wake because no one else had been able to. Lizzie was, however, good at making tea, so for the last couple of hours she'd stayed by the kettle, hoping that by keeping busy, she would gradually forget why they were all there.

The muted babble of voices from the lounge had kept at a constant pitch over the last hour or so; it was more wearing, she thought, than if it had risen and fallen, if there'd been the occasional shout or ill-placed burst of laughter. No, this hushed droning was exhausting, and she was relieved beyond all measure that she had a reason for staying hidden, that she didn't have to stand in amongst the hot bodies of the mourners and search her broken heart for something to say.

When she'd arrived, the kitchen had borne the signs of days of food being hastily prepared and then equally hastily disposed of. A half-eaten bowl of cereal had stood by the sink, the milk, the colour of caramel. Douggie's plastic Mr Men cups and plates were still stacked on the draining board where they'd been left the morning of the picnic, and Lizzie had taken a deep breath and put them carefully away in the cupboard next to the cooker where Sara always kept them. She'd felt furtive when she'd done this; like she was committing a crime, and she'd really hoped it had been the right thing to do. There'd been no corresponding bolt from on high, no soundless scream when she'd touched them, although half of her had expected either or both of these things to happen, so she'd cleared the rest of the kitchen and wiped down the surfaces and had swept the floor, but the room had still felt dirty like it needed to be scrubbed down with bleach until her fingers bled.

"How you doing in here?" Faith asked with false brightness, carrying a tray loaded with dirty cups and saucers into the kitchen.

"Oh, OK," Lizzie replied, lifting the lid of the teapot and stirring the tea. The heat travelled up the spoon and scalded her fingers. She dropped it with a clatter on the counter.

"Hey, watch out!" Faith said, stacking the dirty crockery in the dishwasher.

"It doesn't matter. Just leave it. I'm OK," Lizzie snapped. She wanted to cry; more than anything she wanted to curl up in the corner of the kitchen and weep: for the fact that Douggie had died, because she still had Clemmie and Ben, and because she had no idea how she was ever going to help Sara through it all.

"You seen Sara since we got back?" Faith asked, putting a steadying hand on Lizzie's arm.

How can she be so calm now, Lizzie wanted to know, after what she'd done in the church, how she'd held onto the coffin for a moment, how she'd cried and how together they'd stood at the tiny graveside, their feet stirring up the summer-dry grass of the churchyard and had looked at the ground, not daring to look at one another? *Surely, Faith should be crying now?* Lizzie thought, and she wished that Faith would, so that she could too, and they could hold one another in the hot kitchen and give each other the strength they obviously needed to get through the next weeks, months, the years that would follow this.

But all Lizzie said was, "No. Sara went upstairs, and I haven't seen her since. Do you think I ought to go up? I could take her a cup of tea."

"That would be nice," Faith said, smoothing down the silky material of her white blouse as it tapered over her waist and onto her hips and the straight black skirt she was wearing. In her smocked dress and wedge-heeled sandals, Lizzie felt fat and frumpy in comparison. She wished she could look cool and unflustered like Faith. *Why had she worn this stupid dress?* she asked herself.

Taking a cup of tea, she walked slowly out of the kitchen, weaving in amongst the scattering of people in the hallway and climbed the stairs. In reality, she wanted to run; her heart was beating fast with the fear of being caught and spoken to. She had nothing to say to these people; nothing at all, not even to Ben or Anthony. Harvey had gone to check on the children and, as she stood outside Sara's bedroom door, she envied him this job, wished she'd gone instead.

She tapped on the door. "Sara?" she said. "It's me. Lizzie. I've brought you a cup of tea."

"Oh, come in." Sara's voice was hoarse and ragged.

It took Lizzie's eyes a couple of seconds to adjust to the gloom. The heavy curtains had been drawn and the windows must obviously still be shut because it was sweltering in there, and it smelled of staleness and grief.

"Here," Lizzie said, putting the cup down beside the bed. Sara was curled up on it, fully dressed, still with her shoes on, but she looked no bigger than a comma on the pale counterpane. "Try and drink it while it's hot."

"Thank you," Sara said, but she made no move to sit up.

"Shall I open a window? It's warm in here, isn't it? It might make you feel a little better, to get some air, you know," Lizzie stumbled on, cursing herself for saying this. How could anything make Sara feel better?

"OK, if you want to," Sara did uncurl slightly as she said this. Her face was flushed with crying and her hair had started to tumble from the half-hearted bun she'd put it in earlier.

Lizzie went over to the window and carefully, without drawing back the curtains too far, opened the two casement windows. Sounds flooded in; the birds were singing, and the leaves were rustling in the trees behind the house and somewhere, on another part of the estate, they could hear children playing. They were shouting and laughing and, turning round back into the room, Lizzie saw Sara put her hands over her ears to shut out the noise.

"I'll get back downstairs then," Lizzie said, standing awkwardly, not knowing what to do next. "People should be making tracks soon I guess, and Faith and I'll need to clear up."

"Thank you," Sara whispered. "For helping out today. I'm sorry I haven't been…"

"It's OK," Lizzie interrupted her, sitting uneasily on the end of the bed. "No one could expect you to."

"No, I mean it," Sara said huskily but somewhat urgently. "I mean thank *you*, for everything. *You*, Lizzie. You've been a good friend. A really good friend."

"You would do the same for me," Lizzie replied, standing up and rearranging the bulky material of her dress.

What Sara said next puzzled her then and continued to do so every time she thought of it again in the years that followed.

"No," Sara said, wrapping herself up into a ball again and closing her eyes. "No, Lizzie. I don't think I would be able to, really, I don't."

"Well?" asked Harvey, squatting down in front of Ashley who had his head bent over a puzzle on the floor of a neighbour's house. "How it's going?"

"OK," his son replied, not looking up.

"Need any help?"

"No, thank you."

Harvey sighed and stood up, his knees cracking as he did so. He ached all over and seemed to have done so for days.

He tried Blake next. Blake was sitting on a low wall in the garden, kicking his heels against the brickwork.

"Hey, champ," Harvey said. "What have you been doing?"

"Nothing much."

"Had anything to eat? You hungry?"

"Na, we had some biscuits and stuff. Anyway, I'm not really hungry."

Then there was a silence; one too heavy for a father and his son. *It should be up to me,* Harvey thought. *To break it.* But he had no idea what to say.

"How much longer will you be?" Blake asked at last, picking at a scab on his knee. Harvey wanted to tell him to stop it but didn't have the heart to.

"Not much longer, I shouldn't think. Mum'll help clear up I guess but you, me and Ashley can go home if you like. Shall I go and ask Mum if that'll be, OK?"

Blake nodded.

"Right then," Harvey said. "I'll just check on Clemmie and then I'll go and see Mum. Shouldn't be long. OK, champ?"

He knew he was filling space with words. He knew he was being lame, but the sight of his son's face as he lifted it up and looked at him, at his son's deep eyes and the grief in them wiped his mind clean, leaving him stuttering and unsure.

"Dad?" Blake said, still fixing Harvey with that stare.

"Yes, son."

"I wish I'd been there. I wish you'd let me say goodbye."

Fuck, thought Harvey. *Fuck, fuck, fuck.* "Trust me, Blake," he said. "You wouldn't have wanted to, not if you'd been there. It wasn't nice, really it wasn't."

"OK, but…"

"No, Blake. Leave it will you? Can we talk about it later maybe? When we're home when today's over?"

Blake didn't reply. Instead, he lowered his head and began kicking the wall again.

Fuck, thought Harvey again as he stepped back into the house in search of Clemmie. *How are we ever going to get over this? I shouldn't have said that. What damage is still being done? Will it ever end?*

He found Clemmie asleep on a sofa in the den. The neighbour who'd offered to have them for the day had grandchildren of her own and had told Faith that it would be lovely to look after the poor little dears. "They can play with my grandchildren's toys and watch their videos," she'd said. "Don't worry," she'd added. "All will be well."

Disney's *Beauty and the Beast* was playing on the screen; it had got to the part when the crockery and cutlery were singing and dancing and Harvey watched it mesmerized for a while. Then he tiptoed across the room and switched the set off. Clemmie stirred but didn't wake. He stood watching her for a long time as the sun beat down outside and his sons stayed in their sad, silent worlds elsewhere in this stranger's house and all was quiet and Clemmie frowned in her sleep, uttered a choked sob and then turned over to face the back of the sofa, so all Harvey could see was the back of her head and her spine curved over itself under the thin material of her pink summer dress.

On the Saturday after the funeral, Ben woke with a start. His heart was thumping, but he had no idea why. Had he had a bad dream? Was there something he'd forgotten? He lay still, waiting for his nerves to steady. He looked over at Lizzie, who was lying on her side, facing away from him so all he could see was the jumble of her hair and one smooth pale shoulder peeking above the duvet. He was sure there was something he should have done or something he should be doing; otherwise, why would he be panicking like this?

Then he remembered. He'd promised to take Clemmie to the park on her bike on that long-ago day when everything had changed, and he'd completely forgotten about it.

Why had he forgotten? He thought back. Sara and Anthony had eventually come home from the hospital at around two in the morning after Douggie's accident and Sara had rung him almost straight away. He hadn't been asleep, but the sound still made him jump. He reached out for the phone by the bed.

"Hello?" he'd said quietly into the mouthpiece for fear of waking Lizzie.

"Ben?" her voice was muffled.

"What can I do to help you?" he'd asked, without any preamble because he'd had no notion of what else he could have said. Lizzie had stirred in her sleep but hadn't woken.

"Nothing. I just wanted to hear your voice, that's all."

"Do you think you can sleep?"

"No. I doubt it."

"Where's Anthony?"

"Downstairs."

"Shall we come round tomorrow, Lizzie and I?"

"No, it's OK. Just give me a few days but," she paused; she sounded so very tired. "Would it be OK if I call you, now and again?"

"Of course, anytime," he whispered, wondering if she'd meant 'you' as in him, or 'you' as in him and Lizzie. He rather hoped it was the latter. "Shall I say goodnight now?" he'd said at length when it seemed that Sara wasn't going to say anything else.

"Yes, OK. Goodnight, Ben. Thank you," she'd said and hung up the phone very slowly. He'd imagined her then as an old woman, one who had to move deliberately and delicately for fear that she would break. He certainly didn't feel he deserved her thanks, not at all.

After that, the days settled into a routine of sadness and quietness. Clemmie hadn't asked about the bike ride, and he'd been too distracted to remember about it. All his energy seemed to be directed towards the grief pressing against the walls of number six, and he was torn. On the one hand, he wanted to try and keep it contained, so that it didn't creep too near to him and his family and, on the other hand, he wanted to absorb as much of it as possible, to try and make some of Sara and Anthony's heartache his own.

All this took a huge amount of effort; as did making himself available to Lizzie, Faith, Harvey and the children. It was as if he was too scared to own up to his own sorrow, to admit that he too had loved Douggie. Stopping himself from mourning him properly because he was scared of what it may unleash had made him forget the bike ride. Until now, that is.

He swung his legs out of the bed and crept to Clemmie's room. She was coiled up in the bedding like a hamster, and he smoothed the hair away from her face and whispered, "Hey, Clemmie. Fancy going for a bike ride in the park after breakfast?"

Her eyes snapped open, and she smiled broadly at him, making his heart somersault.

"Yes please, Daddy," she said, holding on tightly to one of her stuffed toys. "Can Barnie come too?"

"Sure, we can put him in the basket on the front of your bike, can't we?"

She nodded happily and said, "Is Mummy coming?"

"No," he said. "It's just going to be me and you and Barnie. Is that OK?"

She nodded again. He felt bad about not including Lizzie, but he also felt that this was something he had to do on his own; it was, he confessed to himself, part of him making amends for all the failings in which he'd played a part, and which had led up to Douggie's death and the hiatus they'd all been, he'd been in, since.

Lizzie didn't wake, so he and Clemmie stole downstairs and feasted on Rice Krispies, giggling when they snapped, crackled and popped, saying, "Ssssh, you'll wake Mummy," to their bowls and trying to quell the noise with their hands. Then Ben left Lizzie a note and they crept out of the house, getting Clemmie's bike out of the garage and wheeling it to the end of the drive. It was just before seven o'clock and the estate was still slumbering.

"Can I cycle on the path?" she asked. "Please, Daddy."

"Yes, but don't make too much noise and don't go too far ahead, and be quiet as you go by D..." He had to stop himself from saying, 'Douggie's house'... "When you get to Sara and Anthony's house. OK?"

"OK, Daddy," she said happily and cycled off, her stabilizers bumping along the pavement.

He followed, walking briskly, trying to convince himself that this was just an ordinary day, that the leaves on the trees were stirring in an ordinary way and the birds were singing just their ordinary, everyday songs. But deep down, he had this uneasy feeling that today was actually the start of some completely new time in his life when all he'd known before had been melted and, when cooled, would be reformed into a series of unrecognizable shapes.

Clemmie was waiting patiently outside number six, chatting to Barnie the bear in the wicker basket hanging from her handlebars.

"Righto," Ben said when he reached her. "Best we walk your bike over the main road to the park, eh?"

With one hand steering the bike and the other holding onto Clemmie, they set off.

If he'd looked up, he would have seen Sara's pale face at her bedroom window watching them and, if he'd waited just a fraction longer, he would have seen her lift up her hand, press it against the glass and then let it drop to her side.

Sara stayed at the window until Ben and Clemmie were out of sight. Then she returned wearily to the bed and lay down on the covers, still dressed in the clothes she'd worn to the funeral. All she'd done was take off her tights; she liked the early morning chill to wrap itself around her toes. She had no idea what to do. She should clean something or cook something maybe or wash some of Anthony's clothes, but she couldn't imagine herself doing any of these things. The hospital lights still seemed to have her captured in their beams.

What she mostly remembered from that night were the lights and the squeaking of doors. The doctors had told her and Anthony to wait in a private room at the end of a long corridor. Outside the room, people bustled backwards and forwards; she could see their shadows come in and out of view in the opaque glass viewing panel in the door. As each one appeared, she wanted to stop them and say, "tell me it's a mistake. Tell me he isn't dead." Towards dawn, she'd changed this to, "Just let me be with him. Let me hold him, please."

In the end, she'd had about an hour with him. They let her sit with him in a small, softly lit room and she didn't let herself think how they'd got him there, how they'd lifted him onto the bed, tucked the sheets around him, who had closed his eyes. It was very quiet; Anthony stood behind her, his hands on the back of her chair and they didn't speak to one another. There was absolutely nothing either of them could say. At the end of the hour, a nurse came and led them back to the noise and the lights and an array of official forms and the horror of breathing in and out, and walking, and talking without their child, who the hospital referred to as 'Douglas', and when they'd got home, Anthony had stayed downstairs and she'd called Ben from the bedroom, not caring if Anthony heard or not; she'd just wanted to hear Ben's voice and she hadn't wanted to ask herself why this should be so.

Curled up on her bed now, she imagined Ben in the park with Clemmie, him running and laughing and Clemmie laughing too. She had to work very hard to keep the hate at bay; it wasn't their fault, no more than it was Faith's or Harvey's or Ashley's or Blake's. It was no one's fault really, although it was very tempting to blame Anthony; after all, he was Douggie's father, wasn't he? He was supposed to protect Douggie. It had been his job, as well as hers. And if Blake hadn't moved Douggie... She didn't even want to go there.

There was, she admitted, nothing anyone could do to change what had happened, although it was tempting to rewrite history and she did this constantly. But, when the rewriting was over, she'd come to realise that there was no alternative and it was living with the knowledge of this, she knew, which was going to be the thing that was going to fill all the available space in her life from now on.

Then she heard a noise in the back garden; a rhythmic thud, thud, thud and gradually she uncurled, slid off the bed and moved towards the bedroom door. The carpet felt cold under her bare feet. The sound was getting louder with each step. Outside Douggie's room, she pressed her back to the wall and slid along it, holding her breath. She had no idea why she was doing it this way; it just seemed the right thing to do. She had to keep her distance. What would happen if the door opened and Douggie stood there? What if it was all a dream, how could all the grief be undone? No, she slid on, towards the guest room. Once inside it, she walked carefully over to the window, not daring to look back over her shoulder in case Douggie should be following her, saying 'Mummy' in his small boy's voice.

Anthony was in the garden, digging a hole at the side of the path. Next to him in a pot was a small tree with flat, pear-shaped leaves the colour of newly mown grass.

She opened the window. Anthony looked up. A half-smile flickered across his face then vanished.

"What on earth are you doing?" she asked, her voice cracking.

"I'm planting a tree, what does it look like," he snapped back, his eyes full of misery.

"Why?" she asked again.

"For Douggie, of course."

"What sort of tree is it?" She leant heavily on the windowsill, suddenly exhausted.

"It's a Judas tree," he answered, resting against his shovel.

"Oh, I see," she said, shutting the window and moving back into the room, the words 'because we too have been betrayed' hanging permanently between them.

"Do you want to play football?" Blake asked. "I'll let you be a striker."

"No. I'm watching this," Ashley replied from his camp of cushions at the end of the sofa.

"Oh, go on. I'm bored."

"I said no, so leave me alone, will you?"

"You're just dull. I'm going to tell Mum on you."

"Go ahead. I don't care."

But when Blake arrived in the kitchen to be presented by his mother's back as she stood at the sink peeling the potatoes for tea, he faltered. He didn't really want to play football either. He just wanted some company, some chance of forgetting.

"Is it OK if I go to see Clemmie?" he asked.

"Of course, but be back by teatime. OK?" Faith replied, glancing over her shoulder at him. Part of him wanted to cry and part of him wanted to hit something very hard.

"Oh, hello Blake," Lizzie said when he arrived on their back doorstep. "You come to see Clemmie?"

He nodded.

"Come on in then."

"What you doing?" he asked Clemmie, who was sitting at the dining room table with a pad of paper and a box of crayons in front of her.

"I'm drawing," she said, looking up at him. "Do you want to do drawing too?"

"OK," he replied, hopping onto a chair next to her. Looking across he could see a jumble of stick-like figures and a great blue puddle. "What is it?" he asked.

"It's Douggie. And there's you." She pointed to a tall figure in the corner of the page, mostly scribbled over in black. "And here's me and Ashley." The other two people were standing very close to one another and the shape she'd said was Douggie was lying down in front of them.

"What are we doing?"

"We're playing pretend," she said, looking up at him.

"I'm going to draw a castle and soldiers," he muttered, picking up a grey crayon and starting to draw a battlement. Then, with a pink crayon, he drew a row of faces looking over the top of it. "That's the enemy," he said.

From Sara's kitchen window I watched the leaves on the tree Anthony had recently planted stir in the late summer air. The earth around it was still bare and some of the leaves were starting to turn.

So many endings I thought as I filled the kettle in the hope of enticing Sara down for a cup of tea. Anthony had rung earlier and asked me to pop in while he was at work and check on her, so I'd let myself in and called up the stairs, "Only me, Sara. Will be in the kitchen. Am gasping for a hot drink."

I'd been met by silence and, in a way, was relieved. There was so much I should say to Sara, so much I should have said a long time ago, that her absence was a comfort; it helped me avoid, yet again, the lie I'd helped keep hidden, the lie I'd vowed I'd keep from Anthony, Lizzie, Ben and Harvey and the children who remained. It was the price I had to pay for knowing the truth and for being too scared to face up to it when I should have done.

A voice from the top of the stairs: "I'm fine, Faith. Don't worry about me. I am reading and don't fancy a drink. You go ahead though if you want one."

I made my way back into the hall in time to see Sara dart back into her bedroom.

"As long as you're OK," I called after her. "I'll pop in again later perhaps?"

She'd closed the door behind her and didn't answer.

Again, relief washed over me. Then the guilt.

I'd ring Anthony when I got home and let him know she was all right, that I'd spoken to her, and I went back into the kitchen and switched off the kettle and, raising my hand, to acknowledge the tree and all that it meant, left Sara to her silence, once again carrying her secret with me back to my house, my life, my friendships, my marriage.

All I had to do was to preserve what we had, let what we knew about each other be the version of us that we all believed in. It was up to me to keep everything in place; the alternative was unthinkable. I could not falter, not make any mistakes. There could be no letting go; the truth would only bring chaos and heartbreak, more than we'd had already. It was up to me, and I would succeed, wouldn't I? I would not let anything, or anyone, deflect me from my task, would I?

Part 2 – Spring, Fourteen Years Later

It can be the small, unassuming incidents that sometimes have the biggest impact. When something portentous happens, we expect a roll of drums, people shouting, and waves crashing against rocks at the base of cliffs. We expect doors to slam, footsteps running through the dark, rain on windscreens, and wipers batting back and forth like heartbeats. But it's not always like that.

It's not like that for me.

When Lizzie and I get in the car, I glance over at her and, in the slanting of light from the lamps at the end of the parking bays, her cropped blonde hair looks silvery and there are new lines around her eyes, just a faint cobwebbing like someone has scribbled very gently on her skin with a pencil. Clemmie, I think. It's bound to be Clemmie she's worrying about.

"You, OK?" I ask her.

"Sure. Just tired, that's all."

I'm not surprised.

It had been busy in the shop, for a Wednesday: a steady stream of customers, which is good, obviously. Lockdown was hard; we almost lost the business, but we survived, just, and whilst it's tiring when it's busy, we don't, we can't complain.

She nods and I reach over and hold her hand for a brief moment, then put the car in reverse and we start for home.

We chat about the film we've just seen and then she says à propos of nothing really, "We had an email from an artist called Nic Bradley today. He wants to know if we'd like to show some of his paintings in the shop. I've left the email marked as unread on the system. Perhaps you could reply to him when you can? You do the pictures, and I do the books in the book swap corner, right?"

"Right, I say." And add, "Sure, I'll answer him when I can."

And there it is. Although I don't know it at the time, there is a small, unassuming incident, one that will change everything.

Before we set off, I put on my driving glasses and flipped the sun visor up and, as I did so, I caught sight of my eyes, eyes which, when we first met, Harvey said were the kind that couldn't lie; they were too clear, too bright for that, he said.

He called them windows into my mind, but I've known for a long, long time that if he were ever to look too closely, these windows would reveal things he wouldn't actually want to see.

Ah, Harvey, I thought. Husband, father, friend. A man mostly unchanged since we married: a solid, square man with a broad face, hair that once shone bronze in some lights, amber in others, and which has now faded to the colour of sand with a scattering of grey. Only the slight slackening of the skin around his mouth occasionally makes him look more vulnerable now, a fraction less certain. This uncertainty is, however, only ever a temporary thing; like a flash of sunlight on water it soon goes.

Unlike me who is riddled with doubt and, more recently, a bubbling kind of anger and a seething mass of regret, both over what I didn't do, and what I did.

I know I've reached the time in my life when it's highly unlikely I'll ever air kiss a famous film star, go hiking in Kathmandu, or ride bareback through shallow waves as a tropical sun sets on the horizon.

Instead, I am an ordinary, middle-aged woman with light hazel eyes who still wonders what my parents could have been thinking of when they'd named me Willow.

Their flower power moment must have lasted about a year; the year in which I happened to have been conceived, born and christened. I am sure that, had they waited, they would have named their child something sensible like Anne or John.

Therefore, I often stay in my seat, watching the credits roll at the end of the films Lizzie and I have watched over the years at the Kennet Centre and have started doing so again now restrictions have lifted, and scroll through the names on the screen and choose myself another one, so I don't have to be known by my middle name of Faith, because faith is the one thing no one should have in me, not now, not any more, not after what I did do, what I didn't, not after what happened because of me.

I didn't like the name Willow and had lost faith in the name Faith.

"See you tomorrow," Lizzie says as we draw up outside number four.

"Sleep tight," I say.

When she gets to her doorstep, Lizzie turns and waves before going in. Her hand raised; her palm white in the pale spring moonlight.

When I reach my own front door, I pause and gaze at our little bit of Penwood Heights on its spur off the main estate: our house at number two, Lizzie, Ben and Clemmie at number four, Sara and Anthony and the space left by Douggie at number six. Each house in its own pocket of garden, with its own drive, garage, and painted front door. I guess in estate-agent-speak ours would be called executive homes, with their four bedrooms, en suites, family bathrooms, reception rooms, kitchens-with-islands, and utility rooms. But to us they're just our homes: the three of them in a small crescent backing onto woodland, near enough to one another to provide comfort, far enough apart to give us our own space.

When I think of our houses, I often remember Scout Finch standing on Boo Radley's front porch at the end of 'To Kill a Mockingbird' and seeing both her life for the first time as he sees it and his from a different angle too and I wonder if this is the same for the six of us.

I unlock the door and go in.

"How was the film?" Harvey calls out from the study.

"Good thanks," I reply, making my way to the kitchen and switching on the kettle before going in to see him. "How was your evening?" I ask. "You been working the whole time I was gone?"

"Pretty much," he replies. "We've got that proposal to do. Ben wants to check it over before we present it. Thought I told you? We've got a meeting with Paradigm Developments tomorrow at three."

His face glows in the light from his laptop screen.

"So, you have," I say, absentmindedly running my hand along the back of his chair. His shoulders gave an involuntary flinch, as though taken by surprise. "Cuppa?" I ask.

"Lovely," he says. "Won't be long, then I guess we should take a look at the headlines and go up."

Back in the kitchen, I hold onto the edge of the counter. I want to stamp my feet like I did as a child, a behaviour Mum's never grown tired of reminding me about, and just let all the rage out. I want to stop having to try to balance on the tightrope of my life, to miss the boys now they've both gone back to uni and to admit to Harvey that I feel trapped.

But he doesn't encourage such displays; has rarely done so since our very early days together. He was then, and still is, taut, and controlled, his solid body packed with energy and fizz, rarely inviting intimacies. He'd been a man of silences when I married him, gratefully and on the rebound, and, even after all we've been through, sometimes I think he still is.

He'd started working from home when he and Ben had set up their partnership, and obviously worked here during lockdown, and he's still here, although now the house is quiet again; it echoes the sound of my breathing, and it stays too tidy.

It was hard having our sons leave the first time, then they came back for lockdown and now they've gone again – a double loss.

I make the tea and take it through to the lounge where Harvey is settling into his chair, reaching out for the remote and saying, "Glad that's done. Now let's see what I should be worrying about in my bed tonight."

"Did you all go to the cinema?" Harvey asks later as he places his toothbrush back in its pot by the basin in the en suite.

"All?"

"Yes, you, Lizzie and Sara?"

"No, Sara didn't come. We invited her of course, but she said she was busy."

"Anthony away again I suppose?" he says, folding his towel over its rack and smoothing it out so it hangs in perfect right angles.

"Guess so, he's back to staying away mid-week."

"Whatever floats their boat." Harvey's tone is dismissive as he turns off the light, leaving me standing in the dark, my fingers itching to rumple the carefully folded towel and then write my confessions on the mirror with his toothpaste.

Having watched Faith's car pull into her driveway, Lizzie closes the front door. She stands in the hall for a moment, gazing at the dresser. There she sees the two pot pigs she'd bought Clemmie at the school fair when Clemmie had been in year two. They are sitting between a photograph of Ben's grandmother and a Coalport teapot Lizzie had found on a bric-à-brac stall at an open day at a garden centre years ago.

"Can I have them please Mummy? Look at their little bitty noses. I have to have them," Clemmie had said pointing a stubby finger at the pigs.

"Well..." Lizzie prevaricated, wondering if this should be a battle she and Clemmie should have in public. She didn't want Clemmie to have them. They were too fragile, too piggy. But she had to pick her fights with her daughter, otherwise, they would be clashing swords all day. Clemmie had always known exactly which buttons to press to get to Lizzie and Lizzie, so befuddled by the images of 'how it should be' rather than how it actually was, hadn't always reacted for the best.

Other people's children, the ones she looked after at the nursery where she worked and where she'd first met Faith when Blake had started there, and before they'd moved in next door, had always been so much easier to handle than her own daughter.

"Can I? *Please* Mummy." Clemmie's voice had been wheedling and just a fraction too loud, so that other parents had begun to look round.

The ample-bosomed teacher behind the counter had smiled cautiously at them, probably fearing Clemmie would break the pigs, and there'd be china pieces over the gym floor causing a health and safety issue she could really do without.

"Of course, you can, darling," Lizzie had said, fumbling in her bag for her purse and handing the money over to the teacher, the set of whose face had, in the meantime, changed into something hard and disapproving, although why it would Lizzie didn't know. Wasn't the whole point of the stupid fair for her to spend her money on things she didn't need in order to raise funds for the bloody PTA?

Well, that's another failure mark on the bedpost of my life, Lizzie had thought as she'd taken Clemmie's hot little hand and they'd walked out of the school hall, with Lizzie carrying a bag in which the pigs languished in blue tissue paper, and Clemmie smiling broadly, another victory firmly under her belt.

Since then, the pot pigs had become a weathervane. Clemmie had ordained that when the pigs face one another, she and her mother are friends, when they face apart; it means that they've fallen out. Even now Clemmie is nearly twenty and should know better, the blame for these fallings out always seems to lay firmly at Lizzie's feet and Lizzie has to confess as she stands in the hallway, her handbag still hanging over her shoulder, her new shoes pinching her slightly, that the pigs have spent the majority of the last fourteen years tail to tail, their noses resolutely in the air.

"What did you go and see?" Ben asks from the doorway to the kitchen. He's leaning up against it, his jeans a smidgen too low over his hips so that a dart of flesh shows at the bottom of his t-shirt. Lizzie's heart gives a typical flip; she never grows tired of looking at Ben's body. It has always been, and still is, remarkable.

She tells him the name of the film as she brushes past him, drawing in the clean, woody scent of his aftershave.

"How was it?" he says, following her, running his hand distractedly through his thick dark hair. His hairline has receded slightly over the years, but not much. Together with his body, his hair and his large, fathomless brown eyes are still his crowning glories, not that he knows it. Ben was and always has been totally unaware of the pull he has over others.

"It was OK," she replies, putting her bag on the breakfast bar and surveying the wreckage of supper things in the sink. "Clemmie in?" she asks after a pause.

"Yep. We made some pasta." He hesitates. "But she had hers in her room. Harvey wanted me to go through a proposal..." He tails off. Lizzie knows he knows what's coming.

"Did you see how much she ate? I mean actually see it?" she asks.

"No," he says, looking down at his feet. "Look, we can't watch over her twenty-four hours a day. We have to trust her. She's said she's better..."

"I know, but I can't help worrying."

"I know, love," he says, crossing the room and putting his arms around her.

She nestles her head into the crook of his neck trying very hard to stamp out the images in her head of Clemmie taking a plateful of food upstairs and then, when Ben's safely ensconced in the study, creeping back down, carrying it out the back door and burying the contents in the garden. Lizzie's memories of analysing the plates in the dishwasher for evidence, and then taking a torch and scouring the flower beds like some sort of mad, nocturnal forensic scientist are still too fresh for her to let go of.

Clemmie not eating has been a constant refrain in their lives for two years now and trying to cope with it is, Lizzie often thinks, like trying to hold water in her hands.

"She said she's got some work to do tonight." Ben's mouth is against Lizzie's head, his lips brushing her skin under the short tufts of her hair. She shivers a pleasure-shiver, totally out of place in the circumstances. "Some research on different manicure techniques apparently," he adds. "She did have a few pots and things in her bag anyway."

"I'll check in on her later, not sure I'm brave enough right now," Lizzie says, disentangling herself reluctantly from him.

"Understood." He turns his broad back away from her and opens a cupboard door. "Fancy a nightcap?" he asks.

Next door, Sara turns off the porch light, locks up and slides the security chain into place. This is her favourite time of day.

With Anthony safely at the Soho Hotel in Dean Street, along with the celebrities and foreign businessmen whose favourite stopover it has become again, and with his shirts in their dry-cleaning bags, his three pairs of work shoes neatly stowed under the dressing table and his phone on charge by his bed, Sara can relax.

She does miss him, of course, she does. But this new routine which they've slipped imperceptibly back into seems, on the surface, at least, to be the perfect solution. No more obscenely early starts for him, scraping ice off the car to drive to the station; no hot, tired, crumpledness after a sticky summer day in London and then the bear of the commute back. This way, he stays in town again on Monday, Tuesday and Wednesday nights, coming home late on Thursdays and working from home on Fridays.

It's on Fridays she hears him murmuring into his phone or tapping the keyboard of his laptop and, sometimes, sees him stretch his long bony body, the sun glinting off the top of his almost-bald head as he stands on the patio and looks out at the garden with a look of surprise on his face, almost as though it's the first time he's ever seen it.

Lockdown had been almost impossible to bear. Both of them here, the walls humming with all the things they've still never talked about. How they got through those long months, she doesn't know. Her writing helped to distract her, and his long cycle rides gave them a break from one another. Too many meals eaten in silence, or in front of the TV.

They had been polite and careful with one another. Too polite, too careful perhaps.

It is much, much better now they are back in their old routine because it means that for most of the week, she can choose. Her days can be spent how she likes, and she can extend her arms and legs across the bed when he isn't there; let her toes feel into its cold corners and the chill punish her; let her fingers make herself come, a needful pulsing so much better than she's ever achieved with him. She can also remember what it felt like to hold Douggie and cry into her pillow without worrying that Anthony will notice.

Turning off the lounge lights, Sara goes into the kitchen. It is, naturally, a lovely kitchen. Anthony's money has given her that much. She had it designed and fitted two years ago and it's got self-closing drawers, a massive US-style fridge with an integral ice maker, a Belfast sink (only just still in fashion – 'A sort of retro statement, darling', the designer had said), an island in the middle with jaunty cocktail stools angled around it, and a hob with an industrial sized extractor hood above it which looks like it's been taken from the set of *Minority Report*.

The lighting has also been designed to be low, almost horizontal, so it won't shine in her eyes or beat down on the top of her head. She's never been able to stand bright lights, not since that night in the hospital. That's why she doesn't like going to the cinema with Faith and Lizzie; it's all very well while the film's running, but then they have to go down the steps into the bright white foyer and it's this unforgiving light reflecting off the walls and straight into her eyes that reminds her.

Sara knows that Lizzie and Faith think that she should be over it by now; should have been able to move on. But what do they know?

After she puts on her pyjamas, Sara pads along the landing to take just one more look. She opens her writing room door, creeps stealthily across the carpet and rests the flats of her hands on the cold cover of the lever arch file neatly positioned in front of her computer screen and keyboard. Book five, written by her alter ego, Hermione Hart, is almost ready to go. The spines of the other four stare out at her from the shelf above her desk. They're held in by a pair of bookends Anthony gave her for their fifteenth wedding anniversary and they contain the stories she's wanted to tell her child and not been able to.

Yes, she thinks as she softly closes the door and makes her way back to her bedroom. *At least I have my books, the support of Suzanne, my agent and Magda, my editor, and the option, if I ever wanted to, to break out of the anonymity I've cloaked myself in and publicise my books in bookstores and at readings.* She's told herself countless times over the years that she does have somewhere to go, something new to do if ever she is brave enough. Her social media presence is a construct, as the books written by the real her pile up on her shelves and she mourns her loss constantly and completely.

Beside the bed her phone is ringing. She leaves her books and answers it.

It's Anthony.

"Hello?" he asks as he always does as if he's afraid that one day she won't be there and that some stranger in a hazmat suit will answer.

"How was your day?" She tries to sound loving as she always does, knowing it's much easier to do loving from a distance than close up.

"Knackering, as usual," he replies. "Did a two-hour Zoom call with the US. Bonnie's voice can get wearing after a while."

As Sara has no idea who Bonnie is, she doesn't reply but just lets Anthony continue.

"Had the risotto again tonight for dinner. Room service this time; couldn't face going downstairs. What about you?"

Sara sits on the bed, crosses her slim legs and, whilst cradling the handset under her ear, expertly winds her long black hair into a knot at the back of her head; her neck feels suddenly cold without the blanket feel of it.

"Did another read-through of the last chapter, checked some emails, updated the website, you know that sort of thing. Faith and Lizzie invited me to the cinema…" She leaves the rest of the sentence hanging.

"Did you go?"

"No, didn't fancy it."

"That's a shame, you might have enjoyed it."

"Well, it's too late now, isn't it?" Sara doesn't mean to snap but knows that as it wings its way through the ether, her voice must sound hard and unforgiving.

She's spent years trying to forgive Anthony. Fourteen years, and still she hasn't been able to.

"Oh well, see you tomorrow then, I suppose," he says resignedly.

This was how all their conversations went and, most evenings, Sara wishes he wouldn't ring to say goodnight. Should he stop, however, she knows that one day he may stop coming home at all.

Saturday

It's afternoon and, as he crosses the hall, Harvey glances into the dining room and sees Faith, one hand on the back of a chair, the other holding a knife in mid-air. *She looks like a painting by Vermeer,* he thinks. *Life-like, but so very still.*

The table is almost laid. They're going to have one of their god-awful dinner parties tonight.

"To celebrate your and Ben's new contract with Paradigm," she'd said when Harvey had asked her what the occasion was this time as they were getting dressed that morning.

"Oh," he'd replied. "Suppose it was a joint idea? Yours and Lizzie's?"

"Of course!" Faith had put her hands on his shoulders and kissed him lightly. She'd smelled of washing powder and toothpaste and his heart had bumped against his rib cage.

As she brushed past him, smiling over her shoulder at him, he'd been filled with a sharp, keen need to hold her, feel the soft skin at the base of her spine, have her lie down under him; be reminded again of why he'd loved her so much for so long, believe for a moment he was better at showing it.

However, the moment had soon gone and now she's moved from the dining room back into the kitchen and is clattering pans and humming under her breath as he saunters into his study and moves papers around on his desk for a few minutes, waiting for the butterflies in his chest to stop flapping their webby wings.

There are times these days when a savage fear that she will leave him overtakes him and leaves him breathless.

After tidying his desk, Harvey moves into the lounge and sets about picking up the newspaper he'd left in sections on the floor by his armchair. He makes a satisfying amount of noise to indicate that he's doing 'a useful thing'. The time is fast approaching when Faith will start to get twitchy; it always seemed to happen about four o'clock on dinner party nights.

Harvey dislikes these evenings intensely but has never had the heart to tell her. Of course, he likes their guests individually; he's very fond of Lizzie and gratified that her and Faith's coffee shop is doing well once more, and he obviously gets on well with Ben, after all, they run a business together too. He also likes Anthony and Sara; has known them both for years as well and, in the hugest of coincidences, Anthony had actually been at school with Faith, so he's more like a brother to her than a friend and, for that fact alone, he has to like Anthony.

It's just that when they're all together he feels a bubble of resentment lodge somewhere at the base of his throat. Maybe it's the candles and the fancy china, or maybe it's because he feels that Faith is diluted by everyone else being there. It's like he can't reach her, that there's something in the way, an obstacle, a truth he's not party to.

She's never told him much about her past. He knows there was a man she had loved, someone she worked with, and that he'd probably been married, but other than that she'd always said what came before didn't matter.

"When we met," she said, "the present got re-set; what we have now has wiped out all the mistakes we'd made back then."

Or maybe it's also because it is at times like these that the weight of everything the six of them have been through together just seems to be too heavy for him to bear. It's almost as though they know each other too well; there are no secrets any more. The worst is known.

It's like we are all colluding, he thinks. *Each of us is pressing down hard on the edges of a surgical dressing, knowing that the wound underneath is still raw and weeping.* And there are times he fears the dressing will peel off and all the pain, in all its sharp detail, will be exposed again. This means that he can never really relax and guesses, as he puts the newspaper in the rack and tidies up the remote controls, this is why he sometimes feels a little resentful.

Harvey prefers, as he knows Ben and Anthony would also, to be safely tucked in a corner seat in the Queen's Head, watching Sky Sports and sinking pints like they do on the Friday nights their wives get together. There'd be no need for small talk or to try to unravel what their wives' conversations actually mean; it would just be blokes, the occasional sentence about the game, the odd pertinent political observation, but otherwise blissful silence; sport, and silence.

"Anything I can do to help?" he asks Faith from the doorway of the kitchen. She's standing at the sink with her back towards him and the table is covered with piles of ingredients like some sort of field hospital.

"No, I'm dandy," she says, rinsing lettuce leaves in a colander.

"I'll mow the lawn then, shall I?"

"That would be nice, thanks," she replies, shaking the salad, water droplets falling onto her arms where they lie like pearls for a second before trickling off into the washing-up bowl.

As he hauls the mower from the shed, Harvey doesn't really want to wonder why this job has made it onto his list; the clocks haven't gone forward yet and it'll be dark when their guests arrive and anyway, they've all seen the house in varying states of disarray before now. Why Faith needs everything like a photo shoot in *Homes & Gardens*, even the parts of the house that won't be seen, he'll never know.

In bed that morning, she'd said, "All you have to do is mow the lawn and sort the drinks, I'll do the rest." And she'd smiled as she'd sighed gently and turned away from him, shuffling her bottom into him as he'd draped an arm across her hips and become hard at the feel of her skin through the satiny material of her nightgown, but that moment had passed too.

He wheels the mower down the path and then, lining it up in his usual starting place, he fires it up. The air fills with fumes and noise. He flexes his shoulders and begins to push. He likes doing this; he likes the sense of order it imposes, the straight lines, the light/dark stripes, the feeling that he is, somehow, in control.

However, what he doesn't like is how the footprints he leaves in the spongy, just-mown grass remind him of his father. The scent of the cut grass lodges at the back of his throat and takes him back to his dad and Sunday afternoons, tobacco smoke and *Final Score* on TV. It is, he knows, better to remember Dad that way, and not the rasping, skeletal creature he'd been at the end, with thin, yellow skin and eyes that had looked glued shut. Both his parents were gone: Dad a few years ago, his mum not long after Douggie. *Death can be so fucking unfair,* he thinks.

As he turns the mower at the top of the garden, he pauses briefly, looking back at the house. The trees in the wood behind their house continue their whisperings; their newly emerged leaves in conversation with one another and he sees Faith's head bent over the sink and wonders what she might be thinking.

Probably about the boys, he reckons. They'd been back for a weekend recently, giving her the standard gifts of eating her roast dinners and letting her do their washing, and then had disappeared again with their bags on their backs: Blake with his jeans halfway down his hips, Ashley with his guitar slung over his shoulder. They'd loosely promised they'd be back in the summer but wouldn't commit; there was travelling to do, jobs to get, girlfriends and mates to consider. He couldn't criticise them for this, lockdown had been hard on them too.

Have I paid the deposit on Blake's house share in Cheltenham yet? he wonders.

Oh yes, he remembers. *I did it when Faith was at the cinema.* He feels an unwelcome flutter of nerves as he thinks of Blake's results. Will they be good enough for him to start the PGCE course he wants to do in September? Ashley, on the other hand, at the end of his second year at Aston, is talking about going to Prague for some sort of music festival in August.

Faith hasn't said anything to Harvey about how she feels about this, or about Blake's choice of career, but he knows that however proud she is of them now, she also keenly misses who they'd been when they'd been younger, when they'd been small enough to fit on her lap, when they'd needed to hold her hand at pedestrian crossings.

He probably doesn't acknowledge how hard it must be for her now they've gone. In fact, her sadness over the fact they have does annoy him sometimes; at least they are still a family. Not everyone is as lucky.

Bending down to empty the cuttings from the box, his back creaks slightly. He presses a fist into the base of his spine to ease the knot of muscle and bone. Then, standing at the compost heap, he has a sudden image of his mother in her apron hanging out the washing on a blustery late spring day much like this one.

As he hooks the box back onto the mower, he remembers the one time he'd allowed himself to cry, once they'd both died, his face pressed against the pillow, Faith's hand resting on the back of his neck. It hadn't helped. His parents had been like the foundation stones of his life, their line of sight always focused on him. Not like Faith's parents who, after their exercise in downsizing, now ran a small holiday cottage complex in the west of Ireland. They always seem to be looking out to sea, away from Faith, and she has learnt to cope with their lack of attention, concentrating hers instead on her sons. He, on the other hand, having been used to being under the constant scrutiny of his parents, missed it passionately now it was so totally gone.

You are a hypocrite, he tells himself. *A bloody hypocrite*. He should be more understanding about what Faith's going through. And then his thoughts scatter again and he's thinking of his own parents once more.

The one and only good thing to have come out of their deaths was the inheritance he'd got once he'd unravelled his dad's muddy paperwork and sold his childhood home to a young couple from Pakistan who had bowed to him when they'd met him, and who had always left their shoes at the door when they came to do yet another viewing with their tape measures and supportive elderly relatives. The money had meant he'd been able to leave his job working for a FTSE 100 service company based in Victoria and set up his own project management consultancy with Ben. Stopping the daily commute and getting away from the internal politics and form-filling had been a breath of fresh air…

He stands and surveys the mown lawn, looking down to kick the stray grass cuttings from his shoes.

Whenever Sara steps from the shower she always reminds Anthony of a fish, silvery and elusive. Water channels between her small breasts and down to her navel and, whilst he always tries not to, he can't help looking at the faint stretch marks on her skin which bear witness to the fact they'd once had a child. These marks seem to Anthony to be almost cruel in their tenacity. They seem, like the memories and the grief, permanent and inviolable.

She hates showers, he knows she does. She still hates water.

"What time are we due at Harvey and Faith's?" he asks sitting on the edge of the bed and opening the top drawer of his bedside cabinet. He picks out a pair of cufflinks and holds them up to the light. It's almost dark outside now and the wind has risen slightly, making the leaves on the Judas tree outside their window rustle a little too loudly, a little menacingly, he thinks.

"Eight," Sara replies, wrapping her tiny body in a huge white towel, her hair snaking over her shoulders and curling slightly at the ends in the way he loves. He wishes she'd leave it to go curly as it would naturally, rather than iron it to within an inch of its life with her hair straighteners; but this is a battle he doesn't dare have with her. The times for such light-hearted challenges died along with Douggie.

"OK, think I'll shave now and then check emails if that's all right with you."

"Sure," she says lightly, a little carelessly, from inside her walk-in closet.

He can hear the tinkle of coat hangers and the rustle of dry-cleaning bags.

"How did your writing go today?" he asks.

This is sometimes a safe area of conversation, sometimes not. He hopes that tonight it will be the former and, in any case, if they didn't talk about her writing or his work, he often wonders if they'd have anything to talk about at all.

"Not bad, thanks," she says, walking back into the bedroom, a black dress draped over her lower arm, a pair of strappy silver sandals hanging from her other hand.

"Did some proof reading," she adds. "And then plotted out some ideas for the next one. I need to check in with Magda about the timetable for the copy edits, but I can do that on Monday."

She lays the dress on the bed, but it slides off like some sort of black waterfall, landing in a heap on the carpet.

"Bugger," she says softly, bending down to pick it up, her towel unravelling slightly so that he catches another glimpse of pale skin.

They haven't made love in months. In fact, he can't remember the last time they did. Maybe tonight, if they both drink enough they could forget just for a little while, and pretend they are who they used to be.

When he's away from home he misses the warmth of Sara's body in the bed next to him, the gentle rhythm of her breathing, but he never knows how to tell her this, never dares break down the walls she's built around herself, the ones on which she'd written in large white letters, 'Don't touch, I hurt'. He never knows either how to tell her how much he hurts too, how Douggie had also been his son, how sorry he still is for what happened, for not being able to stop it from happening.

He misses his wife when he's with her too.

"Lizzie and Ben'll be there I suppose," he asks from the en suite, as he squirts shaving foam into his palm.

"Guess so," Sara replies quietly, and he pulls the door shut, suddenly wanting some privacy, some time away from her palpable grief.

Afterwards, with his skin stinging and his nostrils filled with the clean smell of his aftershave, he wanders back into the room, his t-shirt flung over his shoulder.

"I don't think I can go," Sara says in a small voice. She is sitting in front of the dressing table with her fists clenched and her body folded over itself. She is wearing a silky robe now, tied too tightly at the waist like it's some sort of punishment.

"Of course, you can," he says. "It'll do us good to get out. Remember lockdown? We should make the most of every opportunity we get these days. And, anyway, we won't have to try too hard with them, they know us too well for that."

"That's just the problem," she says quietly. "They know what happened, they were there. I can't pretend with them."

"It was so long ago darling. Surely we can move on just a bit, just occasionally. You know that Faith and Lizzie love you, no matter what."

Sara turns to face him and once again he knows he's said the wrong thing. There's that hard glint in her eyes, the one that hadn't been there when he'd met her at a mutual friend's wedding just over twenty years ago, the look that shakes him to the core these days whenever he sees it because he knows that he will never be able to make things better and that, like her stretch marks, it too will never fade.

Later, when Ben looks across the dinner table at Lizzie, he feels a little jolt somewhere between his shoulder blades. He's grown to love the mobility of his wife's face and the way the tufts of her hair curl over the tops of her ears. She's wearing her favourite linen top tonight; it falls away from her shoulders, skimming her breasts and, for a second, he fantasizes about touching them, imagines her nipples hardening, her skin puckering around them through the cool material.

She'd been tired when she got in from the shop earlier. Just one weekend off from *Flick's*, her and Faith's coffee shop, in every two, isn't much of a break for her, but he knows she and Faith can't afford to man the shop with weekend staff all the time, so they take it in turns to run the place with Dana and a Saturday girl. When Lizzie was getting changed certainly hadn't been the right time to suggest they make love, much as he wanted to. He looks at her breasts again.

To his right, Sara is sitting rigid and tense like some small firework, her hair a glossy sheen shading her face from sight. At the top of the table, Faith watches her guests with her clear hazel eyes, checking the levels in their glasses, making sure they're enjoying the food, and Ben feels as though he's under scrutiny.

He and Faith lock eyes for a second and he is bemused as it feels like he's done something wrong but isn't sure what, like she knows some secret about him that he doesn't know himself. He knows Faith doesn't mean it, just as he knows that any moment and, on his left, Harvey is just about to embark on one of his rants about the economy and how it's all the fault of… blah, blah.

Ben has no time for such luxuries of conjecture. Since he'd decided to throw in his lot with Harvey in the partnership, things have been leaning for him and Lizzie financially. He has no nest egg to fall back on, his parents still lurking unhappily in the background waiting for him to take responsibility for their care when they become too incapacitated. True, he and Lizzie have the income from *Flick's*, but this is uncertain and irregular. Faith and Lizzie haven't been doing it long enough for the income stream to be guaranteed and it's a fickle market, lockdown and the furlough scheme notwithstanding. An increase in shop rental could still mean the difference between success and failure.

He also has Clemmie to worry about. Neither he nor Lizzie have ever really known how to deal with Clemmie, and they have no idea what she's going to make of her life now, even though she's nearly twenty, back at Newbury College doing a beauty therapy course and, to all intents and purposes, on an even keel foodwise. Living with Clemmie is, he often thinks, like living with a forest animal; you never quite know what direction she'll dart in next.

Lizzie is laughing, "You should have seen them, talk about fish out of water, weren't they, Faith?"

Faith's laughing too; a private joke about some of their customers no doubt. Ben feels himself bristle.

"They were dressed in these strange cloaks," Lizzie continues. "Some sort of pagan group or another. Carrying whistles and drums and one had an accordion. A couple of our ladies, you know, from the Blue Rinse Brigade, almost fled in fear. It was as much as we could do to make them stay and finish their cake!"

Ben hates it when Lizzie and Faith go into a huddle about the shop. However proud he is of their achievement and however much he loves Lizzie, he thinks it is insensitive, especially in front of Sara, who never boasts about Hermione Hart's book sales, or about the fan mail her publisher must get from eight-year-olds wanting to know how to become like the characters in her stories: fearless, resourceful and brave, ready to tackle and beat all the sinister goings-on of the adult world.

"Here," Harvey says, topping up Ben's glass.

"Cheers mate," Ben answers and then leaning across, says to Anthony. "Did you see the match today? It was offside, surely! Never really feel I can trust VAR. Know I should, but…"

Then Sara's voice, tight and low asks, "How is Clemmie doing? And Blake and Ashley?"

"The boys are fine," Faith answers, adding. "Thank you for asking, Sara."

Sara fixes Lizzie with a look Ben finds uncomfortable. "And Clemmie?" she asks.

They all know how much effort it must be for Sara to take an interest in the children who are still alive and sometimes Ben wishes she wouldn't; it's too real a reminder.

"Oh, you know," Lizzie is saying. "She has her moments. It's not easy though. It never is with Clemmie…"

"You spoil her, and indulge her too much, that's what I think anyway." Sara's voice is still tight and low, but it has an edge to it.

Oh God, no, thinks Ben. *You mustn't do this.*

Silence descends over the table. Anthony fidgets in his seat, Faith clears her throat and taps the side of her glass absentmindedly.

Sara has broken the golden rule: no one must ever voluntarily comment on the others' children; never interfere without being asked to.

And yet, and yet, it must be so hard for her to watch them all grow and change, bear witness to their daily triumphs and disasters.

He sees Faith and Lizzie swap glances and their tacit agreement not to rise to the bait. They have to forgive Sara, and another thing he hates is their pity. It shouldn't have to be like this.

"Sara?" Anthony says his wife's name and she looks down at her lap.

"Sorry," she says. "I didn't mean that."

Ben knows both Lizzie and Faith know that she did mean what she said. And she's probably right; they all indulge Clemmie, and they dance around the boys too. Some things are too frightening to confront. Maybe if they'd got grief counselling for them when they were children…

Ben can't finish this thought. There is no point in going there. It's all water under the bridge.

Another silence. More seconds stretch. *Who will it be who speaks first,* Ben wonders.

As ever it's Faith. "More wine, anyone?" she asks, then says. "Harvey, open another bottle, eh?"

Chatter resumes, and Anthony rubs his eyes. *You look knackered,* Ben thinks and then he glances at Sara. She's still looking down, at her plate this time, and he's glad she hasn't seen him watching her because something has stirred deep within him that he doesn't want to recognise now either; not here, not tonight.

Sunday

As Blake enters the kitchen the next morning, the cooker clock flicks from 05.52 to 05.53.

"Fuck," he mumbles under his breath as, in the gloom, he surveys the wreckage of pots, pans and plates left by his housemates. He hates their slovenliness. *Ah well,* he thinks. *Not long to go now.* His finals are looming and then, if he can get onto the PGCE course, he'll be moving out of this shithole, his dad should hopefully have paid the deposit on his new place by now. He knows he's fortunate. His parents are good to him; they all have a lot to forgive each other for as it is.

He pushes his dark hair out of his eyes. For all his height and breadth, as he stands at the sink, his shoulders look bowed as though he's carrying a great weight. His mates at school used to call him Heath, after Heathcliff, and he'd liked this at first. Now he's read the book properly, he realises it was kind of a double-edged compliment if it was one at all.

Hints of dawn were starting to creep across the sky as he walked back; early morning workers were starting up their cars and motorbikes – an unremarkable morning. Then again, it had been quite an unremarkable night.

There'd been the pub, then the club and the girl – a normal Saturday night. He can't remember her name now, if he'd ever been told it that is, and they hadn't had sex. He'd fallen asleep on her sofa at about two, he reckons and had left without saying goodbye. She'd been very pissed, and not all that attractive as it turned out. Glancing in at her crashed out on her bed, he hadn't felt the faintest hint of regret.

He wasn't being very gallant he knew, but then he wasn't into the making coffee, having conversations, swapping numbers sort of thing. He'd done all of that with Gabs and he wasn't about to start doing it again, not now. There are too many other things on his horizon, and he's still too pissed off with Gabs – that had been one disastrous relationship in the end.

Plucking a crusty mug from the pile in the sink he squirts washing-up liquid into it and rinses it out under the tap. Around him are the sticky remains of a Chinese takeaway and moonscapes of cereal, resembling in part the papier-mâché creations Mum used to get him and Ashley to copy from *Blue Peter* when they were kids.

He dries the mug with the last sheet of kitchen towel and puts the kettle onto boil. He's hungry but can wait until *Pete's Caff* opens at nine. In the meantime, he'll have a coffee and a doze. Then he guesses he ought to crack on and do some work and call his parents. The Sunday night call was something Mum had insisted on when he left home again after lockdown.

Throwing himself on his bed, he stretches out his long legs and then plugs in his headphones. Biffy Clyro drums away in his ears. He closes his eyes.

"Oh my God, she didn't, did she?" Clemmie says into her phone.

"Yeh, on the pavement right outside Pizza Express. It was vile," Jasmine's voice sounds a bit tinny on the other end of the line.

"Gross!" Clemmie says, but she doesn't really think it is. Yes, throwing up on the High Street after too many Bacardi Breezers wasn't her idea of a good Saturday night out, but she can't help remembering how wonderful it feels when her stomach is completely empty, as though she's being cleansed from the inside, scraped out, purified. Having her skin taut over her bones, her stomach flat and her breasts tiny is still her idea of heaven.

"Glad I left when I did," she continues. "Did Baz stay?"

"Yeh, saw him later, at the bar. He was talking to that slapper, Dana. You know her, she left in year eleven. Didn't stay on."

"Much good staying on did me!" Clemmie laughs as she said this, ignoring the reference to Dana.

"Still, it was worth a shot, eh?" Jasmine counters.

Clemmie can hear the snap, snap of her friend's chewing gum. Her stomach churns. It's been a while since she's eaten. Although much better in the eyes of others, especially her mother, Clemmie secretly still hankers after the days when she didn't eat. The thought of food still disgusts her and she's not really able to sit at the dinner table with her parents with equanimity yet. Her mother finds this hard; she knows she does, but there are times when Clemmie just doesn't care what her mum thinks; she has enough problems marshalling her own emotions. All the years of trying to distance herself from her parents have been exhausting and, now she's back at college with Jaz and that lot, she has high hopes that one day she'll be able to get a job and a flat of her own, to move out for good and be in control all of the time.

"Guess so, Jaz," Clemmie says, adding. "Two E's and a D at A Level are better than nothing!"

"What you up to today?" Jasmine asks, after a pause.

"Not much, just hanging out, might do a bit of reading up for tomorrow's practical. Sort my stuff out that kind of thing. What about you?"

"Same, but hey, d'ya fancy going to 'Spoons later?"

"Yes, let's do that. Laters, Jaz."

Clemmie drops her phone onto her bed and stands gazing out of the window. A sharp spring breeze is tugging at the shrubs which line her parents' driveway. She opens her window and leans out, breathing in the busy air.

Ashley loves this bit. How he'd missed it during the pandemic. That first beat, the heat of the spotlight, the way he can hold the audience's anticipation in the palm of his hand just for a second before the first number starts. The crowd at The Jolly Angler is mainly made up of old, fat blokes with tattoos and shaved heads, but underneath, these guys are good fun.

"Four, three, two, one," he mouths at Will on bass.

Joe taps his feet, pumps the accordion and they're away.

'Skank for me, skank for me', they sing, jumping up and down in time to the music.

Ashley loves how he can look down at his guitar and then raise his eyes to the crowd and pretend he's seeing them for the first time over and over again. It seems that each chord change is a new start, that with each new song, he can wipe out the mistakes of the past. Here he has no history; it's just him and his mates on the stage and when they're done, they will pack up, squeeze their gear into Will's battered Škoda and go back to hall.

Then when he's in bed, he can relive the evening minute by minute and this will fill the night, helping him not notice he's not sleeping again. When dawn comes, he'll join the crowds going to lectures and hunt out notice boards around campus where he will put up posters about their next gig. 'Find us on Instagram', the posters say. 'We are the future!'

"Cheers, that was great," the landlord says as they finish their set. "Same time next week?"

"Sure!" Will says over his shoulder as he starts to unplug wires and pick up their empty water bottles.

"Get yourself some drinks on the house then," the landlord says to Ashley as he invites the next band onto the stage.

"Ta mate," Ashley replies, wondering not for the first time what his parents would think if they could see him here.

They have no idea about his band, the streaming, the YouTube hits, his secret dreams of a record deal, of concerts at the O2, of fans, and his belief in his music. They know about his guitar, but they'd stopped asking about the actual music years ago. Also, they have no idea how often he wishes he looked more like Blake; tall, broad, and capable. Well, Blake looks capable at least. Ashley knows his brother, like himself, has a fault line that runs the length of his chest, through his heart and down. He doesn't think his parents know about this either. As long as he phones on Sundays, goes home occasionally and doesn't go too overdrawn, they pretty much stay off his back. Not like some of his mates, their 'rents are complete nightmares. But, Ashley thinks, as he wipes sweat from his brow with the sleeve of his hoodie and picks up a pint, it would be nice sometimes to have his mum hold him like she used to do when he was little. It's as though there's still some hurt, she needs to protect him against; still some damage only she can repair.

Monday

Opening up the shop each morning is my favourite time of day. It's the blank canvas I love; the chance to start again, the feeling I have that we will somehow be an event in the lives of people I don't yet know. I imagine the strangers who will come, the stories they will bring with them.

I bend down to unlock the bottom lock of the front door of *Flick's*, pick up the newspapers and step inside. I don't look at the headlines.

The building is Georgian, a one-time pub and then a bank and now our coffee shop. It has wide, low windows reaching almost to the pavement on Northbrook Street. We painted the woodwork a green so dark that, in some lights, it looks almost black – a bit like a magpie's wing. Our contrast colour is light grey. The tiled floor is original and is now worn and silvery. The fixtures and fittings are a mixture of light and dark woods, the seats are also upholstered in shades of green and grey and, on the walls, hang pictures by local artists. In the far-right corner, there is the book swap shelf where customers leave their used books and pick up those left by others. It's a jumbly, homely kind of place and I adore it; it has become a second home, my safe place.

I enter and the sweet smell of lemon polish hits my nostrils. "Thank God for Brenda," I say to myself for the umpteenth time. I lift the flap on the alarm control panel, punch in the alarm deactivation code and go into the back to take off my jacket.

As I switch on the coffee machine and pour beans into the hopper, I hear the door open.

"Morning, Mrs M," says a bright light voice, a bit like tinsel.

A short giggle follows as Dana trips slightly as she hurries round the counter and stands beaming at me. She really is the worst waitress in the world I think, also for the umpteenth time.

When Dana applied for the job, I assumed we'd be getting someone like the Dana who sang 'All Kinds of Everything' at the 1970

Eurovision Song Contest. Instead of the sweet, contained thing we imagined, we got Dana the Dynamo. Yes, she's cute, kind, thoughtful and always cheerful but, with her tumble of black curls, her bright-blue eyes, her flawless complexion and her tiny waist and size three feet, this Dana speeds through life like a missile. We have both lost count of the number of cups she's broken, the drinks she's spilt, but what we can never forget is how this young thing, this girl who left school at sixteen with three GCSEs has lit up our life. There's no question of ever sacking her; she'd been at the same school year as Clemmie and Ashley, but they hadn't been friends apparently, and she handles the shop's social media accounts with breathless ease, a thing neither Lizzie nor I can get our heads around.

"Morning Dana," I say. Adding, "When you're ready, could you stack the cups on the hot plate and put the music on? Lizzie'll be here in a mo with the bread and cakes and then we'll need to get cracking."

"Righto, Mrs M." Dana skips into the back, tugging her jacket off as she does so and knocks into the doorframe with an elbow. "Ouch!" she exclaims and then laughs happily.

I smile as I polish the steam arm of the Lisa 3 Espresso Machine, our pride and joy. The day it arrived, all gleaming and clever was the day Lizzie and I finally believed our dream of running our own coffee shop may actually be coming true.

This morning is one of scurrying clouds. Some are bright white like cotton wool; others are thick and slabby like slate. The sun shines intermittently, throwing patches of light onto the street in between the footsteps of the early morning workers. I stand at the window for a moment, ready to slot the day's newspapers into the rack on the wall, but I still don't look closely at them, noticing instead a postman striding jauntily along the pavement. Two lovers are wrapped in each other's arms in front of the Salvation Army shop. They are like a still life or a Hopper painting and I wonder if this is a snatched moment, whether they have each come from different houses, different families, different partners, or whether these are the closing moments of the night they've just spent together and the prelude to another? I hope it's the latter. Then a woman in jodhpurs marches past; she's wearing a Barbour and has skin weathered by the wind. She looks in the window and grazes me with clear, fearless eyes of the most amazing blue, and then she's gone.

"He rang!" Dana whispers, as she gently prises the papers out of my grasp.

"Who did?"

"Steve!" Dana says the name with a small gasp, as if in prayer.

"Oh, what did he say?"

"He suggested a drink at the *Snooty Fox* on Saturday. Should I go?"

"If you want to. You like him, don't you?"

"Oh yes, he's…" Here Dana pauses, fixes me with her amazing eyes and beams, "He's divine!"

The problem is that we've been here before. Dana's had her heart broken a thousand times, each time believing it to be the very last time, that next time whoever she meets it'll be for keeps. Frankly, I can't understand how the boys Dana meets never stay around for long and have often wished that either Blake or Ashley would take this little slip of a thing under their wing, but this has never happened; the few times they've met it's been awkward like they were estranged siblings rather than anything else.

"I remember her from school," Ashley had said, looking down at his feet for some reason. "She was very quiet. Clemmie didn't like her for some reason," he added. "So, we never hung out much, but she seemed OK. Left at the end of year eleven, didn't she?"

Then the moment had gone; Ashley had left for university; Clemmie was at college and Dana came into the coffee shop every day like it was her first and she treated every boy she met as if he was the first too.

"Just be careful, Dana," I say, giving up on the newspapers and passing them to her. "Remember what my mum told me when I was your age!"

"Yes, I know," Dana replies, unfolding the papers and slotting them into place. "Never give all your heart away. Keep some of it back, because when they leave, which they always will, you'll need it for…" she pauses as if hunting for the right word… "For self-preservation," she says triumphantly.

"Well remembered," I say, giving Dana's arm a quick squeeze. "Now go and put the music on. We'll start with Michael Bublé this morning, I think."

"Righto, Mrs M." Dana's voice trickles away as she hurries over to the counter and starts the music. Her head disappears for a moment as she squats to turn the speakers on.

Lizzie is running late. Clemmie has overslept again and there's been shouting.

"Clemmie! It's eight o'clock!"

Lizzie was standing at the bottom of the stairs, her fingers gripping the bannisters.

"I know!" Clemmie had bawled at Lizzie from the landing, her face still crumpled with sleep, and then she'd slammed the bathroom door.

In Lizzie's picture-perfect world, it would not be like this. Instead, she and Clemmie would be sitting at the breakfast bar, sipping orange juice and eating toast, chatting companionably. It would be seven-thirty and the sun would be shining in at the window. Clemmie's bag would be packed and ready by the front door and there would be laughter. Ben would come into the kitchen and give both his girls a kiss on the cheek before breezing out the door, his step light and springy.

But in the real world, Ben had already gone to work as he and Harvey had meetings in London today, and there was no cosy kitchen scene. It sometimes seemed to Lizzie that he was back deliberately arranging these early morning meetings just to avoid being at home when Clemmie had to go to college. They'd been spared a lot of hassle during lockdown but, on the downside, they'd also had to live with Clemmie's frustrations at her secret online life.

When they'd finally got into the car this morning, Lizzie hadn't been able to stop herself from saying, "I'm going to be late, you know."

"I'm *sorry*!" Clemmie had snarled under her breath, eyes glued to her phone, her bony shoulders sagging under her hoodie.

"It's just I've got to go to the bakers and…"

"Look, I said I'm sorry, didn't I? Just leave it will you, Mum? You're always on my case." She leaves it for a beat for maximum impact and then says, "It's just so not fair."

Lizzie counted to ten, put the radio up a fraction and concentrated on not responding. Always torn between whether keeping silent at Clemmie's gross injustices was the coward's way out, or the epitome of wisdom, unfortunately for both of them, Lizzie often alternates between the two. Today's plan was to keep quiet and let the moment pass. She listened to Zoe Ball instead, marvelling at how she's always so bloody cheerful.

At the bakery in Highclere, the bread and cakes were ready as usual, and Lizzie put them in the boot of *Flick's* van thinking, not for the first time, whether she and Faith should consider having them delivered each day. It would cost more that was true, but it would save this extra pressure. Once again, as Lizzie closed the door of the van with an angry thump, she wondered what it would be like if she wasn't held hostage by Clemmie's moods so often; if she was able to break free and say, "Just get on with it yourself."

Sara had had a point when she'd said what she'd said on Saturday night. An unwelcome truth, but a truth, nonetheless.

Lizzie and her daughter never seemed to get to the end of the 'push me/pull you' game and, as she stopped outside college and Clemmie opened the door and got out, Clemmie didn't say thank you for the lift, nor did Lizzie expect her to.

"May see you later," was all Clemmie had said, before she set off, head down, still looking at the screen of her phone.

"Fine," Lizzie answered as she started to indicate and then pulled away. She didn't look back at her daughter but turned the radio up even louder until the music started to hurt her ears.

"Oh, there you are!" Faith says as Lizzie steps out of the van in the service yard behind the shop.

"Yes, sorry. Clemmie was running late."

"No problem, let's unload, shall we?"

"Dana here?"

"Yes, full of some boy or another!"

"What? Another one?"

The women smile at one another as they carry the trays inside.

"I'll get Dana to lay out the cakes and start serving, then we'd better get on with the sandwiches."

"OK," Faith replies happily, and Lizzie looks briefly at her friend, admiring once again Faith's sense of equanimity.

They stand side by side in the kitchen making sandwiches. In the shop, the buzz is starting and Dana flits about behind the counter making coffee and serving cake. The sandwiches are on sale from ten, in time for the lunchtime rush.

Lizzie takes a handful of grated cheese, her hand warm in its hygienic glove, her breath hot behind her mask. If someone asked why she liked to cater for other people, she knows what her answer would be. It circles her mind most days, this need to sustain others. She feels she has failed with Clemmie, and that her daughter not eating is another sign of her failure as a mother and provider. It's the ultimate form of rejection, she thinks angrily as she puts the cut sandwich in its *Flick's* wrapper, writes today's date on the sticker and places it on the trolley ready for wheeling into the shop.

They've tried counselling of course and medication. The doctor had prescribed Sertraline, but Lizzie doesn't know whether Clemmie is taking it or not, and he's referred them to a clinic at the local hospital but, with Clemmie now over eighteen, the wait for the NHS is too long so they've gone privately, have sat in some woman's dining room where Lizzie feels inadequate and exposed.

The sessions haven't gone well so far. Clemmie's proved so resistant and Lizzie so tearful that, after six sessions and when Clemmie then appeared, on the surface at least to be eating a bit more, they've decided to have a rest. Their next appointment is in a couple of months' time, by when Lizzie hopes this nightmare will be behind them and someone will have taken a sledgehammer to the wall between herself and her daughter and reduced it to rubble. She rarely thinks of what might have caused it – what happened that day all those years ago – it seems too big a thing to unpick. No, it's better to concentrate on the now and try and find a way forward, isn't it?

"Right," Faith says, as she wipes down the surfaces and peels off her gloves. "On to the next bit!"

Lizzie takes her turn serving while Faith puts out the sandwiches and Dana does the first round of clearing the dirty crockery and stacking the dishwasher. *It's a good system,* Lizzie thinks. *We all work well together, don't we?*

"Can I help?" she asks a portly lady of about seventy who's standing in front of the counter, fishing in her handbag for her glasses, putting them on and peering at the menu on the chalkboard above Lizzie's head.

"That one, the second one down, dear," she says. "Sorry, I don't know how to say it right."

"Cappuccino," Lizzie says, smiling, laying a spoon on a saucer in front of her and then turning round to the coffee machine.

"Precisely," the woman says, taking some money from her purse.

The woman has light brown eyes and soft skin, and her face is almost girl-like Lizzie notices, but her figure is stout and clad in bulky woollens. She's not wearing a wedding ring.

Lizzie loves watching the customers, seeing where they'd fit in the categories she's invented. There's the Blue Rinse Brigade she and Faith had laughed over: the clutches of grey-haired friends who most likely play bridge together, or outdoor bowls in fine weather. These people may have been friends forever like her and Ben with Sara, Anthony, Faith and Harvey, or they may have just met at a pensioners' club perhaps, where they've gone to try and fill the gaps in their lives their lost loves have left.

Then there are the well-dressed ladies who meet for coffee or lunch and gossip about other well-dressed ladies who meet for coffee or lunch.

She'd heard one once, all Prada glasses, Jimmy Choo shoes and Louis Vuitton handbag actually say, "Well you know, she was just being so thin that day *and* just going on and on about how much he earned that I just couldn't take it. Perhaps if I hadn't been feeling so fat myself, I may not have snapped like I did."

"What did you say?" her companion had asked conspiratorially.

The other woman whispered something across the table that Lizzie couldn't hear. There was laughter. Neither woman had an ounce of fat on them and were sipping skinny lattes. Lizzie wanted to plonk a huge slice of cake down in front of both of them and say, "Right, eat that or I'll confiscate the chihuahuas you've no doubt got at home!"

What hurts Lizzie the most though are the women with pushchairs. She'd see them when they were huge and pregnant, and then later, they come with their babies, who in a flash become toddlers and then when these children are at school, the women come back, calmer now, but still as tired. These are the women Lizzie wants to warn. "Please take care," she wants to say. "Your children will break your heart."

"Excuse me?"

"Oh sorry!" Lizzie looks up. The portly lady has left with her coffee and Mr Brown has arrived. "Must be ten-thirty," Lizzie says, glancing over at the clock.

"On the dot!" Mr Brown replies.

"Coffee with hot milk to the side, no sugar and a slice of flapjack?" Lizzie asks, smiling up at him.

"Correct!" he replies. "As usual."

Mr Brown has taken to coming back in most days at ten-thirty on his way to the Legion for lunch. His routine pleases Lizzie and Faith no end.

"Morning Mr Brown," Faith says from where she's standing in front of the coffee machine. She locks the group head into the machine.

Mr Brown's beady eyes twinkle. It seems to Lizzie that though he's an old man, Mr Brown still has things to do, and still wishes his young wife hadn't died. They'd only been eighteen when they'd married and he'd mourned her for sixty years, so he'd told them once.

"Dreadful business this, isn't it?" he says.

"What's that?" Lizzie asks as she places a slice of flapjack onto a place.

"This child," he says. "The boy who drowned on a school trip. Can't imagine what his parents must be going through. It's on the front page of the paper. Guess it must be all over the internet as well. What an intrusion. Poor people. Never had children of my own of course, but even so..."

Mr Brown's voice trails away as he waits for his coffee. Lizzie and Faith can't look at one another. There's nothing either of them can think of to say to him in reply. Neither looks over at the newspapers in the rack, but both are grateful that it'll be Brenda's job to put them in the recycling bin at the end of the day. The headlines would be far too painful for either of them to bear.

At lunchtime, Clemmie and Jaz come in. Lizzie dislikes the way their hair is scraped back from their faces; it makes them look hard and unforgiving.

"Hi Mum," Clemmie says. "Two lattes to go. One skinny."

Faith leans over from where she's toasting a ciabatta. "Wouldn't hurt to say 'please', you know!" she says lightly.

Lizzie allows this. This kind of intervention is permitted. Although they don't expect their kids to pay and never have, Lizzie agrees that manners are necessary.

Clemmie scowls and Lizzie doesn't know what to say next.

"Did you have a good morning?" she asks at last as she plucks two takeaway cups from the pile.

"Yeh, suppose so," her daughter replies carelessly.

"Hey, Clemmie," Dana says tentatively as she brushes past them with a tray loaded dangerously high with dirty cups and saucers. "How are you?"

It's a good thing she doesn't wait for a reply because Clemmie ignores her, leans her head towards Jaz and says something under her breath. They both look at Dana's retreating back and smile; neither are nice smiles.

"Don't teach you manners at that college of yours then?" Faith says, more sharply this time.

This too is allowed, and Lizzie lets it go, just like she had let what Sara said go too. The path of least resistance is Lizzie's preferred route at all times.

"It's on the syllabus for next term," Clemmie says, looking sheepish and trying to make a joke of it.

"Thanks, Mum," she says as Lizzie hands her the coffee and glances up briefly. "See you later then."

Lizzie watches as they leave, coffee in one hand, phones in the other, Clemmie pushing open the door with her elbow.

Stepping through the gleaming turnstile in the cavernous foyer of the offices in Berkeley Square, Harvey feels stupidly nervous. It's not as though he hasn't faced this kind of meeting a hundred times before, but he's feeling unsettled today. Ben strides easily next to him. They're both dressed in open-necked shirts and jeans like some sort of uniform, and he wishes he'd worn something else. Harvey is carrying a slim document case; Ben's hands swing freely by his side and he's smiling.

"It's going to be fine," Ben says as a pole-thin girl, dressed in a tight black skirt and white top, appears before them and bends her head elegantly in the direction of a brightly lit corridor flanked by tall glass doors. They follow her, watching her hips sway in front of them. Harvey hears a voice of censure in his head. "Don't even go there," it's saying.

"Thank you," Harvey says as the girl holds open a door for them.

"He'll be along in a moment," she says and the way she says *He* sounds reverential. Her voice is almost a whisper.

"Thank you," says Harvey again, cursing himself for not being able to form a whole sentence.

"Tea and coffee'll be along in a minute," she adds as she closes the door.

It woomps into place a bit like a spaceship's door and Harvey wonders if they would be able to escape even if they wanted to. He feels sweat prickling his neck. He sits down and puts his document case on the wide expanse of light-coloured wood in front of him. Ben goes over to the window.

"Great view," he says, turning to look at Harvey.

On another day, a past day, Harvey would have said, "Yes, it sure was!" And, meaning the girl in the corridor, they both would have laughed, but today all he says is, "An expensive one, I shouldn't wonder."

A waitress scuttles in carrying a tray. She puts it on the table in front of Harvey and lifts her smiling eyes at him.

"Thank you," he says again.

"Guess we should wait?" Ben asks, running his fingers along the back of one of the black leather chairs. At the top of the table is what looks like a throne. Both men instinctively sit some distance from it.

The door opens. A small grey-haired man enters.

"Right," he says. "I can give you five minutes. David?" He turns to the young man who's followed him in. "Brief me."

The David person is a slightly larger version of his boss; he has that same air of authority, but he's much younger and doesn't wear his gravitas as easily. His suit is too sharp, his glasses are tinted just a shade too dark for him to be entirely credible. However, as he starts to speak, the small grey-haired man pulls out the vast seat and sits down. It makes him look surprisingly large.

"So, with the late instructions," David says, pulling down the cuffs of his shirt, "and the overrun and the dispute over the party wall, it looks like we're talking about a month's delay and an overspend of a hundred thousand."

The man at the end of the table extends out his arms and drums his fingers on the wood.

"Well?" he asks, piercing both Harvey and Ben with steely, grey eyes. "What's your plan? Surely, it's your job to see this sort of thing doesn't happen?"

This last sentence, although it ended with a question mark, isn't a question, and Harvey knows this. His instinct is to bristle and to catalogue the series of miscommunications with the contractor which has led up to this. He has email trails which show his and Ben's attempts to rectify and pacify, to seek the middle ground and formulate a compromise to please all parties and to keep the building works on track and the costs within budget, but he knows that this bullet-hard man isn't interested in any of this sort of guff.

He wants facts and solutions, nothing more, so Harvey takes a deep breath and says, "We have prepared a report which was sent to David last night which lists the actions we believe are necessary to get the works going again and limit any liability."

He looks at David as he says this and David, for all his slicked back, pinstripe efficiency, shrugs his shoulders very slightly in the direction of the man calling the shots and says, "It all looks like it makes sense, just need you to give it the go-ahead."

There is a moment of heavy silence in the room. Harvey feels like someone is stretching an elastic band somewhere and is waiting for the right moment to let it fly. The small man fixes David with a hard gaze and says, "That's not my job, that's yours. Just do it, David. I needn't be here." And with that, he pushes out his chair and walks towards the door. He opens it with an impatient tug and glances back over his shoulder briefly at David and says, "tell Louisa I'm on my way back up. I will need the car brought round."

He doesn't say goodbye to Harvey or Ben, he doesn't even acknowledge them. David rushes to pick up the phone on a counter running the length of the wall on the other side of the room and punches in a number. Harvey and Ben risk looking at one another as they listen to David speak breathlessly into the mouthpiece.

"Dad's done here. He's on his way back," he says. There's a brief silence while the person at the other end says something and then David adds, "Thanks Lou." And puts down the phone.

As he does so, Harvey thinks there's something about the way David says these which signals something that goes deeper than the usual conversation between employees.

With the small man gone, the atmosphere in the room lightens significantly.

"Tea? Coffee?" David asks, picking up a pot from the tray the waitress had brought in earlier.

"Sure," Ben says lightly. "Black coffee, no sugar for me."

With the drinks poured, Harvey gets out a copy of the report. "Right, shall we go through this now?" he asks.

"Let's do that," says David. "I'm sure we can reach an accord somehow. It can't be beyond the wit of man."

The way he says this makes him seem so much older than his years suddenly, as though his father's departure from the room has given him the space to mature.

Harvey regards him with renewed respect. "Yes," he says. "I'm sure by the end of the meeting, we can have made a significant amount of progress."

There's no ice-cool girl to show them out an hour later. Harvey visits the men's room en route. As he pees, he feels a shuddering in his muscles, like he's run a long race but isn't sure whether he's crossed the finish line yet or not. He thinks he looks tired when he sees his reflection in the mirror as he washes his hands. He wishes he was at home and could hear Faith's radio playing in the kitchen, and smell dinner cooking. He doesn't want to be here in this shiny place with its unpredictable people and he asks himself again whether the payoff of having their own business is enough to see them through the crap of days like this one.

Later, over a pint at Corney & Barrow, Harvey untucks his shirt. He's still hot and feels like a layer of grime has attached itself to him.

"That's better," he says, as the air circulates around his stomach. "God, that was fucking awful. Could have gone tits up, couldn't it?"

"Yeh," Ben says, putting down his glass. "He's always going to be a tricky customer that one. Even more so in the flesh," he adds. "We probably would've done better on Zoom, like in the old days!"

They both laugh. Truth told, no one's found it easy to get back to normal after Covid. A year or so ago, where they've just been, where they are now, would be unthinkable.

"Thanks for getting that report done," Harvey adds. "We would have been fucked without it."

"Deflected attention from us to David, didn't it?" Ben laughs as he says this. "Will be glad to get home tonight, that's for sure and then tomorrow…"

"Thanks again," Harvey says. "Don't know what I'd do without you, you fat bastard!"

"Your round then," Ben retorts, draining the last of his drink and putting his glass down with a thump.

Tuesday

Anthony is sitting on the edge of his unmade bed in the Soho Hotel. It's six o'clock, he's dressed and just about to leave for work. A half-drunk cup of coffee sits on the bedside table next to his elbow. The room is dark, save for the light from a small lamp on the dressing table and the one in the bathroom, a chink from which is sliding through the slightly open door. All he has to do is finish his coffee and go, but he doesn't want to. He looks across at the empty, unslept-on pillow next to his and wishes again that Sara would come and stay with him, just once, so that he could remember her here, so that the hotel would bear some stamp of her presence. It's a brutal, impersonal place without her. He picks up the phone.

"Sorry," he whispers. "Did I wake you?"

"Yes," Sara's voice is mumbly, and he can visualise her dark hair spreading like a fan around her face.

"Just wanted to say I've remembered I've got those tickets for the show tonight. Will you come? I could get off work early. We could have a bite to eat first?"

He knows he's sounding needy, but then he is. It's so lonely here; everyone else seems to walk around in pairs or in company, while he's on his own, trying to be brave, missing his wife and his long-dead child; always missing the life he could have had.

"Oh, Anthony, no, I'm sorry, I can't."

Her voice sounds distant, and he tells himself it's because she is actually a long way away, physically at least. He wishes he could see the look in her eyes to gauge whether she's telling the truth or not. *What else does she have arranged for tonight,* he wonders?

"Do you have plans already then?" he asks a little sharply.

"No, it's just…"

She trails off unconvincingly and he knows why she can't come, it's because she won't. It's just too big and, even now. She's too scared of being found out, of meeting someone in the Ladies or a waitress in a restaurant who'll ask her whether she has children and if so, how old they are.

"Yes, a son," Anthony has practised saying a thousand times. "He would be nineteen now. He died when he was five, you see."

Whereas Sara never wanted to say this out loud, Anthony occasionally needed to; he needed the knowledge to be out in the world. He needed to be out in the world too, somewhere other than work or home and, in the open spaces outside his house, be able to dilute some of the pain.

"Why don't you take someone from work?" Sara is saying. He can hear her moving about in the bed, the rustle of sheets, and feels an unaccountable rage seeping through his bones.

"I don't want to, that's why," he barks. "I want to go with someone I know well, not some casual acquaintance. I want to go with you," he adds quietly but firmly.

"Ring Faith then," Sara snaps back. "You always seem to at times like these."

It was true, though they'd lost touch briefly when Faith first started work, ever since they'd sat in Anthony's bedroom listening to David Bowie when they'd been teenagers, Faith has been Anthony's default setting. There'd never been anything between them, not really, although Anthony's thoughts do stall here. There was that time when... No, he thinks they've always been and still are just the best of friends, or so Anthony believes. He trusts Faith; he has to – she is one of the foundation stones of his life.

"I may very well do that," he says. "It would be a shame to let the tickets go to waste."

"Righto," Sara answers, a little carelessly he thinks.

She still doesn't realise how much gets chipped off each time she does something like this. It's as though she's immune to the damage she causes, but for him, each tiny rejection gets added to the rest so that each fragment, over the years, is slowly building into a solid heap between them. Even if he had the energy, which he rarely does these days, he wouldn't know how to scale it in order to reach her on the other side.

"I'll call you later then," he says, hoping she will catch the sadness in his voice and want to do something to change it, but it's apparent that she does neither.

"OK," she replies. "Goodbye, Anthony."

"Goodbye."

He sits listening to the silence on the other end of the line for a long minute before he too hangs up. Then he calls Faith.

"Hey," he says after Faith picks up on the second ring. "Look, I'm sorry it's so early…"

"What's wrong?" Faiths ask, her voice full of panic and alarm. It is still obscenely early, Anthony realises.

"Nothing's wrong. Look I'll call back later when I'm at work."

"No, it's OK, go ahead. I was just waking up anyway but hang on a sec while I move away from Harvey, he's still sleeping. Can you hear him snoring?" she asks, laughing lightly.

Anthony envies their togetherness; wishes some of it for himself.

"Right," she continues after a moment. He can imagine her sitting on the edge of the bath in their en suite or leaning up against the bannisters on the square landing of their house. "What's up?" she asks.

"You're going to think me silly, but I've got these tickets for *When She Opens Her Eyes* at Drury Lane tonight and Sara can't come…" There's that white lie again – can't/won't – there's a subtle but telling difference. "I'd love it if you could join me," he adds. suddenly aware of a distant siren and he wonders briefly what emergency it is responding to. Ambulances and sirens still manage to put the fear of God in him, even after all this time.

There's a short pause. Just long enough for Anthony to fear Faith'll say no. Then, a tiny hitch in her voice before she says, "Sounds lovely. What time?"

"Seven-thirty. Could you make it for then?"

"I'll check with Lizzie, make sure she can lock up and see to Brenda, but I'm sure it won't be a problem. I've wanted to see it for ages. There's been such a buzz about it on Twitter apparently, so Dana tells me."

He hears Faith's low, friendly chuckle and feels an immense gratitude not only that she is in his life, but that she came into it in the first place and that she stayed, that despite everything she stayed. Without her, he thinks, his life would only be three-quarters full.

"Sure, you haven't got plans with Harvey?" he asks, willing the answer to be no.

Anthony's already looking forward to seeing her familiar body walking along Drury Lane, having it pressed up next to him in the theatre seat.

"No, nothing that can't wait," she says. "I'll call you later to confirm, OK? Once I've spoken to Lizzie and just double-checked with Harvey. That, OK?"

"That's more than OK," Anthony answers. "Thanks, Faith, you're a star."

"It'll be fun," she says before they hang up.

There's a slight spring in Anthony's step as he walks towards the hotel bedroom door. Suddenly he doesn't feel so alone.

The theatre is hot, and the audience expectant. Faith turns to him and smiles. The stage lights reflect off her glasses making her look dazed and transfixed. She waves the programme in front of her face to cool herself down.

He's had a crap day; a deal's gone south, and the US are on his back. Added to this, Martin in finance had rejected his departmental budget proposal and that would mean another day's work to rejig the figures. His call to Sara hadn't gone well either.

"Faith said yes, by the way, about coming to the show, I mean," Anthony had told her when he'd phoned just before he left work.

"That's nice, hope you have a good time," she'd replied, her voice monotone.

It's so fucking hard having a telephone marriage, he thought as he asked what she was having for supper, and she told him she thought she'd have a poached egg on toast or something. She wasn't really hungry, but then she never was. He, on the other hand, was famished and would have to pick something up on the way to the show. *Another hastily eaten sandwich,* he thought. *Another fucking sandwich.*

Anthony puts his phone on silent and is still feeling twitchy when the curtain goes up.

When the play ends, though, he finds himself crying. *Ridiculous,* he thinks. It's not even a sad play, but tears well up and he dashes them away with a hot hand. He doesn't look at Faith and is glad she's not looking at him. Instead, she's clapping hard as the final music fades.

"Wow," she says, turning to him at last, her eyes bright and glittery. "That was fantastic. Thanks so much for inviting me."

"Thanks for coming," he manages to say. "You got time for a drink before your train?"

"Sure," she says, standing and shaking out the creases in her skirt; it's dark red, long and made of some silky material he notices. She's also wearing a denim jacket with a white top underneath it and around her neck is a large paisley scarf. He feels strangely formal next to her in his suit. His shirt's open at the collar and his tie's in his pocket but still, he feels stiff and clumsy.

It's odd, he thinks, as he too stands and starts to shuffle out of the row they've been sitting in, how she doesn't seem to have changed at all over the years. To him, she's still the same capable, easy-going, bouncy-haired girl she'd been when they were younger. Apart from the day Douggie died, he's never seen her ruffled. Although at the funeral… Anthony has to stop thinking here, concentrating instead on picking his way through the discarded ice cream cartons on the auditorium floor.

They go for a drink in Covent Garden.

"Hey, slow down," I laugh as I trip alongside Anthony, my shorter legs having trouble keeping up with his longer ones. "It's just like it was when we walked to school," I say, thumping him lightly on the arm when I catch up with him.

"Sorry," he says, looking down at me. In the streetlight, I notice new worry lines around his eyes. How come my friends are suffering so much? Lizzie, Sara, and now Anthony, all seem so diminished by life at the moment.

I studiously ignore the vacuum in my own life, the secrets pressing against my rib cage, the thing I should have told each of my best friends, and my stunning inability to talk to Harvey about any of these things.

"What did Sara say she was doing tonight?" I ask as Anthony places a glass of wine and a pint on the table in front of us.

"Not sure, she didn't really say," he answers, taking a sip of his drink.

"Probably working on the book," I say.

"Probably," he replies.

"You home on Thursday as usual?"

"Yep, as usual."

"Anything planned for the weekend?"

"Not really. You?"

"Mum and Dad are coming to visit. Seeing that they couldn't come over at Christmas. Apparently, they decided not to take any bookings this weekend, have got someone to look after the dogs and are popping across to see us instead."

"That'll be nice."

"Mmm," I say, running my fingers up and down the stem of my glass. "Not so sure about that!"

My relationship with my parents, like mine with my husband and my friends, has ambiguous corners. I have spent what seems like a lifetime trying to decide what to do: to tell the truth, or to carry on with the lie. Knowing what I know burns me, like someone is holding a match to my skin, and I regret the gulf it creates between me and those I love, particularly Anthony. Yes, most particularly him.

He's talking about the show again; it's a safe topic of conversation and I'm relieved by this. And yet, and yet, always also there in the background is what happened when we were both at university and he'd come to visit one weekend. I'd just broken up with someone; his name was Craig, or something similar. Anthony too was unattached. He was handsome in those days; tall, powerful, dark-haired, with an easy grace. He still is handsome, actually.

Moreover, there was something worldly about him then; girls felt good in his presence, certain that they would be well looked after by him. Having known him as an uncomfortable teenager, I was constantly surprised at how popular he was with the opposite sex.

We'd gone to a party in a small, terraced house. It was hot and crowded. The day had been one of purplish clouds and the possibility of a storm, the air almost fizzed with it. I got to talking to some medical students in the kitchen while Anthony was in the lounge. There was a lot of drink and, after an hour or so, I extricated myself from my position crammed up against the fridge and went in search of him. At first, I couldn't see him, but then as my eyes got used to the darkness of the room, there he was, arms wrapped around a girl, kissing her hungrily. I watched, entranced as his hand snaked its way under the girl's top, and saw his long fingers circle one of her breasts. Behind the thump of the music, the girl groaned and, much to my astonishment, I found myself hating the sound of it.

I went over to them and tapped Anthony on the arm. He broke away from the girl and smiled a long lazy smile at me. His eyes were hooded and full of an expression I'd never seen before.

"I'm going," I said abruptly. "It's too hot and crowded here."

"Oh," he said, gazing at the girl who was shifting from one leg to the other.

"You coming?" I asked.

"What the fuck?" the girl said, stepping out of Anthony's grip. "This your girlfriend or what?" she asked, her face pointy with anger.

"No! Anthony said quickly, We're just friends. Right, Faith?"

"Faith?" the girl spat the word out.

"It's her name!" Anthony replied.

I watched the exchange like a spectator at Wimbledon, but then fixed my gaze on Anthony. "Well?" I asked.

"Think I'll hang around if that's OK," he said, reaching out for the girl again. He was, I realised, very drunk.

"Suit your fucking self then," I said, turned abruptly and stormed out of the room, out of the house, finding myself on the pavement, the air heavy with unbroken thunder and unspent lightning. "Fuck," I muttered, hoisting my bag onto my shoulder and beginning the long walk home.

"Hey, wait up!" Anthony was running after me. Huge, pregnant raindrops started to fall as he reached me. "What's the matter?" he asked, grabbing my arm.

"I don't know," I said, rain spiralling through my hair and seeping into my clothes, thinking now would be a good time to have an umbrella in my bag. It was suddenly very cold. "Time of the month?" I added lamely, hoping he would laugh.

He didn't.

"Come here, you soft git," he said, pulling me to him and wrapping his long, lean arms around me. "You know you're the only one for me! Friends always, eh?"

I wanted to believe him, I wanted to believe our friendship was different to most, that it could withstand more, that it wasn't based on the usual things like sex and duty and accountability but, at that moment with my wet face pressed up against his damp jacket, all I wanted was to have him lie on top of *me*, have his hand circle *my* breast and I had no fucking clue where these thoughts might have come from.

We ran most of the way back to my student flat, me just a few paces behind him of course and we hadn't been able to talk then and when we got in, we'd been so busy getting dry and making coffee, you know that sort of issue avoidance thing, that the subject was left unspoken, unexplored and it has remained so ever since. We'd both gone to our separate beds that night, me in my single bed in my room, him under a sleeping bag on the sofa, and I've never looked too deeply into why I reacted the way I did, and he never explained why he came running after me.

And now we are sitting in a pub in London on a late spring evening after having seen a show, with him married to Sara and me to Harvey and, having been through all we've been through, still not able to ask the question, "What if?" Because both the question and the answer are now too old and too unnecessary.

The other corner, the darker one, the one that contains the more dangerous truth I've battled to quell for so long is one I've never been brave enough to explore either. The time for confessing what I know, for squaring the circle, for righting the wrongs has long gone. I tell myself we have to live with the lives we have now. No good can ever come from upsetting the delicate balance we've all achieved: those of us who know, and those who don't.

I live in fear of things changing though, every minute of every day, like a faint hum in the background to our lives, the fear is there.

"You OK," he asks. "You've gone awfully quiet."

"I'm fine," I lie. Of course, I lie. I've been lying to him for so long that it has become my default setting.

"You can talk to me, you know. About anything," he says.

"I know I can," I reply. "But I'm fine, I really am."

87

"I'd forgive you anything," he adds. "You have always been and will always be the better half of me."

I can't tell him how wrong he is. As much as I want to, I can't. It's that default setting again, the need to protect him, to protect myself, everyone.

So, instead of telling him the truth, I smile at Anthony across the table and say, "Better get going soon, I guess. We both have early starts in the morning."

As Anthony opens the door of a taxi for Faith and says, "Paddington please," to the driver and then saunters to the tube, Sara steps into the bath at home; the water is shallow and hot, just as she likes it. She gasps as it stings her skin. Lying back, she lets the bubbles cushion her. She closes her eyes. To her right is the window, and behind her is an airing cupboard housing the header tank which serves their en suite and which she uses to store her bed linen. There is so much spare time in Sara's life that this bed linen is colour coded and stacked in neat, pressed piles. She's often wished she could pull them out and stamp on them and then just throw them back any old how, but she knows she won't, she can't.

It's been a good day. She's written a thousand words and the cleaner's been in. Her name's Mary and she does a good job, but when she's cleaning, Sara keeps her distance, shutting herself in her writing room. The thought of cosy chats over coffee surrounded by dusters and Pledge is an anathema to her. No, she tends just to leave the money and a note and then hides, only venturing out of her room when Mary taps lightly on the door and says, "Shall I do in here now?" Then Sara finds something to do elsewhere in the house, after all, it's big enough, and waits until Mary's finished, and says, "There you go, dear. All done!" and trundles the hoover back along the landing, ignoring the one door she knows not to open.

Sara lets her hair float, cradled in the foam, careful to keep the water off her face; she'll wash her hair in a minute, slowly, one cup full at a time. She still can't bear the feel of it on her face, of being submerged, of not being able to breathe. She can barely cope with showers, but even they seem less dangerous than baths somehow. Meanwhile, she watches as the water pools around her legs, lapping against her thighs and breasts; it looks so innocent as it does so, so harmless.

It is very quiet; all she can hear are the trees shuffling in the darkness behind the house and the occasional car swishing by at the top of the spur. She wills herself not to be lonely. This is what she wants after all.

Sara's also never really allowed herself to think, *What if? What if the house was full of Douggie and his things? What if he had a girlfriend and I came across them in the kitchen cooking omelettes late at night? What if they were laughing and Douggie was resting his hands on this girl's hips as they stood in front of the hob? What if he was called Doug by now?*

"OK, Mum?" he'd say and turn his big brown eyes towards her, well she assumed they'd still be big and brown. She'd often wanted to pay someone to do a photofit for her, to take a picture of what he'd looked like just before he died and have them do some sort of technical wizardry to show what he'd look like now, like they do with missing children like they did with Madeleine McCann. Well, it would be appropriate, wouldn't it, he is missing after all, missing from her life, missing from life in general. There's no man in her kitchen with his hands resting on a girl's slim waist, there's no deep voice; there's nothing, just emptiness and loss and so much anger she feels it could actually melt her bones.

She opens her eyes; there's a strange rumbling somewhere in the house. She can't pinpoint it, it's more a buzzing, but it's getting louder, then there's a sound of metal breaking and then there's a rushing sound, like applause. She raises her head and strains to hear better. From behind her comes a roar and then a torrent of water shooting out of the linen cupboard, bursting through the doors and falling like some bizarre waterfall into the bathroom. Sheets tumble out like shrouds, and she has absolutely no idea what to do.

Her heart is thundering in her chest, she can't breathe, her arms and legs have turned to jelly and it's as though a stranger is shouting inside her head.

She leaps out of the bath, runs naked into the bedroom and, with trembling hands picks up her mobile from beside the bed. She calls Anthony, but he doesn't answer. *Where the fuck is he,* she thinks? She hangs up. Dials another number.

"Ben?"

"Whatever's the matter?" His voice is both strange and familiar. It makes total sense for her to call him. It makes no sense at all.

"There's water pouring out, in the bathroom, I can't stop it. Help me." She says this last bit plaintively, or she thinks she does, she hasn't really been able to hear her own voice properly, there's still that somebody shouting in her head, and the water's still torrenting out of the cupboard.

"I'm coming, hold on. Try and find the stopcock if you can," Ben says, and the line goes dead.

With some strange presence of mind, Sara runs back into the bathroom and takes the plug out of the bath, the water's about an inch from the top, and it's starting to threaten to spill over the edge. Sheets and pillowcases are strewn over the floor like in her imagination from before, like flotsam from a shipwreck. She grabs a towel and wraps it around herself, then she goes into the bedroom, shuts the door behind her and crouches in a corner. Her hair is sticking to her shoulders, her mind is numb; she is taking short, sharp breaths; she is very cold.

At number four Ben grabs the spare key to Anthony's and Sara's house which Anthony had insisted he and Lizzie keep for just such an emergency as this. Faith and Harvey have one too. They each have keys to one another's houses. Always have. Of course, they do.

However, what Anthony had said was, "With me away so much, it would be good to know there's someone nearby if Sara ever needed anything…" His voice faded at the end of the sentence as he stood, slightly hunched in front of Ben. They both knew that what Sara really needed none of them could provide.

"Where're you going?" Lizzie asks from her armchair in front of the TV.

There's a rerun of *Endeavour* on tonight, one of her favourites. Ben hates detective shows but Lizzie loves them, so he tends to work if she's watching one. Clemmie's out at some pub quiz, he thinks. He's not really sure, as Clemmie doesn't really talk to him much these days.

"Sara's got a plumbing emergency," he says as he rushes out the front door.

He doesn't wait for Lizzie's reply.

Letting himself into number six, he takes the stairs two at a time. The house feels as though it's wailing. Sara and Anthony's have the same layout as theirs, so he hurries to the master bedroom, opens the door and sees Sara huddled in a corner by the window covered only in a towel.

"Did you find the stopcock?" he asks.

She shakes her head.

He doubles back and flies down the stairs and into the kitchen. Wrenching open the door of the cupboard under the sink he bends his head, reaches in and turns the stopcock off. There is a strange moment of silence. He hadn't realised how much noise the water had made.

"Here," he says back in the bedroom, passing Sara a robe he finds lying on a chair. It is made of some sort of floaty material. It is covered in small lilac flowers.

"Thank you," she murmurs.

"Not sure how warm it'll make you. I'll try and find something better in a minute."

"OK," she says in a small, tired voice.

He surveys the damage in the bathroom. *It's not too extensive but it would be worth checking out the rest of the house,* he thinks.

Sara's put the robe on and is sitting on the edge of the bed.

"I couldn't get through to Anthony," she says. "I'm sorry. I'm so sorry."

"It's OK." He goes to the bed and sits down next to her. She is so thin and fragile that he's worried he's going to break her. Pulling her towards him, she rests her head on his shoulder. It feels surprisingly good to have it there. A wave of tenderness rises up in him and he wants to kiss her, not passionately but gently, affectionately. Ben is surprised by this feeling; he thinks he should have forgotten what it is like to be this close to someone who is not his wife.

"I'm just going to check out the rest of the place," he says, relieved to have something to do to make sure the moment passes. "Then I'll organise a plumber and see if I can get hold of Anthony. You get dressed in something warmer. I'll put the kettle on, shall I?"

She lifts her head and looks at him with round eyes, smudged with tiredness and hopelessness.

"Thank you," she says quietly, her lips hardly moving. "That would be lovely."

There's a small damp patch on the ceiling of the lounge where the water has seeped through from the bathroom above, but nothing that a lick of paint wouldn't sort out when it has dried. It hasn't gone into any of the electrics thankfully, but Ben decides to scan each room just in case. He surveys the dining room and the kitchen where he puts the kettle onto boil with water from the hot tap as the mains are still shut off. Then he goes into Anthony's study on the ground floor, all's well there. Upstairs, he checks out the guest room and Sara's writing room, pausing to look at the neat arrangement of papers on her desk and compares it slightly unfairly to the habitual mess Lizzie always seems to live in. Then he opens the last remaining door on the landing, reaches round the doorframe and switches on the light. Nothing in a million years could have prepared him for what he sees.

It's Douggie's room, just as he must have left it the day of the picnic. There is a pair of trousers slumped on the floor as though he had stepped out of them five minutes before. The bed is unmade and there is a half-built Lego castle on the carpet. A book lies open on the windowsill, and the wardrobe door is open so that Ben can see the tiny hangers hanging there, each with a shirt or jumper or pair of trousers hanging on it. There is a quiet film of dust over everything; it's been like this for fourteen years.

"Oh my God," he says out loud.

"Ben?" he hears her behind him. Turning, he sees her small pale face. She's wearing a pair of jog bottoms and a huge sweatshirt; her hair is still damp and is resting in ringlets on her shoulders; he's never seen it that way before.

"Don't tell anyone, please," she says. "Not Lizzie, nor Harvey, and especially not Faith."

"Of course not," he says as he switches off the light and closes the door. "Does Anthony know?"

"Of course, he does," she snaps and then she looks down at her feet so all Ben can see is the light bouncing off the top of her head. She glances back up at him, her eyes flat, masked.

"Why?" he asks after a lengthy pause in which they stand and look at one another. He is reminded of his father when he was a headmaster, and a pupil had done something wrong and been called in to see him. Sara's face is as pinched and worried as a child's who hasn't understood what they've done wrong.

"I just can't let go," she says finally and then she cries, huge round tears spilling down her cheeks.

"It's OK, really it is." They are leaning into one another now and he can feel the blood pounding in his ears. "We'd better make those calls," he says into her hair.

But they stand there as the minutes stretch and widen. Neither, it seems, wants or is able to move. He can feel her heart fluttering against his chest and remembers the soft curve of her neck. They remain frozen and he knows that should one of them move just a fraction, the inevitable would happen.

Then his mobile rings. Gently, he separates himself from Sara as he plucks it from his pocket. It's Lizzie.

"Is everything all right?" she asks when he answers.

"Yes," he says. "Everything's fine."

And it is, and it isn't. The moment of crisis has passed but another is queuing right behind it; another one is always there because they've never confronted what needs to be said, never dealt with the fallout of what happened all those years ago.

Friday

Clemmie texts her mum, 'Gone out. Staying at Jaz's'.

It's six in the evening and the house is quiet, her mum and dad are both out somewhere, but she doesn't care where. She picks up her bag and yanks open the front door, letting it slam shut behind her.

Standing at the end of the drive, she draws in the mustardy smell of their street; the leaves on the garden shrubs and the trees behind the houses seem large and menacing. Spring is turning into summer. Another year going by. Suddenly she doubts what she's just about to do. With a sigh, she strides towards the bus stop.

The journey's not too bad, just one change at Reading and, just before nine, she's at New Street. Ashley had said to meet at a pub near The Mailbox.

'Am here', she texts as she steps off the train.

'Gr8', he replies. 'C u soon'.

His band are already on stage when she gets there, so she asks the barman for a vodka and lime and hunts for somewhere to sit.

"You can sit here, love," says one man, patting the seat next to him and looking up at her with little piggy eyes.

"Ta, but I'm looking for someone," she mutters, as she squeezes round the back of his chair and desperately scans the room for a quiet corner where she can sit unnoticed. She's still not really very good at this sort of thing. She's also not sure why she couldn't tell her mum and dad where she was actually going; it's not like she's ashamed or anything. It's just that...

Mercifully, she spots an empty space at the end of a bench up against the wall; she can just about see the makeshift stage from there. She puts her drink down on the floor in front of her feet and peers around the heads in front of her to try and get a glimpse of him.

If asked to name the moment when her feelings for Ashley changed, she probably wouldn't be able to; it was a general seeping from the sort of feelings you'd have for a brother, to something very different indeed. *Maybe,* she thinks, as she takes a small sip of her drink. *It was when he kind of asked Dana out on a date.* She'd certainly felt differently after that.

They'd been hanging out at school in the link between the H and S blocks; it was pitting with rain and fucking cold. She, Ashley and Jaz were standing huddled in a group like penguins trying to keep warm. Then Dana walked past, all small and compact, wrapped up in some furry number so that only her pesky little mouth and nose showed. Even her eyes were half-hidden by her hood. But it was unmistakeably her; no one else could walk quite like she did. Then, without warning, Ashley peeled off to follow her, saying something like, "Hey, wait up!" but Clemmie couldn't quite hear the exact words because the wind had carried them away. She and Jaz were left with just each other's warmth, but the desertion was worse than that; it was like with Ashley's defection, someone had peeled off a layer of Clemmie's skin, exposing the beating heart of what she'd been hiding from for years, and she hated Dana for doing that to her.

After that, Clemmie had set her mouth to a hard cruel line every time she and Dana saw each other; she'd even sometimes 'accidentally' knocked her against the corridor wall outside History. She never asked Ashley what had happened; whether they'd 'gone out' or anything, with every fibre of her body she didn't want to know. All she knew was that ever since then she'd made it her job to be mean to Dana, and had felt differently about Ashley, not that she'd ever tell him about that either, not in a million years.

Now, she only has eyes for him as he plays, his head bent low so that the stage lights bounce off his mop of sandy hair. Occasionally, when he looks up and smiles, her heart catches at the sight of his freckles. She loves the way he stands, his legs angled like the sides of a triangle, his guitar at his groin, his foot tapping in time to the beat and the muscles of his arms flexing, flashing light, dark, light. The drummer pounds his drums, the boys are singing and jumping now, and the crowd are pulsing to the music; the whole place has been captured by them, and then the number's over.

There's applause. "Thank you," someone says into a microphone. "Back here, same time next week."

Other music plays from speakers on the walls while the next band sets up, there's a hum of conversation and people sidle to the bar to refresh their drinks. She hasn't eaten anything since some toast at breakfast, but she doesn't mind, the vodka has warmed her, has diluted her blood so that it rings through her body. She feels great.

"Hey," Ashley says, his guitar bag slung over his shoulder.

"Hey yourself," she replies.

"What did ya think?"

"It was great," she says, bending down to pick up her drink again so he can't see her blush. *It's probably the vodka,* she thinks.

"D'ya wanna another drink or shall we get out of here?" His head is half turned away from her as he searches the bar for his bandmates.

"Whatever you want to do," she replies, standing and pulling at the tight denim of her jeans. She's feeling light-headed and wonderful; she wants this particular moment, like an insect caught in amber, to last forever.

Later, as Ashley crashes onto Pete's bed in the next-door room, his thoughts turn to Clemmie. He still doesn't know why she comes up to visit him like this sometimes; how she'll follow him from bar to bar, sit and listen to him and his mates dissect the evening's performance and how he's sure she doesn't tell Lizzie or Ben that she comes so, in turn, he never mentions it to his mum or dad either.

How she gets away with it, he doesn't know.

But, at least, he knows where she is when she's with him – a lessening of the worry he carries around with him about her, and about Blake. Ever since the accident, it's always a little bit better when he knows the other two are safe.

He glances around the room. Pete's a strange bloke, he's into the Gorillaz and Michael Jackson and he goes home every weekend to visit his girlfriend, Sacha. Ashley thinks he must be crazy, but at least it means that when Clemmie descends on him, he has somewhere else to bunk down, so he doesn't keep her awake with his own inability to sleep.

They'd tried to sleep in the same room once, towards the start of term; her in his bed, him on the floor, but the night seemed to go on forever as he tried not to sigh and toss and turn and she'd looked so small and fragile under his duvet; nothing more than a bag of bones really.

Around three in the morning, he'd felt this irrational need to clamber in beside her and scoop her into his arms. He could almost imagine the fluttering of her heart next to his, the smooth skin on her arms and legs, and how tenderly he would have to hold her so that he wouldn't risk crushing her.

No, this is far better, he thinks, as he turns off Pete's light. *Far safer.* And he knows she's only a wall away.

Over in Cheltenham, Blake looks at the clock on the wall of his room. "Three a fucking clock," he mumbles, rubbing his tired eyes. The essay's due in on Monday and he's only just started it, is going to have to work all bloody weekend to get it done. Five thousand words on 'Paradise Lost' and he's only done five hundred so far. *Fucking Milton,* he thinks. *What was he thinking of?*

To his right are piles of notes and three musky reference books he'd got out of the library; those by other, more contemporary critics had already been taken out. "Fuck," he says out loud as he stretches back in his chair and hovers his fingers over the keyboard of his laptop.

Downstairs, the doorbell rings out shrilly, and Blake's heart starts to thunder irrationally in his chest. He waits; the rest of the house is silent. The bell rings again. He looks out of his window onto the street but whoever it is at the door is tucked into the porch so he can't see them. He creeps downstairs. There's a small figure standing on the other side of the frosted glass.

"Shit," he says to himself as he reaches out for the door handle. "No, please, don't let it be her. Not again."

But it is.

"Gabs," he says to the girl standing on the step wrapped in a huge woollen poncho thing, her hair a tangled mess of pink and green strands. The light from the hallway is winking off the diamond stud in her nose, her eyes are huge and panda-like with tiredness.

"Blake," her voice is plaintive, childlike. "I know it's late. Did I wake you?"

"Na," he says, leaning up against the wall, suddenly so tired he feels he could curl up and sleep on the mat, right there, right then. "Na, I was working. Got an essay to do."

"Can I come in?" she asks after a pause during which it's obvious neither of them knows what to say. After all, she'd left so brutally the last time, he could almost still feel the edges of torn skin flapping unhealed around his heart. He would be a fool to let her back and they both knew it.

"Sure," he says, opening the door a bit wider and making room for her to step into the hall.

He turns and walks upstairs. He knows she'll close the door and follow him. They've been through this dance a hundred times before.

"What's your essay on?" she asks as she shrugs herself out of her poncho, revealing some sort of black lacy top and long black leather skirt. On her feet are huge DM's, painted over with purple emulsion, some parts of which are peeling off, making the leather look mottled and ugly.

He tells her and then says, "Fancy a coffee or something?"

"No, thanks. Just wondered if I could sleep here, that's all. I know it's late." She's slurring her words; is either drunk or stoned or both, Blake doesn't really want to know. "I've lost my keys again," she adds. "Really sorry, Blakey Boy," she says as she presses her tiny frame up against him.

He feels himself stir; he really wishes she'd go, but then he remembers them fucking, her multi-coloured head on his chest in the grubby light of morning, the spark in her eyes and the perfect pink of her lips. Despite all her best efforts to look otherwise, Gabs is a beautiful girl, at least she's always been to him; still is. But she's also dangerous and unpredictable; she's left him so many times now and, each time he thinks it's for good and he can move on, something like this happens and he's right back where he started again.

"Sure," he says again. "I've got to work anyway, so you can have the bed."

"You goin' to join me?" she asks, her head on one side like a watchful bird.

"No," he says resolutely. "I've got to work, I told you." He knows he sounds sharp and mean, but this time, this time, he's determined he won't give in; he can't.

"Suit yourself," she says, as she curls up on the bed like a kitten. She doesn't take off her boots and within seconds she's asleep.

Blake sits back down in front of his laptop and tries very hard not to watch her. He puts his headphones on. There is music and the minutes tick by, and he writes precisely fifty more words before dawn begins to break.

As Clemmie sips her vodka and lime in Birmingham, Lizzie's back home in the kitchen at number four, getting another bottle of wine out of the fridge.

Friday night is girls' night, she says to herself for the umpteenth time, trying not to feel a habitual tug of guilt of having to throw Ben out of the house every third Friday or leave him staring at his laptop screen while she gathers with Faith and Sara for what has, over the years, become a very necessary sort of community girl hug. It hadn't been the same on Zoom, but they'd done it as often as they could. Being able to do it in person again made everything so much easier.

But then, you'd think, she muses, as she shakes out the dregs of the crisps from the packet into a bowl and tucks the bottle under her arm. *Of the three of us I at least should have been good with kids; it'd been my background after all.*

She'd taken a course in childcare at school after her A Levels and had worked at various play schemes and nursery schools until, just after she'd met and married Ben, she got the job as a supervisor at the nursery where Faith took Blake when he was three.

Hearing Faith chuckle in the lounge at something on the TV, she remembers the first day they came; how Faith's clear hazel eyes had swept the room, alighted on her and how when she'd smiled, Lizzie felt like she'd already found a friend. Then when Anthony and Sara moved out of London and were in their rented house before moving into number six, Anthony had introduced Faith to Sara and then Faith had invited them all over for a barbeque, after which the three of them – the three witches, Ben had laughed a little unkindly she'd thought at the time – had become inseparable, due to proximity more than anything. Then when Clemmie, Ashley and Douggie all appeared at roughly the same time, they did the whole antenatal, postnatal, baby-puke-mopping-up-stuff together. The first five years of that, with Blake forging the way with potty training and primary school and the like had, she'd often thought, on balance, been the happiest of her life.

The next fourteen, after Douggie, have been some of the hardest.

On her way out of the kitchen, she passes the dresser in the hall and sees Clemmie's pigs facing away from each other as usual, and wonders what her daughter and Jaz are doing tonight. She hopes they're just watching YouTube, listening to music, chatting with their friends online, that sort of thing. But somewhere lodged deep down is a worry she's never even told Ben about, the fear of clubs, spiked drinks, small packages of drugs and boys with tatty hair and tattoos. She wishes Ashley was still around, or that he'd decided to study more locally. When Clemmie's with him, she seems more grounded, and safer. This whole not-eating thing had started around the time he'd first mentioned going away to university, after all, hadn't it?

She thinks back to what Sara said recently about them indulging Clemmie. She was right, of course, but still, it's not something they need to say out loud, especially Sara…

This thought stings Lizzie. She should be kinder to Sara. Both she and Faith need to make allowances, don't they?

"What we watching now?" she asks as she plonks the bottle on the coffee table in front of the sofa. Faith's curled up at one end of it, her legs tucked under her and Sara's at the other end, all contained and ramrod straight. Her glass is empty and resting lengthways between her thin legs in their loose black trousers like a shaft of light. Lizzie steps over Faith's bag and says, "More wine?"

"A rerun of *Dad's Army*," Sara says, holding up her glass in one of her perfectly manicured hands. "Lovely," she adds, as Lizzie picks up the bottle and pours. "I used to watch this with my grandparents when I was a child, although why they thought it was funny, I'll never know. Grandpa drank at the Home Guard club every Thursday night for the last fifteen years of his life; we had his wake there too if I remember."

Sara's voice fades as she puts her glass to her lips. The canned laughter from the TV fills the room.

Faith stretches, and says, "Hey, what about me?" And then. "Thanks," she adds as Lizzie fills her glass too.

The three of them settle back down to watch TV. *It's wonderful,* Lizzie thinks. *We don't have to chat all the time; we can just laze here in front of the screen and the fire, like sisters almost, and have everything so very known about each other, even the unspoken things. Is it good, isn't it? I am safe here, aren't I?*

As she drinks her wine, Lizzie remembers that Clemmie must have been about five, around the time of the accident, when her behaviour changed and that Faith in particular had stepped in to help, giving her a shoulder to cry on when Clemmie's tantrums became too unbearable, when she started to break things around the house, and wet the bed again. Lizzie would try and believe her child hadn't meant to do it, but there'd always been a glint of something in Clemmie's eyes when Lizzie put her head around the door in the middle of the night and Clemmie's whimpers had woken her.

Of course, Lizzie hadn't been able to talk to Sara about it then and there'd been times when Lizzie had even wished Clemmie had not been Clemmie, not that she could ever admit it to anyone; it's just that maybe had they had another sort of child, her and Ben's lives might have worked out a little differently; maybe she wouldn't now still fear that one day he would up and leave her. After all, there'd been those few odd months just after Clemmie had been born, around the time Douggie came along actually when Ben had been a bit strange, almost as though he hadn't wanted a child in the first place. His behaviour had hardly been that of a besotted new dad.

"Hey, dreamer," Faith says, picking up a cushion and throwing it at Lizzie. "What's on next? You've got the controls!"

"Sorry," Lizzie exclaims, putting her glass down and turning to her friends. "What shall we do now?"

"It has to be *Dirty Dancing*," Faith says. "It's on Netflix, surely. We haven't seen it in *ages!*"

The other two give a collective moan, but it's an unconvincing one and Lizzie scrolls through the screen, selects the movie and they settle back. They each sip at their wine and now and again glance at one another and smile.

We are OK, aren't we? Lizzie thinks. *There's nothing we need to forgive each other for, is there?*

Outside the trees are unusually quiet for the time of year and I feel like I'm suspended. Despite the apparent sense of ease in the room, I'm on edge. I'm always on edge when the three of us are together. And I don't want tomorrow to come; I really, really don't want to see my parents right now.

So instead of thinking about the unexploded bomb in my friendship with Sara and Lizzie, the unsatisfactory nature of my relationship with my parents or the things about my past I'd always kept from Harvey, I think about the boys.

I'd always thought the term, 'heavy heart' was a bit of a cliché, but since they'd been gone, my heart had become sort of numb, loaded with unspent stuff, and there was always that feeling of suspension like I was constantly waiting for one or other of them to come back to make my life worthwhile again.

In my more sensible moments, of course, I know their leaving is totally the right thing; it's what I'd prepared them for, it'd been my job to get them from baby to adult, but that didn't stop me from being terrified that deep down I'd done something wrong that I'd pay for later.

Blake had been such an easy baby; he'd fed and slept almost to order and had started to walk at ten months. He'd been such wonderful company while I'd been pregnant, and I'd run my hands over my swollen belly and felt the contours of his limbs. Already, I'd trusted him completely.

Ashley had been more of an enigma; I'd taken longer to get to know him, both before and after he'd been born, and what I remember most about my pregnancy is the weight and the pain. It had been a difficult one and I'd struggled to look after Blake too. I'd been sick almost every day for eight months.

I can't remember precisely when I came out of the tunnel, but it was probably when Ashley started school. Life then began to seem possible; there was an element of control and structure I relished. It was as though my horizons had expanded but still, in the dark of the night when I lay awake listening to the night-time creaks of the house, I would get out of bed, tiptoe into the boys' rooms and watch them sleep, always terrified that something would happen to take one or both of them away from me.

It was like living on a precipice that I was on the cusp of falling over every minute of every day.

After checking on Blake and Ashley, I'd slide back between the cooled sheets, hear the soft oomph of Harvey's breathing next to me and remember how I'd drawn him into me the nights they'd been conceived, how wanton I'd felt when he came and my orgasm had pulsed around him; how I'd known precisely then, each time, that my baby had arrived.

"It's such a shame about Patrick Swayze, isn't it?" Lizzie says cutting across my thoughts. "He looks so young and invincible here, doesn't he?"

Sara needs to pee and so she carefully puts down her glass and slides out of the room. It's good to leave them for a bit; she's beginning to feel claustrophobic in there. Mostly she can cope, but sometimes her loss gets between them.

Both when she'd discovered she was pregnant and after Douggie died, she'd begged Anthony to let them move away, to start over where no one knew them, but he'd resisted, saying that they were better staying put, close to their friends, where – in both instances – they had their support network already in place. There'd been no question of moving nearer either of their sets of parents, Sara was still estranged from hers and his parents' grief after Douggie's death was too raw too, so they'd stayed at number six and gradually, Anthony had spent more time at work, holing up in hotels rather than coming home, and she'd begun to write, closeted in the house, barely seeing anyone except occasionally Faith and Lizzie because she felt she owed them something and that, in some way, she was responsible for their and their children's grief too.

Standing in Lizzie's downstairs cloakroom, Sara scrutinises her face in the mirror. The ceiling spotlight is harsh and unforgiving and casts harsh shadows across her reflection. She hates its brightness and switches it off so she cannot see how ugly she is, how she's always been – ugly and guilty.

Sara has spent years plastering over the cracks, she knows this. She's gone through the motions of her life as best she can and thanks God for her writing and her books, without them… Well, that just doesn't bear thinking about. But even so, there's the guilt, not only over what she did, and what happened that day, but over the fact that she'd taken so long to bond with Douggie – the gift she hadn't wanted but had mourned irrevocably when it was taken away.

She bends her head and rests it on the edge of the basin in the dark; it's cool and hard and, for a second, she wants to bash her skull against it, see blood and hear the splitting of bone; sometimes only this would be enough punishment.

She remembers the moment she picked up the pregnancy test and saw the pink dot. *Oh my God,* she'd thought. *I don't want this. Not now.* There were so many reasons why then hadn't been a good time and, even as she hugged the knowledge to herself, trying to convince herself that it would be all right, she knew she was battling on two fronts and that her mixed feelings stemmed from her natural fear, but also the prospect that one day the truth would come out.

What made it worse was Anthony's abundant joy; he'd been overwhelmed by the prospect of being a father and had lavished her with gifts and attention, making it all so much worse. Then when Douggie had actually been born, she'd spent hours watching his tiny, crumpled face in the clear plastic hospital crib, willing herself to fall in love with him.

It took a long, exhausting month until she did so, and she's carried the guilt of this around with her ever since too.

She can pinpoint the exact moment; it's not something you forget.

The midwives were starting to mutter about post-natal depression and Sara's days, instead of becoming lighter and better as Douggie settled into something like a routine, were getting darker and less easy to bear. Anthony went to work each morning and she knew he hoped that when he returned each evening, there would have been some sort of miracle and she'd appear at the door, all smiles, and with their baby in her arms and say, "Here darling, he's just been fed. You hold him for a while so that I can finish off the dinner."

But not only couldn't she breastfeed him, both physically and emotionally it just seemed too difficult, but during those hard first weeks she started to blame Anthony for the fact that she didn't love Douggie as she should; she was starting to spiral. But then one day, it was a Tuesday, she'd just finished giving Douggie his mid-morning bottle, was rubbing his back, holding his little chin in the palm of her hand when he gave an almighty belch and looked quizzically up at her out of his sludge-coloured eyes and gave an almost smile as if to say, 'Well Mum, what did you think of that'?

Suddenly Sara laughed. The laughter rose from deep down between her legs and travelled up in degrees until it spilt out of her, and she nuzzled her face into her son's neck, felt the incredible softness of him, drew in the sweet scent of him, which up to now she had almost disliked, and felt something inside snap. It was as though whatever it was that had held her love in check had been breached and it poured out, unrestrained and unrestrainable. He was *her* child, and that was all that mattered.

Everything changed from that moment. In some ways, she wished that maybe she hadn't loved him so much in the end because, in the end, it made losing him just so much harder to bear.

In Lizzie's cloakroom years later, Sara washes her hands, letting the water run cold so that it's almost freezing on her skin. She wants to be numb; she wants the water to anaesthetize her. Unlike what happened in her bathroom earlier in the week, this small stream of water doesn't terrify her; it seems more like a friend, something which can take the pain away.

"Well?" Harvey says to Ben in their corner seat at the Queen's Head. "What time did Anthony say he'd get down here?"

"About nine, I think," Ben replies. "He's been working at home today so shouldn't be that late."

Harvey glances at his watch, it's just after nine. At that moment, Anthony's tall frame bends itself to enter the low door of the pub. The other two raise their hands in greeting. Anthony lifts his eyebrows at them and mouths the word, "Pint?" Harvey and Ben nod.

With Anthony at the bar, Ben turns to Harvey and asks, "So what are you up to this weekend?"

"Faith's parents are making a rare visit," he replies, his voice flat. Both men know what this visit could mean.

"Tough luck, mate," Ben says, draining the last few drops from his glass.

"Yeh, let's just hope things don't kick off. It's never certain though. Faith gets really stressed and Deborah…" Here Harvey pauses, unwilling to start trying to define the relationship between his wife and her mother.

"There you go," Anthony says, plonking three-pint glasses on the table. "Sorry, I'm a bit late, got tied up with the bloody Yanks again. When I rule the world, everyone will work on GMT so that Friday nights can be Friday nights all over the world!" He flings himself into the seat with a sigh.

"Good idea!" Harvey says laughing and then shuffles out of the other end of the seat. "Need a slash," he says.

"Cheers." Ben raises his glass.

"Hey, thanks for what you did for Sara in the week," Anthony says.

He looks tired, Ben thinks.

"It was nothing."

"Well, it meant a lot to me. Just knowing you're there, next door. You know what she's like around water."

"Yeah, I know. Is it all fixed now?"

"The plumber you arranged came in the next day and dealt with everything. Just got a bit of touching up to do to the paintwork and stuff and then we'll be all sorted. It's why they're getting together at yours tonight, rather than ours though."

"Thought as much," Ben says, looking down at his lap. He wants Anthony to change the subject. He wants to stop thinking about Sara pressed up against him, her head on his shoulder. He wants to forget the warm fragility of her. He wants to forget what he nearly did, nearly said.

Mercifully, at that moment, Anthony's phone buzzes. "Fuck," he says, looking at the screen. "Better take this. Fucking Americans!"

He strides out of the pub and Ben can see him pacing up and down outside the window, the light from the window reflecting off his bald head. From this distance, Ben can't see his friend's kind eyes or worn smile; he can't see the wrinkles that Douggie's death has etched into his skin, but he knows they're there. They all carry them to some extent.

"Hey," Harvey says, sliding back into the seat next to Ben. "You're looking thoughtful. Everything OK?"

"Yes, everything's fine," Ben replies, running his finger round the rim of his glass and then looking up at the TV screen in the corner. "So do you think Chelsea has a chance at the title then?" he asks.

Saturday

The insides of my head feel much as I imagine a battle reconstruction ground might look after the Cavaliers and Roundheads have done their stuff on a Sunday afternoon. We certainly shouldn't have had that last bottle of wine last night and, as I stand in front of my wardrobe looking for inspiration, I remember how Ashley had wanted to join such a group when he'd been smaller. Calls had been made and an introductory session booked but, with the fickleness of youth and much to my and Harvey's relief, he'd changed his mind and had persuaded us to let him have a hamster instead. The thought of all that hessian and mud and shouting…

I run my hands along the clothes in front of me; each one has a memory of my life with Harvey woven into its fabric and you'd think, I muse, as I pluck out my safest black trousers and long silvery knitted top that, like the guys on the battlefield, each garment should therefore be able to provide me with some sort of armour against Mum.

As I get dressed, I wonder again why they are visiting now; it's a bloody long way to come after all and they'll have to make a stopover in Wales to break up the journey which means they'll be arriving around lunchtime today and then leaving again tomorrow. "Hardly a weekend," I say to myself as I sit down to put on my makeup.

Harvey's already downstairs; I can hear him drawing back the curtains in the dining room, hear him clearing his throat as he does so and the sounds of his footsteps across the kitchen tiles. I doubt I'll ever get used to how big and quiet the house is without the boys. There'd been so much shouting when they were smaller; cries of, "Where are my goalie gloves?"

"Blake's taken my Gameboy *again*!"

And from my and Harvey's sentry point at the bottom of the stairs, the ubiquitous, "Hurry up for heaven's sake, or we're going to be late!"

I must call Lizzie to see how things are at the shop, but I'll crack on with the lunch preparation first I think, as I pick out my Ugg boots from the bottom of the wardrobe; I'll change later into some more appropriate footwear for what I consider to be my biannual interview with my parents.

They've never been easy people to love; even when I was smaller and looked up at their world, I'd been aware of a need for wariness. It wasn't something I could define, more of an atmosphere of things not being spoken about, or me being to blame for something I hadn't known I'd done.

It had been OK early on, I guessed. I did remember Mum dressing me in pretty clothes, brushing my hair before bed and Dad's tired step coming up the stairs to read me a bedtime story. They would keep my bedroom door ajar so that the faint light from the landing could shine in and I'd hear them murmuring to one another in their bedroom; their voices had sounded mellow and relaxed then. But, around the time I was twelve or so and had started to baulk at Mum's taste in clothes, you know, changing into my plimsolls on the way to school so that the other kids wouldn't laugh at my old-fashioned sandals, Dad had started to come home later in the evenings and Mum would plate up his dinner with her mouth set into a tight line and then she'd change her own clothes and go out to play bridge, sing in a choir, learn about flower arranging or so she had said; anything it seemed rather than stay in with me, stay in to wait for Dad to come home.

After a while, this seemed the norm rather than the exception; I'd spend hours on my own, watching TV, trying to do my homework at the small desk in my bedroom, and watching the seasons change outside the window. We lived in an Edwardian semi in those days; it was a nice house – solid and unpretentious, but it was on a busy road and on the rare occasions when Mum was in, I'd sometimes see her standing at the lounge window, looking out onto the road, watching the scurry of people and cars, her fists clenched into tight balls by her side.

"Oh, Willow," she'd say, turning round to look at me scowling at her. I hated it when she called me Willow. I wasn't Willow. I was Faith. Then she'd add, "I need to get away from all this noise."

But, she stayed, we all stayed, at least until I finished school and went to university and found that moving out was no hardship at all. I swapped one lonely existence for another, until my first job that is…

Here I have to force myself to think of something else. I haven't allowed myself to think about that particular subject in years. It's always there though, in the background, a distant hum of memory, regret; another faded scorch of regret.

Rather, I concentrate on the day of my last A level and how I'd gone home, feeling rightfully special, like someone had placed a crown on my head so that everyone I passed in the street would know that whatever the outcome, I had accomplished something. But no one had been home. I heard my key turn in the lock and knew from the echo the sound made that the house was empty. I flung my bag down in the hall, threw myself on the sofa and allowed myself to cry for the first time in years. I know I was eighteen, but all I really wanted was a hug, surely that wasn't too much to ask, was it?

Even after all these years, I've never really forgiven Mum for that day. The resentment lodges inside me like an insect buzzing its wings against my bones, reminding me every day of how not to be a mother; maybe that's why I'd been so careful with my own, been too careful, too watchful, I think, as I pass the closed doors of the boys' bedrooms.

"Morning," Harvey says as I reach the kitchen. "How are you feeling?"

"Not bad, at the moment," I reply, walking across to the fridge and getting out the joint of beef for lunch.

"Roast beef then?" he says a little unnecessarily, I think. It's rather obvious after all, isn't it?

"Yes, Dad's favourite." I plonk the container on the counter and stand and stare at the small pool of blood resting on the surface of the joint. For a moment, and unaccountably, I feel like throwing the whole thing through the window, watching the glass splinter around it. I can hear and see it happen in slow motion and then I'm walking out of the house, and into the secret dark of the woods at the back of us where I will hide all day in the shelter of the trees.

But I am Faith, steady Faith, predictable Faith, so I don't. I have worked too hard to contain my wrongs, cover up the fractures, and keep the fear at bay that even I have begun to believe in this version of myself and am not going to give up now.

"It's my favourite too," Harvey says over his shoulder as he leaves the kitchen for his study. He pauses at the door. "Look," he says.

"I'm sorry I won't have time to help much today, got a lot to get ready for next week."

Bloody work, I think savagely. *Bloody typical.* I glance out the window at the lawn which is just on the wrong side of just-too-long and at the flower beds which need weeding and can predict Mum's comment: "It's a shame you don't have time to look after things properly."

I do get the irony of the situation. I insist Harvey mows the lawn when the others are coming round for dinner, and it'll be dark, and no one will see it. And yet, I fail to insist on it when not having it mown will expose me to my mother's critical gaze. I could, of course, mow the bloody thing myself, but I have a hundred things to do in the kitchen and whilst I said I was feeling OK to Harvey, my head still feels like a goblin wearing hobnail boots is tap dancing in it, and the thought of my first job and all that meant has unsettled me.

Instead, I tell the microwave, I shouldn't mind about any of it; my life now is busy and fulfilled and we live in a real world, not the make believe, organic, isn't-everything-now-fucking-marvellous-again world my parents do.

And there really is no point in thinking about Dom, or the other secret. I can't do anything about either of them, not now.

Dumping potatoes in a bowl of water ready to peel them, I concede, however, that maybe I'm being a bit unfair to my parents. I've only ever visited them in Ireland a few times and then I never really tried to get to know the place or understand its appeal. All I felt was a huge wave of resentment that they'd chosen to go there and look after other people, rather than to stay around and…

The water's cold and my fingers are nearly numb by the time I throw the last peeled potato into the pan.

An hour later a car draws up and Harvey comes out of his study; he's hurrying so he can get to them first and assess what sort of visit it's likely to be. *Maybe he does understand,* I think as he opens the front door.

"Deborah, Roger, you made good time!" he says breezily.

In the kitchen, I breathe in and out deeply three times and then walk into the hall.

Mum is always so much smaller than I remember.

Over lunch, Harvey watches Faith carefully. Around them, their furniture and ornaments sit in silent contemplation: the sideboard, display cabinet, and even the floor-length red velvet curtains all seem to be watching too. Sometimes Harvey feels like he is surrounded by their things, like they are wagons penning him in and he wouldn't be able to forge a way through them if he ever needed to escape.

He's also aware of the long pauses between conversations and of Faith's reluctance to say much for fear it will be picked up and hurled back at her by Deborah.

Faith's playing with her food rather than eating it, but Deborah and Roger are tucking in like they've been starving on a desert island for months.

"So," Roger says, in a gap between mouthfuls. "How's the business going?"

The way he says 'business' makes it sound almost distasteful; he's never really supported the idea of Harvey and Ben going it alone. "Far too risky," he'd said in the early days. But then, Harvey reasoned, his father-in-law didn't really have a leg to stand on. He'd taken the huge package he'd been offered when, at age fifty-five, he'd been found to be surplus to requirements at the multi-national IT company he'd worked for as finance director for almost twenty years. He'd watched the company grow, seen it change and evolve into a creature which no longer had room for him; the US had muscled in as usual and had redeployed the financial function to Switzerland.

"We have too many roots here, my boy," Roger had said to Harvey at the time, justifying what he had billed as *his* decision not to go to Zurich, and so he and Deborah had taken the money and moved to one of the remotest parts of southwest Ireland instead, leaving whatever roots he'd been talking about, and Harvey had presumed he'd meant himself, Faith and the boys, flapping like loose sails in the wind. Harvey had thought him hypocritical at the time and still did.

"It's going well," thanks. Harvey answers. "More gravy?"

His father-in-law nods. "Thanks," he says, still chewing.

"We've just got a new contract with Paradigm Developments for a £5 million, 35,000 square foot office fit-out in London. For a firm of lawyers."

But Roger's eyes have glazed over; this is far too much detail. He readjusts the leather-covered buttons on his fawn cardigan to make sure they're all still done up correctly, as if some pixie had arrived during lunch and unfastened them and done them up another way, and says, "I've brought some photographs of the new drainage scheme in the lower field. I'll show them to you after lunch if you like."

There's nothing Harvey would like less than to see shot after shot of a muddy field, with Roger breathing his heavy ex-smoker's breath next to him, so he says, "Well, let's see what the ladies want to do, shall we?"

At this, he glances over at Deborah, who's spearing a carrot with her fork. She must be aware of him looking at her because she raises her eyes; they are a hard and brilliant blue, nothing like Faith's he thinks. Her face has become more weathered of late, and her hands are gardener's hands; in fact, there's nothing soft or pliable about this woman, if there ever had been, he thinks.

She smiles sweetly at him as she finishes her mouthful. "Perhaps," she says, "the men can clear up after lunch while Willow and I have a nice catch-up about what the boys are up to."

Harvey sees Faith flinch at the use of her first name. Her mother is the only person to call her by it. Faith told him this is because she believes her mother just likes to be contrary.

And Harvey knows the boys are the very last thing that Faith would want to talk about. Being reminded that they aren't here and that she has no real idea of what they're doing, apart from the edited highlights they give her on brief trips home or during their Sunday night calls, is like rubbing salt into a wound. And, in any case, he thinks as he gathers together his in-laws' empty plates and his wife's almost full one, what makes Deborah think that Faith has any idea of what's going on in her sons' minds? After all, Deborah patently has no idea what her own daughter is thinking most of the time.

In the kitchen, he surveys the wreckage of the lunch preparation and has to grip onto the edge of the draining board. The Yorkshire pudding pan clatters to the floor as he realises that in the hubbub of their everyday lives, he has no real idea what Faith is thinking most of the time either.

Later, in the shop, Lizzie says goodbye to Dana as she wipes down the serving counter for the last time that day.

"Bye," Dana replies, hopping from one foot to another. She has a date with the famous Steve tonight, and, despite her best intentions, Lizzie is dreading tomorrow morning's inquest in case, yet again, Dana's dreams have been shattered by loutish behaviour and the belief that a quick feel in the car behind Sainsbury's at midnight is every girl's dream.

"Be careful," Lizzie adds.

"Sure will!" Dana replies with a smile and then she's gone in a flurry of denim and dark curls.

Lizzie sighs as she switches off the coffee machine. As she's walking towards the door to turn the Open/Closed sign around, she sees Brenda's comforting shape scurrying up the street.

Brenda is short, plump, grey-haired and always smiling, always believing the best in people. She's been married to Cyril for thirty-five happy years, and they have three children and two grandchildren. Lizzie often thinks if there were medals awarded for 'getting it right', Brenda would be a fixture on the gold medal podium.

"Hello there, dear," Brenda says as she opens the door, letting in a blast of evening air. "Bit chilly out there tonight, sure it is," she says.

She bustles past Lizzie into the back where she hangs up her jacket, puts on her housecoat, the type Lizzie's grandmother used to wear made from blue and white checked polyester, and picks up her tray of cleaning products. "Busy day, dear?"

"Not too bad," Lizzie answers. "Be glad to put my feet up tonight though."

"You doing anything nice?" Brenda asks as she turns the nozzle on the cleaning spray from off to on.

"No, just feet up and takeaway," Lizzie replies. "But first, I'll just quickly check emails if that's OK. Ben should be here in a moment."

"You go on right ahead, dear," Brenda says busily cleaning the already clean tabletops. "I won't disturb you."

To Brenda, the computer is still an instrument of mystery, something which has to be talked about in whispers. She had, she told Lizzie once, "Just got the hang of faxes, like what's her name on the old BT adverts, you know that one that looks and sounds like Joyce Grenfell," she'd said. "When everything moved off at a million miles an hour and emails and podcasts and Bluetooth came in. I still believe in writing a nice letter, dear," she said. "Or sending a notelet."

There are a few emails, some Viagra ones which had slipped through the spam filter, one from their internet service provider saying that routine maintenance would be being carried out at two the following morning and users may notice some interruption to services, and the one from that artist, Nic Bradley, is still marked as unread. Faith has obviously not replied to it as yet. He is, it said, a watercolourist with a substantial back catalogue and gave a link to his website for further information. She leaves it for Faith, again.

As Lizzie's logging off, she hears Ben arrive. "Thank God," she says to herself. She's aware of Ben and Brenda chatting in the front of the shop and wishes that she could capture this moment, freeze-frame it. It is, she believes, one of those perfect ones, where everything's in its rightful place. Part of her doesn't want to go home, to be faced with the laundry and Clemmie, with the vase of flowers in the lounge which needs dealing with, as some of the blossoms have blown over and scattered pollen on the hearth like some weird sort of orange fairy dust. No, she'd rather stay here, suspended, protected.

"Hello love," Ben says, popping his head around the office door at the back of the shop. "You ready?"

He's looking at her tenderly with his wonderful brown eyes and she answers him, "Yep, just coming!"

Later, as Ben comes through the front door with their takeaway and bottle of wine, she passes Clemmie on the landing and says, "Had a nice time with Jaz last night?"

"Um, er," Clemmie replies, leaning up against the bannister in what Lizzie thinks is a studied act of mock indifference. "Yeh, had a great time, thanks. Just stayed in, watched YouTube, that kind of thing."

"Oh, anything good?"

"What?" Clemmie snaps.

"Did you see anything good, on YouTube?" Lizzie says, thinking, *God this is hard. Like having a conversation with a bloody brick wall.*

"Oh, I can't remember." Clemmie slinks along the landing as she says this, her eyes large and watchful.

"Do you want some takeaway? We ordered for you," Lizzie asks her daughter's departing back.

"No thanks, already eaten," Clemmie's disembodied voice replies from the doorway to her room.

She's lying, Lizzie thinks. *Both about the evening at Jaz's and about having eaten.* And she's just about to say something when her phone rings. Ben answers it and she can hear the mumble of his voice, then he calls up, "Hey, Lizzie, it's Faith on the phone for you."

Clemmie's back is still turned to her, Lizzie can see the sharp outlines of her daughter's shoulder blades under her top and can sense a cloud of unhappiness shrouding her brittle frame and she wishes she could do something to help but has no idea what.

She hurries downstairs to take the phone from Ben. "Hey, she says, how's your day been? How's your mother?"

Anthony is standing in front of the wine rack wondering which bottle to have tonight. Sara said something about seafood pasta for dinner but still, he fancies a nice solid red, something masterful like a Barolo; he feels the need to be taken in hand. There are times, like now, he thinks, when he wishes that someone would look after him; he's tired of being the strong one, always making sure he's the right-shaped hole into which his wife's grief can fit.

He selects a bottle, puts it down on the counter next to the hob and goes upstairs, tapping on Sara's writing room door.

"Hi," he says softly to the back of her head. She's sitting bolt upright, her eyes fixed on the screen. He can see words neatly spaced over it and the flashing cursor at the place where she's been forced to stop. For a second, he has an irrational wish to smash the whole fucking thing to pieces, to take a hammer and demolish the screen and its hold over her. But he knows that, in reality, he's just jealous. *Ha!* he thinks. Just jealous. If only it was as easy as that, as simple a thing to admit to. There were times when he hated the fantasy worlds and make-believe people his wife created, not only because they take her away from him but because they cover up the gaping hole of loss which forms the centrepiece of their life, and

Anthony resents this, wishes they had found a way to deal with Douggie's death together. "Shall I start dinner?" he asks. "You said something about salmon and pasta. I can get going on it if you like."

"Oh." She turns in her chair, her eyes glazed and bright. "Yes, that would be nice. I'll be down in a little while, just want to finish this bit."

When Anthony has quietly shut the door behind him and she's heard his steps on the stairs and the sound of him opening a kitchen cupboard, Sara minimises the document on the screen to reveal the email she'd hastily hidden when he'd knocked just now. It's from Suzanne, her agent, asking if she'd do a book signing and talk at a special needs day centre in Thatcham. The manager had said that the children were particularly enthralled (and it is this word which has captured Sara) by Sara's latest hero, eight-year-old Sebastian and his magic toy spaceship and that it would be wonderful to have Hermione Hart visit… blah, blah, blah.

Sara wishes that Suzanne wouldn't do this and force her into deciding. A 'no' would appear unfriendly and unsupportive, but saying 'yes' would mean getting into the car, wearing appropriate clothing, talking to strangers, have them risk them asking her…

She closes down the email without answering it, saves the document she was pretending to work on when Anthony came in and turns off the laptop and her desk lamp. She sits in the dark for a while, gathering up the strength to go downstairs and eat seafood pasta with her husband.

The house is quiet. Mum and Dad are asleep in the guest room and Harvey is dozing next to me; I can hear the small snuffles he makes, the occasional gurgle from his stomach as his pre-bed cup of coffee settles. The day hasn't been too bad; Mum's caustic comments have been well-spaced out and not that ferocious. There'd been the usual stuff about the boys and when was I going to let them come and work on the estate.

"It's time they did something to make men of them," she said as I was stirring the soup for supper.

The image of my sons chopping wood and driving tractors reminds me of meeting Harvey when he'd been a groundsman at the university where I'd been working in the finance office. My second job after university; his fifteenth since he'd got his quantity surveying degree and, whilst he loved not having any roots, moving from house share to house share and biding his time before he got a full-time job, I'd felt imprisoned by the routine and hated my job. I'd wanted my old one back, but that just wasn't possible. There were so many things at that time that just weren't possible.

It was lunchtime and I was walking from my office to buy a sandwich. Harvey had been halfway up a step ladder near a small tree which bordered the quad. He was reaching up with a pair of long-handled clippers. The day had been hot with a savage brightness; even the breeze was hot, and the sun had shone on his sandy hair and a patch of sweat had formed on his back. The branch he'd been cutting cracked suddenly and I'd stopped walking, unable to move any further, momentarily spellbound by the sound. The branch tore itself from the trunk and fell with a roar to the ground. I'd jumped back, even though it was nowhere near me really because he'd cordoned off the area with poles and tape, but I must have screamed because he'd looked down from his vantage point on high and had fixed me with his bright, intelligent eyes and that was it really, although it wasn't. There would be much more to it than that.

And now, as I lie back in bed, with the trees shuffling outside the window and my parents in the next room and my sons miles away with their own bank cards and passports and secrets, I have no idea where the years have gone, can barely remember what led me here to this, and absolutely no idea how I am going to carry on knowing what I know while still full of the indefinable but weighty memories of Dom.

I turn onto my side. Harvey grunts in his sleep. I tuck my hand under my pillow and force myself to think of something practical. *Oh,* I think. *I haven't replied to that guy, Nic Bradley, yet. Maybe his work will prove interesting,* and I close my eyes to block out the light from the landing which is seeping around the door. *It's time we had something different in the shop.*

Monday

It's evening, Brenda's gone, and the shop is quiet. I don't often see it like this; only first thing in the morning and occasionally if I stay late. Its end-of-day quietness is different from its morning. Then it's a hopeful silence, a pending one. Now it's just weary. The floor seems tired, and it's as though someone has filmed the day and kept it playing on a constant loop in my head and I find, as I log on to the computer in the back, that I can't see clearly.

I pick a fleece off the peg on the back of the door and put it over my white blouse. It hangs low over my black skirt. My toes are chilly now I've stopped moving about. It's still surprisingly cool for the time of year. I'd hoped that the merge from spring into summer would have brought comfort, but the weather has just been more of the same blustery, squally showers, I think, as I move the cursor onto the email icon on the screen.

As I wait for the messages to download I clean my glasses and remember Mum's visit to the shop yesterday, not quite sure why these two things should be linked in my mind.

"It's more pokey than I remember," Mum had said, peering at the fixtures and fittings as if she was marking them out of ten. "Did it used to be bigger?"

Turning to face me, she looked me up and down and I saw the brittle grey flecks in her hair as they spiralled from the crown of her head.

"No, it's always been this size, Mum," I said, noticing with a hint of annoyance that Dana was obviously behind clearing the tables. *Probably still recovering from last night,* I thought.

"Hello Elizabeth," Mum had said as Lizzie sailed past with a tray.

"Hi, be with you in a moment."

"No, I'll do it," I said. Ushering Mum to an empty table, I added, "What would you like?"

Breakfast had passed off safely enough, and Harvey and Dad had gone to hit a few balls at the driving range.

"What on earth can I do with him this morning?" Harvey had asked in bed after he'd turned off the alarm. "We've had our usual conversations about work and politics and sports. I guess it's the driving range then," he'd said as he shrugged off the duvet and stood up.

I'd watched his broad back as he walked across the room and felt a stir of desire somewhere deep within. He was so comfortable and safe, so known, yet... I didn't have time to finish the thought as my alarm started to sound. Switching it off, I too had got out of bed.

In the shower, I'd run my hands over my body, tracing the curve of my breasts and placing an experimental fingertip between my legs. My stomach had tightened, my nipples hardening, and I'd leant against the cold tiles, gasping as my skin hit them. The water cascaded over me. I'd opened my mouth and let the water run in and out, had wanted to cry and then came the guilt and furtiveness. I'd washed my hair, my body pulsing gently and, when I turned off the water, I'd felt very tired.

And what hurts the most is that the person I'd thought of when I was doing all this wasn't my husband. It should have been, but it wasn't. Still, after all these years, it wasn't. I told myself I thought of him only at times like this but, in my secret heart, I knew Dom was still there. He was always there. He'd been my first real love. I'd been disloyal to Harvey from the start of us, and I'd been disloyal to my friends for years and, in truth, despite everything we'd all shared, because of it, I still was.

"That's sorted then," Harvey said from outside the door as I stepped onto the mat and wrapped myself in a towel.

"What is?" I'd asked, trusting he wouldn't notice anything different about me.

"The driving range," Harvey said. "I've booked us a slot. You still taking your Mum to the shop?"

"Yes," I replied, rubbing my hair with a towel, glad he couldn't see my face.

At *Flick's* Mum said, "Sugar?" Her voice wasn't kind and she leant over the table to pluck a sachet off the tray, flapping it impatiently against the palm of her hand to make the sugar fall to one end, the grains making a shivery sound against the waxy paper.

"Sorry, Mum," I said, noticing with relief that Dana was approaching with an empty tray.

"Hello, Mrs M," she said brightly. "Just getting these tables done."

"How was last night?" I asked.

Dana stopped mid-step and sighed. "It was great, Mrs M, just great."

I stirred my own coffee, waiting for Mum to say something, but it was mercifully noisy in the shop and anyway, what was there to say?

"I wonder how Harvey and Dad are getting on." I ventured at last.

"I expect they're OK," Mum had replied, scrutinising a woman with a double buggy trying to negotiate the door.

"Here let me." I jumped up and held the door open. The woman smiled gratefully, and I sat back down wishing I was anywhere in the world but here, now, with Mum and all this space between us.

When we got home, we had lunch and it passed off OK.

"Just cold meat and salad, I'm afraid," I'd said.

"Just as well," Dad had replied, his face still flushed from spending the morning in the open air. "Don't want to fall asleep at the wheel!" He laughed when he said this, but it was an uneasy laugh. He didn't look at his wife or me but leant over to pick up the salt and pepper.

And then they'd gone, and I'd watched as their car went round the corner and disappeared. I'd waited at the end of the driveway to make sure they weren't coming back before going in and stripping their bed. It was then that I'd cried; huge, hot tears splashing onto the duvet cover, and I stood and watched them as they dried, imagining each one had left a small round mark, like a stain.

"I wonder why they came," Harvey said later.

"I've no idea," I replied, grateful that the phone had started ringing. It was Ashley. "Blake will call later," I told myself as I heard my younger son's voice say, "Hi Mum, it's me."

Blake had called and, as I click on the unread emails in the shop the following evening, I worry at the memory of the slight caginess in his voice, as though he was hiding something.

I go back to the one from that artist Lizzie had told me about.

To: Flick's
From: Nic Bradley
Subject: Art

'I noted with interest that you show work by local artists in your shop and wonder if you would consider letting me hang some of mine. I would also be happy to come into the shop to answer questions or talk about my paintings in more detail if desired. For more information about my work please visit my website, www.nicbradleyart.co.uk'

There's something familiar about the surname, I think as I wait for the website to load. *I hope his paintings are OK as I hate having to say no.* There's no picture of the artist on the site, but there are testimonials from galleries and shops and from satisfied customers, there is also a page devoted to his technique and how he came to take choose watercolour as his medium and there are examples of his work.

My fingers pause over the keyboard as my eyes soak in the images. They are stunning, with a controlled use of colour and shape. Whether a landscape or a still-life, whether abstract or a portrait, they breathe life, and have texture. Even through the computer screen, I feel I could reach out and touch the canvases and they would feel warm and soft. I hit 'Reply'.

To: Nic Bradley
From: Flick's
Subject: Re: Art

'We would love to show your work. Please can you come into the shop any day next week to discuss the timings and arrangements?'

In my hurry, I don't sign off at the foot of the email but close down the computer and shift my shoulders inside the fleece. Brenda has already left, leaving the scent of lemon polish behind her. I must have missed her saying goodbye. I tap the code into the burglar alarm and, taking the keys from my bag, leave the shop, turning and bending down to lock the door. A McDonald's wrapper skitters along the kerb as the light evening breeze tugs at my skirt. The low sun is warm now on my face and I am smiling but have no idea why.

As Faith leaves the shop, Nic Bradley raises both hands and clutches the sides of the board on the easel in front of him. The paper is blank; stretched and ready, but blank. This is his favourite moment. He lets go of the board and turns in his chair to pick up his soft pencil from the table by his right elbow and then he pauses, the lead just millimetres away from the surface, a whole world in waiting.

The room faces west, not a good light for painting, but the view is at its best from here. His tubes of Winsor and Newton paints are lined up in rows like toy soldiers, colour coded with their labels showing. His sable brushes are clean and dry, and his regulation ten pots of clean water are within reach. He is almost ready.

All is beautifully still on the hilltop overlooking the sweep of the valley, each field a different green, like a patchwork quilt. All he can hear is the distant croak of a crow issuing its early evening complaint and the faint ticking of the clock in the hallway. This is regulated to his heartbeat, it seems, just part of the synchronicity of his life now. A balance he has paid heavily for.

He has an uneasy truce with his kids. He sees his daughter occasionally, but she has her own life and family now and, given what happened, there isn't much space for him within either of these things; his ex-wife takes up a great deal of room and she makes a lot of noise about it, two things he has fought hard to escape. His son is a different matter; they haven't spoken for some time. He works in South Africa now and rarely comes home and doesn't really keep in touch. Whether he does so with his mother is something Nic has never been able to discover.

The paintings help of course, as does the fact that they each bear the evidence of this separation. Nic loves the fact that he can sign them 'Nic Bradley', as though by changing his name, he has allowed himself to become a different person from the one who eventually left behind such a mess of shouting, torn clothes and guilty credit card slips.

He'd spent years building a life, only to destroy it in a matter of months.

He starts to trace the outline of the landscape in front of him. He supposes it's like trying to paint someone you love; the stakes seem to be higher than when it's someone or someplace anonymous.

Time passes and he bends nearer the paper, it's like it's sucking him into it, absorbing him like it absorbed the water, a merging with the valley and sky. The sun sinks lower, sending probes into the rose garden he's planted outside the studio. It's nearly time to stop for the day. Before he does so, though, he picks up some colours to conduct his daily experiment. Today he mixes olive green with quinacridone gold, adds some water, takes a brush and sweeps the margin of his paper, in the border of inches which will be cut off later.

He waits for it to dry, wonders if it's anywhere near the colour of her eyes, whether it's nearer than he's ever got before. But the problem is he can't quite remember them. He should, he knows, after all that time had been the happiest, if the hardest, of his life.

The stuff that had followed when he'd lost her and then, a year later, when he'd left his wife and kids in an attempt to make things right and to try and heal his wounds, had been some of the worst, so maybe that was why now he can't quite remember the exact shade and shape, a kind of defence mechanism maybe.

The outline done, he stretches his long legs and runs his fingers through his hair; he's tired and will need to make something to eat but, covering the easel with a cloth, he feels an unaccountable surge of grief rise up in his chest; it's a physical pain and he gasps, then coughs, the sound of it echoing around the too empty house. How stupid he is, he thinks, to imagine that his pictures can be enough, can provide the company he so badly needs.

Since he sold the business and retired to the country, having been slapped on the back and told what a lucky sod he was to be getting out and getting out rich and healthy enough, he'd worked hard at convincing himself that this was indeed the very best solution, that the art classes, the drinks down the pub, the odd game of golf and a bottle of single malt by his side in the evening when he watched the news on TV was enough. But it so obviously wasn't, not when there was nobody to share it with, not even an exact enough memory of the girl he'd loved too much in the end.

His footsteps make a clip-clop sound on the slate floor as he walks to his study to check his emails. There's one from that coffee shop in Newbury, *Flick's*, saying they'd like him to exhibit his work.

"Well, that's something I suppose," he says out loud as he replies suggesting a date and time to visit.

Thursday

I wake just before the alarm, lean over to the bedside cabinet and switch it off and then plump the pillows under my head, quietly, so I don't wake Harvey. He's lying on his back, breathing evenly; his face is relaxed, and his lips are slightly open. He looks younger like this. He reminds me of who he was when we met.

"Hi," he'd said, popping his head round the finance office door later on the branch-cutting day. "Remember me?"

I'd looked up from my screen to see his fresh, hopeful face beaming down at me.

"Just checking you're OK."

"How did you know where to find me?"

"It wasn't hard; just asked the lady selling the sandwiches. She said you worked in finance, so…" He swept his arms wide, still smiling, "Here I am!"

"Well, I'm fine thank you," I'd replied, moving some papers on my desk in an attempt to look busy. Truth was I'd spent most of the afternoon in a state of inactivity because just after I'd got back from lunch, Dom had called.

"I'm sorry," he'd said. "It's Rainbows tonight. I have to get back to babysit."

"Of course," I said, hoping he hadn't picked up on my disappointment, but this was the third time this had happened recently. He would say he was coming over after work as planned, then he'd ring halfway through the day with some reason why he couldn't. I didn't want to think the obvious, but it was hard not to. Carrying on believing in him was getting harder and harder to do. It would, I knew, be up to me to break the deadlock. One day, if I was brave enough.

"So," the tree guy interrupted my thoughts. "Would you like to grab a drink after work? We could go to the Union, or somewhere else if you'd prefer."

The sun was pouring through the half-open windows, a slight breeze tugging at the broken Venetian blind so that it clattered every now and again. I felt coiled, furious, and frustrated; I'd wanted my life to be much more than this.

My new job was boring and samey, my colleagues stuffy and flat sandal wearing; I felt I had nothing in common with them and more than once I'd wondered why I'd agreed to leave Dom's business and move here.

It had seemed such a sensible thing at the time.

"It's going to be impossible for us," he'd said, moving his mouth from one nipple to the other as we lay in bed early one evening soon after the rainy night in the motel. "I won't be able to keep my hands off you!"

In reply, I'd opened my legs and wrapped my hands around his back, holding on tightly, nodding into his shoulder, wanting to sink my teeth into his skin, hurt him, leave a mark.

Yes, it probably was for the best, I thought.

So, he'd written my references and planned my leaving party, standing up in front of everyone at the pub and saying, "I really don't know what we've done wrong, but she's off to pastures new! Needless to say, we'll miss her immensely." And he'd presented me with a card everyone had signed and a set of crystal wine glasses which they'd all contributed money towards. As I thanked him, shaking his hand, I looked up and saw Tina's glinty eyes on me. It was enough to prove that what Dom and I had decided was most likely for the best after all.

"I'm sorry," he'd said in the car later as he drove me home. "It's the right thing to do, I know it is, but still, I will miss you. I will really miss seeing you every day."

I'd believed him; I had had to.

"Can I come up?" he'd asked, the light from the streetlamp filtering through his hair, his face softened and his blue eyes shining.

I'd nodded; of course, I'd nodded. It was the only thing I could do.

We tried to settle into a routine; two evenings a week he'd come by my bedsit after work, sometimes picking up a bag of chips on the way which we'd share, licking the salt off one another's fingers and drinking bad red wine from the wine glasses I'd got as my leaving present. I'd drink most of the bottle in the hope that it would numb the ache I knew I would feel when he left and he would have one or two glasses, at the most, and then drive back to his family and I would imagine him putting his key in the lock, calling out, "Hi there, I'm home."

I imagined his children running into his arms, crying, "Daddy, Daddy."

It was hateful but it was necessary. I wanted to be able to walk in the park with him, hold his hand and buy ingredients for supper with him. I wanted him to come home to me every night, stay and be there in the morning. I didn't want to be torn like this, but he was like a drug, and whilst there was a tiny part of my heart that told me to be wary, that he'd done this before, that he would tire of me, this tiny part got smaller and smaller as the months passed and as he continued to call and come round and make love to me and I felt treasured and needed and beautiful.

But it was getting harder. It had been nearly a year and his children's social lives were kicking in. His daughter had Rainbows and swimming lessons and play dates with friends, and he was called home to look after his son while his wife drove her here and there. And I knew it would just be more and more like this. His son would start to play football, learn karate or do gymnastics and I would, of necessity, be squeezed out by the size and shape of Dom's duty.

"I have to go, I'm their father," he'd say, sitting on the edge of the bed, with his head in his hands, his long smooth back turned towards me, and the clock would tick inexorably on to the time he'd have to leave so that he wouldn't miss bath and story time.

"I understand, I really do," I'd say, clambering over the bed and placing my head on his shoulder blades, wanting to soak up the misery he was feeling, to mend the tear I'd made in his life. It wasn't supposed to be like this.

"Let's run away together," he said once, his body curved round mine. It was late December and outside snow was trying to fall in unconvincing flurries. It was bitterly cold and the radiators in the bedsit hummed noisily, even the smell of fish and chips was diluted in the freezing air.

"Where to?"

"I don't know, anywhere but here."

I didn't need to say, "What about your children?" It was an unspoken barrier between us, and I'd known he hadn't meant it; the final decision, I knew, would rest with me. In the end, I would have to make him go or we would both end up destroyed. What we were doing was unsustainable in the long run. It was up to me to do 'The Honourable Thing'.

And then there was the jealousy. I'd imagine him fucking his wife on a Saturday night, wiping himself clean afterwards and turning over and going to sleep and I'd imagine the look of triumph on his wife's pointy little face and want to slap it, slap it until the bloody woman cried out, 'OK, you have him, you keep him. I don't want him anyway.'

So, as I sat there in my office on the day the tree man called by, I was nearing the end, nearing the time when I would have to pick up my sacrifice in both hands and present it to Dom and say, "Here, go. I'm letting you go. I can't do this anymore."

"OK," I said, "I'd love to go for a drink. Meet you there at six."

"I'm Harvey, Harvey Marshall, by the way," he said, holding out his hand. I noticed the fine hairs on the back of his wrists and the freckles and the strong-looking fingers and felt a shiver run through me at the thought of them touching me.

"Faith. My name's Faith."

"Can I walk you home?" he said later when we left the bar and stepped out into a velvet evening of tired birdsong and dusty pavements.

"It's OK. I live on the High Street, just above the chippy. You can leave me at the corner if you like. I don't want to take you out of your way."

In truth, I didn't want him to come up; there were too many signs of Dom around the place. Nothing physical like a toothbrush or shaving gear, or a clean shirt hanging in the wardrobe; all the things I wished could be there. But it was more the impression he left, the smell of him on the air. I wondered if Harvey would be able to pick up on these things and guess my secret. The thing about having a relationship in a vacuum was that keeping it a secret, operating in that vacuum, was exhausting.

"Well, how about coming back to mine then?" Harvey suggested, reaching down and picking up one of my hands.

"OK," I said and let my hand rest in his as we walked under the full-leaved trees, the warm air around us like a pillow.

"Here we are," he said, pointing to a small, terraced house. "I share it with a bloke called Rory. I was at uni with him. I'm just crashing here for a while until I decide what to do. It's wonderful having no obligations, just being free."

Following him down the narrow path to the front door, I relished this feeling of freedom, of him having no baggage, of maybe having room in his life for all of me. It would be a welcome change, I thought dryly as I stepped into the house.

Also, the fact that he had qualified in the same industry as Dom seemed to create a connection between me when I was with Dom and who I could be with Harvey. Bonkers I know, but that's how it felt.

It was like a dream. For the next few months, being with Harvey was like stepping into a cool shower after the intense heat of my half-life with Dom, but I hated deceiving both of them but found it impossible not to, to start with.

However, this wasn't the person I wanted to be, and that was before you took into consideration Dom's wife and family. Although I disliked his wife, she didn't deserve this, surely?

Leading a double life was just awful and it gave me an insight into what Dom had been going through and so, gradually, I withdrew from him, schooling myself not to mind when he cancelled coming over, suggesting even that why don't we just wait until the following week? Maybe his diary would be clearer then?

Eventually, I told him it was over.

Harvey had been offered a full-time job with a large contractor and had asked me to move with him. I had to go, I had to get away; I had to start being honest with myself, and with Harvey.

"I can't do this. I just can't, not now, not anymore," I said to Dom, whispering into his neck as we stood by the window of my bedsit. The traffic slid by beneath us, his car parked around the corner as usual, out of sight, just in case.

"Don't, please don't do this."

"Fuck the clichés and the movie talk," I said, having prepared a sweeping speech in the mirror beforehand. "I just want out. I just have to get out."

"Give me another chance, please."

"No, Dom. I'm sorry, I'm so sorry."

The words had been lame and inadequate. There was nothing, absolutely nothing that could describe the pain.

I watched him leave with the tears stuck in my eyes like drops of glue and had to believe that for both of us it wasn't really over; this had to be only a pause. There would be more. There would have to be more.

This is the man, these are the memories of the man that haunt me as I slip out of bed, leaving Harvey sleeping. It's seven-thirty and I go downstairs to unload the dishwasher and put the kettle on. The kitchen tiles are cold under my feet, and I stand by the sink and let a long low sob escape. As the water comes to a boil, I watch the steam weave around the kitchen and then walk into the hallway to the photograph of us – me, Harvey, and the boys – on the table by the phone. I pick it up, trace the contours of the boys' faces with my fingers, see the familiar shape of Harvey's features staring back at me and search their eyes for some sort of forgiveness.

I remember our wedding. It had been hot, the sky a perfect blue. I had pushed aside all thoughts of Dom and had lost myself in the joy of the day. Harvey had looked handsome in his suit, his face full of love and hope. And all around us were family and friends who wished us all the very best life could offer. I'd stood at the altar, and I'd made promises to Harvey and really, really hoped, that despite everything, I could keep them.

I wanted so badly to, and I still do, and I believed it when he promised to honour me, stay faithful to me, love me in sickness, health and all the rest of it.

I didn't think of Dom that day, but I think of him now and how it was all so long ago that it seemed to have happened to a different person, someone who was not, yet was, me.

Part 3 – Before

Everyone had gone, even the cleaners. She logged off her computer, tidied her files, put them in a heap in the drawer next to her desk, switched the phone to answerphone and, casting a hurried look around the office, turned off the light and closed the door behind her.

She'd deal with the agenda for Dom's management meeting tomorrow; now she had to get home, if you could call the bedsit over the fish and chip shop on London Road which she was defiantly renting to piss her parents off, home. She needed something to eat; she was famished, and she should also wash out some knickers for tomorrow. Last week's trip to the laundrette hadn't been as efficient as it should have been, she'd left one of the bags of dirty washing behind and hadn't fancied getting the bus back to fetch it.

"Oh well," she sighed as she popped her head into the small kitchen at the end of the corridor to make sure the cleaners had done their job properly. "There's always tomorrow."

"Pardon?" said a voice behind her.

She jumped, turning around, her heart thumping in her chest, but it was only Dom.

"Oh, it's you," she said. "Thought you might be an industrial spy or something."

He laughed softly, "No, just me."

"What're you still doing here anyway?" she asked. "Aren't you needed back at home?"

"Yes, I guess so," he said, shaking his boyish blond curls and screwing up his face in a wry smile. "But I had some things to finish off, wanted to get a running start at tomorrow. Am knackered now though," he hesitated, a rare flash of uncertainty crossing his face.

This was her first job after leaving university and, in the six months she'd worked for Dom at the small quantity surveying practice he ran, she'd grown used to his different expressions: exasperation, frustration, anger, amusement and the occasional dart of sadness, but rarely had she seen him uncertain.

"I guess you wouldn't fancy a drink?" he asked. "We could go over the timetable for tomorrow's meetings." The words came out a fraction too quickly, one after the other as he leant his muscle-bound body against the doorframe in a pseudo-relaxed way, crossing his arms and gazing squarely at her out of his dark blue, almost indigo, eyes.

He's a dream of a man, she thought for the hundredth time. *He's also married, with kids, and is fifteen years older than me, almost old enough to be my father,* she added firmly as she flicked the kitchen light switch off, plunging them both into darkness.

"Shit," she said. "Didn't mean for that to happen."

She felt his breath hot near her neck as he leaned across her to turn the light back on.

His fingers hesitated on the switch just long enough for her to say, "Drink? OK then, one quick drink can't hurt. Can it?"

"Pint of bitter and..." Dom paused, looking over his shoulder. She was sitting in a corner booth, her legs crossed neatly, and he felt a quiet shudder somewhere inside his bones... "A glass of white wine," he said. The barman had followed his gaze and there passed between the two men a flicker of an unspoken conversation which, if said out loud, would have been deeply inappropriate and which shamed him.

When they'd got to the reception desk in the office, she'd bent down to turn on the lamp on the low table in front of the big bay window which overlooked the four car parking spaces in front of the building and he'd noticed the way her hair fell forward as she did so, saw the slender curve of her neck. He'd never really looked at her that closely before. But now, he saw its graceful sweep, how the tiny hairs lit up in the diffused light, how her head almost seemed too heavy for her shoulders.

She'd worked for him for a while, he couldn't remember exactly how long, but his diary was now well-managed, all documents stored neatly, and she dealt with customers and associates in a firm but friendly manner on the phone. It'd been a risk taking on someone so young, it was true, and he'd never really asked her about her personal circumstances.

There was probably some huge beefcake of a boyfriend in the background; a prop forward or something.

To Dom, she seemed a strange mix of tenderness and worldliness and this fascinated him. In other words, she was an enigma and he liked enigmas. It was a while since he'd had a distraction; maybe it was time to indulge himself. He deserved it, didn't he? Things at home were lacklustre and somewhat shit. His wife… He hadn't wanted to think of her, so these thoughts had circled back to the girl in front of him.

The two of them had walked to a nearby pub, leaving Dom's car sitting silently in its parking place, and now he was placing her wine in front of her trying not to gaze at the buttons of her blouse, the material around which was straining slightly across her breasts.

"Here you go," he said brightly.

"Thank you."

"Right, to task!" he added, sliding into the booth and putting his own drink on the table.

"I haven't got any paper with me," she said, shrugging her shoulders sheepishly. He liked the way her nose crinkled, the sudden dart of her smile.

"Never mind, we can discuss the agenda in outline and then see what we can remember in the morning!" He laughed as he said this; it was an uneasy, slightly cheesy laugh that he wasn't proud of. He was normally better than this.

She sipped her drink, licking a droplet of wine from her lower lip and grinned at him. She shifted in her seat, knocking her arm against his as she did so.

"Oops, sorry!" she said.

"That's OK," he replied, putting a steadying hand on her lower arm, feeling her react, the fine hairs rise. Again, a tremor coursed through him. Things were moving quickly, which was probably a good thing; he shouldn't really be too late home tonight. His wife would be expecting him.

Ah, he thought to himself, as he let an image of his wife's unsmiling face stray inconveniently back into his mind. He couldn't actually remember the last time she'd really smiled at him, maybe if he thought carefully, he could track back, pin it down to just before the first time he'd been unfaithful. Maybe in some weird way, she knew. He'd thought he was a good liar, but perhaps he wasn't. He'd found it a constant struggle to keep up the pretence, to make believe that everything was OK when it so clearly wasn't.

Looking over the top of his beer glass at the girl in front of him, he hoped this time it would work out all right, that he could do this without either one of them getting hurt. He'd never managed it before and it would be such a shame to lose her from the company, but the others had never stayed around afterwards before. It had always been way too uncomfortable.

"Cheers!" he said, raising his glass.

She smiled back at him, and his heart did a tiny, but unexpected somersault in his chest.

The wine was cool and refreshing and it slipped down easily, too easily. She felt herself becoming a little woozy and wished she was lying down on her bed in the flat. Even the smell of fish and chips frying wouldn't bother her tonight, she thought. She could sleep for England.

"You, OK?" Dominic asked.

"Just tired, that's all."

"Better get you home then."

"It's OK, I can walk, could do with the fresh air."

"I won't hear of it. I kept you late, so I'll drop you home. We'll need to go back to the office to get my car though. Is that OK?"

Pushing the table slightly away from her, she tried to stand up. Her legs felt wobbly, and her heart was thumping in her chest. She was surprised the other people in the pub didn't look round at the noise it was making, not that she understood why it should be beating so loudly.

"Sure," she said, picking up her handbag and walking unsteadily to the door. She didn't notice Dominic and the barman exchange glances, hadn't noticed that Dom had drunk one pint to her four glasses of wine.

The fresh air she'd so wanted hit her like a frying pan and she staggered slightly. Dominic was right behind her and steadied her, his hands warm on the thin material of her blouse. She felt an unexpected tremor between her legs. It had been a while.

No, she said to herself. *Absolutely bloody not, not in a million years. He's your boss, he's married, and he's got kids.* Again, there's that refrain. Yet the heat from his body was so close to her and it felt good. She leant into him. She hadn't meant to; it was more an instinctive thing.

They were standing on the pavement outside the pub. He said her name, very quietly and she turned to face him. She lifted up her eyes and the light from the streetlamp shone down.

"Thank you," she whispered.

He looked into her clear eyes with his troubled ones; she wanted to comfort him, to have him rest his head on her chest. All she wanted was the weight of him – she had been alone for so long. Her previous boyfriends had been transitory and too young. Dominic was different, too different, too dangerously different, she thought as he raised a hand and rested it – inappropriately, and wrongly – on her cheek.

"I really ought to get you home," he said gently into her hair. His breath was spicy and exciting, like a fairground ride, she thought.

They walked back to the car in silence, her arm brushing against his now and again. Her breasts felt swollen under the lace of her bra; she hoped he wasn't picking up the signals, but the wine had confused her, all the lines in her life made blurrier than they'd been before.

Opening the car door for her, she slid into the seat. The leather was smooth to the touch. Looking over her shoulder into the back, she saw a soft toy one of his children must have left there its head on one side so that it looked as though it was asleep. She felt like weeping.

"Just here'll be fine," she said at last, the first words either of them had spoken for a while. He pulled into a lay-by. "I'm just there, above the chip shop," she said with her hand on the door handle.

"See you tomorrow then?" he asked, his voice unusually sombre and quiet.

"Of course!" She tried to sound brisk and business-like, but something had shifted between them, some small quiver which had changed everything. The feel of his hand on her face was still there and, as she stepped from the car and watched it drive away, she wondered if and when it would ever fade.

Dom woke the next morning feeling uneasy but without fully understanding why. He lay for a while staring at the heavy damask curtains his wife had recently ordered from John Lewis. The pattern on them made him feel claustrophobic; the huge red flowers were far too big for the room. But he hadn't dared mention this to her. She wouldn't have wanted to know his opinion in any case.

The numbers on the clock by the bed pulsed at him; it was five-thirty. He turned his head to look at his wife. She was pressed up against the far edge of the bed because in between them their four-year-old daughter was spread out like a starfish, her dark lashes resting on her plump cheeks.

He had no idea when she'd crept into bed with them so he must have slept soundly for some part of the night at least. By rights he shouldn't have done because when he slipped under the covers carefully so as not to wake his wife, he had lain awake and watchful for a while, thinking back to how he'd felt standing outside the pub. He tried to tell himself that this was no different to the other times, but there was something unusual about this girl; maybe it was the fact that he just hadn't noticed her until now so what he had noticed had taken him by surprise? Maybe it was just that it'd been a while since his last conquest, and he was worried that he was losing his touch? Maybe it was just that suddenly the stakes seemed to have risen? There did seem an awful lot to lose now.

Shifting position slightly, he rested his large hand on his daughter's small one; her fingers twitched, and she sighed in her sleep. He felt an overwhelming need to hold her, but he didn't. Instead, he pulled back the duvet and swung his legs out of the bed. He wanted to leave for work before the house woke up. There was no way he could cope with the uniform, lunchbox, games kit and breakfast chaos which usually punctuated school mornings. Today also wasn't the day for him to have to deal with his two-year-old son's Weetabix carnage. On his way to the guest room where he kept his clothes, he stuck his head around his son's bedroom door and watched the Bob the Builder cover rise and fall in time with his breathing.

He dressed quickly. He didn't leave a note. His wife would know where he'd gone. He couldn't face her this morning either.

Later, from behind his half-open office door, he was aware of the other staff arriving; their early morning chatter filling the corridor, but he kept his head down, his eyes fixed on his computer screen, wishing he could postpone the management meeting so he wouldn't have to be in the same room as her for long. Someone tapped on the door.

"Dom?"

"Oh," he said, picking up a pen and clicking it on and off rapidly. "It's you."

"Yes," she said. She looked very delicate this morning, as though she'd been fashioned from tissue paper. She was wearing a long flowery skirt and a white knitted top with a round lace collar; she couldn't have looked more innocent if she'd tried. "I've typed up the agenda for today," she continued. "I hope I've remembered everything."

"I'm sure it'll be fine," he said. "We'll manage. We always do."

"Do you want me to take the minutes as usual?"

"Yes please, and oh," he paused, stretched back in his chair in an act of studied indifference and said, "I presume you'll sort the coffees and stuff out if that's OK?"

"Yes," she replied shortly and, putting the agenda down on his desk, turned to go. He watched her, remembering last night and how he'd turned the car around, saw her slip through the door at the side of the chip shop, and how, with every atom in his body, he'd wanted to follow her.

Time had taken on a sluggish feel; every day seemed to hang like a lead weight from the tips of her fingers as she trudged through her work. Dom was avoiding her; she was sure of it. She'd even taken to staying late. Her files had never been tidier, and she hoped that he'd pop his head round the door on his way out, see she was alone, and they could take up from where they'd left off. What had happened when they'd stood outside the pub and he'd touched her face with his large warm hand had, she often thought, kind of branded her, making her no good at anything else, or for anyone else. He shouldn't have done it. She shouldn't have let him. But it was done now and couldn't be undone.

When she did manage to tear herself away from work, she'd go back to her bedsit above the chip shop and stand stupidly at the window, willing his car to draw up, hoping against hope that it wouldn't, because if it did, she would have no idea what to do, how to say no.

In her more rational moments, she knew, however, that it was probably for the best; getting involved with someone at work, and your married boss at that, wasn't a smart move, not for your first job, well for any job, really. But still, it was getting harder each day, harder to keep on pretending, so on her way to work that morning, she'd picked up a copy of the local paper from the newsagents on the corner by her bus stop. She'd start looking for a new job at lunchtime.

At about eleven, the phone on her desk rang.

"It's Tina," came Tina's imperious voice from reception. "Where's Dom?"

"He's still out at Bandon's, shouldn't be long though. Why?"

"His wife's here to take him to lunch."

An inexplicable rage coursed through her. It wasn't in his diary. He hadn't told her.

"Does she want to wait?" she managed to ask.

There was a pause as Tina obviously spoke to this wife who'd come crashing into the bit of Dom's life over which she didn't have any rights.

"This bit's mine," she said to herself as she clutched onto the handset with a grip so fierce, she was almost getting pins and needles in her fingers.

"Yes." Tina's voice came back on the line. "She's on her way up. She says she'll wait in his office. Can you get her a cup of coffee?"

"Of course, I can," she snapped back and put down the phone with a heavy clunk, knowing that Tina would most likely take her to task over it later. Everyone had to suck up to Tina, or else. That was kind of an unwritten rule and she'd just broken it big time. "Oh well," she said to herself. "I've got bigger fish to fry right now."

She smiled at the irony of this, pushed back her chair and walked to the door of her office, really hoping that no one else was around; she would hate for this encounter to have an audience.

Dom's wife was, by this time, at the top of the stairs. She was a small woman, mouselike, with sharp eyes and a thin mouth. She looked coiled and expectant.

"Where is he then?" she asked, her voice not kind, nor polite even.

"He's at a meeting at Bandon Architects. Should be back soon though. He must be running a bit late. Can I get you a coffee while you wait?"

"OK," his wife said, striding into Dom's office and pulling the door behind her.

As the door swung shut in her face and his wife moved mercifully out of view, she couldn't stop herself from muttering the word, 'Cow', under her breath as then she walked towards the kitchen to put the kettle on.

The woman was sitting in Dom's chair behind Dom's desk and, as she put the coffee down, she felt this overwhelming temptation to spill its contents into her sanctimonious lap, but she didn't. She left her there, dressed in her ill-fitting Laura Ashley number and her stupid little shoes and went back to her desk to carry on typing up a report on the new supermarket development on the western edge of town.

About half an hour later, she was aware that Dom had returned. She recognized his footsteps in the corridor, heard him open his office and the exchange of words which followed. She couldn't hear exactly what was said but neither tone was friendly. Then there was a silence. She carried on typing but inside she was running, running through a field and Dom was running with her. He wasn't fully drawn in her mind, but she knew it was him. He had the right shape; his body made the right sounds. She could see the sun glinting off his golden hair as he ran by her side. They were both laughing.

"Hey," he was in the room with her now and he'd said her name. "Will be about an hour. Is that OK?"

"Sure," she answered, wondering what it would be like if she really had the option of telling him not to go.

He hesitated by the door, his hand on the handle. Then he came over to where she was sitting. The sun was hot on the back of her neck. She could sense his wife in the room down the corridor; some sort of unexplained fury was seeping along the carpet.

She rested her hands on her desk and then he touched her, touching the bit between the end of her cuff and her wrist, where the skin is softest.

"I'll see you later, then," he said gently and then he walked away to join his wife and she heard them go down the stairs together, heard the swish of Laura Ashley fabric. She looked down at the place his fingers had touched and was surprised to find there was no red mark there; she thought there ought to have been. Like when he had touched her before, it carried on stinging long after he'd gone.

Dom came back alone. He checked in with her and then spent the afternoon on the phone so she didn't see him or speak to him much after that, and when five-thirty came and she left the office he was still working with the door closed, so she didn't pop her head round it to say goodnight but, in the bin next to her desk, the newspaper she'd bought earlier in the day had been folded and tucked down one side next to her empty coffee cups ready for the cleaners to come and spirit it away.

The day his wife came into the office was, for Dom, like a marker in the sand. From that moment he could imagine himself as William in Brenda Bainbridge's *Sweet William*, a book he'd come across at a jumble sale once, and having his wife surprise his mistress with a birthday cake for him which the two of them would share. Such things were possible, weren't they?

His wife's visit that day had been designed so that the two of them could go to lunch to discuss plans for that year's holiday. They'd left it far too late to book something good. "There's only the dregs left in the travel agent's window," his wife had said to him that morning.

She'd made arrangements for a friend to look after his son and do the school run for his daughter and so he and she had sat at either side of a table at a pizza restaurant in town and the bidding had started.

"I fancy somewhere warm," he said. "A hotel, maybe with a golf course, but definitely a pool and a kids' club, so that they can be entertained during the day, and we can relax." He'd looked meaningfully at his wife when he said this, but she hadn't responded, "And then we can spend some time with them during the early evening, maybe get a babysitter or something…" He tailed off, realising his words were landing on stony ground.

"I," she responded, looking at him with her hard beady eyes, "was thinking more along the lines of an activity holiday, maybe camping.

This country definitely, so we don't have to worry about constantly putting sunscreen on the children."

There, the battle lines had been drawn and when he'd got back to the office and looked into her room and saw her sitting there with her small head on its delicate neck and the smooth skin on her upper arms, he'd seen the surprisingly welcome but bloody inconvenient other line in the sand clearly in front of him. He'd decided that his late night and early morning doubts, his policy of avoiding her as much as possible were as unnecessary as they were unwelcome. There were, after all, some things you just couldn't deny.

As it happened, a week later, the company won a contract for a large retail development just outside Wolverhampton which meant he couldn't go away at all.

His wife had stood in the kitchen of their house with her arms folded and said, "Well, what do you expect me to do now?"

It seemed she just couldn't see the direct correlation between the amount of money he earned and the house they lived in, and that they were saving for their children's future and that it was because of his salary she was able to order hideous curtains for their bedroom from John Lewis.

"I suppose I could take the children to my mother's," she'd said and had turned her back on him and made a large noise with some saucepans.

All Dom could feel was a wave of relief washing over him at the thought of a week away from the sweep of her baleful glare.

"I'm going to visit the new site," he told the office on the Monday of his family-free week, nodding his head ever so slightly at her as she sat behind her desk. "And would like *you* to come with me to take notes."

As he said this, Dom made an air sign of writing which she thought to be a bit ridiculous, but she knew she'd go; it was her job to.

She made sure she had a spare Dictaphone and tapes with her and a spare notepad and pen. It was only fifty miles there and fifty miles back. They could do it in a day.

Tina was watching them get in the car out of the window in reception, her back stiff and straight, her face expressionless, but she could tell what she was thinking, she could hear the scornful, 'Ha!' coming from Tina's mind. She was imagining Tina saying, "Seen it all before."

Dom put the car in reverse and set off up the road to the T-junction.

Looking over her shoulder, she noticed there were no soft toys in the back this time.

The site visit went well but went on much longer than she'd anticipated. It also started to rain, real steel-like rain; not sequin rain, but hard, unforgiving, hot, stormy, summer drops which splashed onto the car windscreen and caused Dom to screw up his eyes so that he could see better. Outside Birmingham, they hit rush hour traffic.

"Bugger," he said. "Looks like we're going to be late home."

He glanced across at her, but she said, "It's OK, I don't have anything planned this evening."

"No date?" he asked.

"No," she said, deciding not to say anything else. There wasn't much point, was there?

His car phone rang, and his wife's name came up on the screen. "Do you mind?" he asked.

"Of course not."

She tried not to listen to the conversation, but she couldn't help it. Both Dom's and his wife's voices were clipped and distorted by the reception and the sound made by the windscreen wipers as they flashed back and forth and they spoke only about the children, her mother, and the weather.

"I'm on my way back from Wolverhampton," he said.

His wife didn't ask how it had gone and he didn't say he wasn't alone in the car. They hung up at the same time without really saying goodbye.

A wet, purple dusk was falling when the lights on the dashboard of the car started to flash.

"Shit," Dom said. "Looks like we have a problem. I knew I should have got the thing serviced."

"I'll book it in tomorrow, shall I?" she offered.

"Might be too late by then," he answered, as he swerved the car into a lay-by and switched off the engine. He thumped the steering wheel; the windscreen wipers were still ricocheting back and forth.

He leant across her to the glove compartment, and she could feel the heat from his body. As he bent forward, she looked at the back of his head, at the way his hair curled over his collar. She wanted to reach out and touch it.

"Sod it," he said, sitting back up and opening up the car's instruction manual. "I think we'd better get the AA out."

He rang. They came. They couldn't fix the car, so they towed it away. Dom called a local cab company and checked the two of them into a motel.

"Knew I should have splashed out and added Relay to my policy," he told her. Then, "Two single rooms please," he said to the lady behind the desk as they stood in front of her, dripping from the run across the car park.

The receptionist gave them a key each, and a toiletry set: toothbrush, toothpaste, and soap. "That'll be an extra five pounds each," she said.

"No problem," Dom replied.

There was, she thought, something dream-like about the whole evening as she took the key Dom held out for her. His eyes were almost grey in the yellow light of the corridor. "I'll hire a car in the morning and get us back," he said. "It's pointless trying to do so now, what with the weather and the traffic."

She chose to believe him. It was, she thought, a bit like being in a play that someone else had written the script for, so she nodded. "I can write up the notes this evening," she said, pulling her wet coat around her. "It'll save time tomorrow."

He turned abruptly away then and unlocked the door to his room. For some reason, her hands were shaking as she did likewise. She supposed it was because she was cold.

She showered, dried her hair and got back into her still unpleasantly damp clothes. She also did her teeth. Turning on the TV, she sat in the armchair and watched a programme about farming. At about ten o'clock there was a light tapping on her door.

"Yes?" she said, her voice cracking slightly from lack of use.

"I thought you might be hungry," Dom said, peering round the door, a carrier bag in his outstretched hand. "Got some sandwiches from the garage next door. They don't look very appetising, but they're better than nothing. There's a bottle of wine as well, although it's probably like paint-stripper." He laughed uncomfortably as he said this and she couldn't help thinking back to when he leaned against her outside the pub, when he put his hand on her face, when he touched her wrist in the office, and felt that there was a chasm between them now, which she had no idea how to cross, if she should cross it at all, that is.

She switched off the TV and got the plastic toothbrush mugs from the bathroom while he opened the wine with a corkscrew on his penknife. She'd never seen the penknife before. "Present from my dad," he said, putting it back into his pocket. "He died when I was a teenager actually."

"I'm sorry," she said.

He passed her a sandwich; cheese and pickle with today's sell-by date on it. The wine tasted foul, and her hands were too uncertain to open the plastic sandwich wrapper, so she put both it and the beaker down on the floor and said lightly, "May save it for later. Not so hungry at the moment."

He came to sit by her on the bed. She had a feeling she knew what would happen next and she was right. He took her face in his hands. They were hot, like electricity.

"I…" he started saying.

"I know," she said, leaning towards him and letting her lips brush against his. It seemed the easiest way to cross the gulf which, as he opened his mouth under hers, seemed no gulf at all.

"Do I need anything?" he asked.

"No," she replied. "I have it covered."

"You sure about this?" he asked, locking his eyes onto hers.

She couldn't look away even if she'd wanted to. "Yes, I'm sure," she said.

She'd never had anyone make love to her like that before, or, she would later realise, since. It was perfect and round like a circle and right and easy and afterwards, as she sat on the chair by the window dressed only in his creased shirt with her legs tucked under her watching the rain splash into the puddles on the pavement, she turned to him and said, "How many?"

He lifted his head from the pillow, ran his hand through his hair which shone like butter in the light from the streetlamp outside and said, "Not many."

"We talking one or two, or ten or twelve?" she asked.

"One or two."

"And what happens now?"

"That's up to you really, but now I think we should get some sleep, don't you?"

Already she could imagine the exhaustion of having to stay one step ahead all the time; of having to have a catalogue of lies to choose from each time he came to her, lies which she'd have to tell herself and be ready to tell other people, people like his wife, or Tina or the guys in the office, or her parents when she suddenly couldn't go and stay for the weekend like she'd planned because Dom could get an hour or two off from his duties at home, using work or a drink with the lads as an excuse to come and see her. It was like they were already in some sordid TV drama.

She knew she was a living, breathing cliché. *How many have been in this situation before me,* she wondered. *Not just with Dom, but generally, the world over: books, films, and secret histories are littered with the remains of futile affairs that seemed so urgent and necessary at the time, so justifiable.*

Yet, as she stepped across the battlefield of their discarded clothes, she could also already imagine standing at her window above the chip shop and seeing him step out of his repaired car, seeing him look up at her and smile and she wanted this, she wanted this very badly indeed.

She must have slept because, on waking, she was still full of a dream; her mind was filled with the sound of rain and movement. There'd been lights and voices in her dream and again she had felt herself running. The voices had started off speaking quietly and then they'd got louder until, as she woke, they were reverberating around in her head, and she felt that she would never be able to breathe properly again.

Dom stirred in the bed next to her, grey light from behind the curtains falling onto him. Her heart was racing. What was she doing here? How had it happened?

She tried to remember. Last night when she'd sat by the window it had all seemed so simple. All she had to do was to walk back across the room and slide in next to him. She'd known he would reach out and draw her near to him until her back was pressed against the curve of his body and that she would close her eyes and want to make the moment last forever. It had all been so right then.

But now, as dawn crept in stealthy steps across the carpet and she tried very hard to shake herself loose from her dream, she knew that she was only borrowing him, that he was on temporary loan, an unsanctioned and unallowable loan. There was nothing, absolutely nothing of his that belonged to her, that she had any entitlement to and that it would always be like this, every time. She had no idea how she was going to survive it. She knew it could never happen again.

Turning onto her side she watched his eyelids flutter and wondered whether he was dreaming too. His skin smelled of rain and wine and sex and she wanted to put her mouth to it and drink in its scent one more time. She reached out a hand and rested it on his chest. His heartbeat was slow and measured.

"Morning," she whispered, wanting to pretend that she could say it every day, that she could start every day like this, that this first time wasn't going to be the last.

Dom's eyes opened and he blinked. She felt that her life was resting on a blade edge. What would happen now? Would he sit up horrified and say, "My God, what have I done? Get out, get out of here." Or would he look at her, his cobalt-blue eyes hooded with desire and stroke the soft skin at the top of her arm like he'd done last night, and he would kiss her and want her again? What would she do should he do either of these things?

"Morning to you too," he said, smiling lazily at her.

"I thought you were asleep."

"Just dozing." He stretched and the thin sheet slipped off him. His cock was hard and beautiful, and she wanted it in her again. Her breasts tingled, her whole body did. *No,* she thought. *Leave, I have to leave now.*

"Well?" he said. "What do we do next?"

"I should get up," she said. "We need to get back."

"Do we?" He gazed at her, and she felt herself wavering like she was being mixed with water and dissolving. She didn't have the strength to fight so, in reply, she leant on her elbow and reached over to kiss him, tentatively at first, then deeper, and deeper.

"Mmm," he said. "You taste good."

He lifted her onto him, and she straddled him, lowering herself onto him, gasping as he entered her. He held her with his eyes and his body, with his rising and falling until he came and she could feel the pulsing of him, almost familiar now it was the second time and she felt herself crying as she realised that she did have something of his, she had this moment and that nothing anybody else ever said or did could take it away from her, and that she would do whatever she could to preserve it, him, them, this – whatever it took to have it again, to keep it.

Still looking deep into her eyes, he used his thumb. She was rigid on him, building it until she came, still shuddering as she bent forwards, resting her head on his chest, their hearts matching beat for beat and the traffic sliding by outside the motel window and somewhere his wife and children were waking but that didn't matter. *This is right*, she told herself. *This is how it is meant to be.*

He hadn't meant for it to happen again. Last night had been necessary, cathartic. *Get it out of your system*, he'd told himself as he'd queued up in the garage clutching the wine and the sandwiches and, as he dropped off to sleep he told himself again and again that when morning came, they would rise, dress, leave and he would explain quietly and gently that it could never happen again, that it had been fun but that he was married and, as she would know by then, he'd done this sort of thing before and that she shouldn't waste herself on him; there were far better men out there. He would be sad for a while, mourning the passing of the chase, the would-she/wouldn't-she tension that had run through him during the past few weeks, but he'd never been able to sustain something like this before; it had never seemed fair on himself or her, or more especially on his family. No, this would follow the pattern of the other times, and no one would get hurt.

As he woke, he was decided, but then he felt the pressure of her hand on his chest and heard her say, "Morning," as though she did so every day. Her voice was gentle, cooling, and healing.

"Morning to you too," he said, smiling lazily at her. He was stalling and he knew it. She looked luminous in the grey light of morning, her sweet round face, her eyes clear and bright.

"I thought you were asleep," she said.

"Just dozing." He stretched and the thin sheet slipped off him. He was hard and he wanted her again. Her breasts brushed against him; they were small and plump, and he wanted his mouth on them, to feel her flesh tingle, her nipples harden. *No,* he thought. *Tell her, tell her now.* "Well?" he said. "What do we do next?"

"I should get up," she said. "We need to get back."

"Do we?" There was a fraction of a pause; a dangerous one, one that separated what should happen and what they both wanted to happen.

So, he lifted her onto him and slid himself into her. She gasped. He came quickly, needfully, watching her, watching her bite her lip, her hair tousled and tumbling around her ears. Then he used his thumb and felt the hard nub of her and the muscles inside her draw him in as she came. She rested her head on his chest and he placed his hand in her hair. He tried not to think of his wife or his family waking. All he knew was that what they'd done hadn't just been sex; it had been the beginnings of something else, something which had taken him by surprise.

He said her name, his lips grazing her shoulder.

"Mmm," she answered sleepily. He ran his hands down to her waist and held her, cradling her, still in her.

"It's going to be OK, isn't it? We're going to be able to do this, aren't we?"

"Yes, Dom," she murmured against his skin. "It is. We are."

Outside the room, the housekeeping staff were starting to wheel their trolleys down the corridors, dusters hanging like limp flags from the waistbands of their uniforms and Faith and Dom pretended to sleep, both wishing they had a crystal ball and that they could see into the future and know that it was going to be OK, that they were going to be able to do this, that 'The Honourable Thing' both knew lay in their power to do would stay in the shadows, wouldn't get in the way of the here and now and the future of this.

Part 4 – Late Spring, Twenty-three Years Later

It's Wednesday, and Nic Bradley slides the car park ticket into his wallet and then leans in to pick up his portfolio case from the back seat. He's unusually nervous, but he shouldn't be. He's done this many times before but putting his work in front of people is still a difficult thing for him to do. However, as he's sitting in his studio, brush in hand, he does sometimes wonder what the point of it is if he doesn't let his pictures speak for him. If he keeps them to himself, it's like he's being gagged, that the story he wants to tell is being whispered in back rooms to shadowy people and not, as he thinks it should be, shouted out from the rooftops. "I cocked up," he wants to holler in amongst the concrete pillars of the multi-storey. "And I want you, whoever you are looking at my paintings, signed with the name I gave myself to hide my regret, to read this in every brushstroke, every shade of blue and to know this and know how sorry I am."

You'd think, he muses as he strides to the lifts, *that by now I would have been able to let it go.* But he'd loved her, and he hadn't expected to. It was supposed to be a mild flirtation, just something to pass the time like the others had been, and he'd expected that when it was over, he would have been able to move on, still married, still with his kids, still with everything intact. What he hadn't counted on was the destruction, both that he imposed on himself and that done to him by others.

That first night and the following morning in the motel near Birmingham – part contrived, part-accidental – had, he sometimes thought later, sealed it for him. From somewhere deep down, near his navel, something that had been embedded and hidden had come loose and a torrent of feelings had crashed over his head, and he'd wanted her again and again and again. He kept on wanting her. In the end, he'd had to try and persuade her to stop working for him.

"Look," he'd said. "I just think it's best. It's going to be too difficult otherwise."

"But it means we won't see each other as often," she said, her face open, smooth, loveable, her eyes clear and shining. She'd turned round to look at him, spoon in one hand, coffee jar in the other in the tiny kitchenette of her bedsit. She'd been naked and he hadn't been able to drag his eyes away from her. Her breasts still bore the blush from his stubble, her tight, flat stomach led down to where he'd tasted her. He'd wanted to wrap her up and never let her go. "Well?" she'd said. "We won't, will we?"

"No," he'd replied. "But I still think it's for the best. Tina's going to guess before long."

Thinking back, it was about then that he'd wanted to start the whole shouting thing. He'd wanted to be able to stand on a desk in the middle of the office and say, "I love her! I want to be with her, not my wife." But he knew that just like the whole unrealistic wish thing with the pictures now, the thought of his kids and his duty to them then had held him in check, kept him silent.

Her leaving party had been torture. He'd had no idea what to say when inside he was breaking. Something fucking meaningless like, "We'll all miss her. We wish her well." That sort of thing had issued from his mouth and, after he'd presented her with a measly gift of wine glasses and a card, she'd shaken his hand, his hand! He'd wanted to pick her up and kiss her deeply on the mouth, right there, right then with everyone looking on. But he didn't. Instead, he'd driven her home and they'd made love quietly and somewhat sadly. Even back then he'd had a sinking feeling that the ending had just begun.

He'd tried really hard. Twice a week he'd make excuses to stay late at work or have after-work 'meetings'. "Just boring networking things," he'd say to his wife. But she hadn't seemed to care, had kept her back turned to him in the kitchen of their home and said, "Whatever Dom, do what you please. You always do."

Then the kids started to need him more. His daughter got involved in stuff and needed to be taken places and he had to go home to look after his son. He should have wanted to do this more than anything else and, on an instinctive level, of course, he did. He loved listening to his son gabbling about *Thomas the Tank Engine* and he'd pretend to get the names of the engines wrong, just so his son could correct him. "No, silly Daddy," he'd say. "That's Gordon, not James!"

So, the, 'I'm sorry', calls to Faith became more frequent and he felt powerless to do anything about them. She'd tried to be brave, he could tell from her voice, but he also knew that with each and every call, he was pushing her away when really what he wanted was to pull her nearer, be in her, be around her, be part of her.

At the end of their second summer when the leaves were melting to browns and golds and coppers, he sensed she was fading. Her voice changed on the other end of the phone, she was less easy with him, less open, and it shattered him to know this and to know that he had no right to stop her from going. In the end, she'd said something like, "Fuck the clichés and the movie talk." And had just told him bluntly that she wanted out. He remembers begging and then crying with his head on the steering wheel of his car and the well of resentment that had been bubbling under the surface surge up and threaten to engulf him. He'd had to believe it wouldn't be forever; he had too much invested in it for that. But she went. She left her job, left the bedsit but didn't leave any trace of where she'd gone. It was easier to disappear in those days. Less so now with other people's lives played out on social media, He assumed there was someone else and on occasions, he even hoped there was because he hated the thought of her being alone, but never discovered who it might be because this was before everyone plastered their lives all over social media. He never looked her up and assumed she'd changed her name anyway. Such self-control. Such a sundering.

And he'd really tried to do the whole husband/father thing, but his heart wasn't in the former and, a year later, when his wife finally confronted him with credit card slips from his time with Faith which he'd kept as mementoes and she'd picked out of his wallet while he'd slept and had harboured like poison, he was almost relieved. There'd been a lot of angry whispering while the kids were in bed and, in the end, he'd left, doing the whole doorstep weekend dad thing and he'd missed his children with a keenness that had staggered him, but overriding this was the sense that he'd escaped from a marriage which would have diminished him so that eventually he would have become unrecognisable even to himself. He had to hold onto this belief; all through the years which followed. It was the only thing that kept him going.

He'd never married again. There'd been other women, some –
not many, but no one had ever come close to Faith, or to that time when he
discovered that there could be so much more to life, to love, than he'd ever
imagined.

In the lift, he reaches the ground floor, tucks his portfolio case
under his arm and heads out into the street.

On my way to the shop, I take a detour, turning left by St Nicholas Church
and down to Newbury Lock. The water this morning is languid, still
stretching its limbs into the soon-to-be warm air. My relationship with
water, unlike Sara's, has over the years settled into an uneasy truce, and
there are still times when I love to watch its meanderings and the glide of
swans and their reflections in it and the unsettling and resetting of their
feathers, the odd quill floating downstream and away.

I also love the solid dark wood of the lock itself and the power
stored in its gates and levers, but today all is quiet, only the odd rustle of a
hidden creature along the bank, the sound of a jet overhead and the distant
rumble of traffic. I want to stretch up my arms and feel the bones in my
back tumble. I want the muscles to flex and bend and fall away until there
is nothing left of me but a heap of skin on the ground. Instead, I hitch my
bag further up my shoulder, thrust my hands into my jacket pockets and
make my way back onto Bartholomew Street and the shop.

Later, when Lizzie and Dana have both arrived and the
sandwiches have been made and the eleven-thirty lull is just looming, I say,
"OK if I pop into the back and do a bit of admin? There's the orders to
reconcile and I need to check the petty cash tin."

"Sure," Lizzie says, smiling over her shoulder at me before she
lowers her head to read the temperature of the milk.

I pull the door shut so that I can only see a sliver of the shop and
the shadows which flit back and forwards. I put on my glasses, switch on
the computer and wait for the menu screen to load.

As I wait, I gaze idly at the notice board on which Lizzie and I
pin all sorts of stuff which, at the time, seem vitally important but which,
on reflection and when the date of the exhibition, book launch, or theatre
production has passed, leave just a faint stab of regret at something not
done; an opportunity missed. I skim over the card Harvey gave me when

Ashley finally left for uni. On the front was a picture of a puppy and the words, 'Mums are for life, not just for Christmas' and inside he'd written, 'They will always need you. I will always need you. All my love, H.'

I live my life on too straight a road, I sometimes think. There is here and there, and my job is to travel, just that, just to journey. I should seize things more, experiment, make difficult choices, sleep better, be more honest with Harvey, forgive myself my early wrongs, and celebrate the fact the boys have gone, not mourn it. Yes, I tell myself, as I manoeuvre the mouse to click on Excel and open the stock control file, I should take more risks with my life, I should make the journey more interesting, own up to my mistakes, and allow the messy things to life to intrude.

Half an hour passes and there's a tap on the door. I look up at the slice of light but can't see who it is. I guess it's Lizzie. I'm right.

"Faith?" Lizzie's voice is light and easy. "It's the artist guy, Nic Bradley. He's brought his portfolio to show us."

"Oh," I reply, standing up and smoothing down my skirt which is practical, and my customary black, and covered by my apron with the *Flick's* logo on it. I take off my glasses, run my fingers through my hair and go towards the door. I've forgotten he's due to come in this morning, but now he's here, I'm glad. It'll break up the morning; give me something different to think about.

I open the door, and there is Lizzie, small, silver-haired, smiling, and behind her is Dom. Dom, from my past. Dom, the man I have spent more than twenty years trying to forget.

"You?" I say.

I know I must have gone pale, my skin must be almost white, and my eyes huge. My lips are dry, and my heart is pounding. It takes my brain long seconds to catch up with what I'm seeing. How can this be? Lizzie had said it was Nic Bradley, not Dominic Bradley. Then I knew why the name on the email had seemed familiar. Bradley, that had been Dom's surname. I'd tried so hard to forget this too, not search for it on the internet. So hard.

"Faith?" he says, and the world stops turning. Right there, right then, it just stops.

"Oh my God."

What else is there to say?

All the years of wondering and wishing and here he is, standing behind Lizzie in our shop with a folder under his arm. He looks no different and yet is so totally unfamiliar. I can recognise every expression on his face, foresee the movement of his arms and legs as he walks towards me, and yet I know I don't know him at all. Not anymore. There is a gap, a huge crater of missed moments between this one and the one when we'd said goodbye, when Dom had driven away from my bedsit above the chip shop in a different town in a different time, before my children were born, before Douggie, before everything that had happened since because I'd let him go, because I had carefully constructed a world of lies, a world without him in it.

"Oh, do you two already know one another?" Lizzie asks, her voice a little unsure, trying it would seem to break the deadlock, to kick-start the world spinning again.

Dom is the first to speak. "Yes," he says. "We used to work together, a lifetime ago. Right Faith?"

I nod, wondering if I will ever be able to speak again.

"Oh well, that makes it a lot easier, doesn't it?" Lizzie says, laughing and turning to go. "I'd better get on if it's OK with you." She looks up at Dom and adds, "I'll leave you in Faith's capable hands."

Lizzie obviously has no idea what she's doing, and I want to shout, "Don't go! Stay! Stay in between us just where you are. Don't let me get any closer to him than this. Please."

But Lizzie has gone, and I can hear her talking to Dana at the counter and the murmur of our customers' voices and the sound of steam hissing into milk.

"Come in," I say at last. "I guess you'd better come in."

It is awkward in the office. There isn't much room, but we dance around one another uncomfortably until I am seated again by my desk, and he's pulled up a chair and is sitting in it, with his long legs crossed and his folder resting against the wall.

He laughs a strange, half-formed laugh and says, "Maybe I should have known?"

"Why would you have done?" I glance at the computer screen as if it holds the answer to this question. It doesn't.

154

"I don't know," he answers, smiling at me and brushing the hair back from his forehead.

His hair is greying but still tousled and wanton like it had been years before. His eyes are still indigo blue and his body lean and muscular. I feel dowdy and unkempt next to him, that I have aged two years to his one. It's as though I've nearly caught him up.

"You haven't changed," I say.

"Oh, I have." He laughs again and a shiver travel from the base of my skull down my spine. He is everything he used to be and yet…

I don't finish the thought because he reaches out and touches my arm like he used to do years before. "It's good to see you," he says. "It really is. We have so much to catch up on. Don't we?"

To my beleaguered mind, this last question seems more of a challenge than anything else and one which I feel supremely unqualified to answer. What I do know though is that deep down, beneath everything that has happened during the 'so much' we have to catch up on, there is a thick layer of guilt and regret and right at that moment, I am filled with panic, fearing that should we pull apart the covering, should I get the chance to tell him the small stories and the huge ones, this layer will be exposed like lava and I will have no control over its ferocity and the direction of its flow.

He's still reeling; it feels like his head is not attached correctly to his body, that there's a slice of his neck missing. Here she is, after all this time and her eyes are clear and bright just like they used to be and her skin is soft and her hair, shot through with gold highlights to hide the grey, stops just below her ears in exactly the same place it used to. She's slightly plumper, more rounded and he likes this, and he remembers her smooth limbs beneath him, his hands on her shoulders, and looking at her mouth as it broke into a smile whenever she said his name. He can see it all again in his mind like it is happening now, even though they are in a small office at the back of a coffee shop in a town he has visited many times in recent years, but never thought she might live there too and he has his paintings to show her, the ones he has signed with his made up name, the ones which he painted as a way of saying he was sorry for what he'd done, for letting her get away.

"Would you like a coffee?" she asks, standing up abruptly and squeezing past the back of his chair. She seems desperate to get away.

She's gone in a flash, and he's left looking at the notice board on the wall with its jumble of pamphlets and adverts, a chart giving details of weekend rotas and a card saying 'Mums are for life, not just for Christmas'. His eyes stray to the papers on the desk and the computer screen which has changed to a screen saver, a photograph of two boys and a girl, sitting cross-legged in someone's back garden. The girl is in the middle and the boys have their arms draped over her shoulders. She's not smiling, but the boys are grinning self-consciously. It looks hot. They would be in their mid to late teens, he guesses. He remembers his own kids at that age; gawky, unreasonable, ever ready to blame someone else for their own shortcomings. He wonders whether any of the ones on the screen are Faith's children and he scrutinises their faces for a resemblance, but can't see any, or doesn't want to. He's honest enough with himself for that.

She returns, somewhat breathless. "I…" she starts to say, then stops, leaning across him to put the cups down on the desk, several sugar sachets drop down next to them. "I didn't know if…"

"Yes, two sugars, like before," he laughs. "Some habits are hard to break."

How right you are, he says to himself, as he moves his coffee nearer him and picks up the sugar. He doesn't want to look at her right now but is aware of her sitting down again and picking up her own cup in two unsteady hands.

"Your kids?" he asks, pointing at the screen saver.

"The boys are, yes," she replies. "Blake's on the left, Ashley on the right. Lizzie's daughter, Clemmie is in the middle of them." She sighs as she looks at the picture. "It was taken years ago. They're a lot older now."

"Yes," he says, taking a sip of his drink. It scalds his lips.

"Your children? Are they well?"

"Fine, thanks. What I see of them."

They both laugh uncomfortably at this, but he doesn't tell her the rest, the whys and wherefores of his relationship with his son and daughter.

As she drinks, he studies her, and notices the worn gold ring on the third finger of her left hand.

"Married?" he asks.

She nods. "Harvey," she says.

"Was he…?"

"Yes," she answers. "We married later that year."

"I see. I thought there was someone else."

"And you?"

"It didn't last."

He knows he should tell her that he had left soon after, that he couldn't live with the lie of it, that his wife had thrust the evidence in his face and snarled, "Some young tart, I suppose?" He also knows that he should tell her that there had been no one else since, not who'd lasted anyway. There'd been a few, those brief flings and lucky escapes and the odd moment in the morning when he'd turned over in bed to look at the face next to him on the pillow and wondered what it would have been like to find hers there. But he didn't tell her any of this. What would be the point? He was going to arrange for his paintings to be hung, he would visit the shop two or three times, and he may even never see her there again; it may be the other woman he deals with and Faith will pack up at the end of the day and go home to her husband and sons and the whole stupid fucking life she lives with them, the life that has no room for him in it.

"I'm sorry," she says. And he wants to ask her, 'What for'? Is she sorry that she left him, that she didn't give it a chance, that she didn't wait for him to come to his senses and work out that he could still love his kids but not their mother? Or is she just sorry that his marriage didn't work out, and does she want to know if he's single now? Would it make any difference?

She interrupts these thoughts when she says, "I guess we'd better talk about the pictures, if you still want to that is."

And she laughs lightly, but uneasily, as he gathers the folder up and opens it, pulling out the view from his studio and saying, "Of course, I do. This is what I see from my studio by the way."

"It's lovely, Dom. It really is. But would you want to sell it?"

"Sure. After all, I can see it every day, can't I?"

It's all over within minutes and he's back out in the street, standing with his back to the dark green door of the shop, wondering if it had all been a dream.

157

"Can I call you?" he'd asked, as she proffered him her hand again, like she'd done at her leaving do. He doesn't want to shake it. Instead, he wants to gather her to him, press her against his chest and breathe in the smell of her.

"About the pictures?"

"Well, yes and…" he'd hesitated… "Maybe we could, you know, meet for a drink or something." And although he really didn't want to say it, he did, "For old time's sake?"

"I don't know," she answered.

"Maybe with Harvey?" he said, wishing he could pull back the words immediately and stamp hard on them. What a stupid idea! Just think, the three of them and the air thick with everything he and Faith couldn't say.

"If we did," she'd said, her hand on the door handle. "Probably best without him, don't you think?"

He holds onto these words tightly as he crosses the bridge back to the car park. After all, she hadn't said no, had she?

Her mum's wittering and Clemmie hates it when she does this. Why can't she just stay quiet? They're in the car, stuck in rush-hour traffic and the day has suddenly grown hot like someone's turned a heat lamp on.

Her mum's voice is quiet, a whisper almost. "I didn't think I'd be able to get away," she says.

Clemmie doesn't bother replying but gazes out of the window at a woman, well a girl really, no older than her, pushing a buggy along the pavement. The girl's dressed in low-slung jeans and a too-tight top so that the bulges left over from childbirth are showing. Clemmie has to look away; the sight appals her.

"Faith went all strange on me today. She's hardly ever like that," her mum continues in that strange half-whisper, drumming her fingers on the steering wheel in time to the tinny music playing on the radio. Clemmie wants to crash her fist into the dashboard to make both noises stop, but her mum's carrying on, "This bloke came in with some paintings, they used to work together or something, years ago…" Her mum pauses to run her fingers across her temple before saying, "…Well, Faith was really quiet after he'd left. I said to her, 'You sure it's OK for me to go with Clemmie'?

and she said, 'Sure', but I could tell she wasn't really listening. I didn't want to leave her to cash up and lock up on her own really, I mean Dana's there but…"

"Yeh, whatever, Mum," Clemmie says at last, in an attempt to break the flow. She didn't really want her mum to come, but every once in a while, the counsellor suggests it, and says it would be good for them both.

What the woman, Megan, doesn't realise is that it's all an act when Clemmie's there in that dining room: Clemmie facing the garden, watching fat pigeons swagger across the lawn; Megan facing the clock, with its silent ticking, on the wall behind Clemmie's head. Clemmie can feel the seconds pass by as if they are touching her. And then she has to leave, step out into the street, be her parents' daughter again, and have the guilt of what happened to Douggie push itself to the front of her mind again so that everywhere she looks all she can see is him in the water, the trails of blood; all she can hear is the hammering in her ears; all she can taste is the glob of sick stuck in her throat.

Inside the room, she can play the part; it is so much harder to do it outside, in the real world.

"Oh, thank God," her mother says, easing the car into a space outside Megan's house. "Didn't think we'd get a spot, not at this time, with people coming back from work and that." She sighs loudly as she puts the car into neutral, puts the handbrake on and switches off the ignition. The ensuing quiet is uneasy.

"I don't have to come in, you know," her mum says. "I don't mind."

"Nah, it's OK," Clemmie replies, picking up the handles of her bag and reaching out for the door handle and saying, "Come on, let's get it over with then."

Megan is short and plump with bright red hair and masses of jewellery; she jingles as she walks, her hips rolling comfortably from side to side down the corridor. "It's lovely to see you both," she trills as she pushes open the dining room door. "Come on in, make yourselves at home. Anyone fancy a cup of tea? I'm gasping!"

"That would be lovely," Mum says, sitting down in one of the three chairs around a small circular table. On the table is a vase with flowers in it, but Clemmie doesn't know what sort they are. Their scent is pungent though, it fills the room, making the air in it heavy.

"Nothing for me, thank you," Clemmie says.

"So how have things been?" Megan asks when they're all settled, two mugs of steaming tea on the table between Megan's side and her and her mum's. "Clemmie? Let's hear your news first," Megan says. "Mum can just listen for now. OK?"

Clemmie is looking down at her lap. She can see the individual fibres that make up her jeans; they are cross-hatched and are different shades of blue and she wants to scream, most of all she wants to scream.

Ashley knocks on the front door of the small, terraced house in King's Heath. A guy called Dave opens it. "Watcha," they say to one another, and Ashley turns sideways to let himself, and the guitar bag slung on his back, into the small hallway.

The house is dark and musty; there's no light bulb in the fitting in the hall ceiling and everywhere is the smell of old fried food, but it's the cabin in the garden he's come to visit. There they can practise without fear of disturbing the neighbours and they give Dave a tenner each time to cover the electricity and stuff like that. Some kind bloke had put it up years before, and they only found out about it by accident when they were talking to Dave, who rents a room in the house, down the pub one night. It was the ideal solution to their band practice dilemma. There was no way, after all, that they could do it in their rooms in hall and whilst the cabin's unheated, rather crummy and dilapidated, it's still quite sound-proof and, in the colder months, there's a small electric fire which keeps their fingers warm.

Joe's already there. "Hi, Ash," he says. "Want a beer?" He holds up a can of Stella.

"No thanks," Ashley replies.

Will arrives shortly after. "Si not here then?" he asks.

"Nah, he's shagging some girl," Joe replies, laughing. "Lucky fucker."

"Come on then," Ashley says. "Let's get started. We can work without him, can't we?"

They tune up, Ashley's fingers hover over the neck of his guitar. He plays a chord, then another and slowly the track builds. It is only in the middle of the song when the music surrounds him completely and he is lost to it, blind even to Joe and Will, blind to the cabin walls and floor, to the drums Si should be sitting at, can he really forget, can the voices in his head stop their chanting, 'It was your fault, your fault, your fault.'

Blake turns over in bed. Six o'clock sex, he thinks, is the best. There's something primitive about it that makes it more like fucking; no danger of getting emotionally involved at six o'clock in the evening.

Gabs sighs and stretches, and the duvet slips off her narrow shoulders revealing her small round breasts and the tattoo of a butterfly just above her right hand one. He bends down to kiss it, imagining he can feel the wings beating against his lips.

"What you doing later?" he asks her.

"Dunno," she replies sleepily. Her multi-coloured hair is crashed out on the pillow, her dark eyeliner smudged making her look owlish. Her skin is very pale, and he can remember the soft sound of her cry as she came. "Might go out with Bella and that lot. What about you?"

"Got to do the corrections to that essay. My tutor's come back with some useful comments. Hopefully will push my marks up."

She smiles at him. "All work and no play make Blake a dull boy," she says, her small hand snaking its way under the covers to his cock, where it rests tantalisingly on it.

"Does it?" he answers, laughing, growing hard at the thought of her again. He rolls onto her, sliding himself into her again. He comes quickly. "Oh fuck," he whispers into her neck.

Later, she curls up next to him and he rests his chin on the top of her head. Their breaths are in unison, and he sleeps, slipping down to where the memories can't find him. He wakes just before nine; it's almost dark outside and he's thirsty, very thirsty. He turns over again, but this time Gabs is not there. Sitting up, he looks round for a note, but she hasn't left one; he didn't really expect her to, and he has no idea if and when he'll see her again, or even if he wants to.

Friday

The shop phone is ringing. I can hear it as I reach over to pick up a saucer from the pile. "Extra shot?" I ask the customer.

"No thank you," the customer replies, shifting impatiently from one foot to the other.

The answer phone kicks in and once again I wonder if it's Dom. As with each time the phone has rung over the two weeks which have passed since he came into the shop, I half-hope it is, to get it over and done with, and I half-hope it isn't because I have no idea what I'm going to say to him.

"OK if I pop in the back?" I ask Dana, wiping my hands on a cloth and moving out from behind the counter. The customer moves away, Americano in hand.

"Sure thing, Mrs M," Dana beams, swapping places with me and dropping a spoon on the floor as she does so. "Oops, silly me," she says, laughing gaily, picking it up and putting it with the dirty crockery stacked ready to be taken to the dishwasher in the kitchen.

I hurry to the office. The red light on the phone is blinking wisely. It knows who rang and I don't. I take a deep breath and push the button. The machine whirrs and clicks and a female voice booms out at me, "Oh, hello, this is Veronica from Kitchen Supplies UK. We have you down to reorder dishwasher liquid this week. Perhaps you could ring us back to confirm the exact quantities?" She leaves a number, but I'm not concentrating. Instead, all I can feel is a rush of hot blood from my head, down my legs to my feet. I curse myself for being so stupid.

Why should he call, after all? Ours is just a business arrangement. He probably has a number of coffee shops or galleries in which he hangs his pictures; he probably charms all the female proprietors of these establishments and then goes home to his paintbrushes, his whisky and his dog (yes, he probably has a dog) and doesn't give any of these people, including me, a second thought. Just because of what happened all those years ago, it isn't a given that there should be anything out of the ordinary between us now. But, still, I remember how he touched my hand, the familiar feel of his skin on mine…

As I'm hunting for a pencil to scribble a note for Lizzie to say that Veronica called, the phone rings again. I pick it up hurriedly. "Hello," I say. "*Flick's.*"

"Oh," says the voice on the other end. "I didn't think you'd pick up. It's Nic, I mean Dom." There's a pause during which I have to swallow hard. "How are you?" he asks.

"I'm well, thank you," I manage to reply, frantically looking around the office for something to concentrate on to help me breathe in and out. Why does it matter so much now? Dom is history; he was history the moment I left him and married Harvey, and he certainly was after the boys were born. So why is my heart pounding now, why do the times we spent together keep playing on constant loops in my head? Why does it matter so much what he is thinking?

"How are sales going?"

"Sales?"

"Of the paintings?"

"Oh, good. We've sold two so far."

"Yes, that is good."

Shit, I think, as the silence between us deepens. *What should I say next?*

"How shall I get the money to you? I can pay you online if you like," I ask at last.

I can hear Dom breathing and then he clears his throat. "Is there any chance," he says, "you could come and see some of my other work? Er, I mean, paintings to replace the ones that've been sold. It would be nice to see you, you know, catch up properly," he adds.

Standing there in the office, with the bustle of the shop just the other side of the door, I realise I'm busy working out a way to make this seem as innocent as I want it to be.

Surely, I've had enough of secrets by now? Surely?

"Faith?" he says.

163

"Oh, yes, sorry, just going through my diary in my head. When did you have in mind?"

"How about next Thursday evening? After work? Could you pop over? It's only about a twenty-minute drive."

Harvey'll be away in Paris on Thursday, not that that should make a difference, I think, but it would mean I needn't get home to get the dinner ready and Thursday's not Friday, my night with Lizzie and Sara, so, there really isn't a reason why I can't go, is there? But, still, the idea of being alone with him is an uncomfortable one.

In my mind, I can see us: standing side by side looking at a picture on an easel, his arm near mine, his hand hanging down, and I will imagine it touching me again like it used to do. How could it be otherwise? Yet, this wouldn't matter. My marriage is strong enough. Isn't it? I am strong enough. Aren't I? This is a business transaction, that's all. Over twenty years have gone by; I am not the same person I was before. I have much, much more to lose now.

"Yes," I hear myself saying, "Thursday, about seven. Should be fine."

He gives me the postcode and his bank account details, and we hang up. I find that I have scribbled around them; I'm not sure what I've drawn – it either looks like a pair of bird's wings or a heart.

"Who was that?" Lizzie asks, popping her head around the office door.

"Veronica from Kitchen Supplies," I say. "I've left a note, it was about dishwasher liquid."

For some reason, I don't tell Lizzie about the second call. I'll tell her on Friday when I've chosen some other paintings. It isn't that big a deal; I don't need to involve Lizzie in this, just as I don't need to broadcast my plans to all and sundry.

After all, my main job these last few years has been to protect her, protect all of them, hasn't it? And I'm not going to stop now.

Wednesday

"Thought I'd take a short-sleeved shirt," Harvey says the following Wednesday evening as he's packing his overnight case. "Have you seen my grey one anywhere?"

"It's in the ironing pile," I reply, as I hang up my skirt and slip my nightdress over my head. "Do you want me to press it for you?"

He comes over to where I'm standing and puts his arms around me. "What have I done to deserve such service?" he says, chuckling and moving his hands so they are resting on my hips.

I wriggle out of his grasp. "Nothing extraordinary; you're just good all the time," I answer, throwing what I hope is an easy and relaxed smile over my shoulder as I leave the room.

Downstairs, as I wait for the iron to heat up, I can hear Harvey trundling about upstairs and the sounds of cupboard doors and drawers opening and closing, and I am filled with a fierce stab of love for him. But, despite my best intentions, under this layer of love is a foreshadowing of new guilt, a backstory of old.

I iron the sleeves and collar, then the yoke and then in between the buttons on the front and then the wide expanse of the shirt's back. I imagine him wearing it; the familiar smell of him, his comfortable shape, and I think about Dom and how there is no way that I could ever go back to the way things were between us. What if there are unresolved issues? They are nothing, just nothing compared to this, to what I've got now – my obligations to my family, to my friends. I hang the shirt on a hanger, put the iron on the side to cool, collapse the ironing board and go upstairs.

"Hey, thanks love," Harvey says, hanging the shirt on the outside of his wardrobe door ready for the morning.

"Got your passport?" I ask later, as I set the alarm and switch off the light.

"Mmm," he replies sleepily, reaching over to kiss me briefly on the lips before he settles his head back on the pillow.

"Night then," I say.

"Night, Faith."

He's asleep within minutes. I lie there, staring out into the dark listening to the smooth rhythm of his breathing.

Thursday

"Sure, you don't want me to help you clear up?" I ask Brenda at six o'clock as she dons her housecoat and picks up her mop.

"No, my dear. Why should I? It's my job. You get on home and put your feet up. You look exhausted."

"Well, yes, I am a little tired, I say." Adding, "If, you're sure?"

"Get on with you. I'll see you tomorrow."

Brenda is picking up the discarded newspapers and begins to hum. I wish I was her for a moment. How simple life would be then.

I'm driving; the fields are flashing by, and cars with other people in them going places are too. These people are busy, they are thinking their own thoughts quietly and privately. I feel like I'm carrying a sign on top of the car that says I'm going to see Dom, that we'll be alone again and that I have no idea what is going to happen.

My mobile rings. It's Harvey.

"Hi," he says, his voice distorted by the distance and the poor reception. "You driving? Can you talk?"

"Yes, I'm hands-free. How are you?" I reply.

"Yes, it's going well." His words are blurry like he's been drinking. "We're just having a meal and a couple of beers. How are you?"

"OK, thanks."

"What are you doing tonight?"

What should I say? Telling a lie now would be colossal, and would make me guilty by association, so I say, "I'm just popping over to see some guy's paintings for the shop. Shouldn't be long."

"Oh," he replies, he's obviously not listening. I can hear chatter in the background and the sound of tinny music as he says, "I'll text when I get back to the hotel. OK? I'd better go now. It's Ben's round."

I can hear laughter. I mouth, "Goodbye." Then wait for him to mumble, "Bye, Faith." And he hangs up.

The road sweeps out in front of me like a silver ribbon; all is lilac and soft. It is a beautiful evening.

The sat nav tells me I've reached my destination and I pull up outside a soft-stoned house nestled in a clutch of trees on a hillside. The walk down the driveway is steep, and I have to watch my step in the cobbled yard. There are flowers everywhere, baskets and tubs of them and the house is well-kept and orderly, like a scene from a postcard. I lift the cast iron knocker on the door and let it fall.

Dom has tried to keep busy all afternoon. He's sorted his paints, cleaned his brushes and arranged some more pictures to show her by resting them against the back of the sofa and chairs in his studio. He's done a load of washing and made some small pastry concoctions from a Mary Berry recipe which, when he sees them cooling on the wire tray on the kitchen table, make him feel quite foolish. He also watches the clock quite a lot, but it doesn't seem to want to move any faster. At six o'clock, he pours himself a small whisky and sits in the lounge looking out at the view. The evening shadows are creeping along the valley and the sun is beginning its descent over the hilltop on the other side. Sheep spot the landscape, and the trees look like they're made from modelling clay; everything is still and waiting.

He is trying not to remember how it had been before; the evenings when he'd hurried out of work and driven to the High Street, parking on a side road and letting himself into her bedsit with a key she'd had cut for him. He tries not to think about the needful rush of their lovemaking and how he'd lie in her arms afterwards and trace his fingers along the soft skin at the top of her legs and never want to leave. She'd got to him like no one else before or since and, when it came time to call a halt to it, when he became so torn he feared he would be ripped apart permanently, he hadn't fought for her, he'd left his key and he'd left her and he hadn't looked up to see if her face was at the window watching him return to his car and his wife and the life he should have been leading.

They used to laugh about what they called THT, 'The Honourable Thing'. It had seemed innocuous to start with. It became massive in the end.

There's a knock on the door. Hastily he puts down his whisky glass, stands and shakes out the material of his jeans. He's wearing a pale-pink shirt, hanging loose and unbuttoned at the collar showing a narrow band of his now grey chest hairs.

This is like being sixteen again, he thinks.

He opens the door.

"You found me!" he says, standing back to let her in.

She is stiff and uneasy, and she laughs a small, narrow laugh as she says, "Yes, sat nav got me here without any problems!"

Standing in the hallway, he can see she is scanning the walls and furniture. She's wearing simple black linen trousers and a long white crocheted tunic-type top under which he can see a black camisole, the thin straps over her slender shoulders, and a hint of skin. There isn't much jewellery, just a simple wedding ring and a couple of bangles and a string of wooden beads. On her feet, she's wearing Birkenstocks and he can see her toenails; they're painted bright red and for some reason, this disturbs him, and makes him feel vulnerable.

"You have a lovely place here," she says, following him down the hallway and into the lounge.

"It suits me," he answers. "Not too big, not too small, you know just like Goldilocks!" He knows he's just speaking for the sake of it. "Would you like a drink?" he asks. "I can make some Pimms, it won't take me long."

"Sounds lovely," she says, "but not too strong for me. I'm driving."

As he's mixing the drinks, he can sense her presence like a light in the other room and he thinks back, remembering the taste of stale wine on his breath as he drove home after making love to her and of the mints, he'd keep in the car to try and fool his wife.

He loads a tray with the jug, two glasses and a plate of the stupid little canapés he's made and, when he goes back into the lounge, she's standing at the window with her back to him. Unbidden comes an urge to wrap his arms around her, to fold her into him and to let out a breath he seems to have been holding for over twenty years.

Instead, he says brightly, "Here we are! Refreshments!"

"Lovely," she replies, turning to face him so that her face is in shadow, and she seems somehow unreal to him.

"Let's take them through to the studio, shall we?" he suggests, raising an arm and pointing to the door at the far end of the lounge. "After all, we're here to work, aren't we?"

"Oh, yes," she says.

They walk into the studio.

"Oh, Dom," she says, as she surveys the room; bathed golden in the evening sun. "It's lovely here. You're very lucky."

"Mmm," he replies, putting down his glass and fussing about with one of the pictures, moving it slightly to the right and then back to the left again. He doesn't feel lucky. She so obviously belongs to someone else, has a massive history with him, and has kids for God's sake.

"These your children?" She's put down her drink too, and her bag, and picks up a framed print from the low windowsill.

"Oh yes, it was taken a few years ago now. Probably the last time the two of them were knowingly in the same place at the same time."

"Don't they get on?"

"It's not easy. My ex-wife can be…" He pauses, he doesn't really want to go down this route, but he has to be honest. "…Divisive," he says. "She's a great one for divide and rule; I've never really been able to make amends, to put my side of the story across. But we get on OK I suppose, me and the children, after a fashion. We speak occasionally, and I do get to see the grandchildren, my daughter's kids, now and again." He's not sure why he's lying, but he feels it's probably safer than telling her the whole truth.

They chatter on and he feels he's telling her more than she's telling him, like he's opening up his chest and laying bare all that is written there. She puts on a pair of glasses from a case in her bag on the floor by the window and chooses two pictures; one is a horse cantering across a shoreline which, he has to admit, is one of his favourites, and the other is a still-life of a bowl of peaches.

"They look almost good enough to eat," she says, laughing, as he wraps the pictures in brown paper and ties them up with string.

"There," he says. "I'll leave them by the door, shall I?"

"Good idea." She puts her glasses away and when he gets back from the hallway, he clears the remaining pictures away from the sofa and they sit; her on the sofa, him on a chair but the studio isn't that large and together they seem to fill it.

"Do you mind being in here?" he asks. "Wouldn't you rather go back into the lounge?"

"No, I prefer it here. I like to imagine you working. I never knew you painted. Did you do so before? I mean, when…"

He knows what she means.

"No, he says. "It's a new hobby. Something I took up when I retired." And then he adds, "You can come round anytime and watch if you like."

But it's a silly, glib thing to say. How could she? She probably has every minute of every day packaged up neatly. No wistful staring off into space for her. No, she has her business, her marriage, her sons, her friends; all of it crafted in the years he hasn't known her, all those lost years.

He is watching her as she picks up her glass, takes another drink and then puts it back down again. She rests her hands in her lap as though waiting for something.

I have no idea what to say now. All the easy stuff has been done; the arrival, the house, the drink, the paintings. Now it's just him and me and all the things we're not brave enough to talk about. There isn't even a dog to distract us. I really thought there'd be a dog.

Eventually, I say, "I'm sorry."

"Whatever for?" he leans forward in his chair, so our knees are almost touching.

"For everything."

"It was more my fault than yours. I was the one who was married. Perhaps I should never have started it."

"Don't say that."

"OK, sorry. But…"

"Look, Dom. I'd better go. We can't change it, can we? Let's just…"

"What, Faith? Let's just do what? I can't forget it; I can't not want…"

We are standing now, and I am trembling. I have to get away. I pick up my bag and step forward. He's there, all his solid bulk, smelling just the same, his eyes the same blue, his hair tumbling over his ears and for a second, I forget. I forget I'm married, that I have children, that Douggie died, and that all the years have gone by. In that second, I am transported back and when he bends down and kisses me it's like coming home, that's it, just that. It's a *'P.S. I Love You'* kiss, the type I thought only existed in movies and, from somewhere deep down, some primitive yearning, there is burning, and I kiss him back, opening my mouth to his tongue and his teeth. His hands are on me, nestled in fists in the small of my back, easing the tension away and we stand there locked and unmoving while all the time a kaleidoscope whirrs around us.

"I have to go," I say, breaking away from him.

"Stay?" he asks.

"No, I can't. I can't. I'm sorry, Dom."

"Don't say sorry. It doesn't matter."

"It does, Dom. It does. I…"

But I don't finish what I'm going to say, because I don't know what it is I want to say. Instead, I walk hurriedly from the house. I forget the pictures in their brown wrapping by the door and I forget I have emailed him my mobile number, stupidly, carelessly, in a mad moment from the car before I set off in case I got delayed en route and he needed to call me. It had seemed a practical gesture, nothing more, at the time, but now, now when I remember, it reminds me of a fuse ready to be lit, ready to sparkle and fizz, ready to scorch me again.

Friday

The second lie comes much more easily, much too easily.

"Did you choose some more pictures?" Harvey asks as he's pulling on his jeans ready to go to the pub with Ben and Anthony.

I'm confused for a moment. "Pictures?" I say.

"Yes, yesterday evening, on the phone, you said something about some pictures."

I feel cold suddenly and wrap the towel around myself more tightly. I'm getting ready to go with Lizzie to Sara's, now the post-flood redecorating has been finished, for our Friday night movie and bottle of wine, but I've not been looking forward to it. In fact, I've been twitchy all day.

"Oh," I say. "The pictures. Yes, those. Well…" I hesitate and Harvey looks at me, puzzled. "…I didn't see any I liked, so I left it for now," I say hurriedly, grabbing another towel from the bed and rubbing my hair hard with it to avoid having to say or hear anything more and there it is, the second lie.

"That was easy, wasn't it?" I tell myself. So much for him being able to see into my soul through my eyes.

I've been lying to him for years, to all of them: the first lies when I was seeing both him and Dom, the colossal secret I've been keeping since Blake was small, this new one. Will I never learn?

When I emerge from the towel, Harvey has gone. Hopefully, he's lost interest and has wandered away, distracted by something else, and I sit on the edge of the bed and put my head in my hands; all I can see is the stack of pictures tied up in brown paper left by Dom's front door, all I can feel is the imprint of his lips on mine. I believe they probably still bear the mark and that everyone I've spoken to today will have noticed them. And, I think, as I step into my underwear and tug on a pair of loose jogging trousers and shrug myself into one of Harvey's old jumpers, glad I don't have to dress up to go to Sara's, there is the matter of the phone call this morning.

I was standing by the lock again before opening up the shop, watching a moorhen scooting across the surface of the water, its head bobbing busily when my phone buzzed. Harvey, I assumed. He'd said he'd ring from Paris to confirm his flight home but hadn't done so yet. I pressed the button to answer the call without looking carefully at the screen.

"Morning, I said," much more brightly than I felt.

"Faith?"

"Dom? Oh, it's you. Sorry, I thought…"

"Thought I was someone else? That's OK! I don't mind, really, I don't," he laughed uneasily, and I squashed the phone so tightly against my ear I could feel its heat. It was, I realised, really good to hear his voice.

"How are you?" I said quickly in the ensuing gap.

"Fine, thank you," he said, slowly and deliberately. "But you left the pictures. After all that!"

"I know, I'm sorry," I said.

"Shall I bring them in?"

"Yes, if you like. Sometime tomorrow would be good."

It's Lizzie's weekend on duty, so there's no danger of me seeing him; I will be safely tucked away at home, with Harvey, exactly where I should be.

"Will you be there?" he asks.

"Most likely," I lied.

This was the first lie and I gasped after I'd said it; it felt like it had been dragged out of me, leaving its roots in my mouth.

"See you soon then," he said.

"OK. Take care."

"I will, you too."

We hung up and I stood looking at the blank screen again, wondering how on earth I was going to rationalise how I felt when the text icon flashed. It was from Harvey, 'Going into a meeting, then the airport. Home by six'.

'Safe journey', I texted back and then dropped the phone back into my pocket as if it was burning.

Lizzie is watching Faith. There's something different about her, something off.

"You, OK?" she asks her, as Sara places a bowl of peanuts on the table in front of them.

"Yeh, sure. Why?"

Faith won't look at her though, she's pulling at a thread in the sweater she's wearing. It's one of Harvey's. Lizzie remembers it from years ago.

Then Faith glances up at both her and Sara and says, "Right, what're we gonna watch?"

There's an air of unease in the lounge, Sara thinks, as she curls her legs under her, and the film starts. Around her are her things, her and Anthony's things: pictures, ornaments, expensive bits of furniture, expensive carpets. The diamond ring on her wedding finger is too large for her now and she's worried she'll lose it. She rarely wears it. Anthony gave it to her too long ago, he gave it to her before Douggie.

His name still has the ability to cut her. It is as though a surgeon is standing above her, scalpel in hand, bearing down on her each time she thinks of him.

The film's introductory music is loud, too loud. She reaches over to get the controls to turn it down and smiles at Lizzie and Faith as she does so. They smile back.

No one knows, Sara thinks. *Absolutely no one knows the rottenness at the heart of me.*

Anthony is tired, bone tired. It's been a pig of a week, and, despite the warmer weather, there is a chill running through the core of him.

They're in the pub: him, Ben and Harvey, but he feels disembodied, like he's watching himself from above.

He knows it's grief; grief he can't lose and doesn't know how to. He sometimes wonders if it's the only thing keeping him and Sara together.

"Your round, I think?" Ben says, playing with his beer mat.

"Same again then?" Harvey replies, standing up and putting a warm hand on his shoulder.

"Sure thing."

"And you, Anthony?"

Anthony nods. *He looks exhausted,* Ben thinks. *All this staying away from home must be more tiring than the commute, surely?*

But he has to stop himself there. No point in thinking too deeply about the quiet spaces in Sara and Anthony's lives. No, he tells himself as he watches Harvey make his way to the bar. No point in doing that, who knows what may fill it if he does.

At the bar, Harvey places his order and, while he waits, he can overhear the whisperings of the couple next to him, not their actual words, just the tone of their voices: intimate, excited, wary.

Ah, he thinks, to go back to that, the unknown, the unmarked territory of first love. When you're young, you think you'll always have a second chance at everything. How wrong that is.

"Here you go, mate," the barman says, placing the third pint on the bar.

"Cheers," Harvey replies.

The condensation is running down the side of the glasses and Harvey watches as it does so.

Saturday

Dom knows as soon as he bends down to open the coffee shop door that Faith isn't there. He can feel her absence in the air and realises she has deliberately misled him, for his sake as well as her own. He's mostly annoyed by this, but also secretly pleased. It means that it matters to her, that he matters to her.

"Can I help you?" the short-haired woman he'd met the first time he'd visited the shop asks as he stands in the middle of the room, the pictures under his arm. She has her hands on her hips and doesn't look very friendly. Around them is the hum of conversation.

"Oh, I've brought some more pictures. I did ring." He doesn't mention Faith's visit to his house; he's not sure whether this woman would know about it or not.

"Did you?" she asks. There's a pause. "You must have spoken to Faith then."

"I did," he says, prevaricating.

"You used to work with her, didn't you? When was that?" Her voice is somewhat shrill, but then he guesses it would have to be because there's quite a bit of background noise in the shop.

"It was ages ago and not for long, just a few months, actually." He shifts his feet uneasily and the paintings bump against his leg.

"She's never mentioned you, that's all," the woman is saying, turning to lead him towards the office at the back of the shop.

"Oh," he laughs uncomfortably. "I wouldn't have expected her to."

"It's just." She stops, turns and puts a hand on his arm and says, "We tell each other everything, she and I, always have."

"As I said, it was ages ago and just for a little while. We were both a lot younger then."

He wants the conversation to stop; he doesn't like the woman's tone, it is too aggressive, like she owns part of Faith and has more rights to

177

her than he does. But then, he reasons, as he follows her to the office, this woman doesn't know, does she? She doesn't know what he and Faith shared, what it meant. How could she if Faith has never told her about him? He's relieved about this because deep down it tells him he was right earlier, that he obviously meant something significant to Faith. Why else would she have kept him a secret?

Thank God he's never been a topic of conversation bandied around over a cup of tea or glass of wine, someone dismissed as, "Oh yes, there was this bloke once. He was married, but then I met Harvey."

Faith keeping him a secret all this time is, he thinks, much better.

"Well," the woman says. "I'll let Faith know you called in. She's not working this weekend. I'm Lizzie, by the way. Faith's business partner." There's another one of those pauses again, "And her best friend," Lizzie adds, unnecessarily in his opinion. He has guessed this already.

"Thanks," he says, resting the pictures against the leg of the desk. "I'll get going then."

"Hey, wait up," Lizzie calls, as he is stepping back into the shop. "Has Faith settled up, money-wise? You know, given you the proceeds from the pictures we have sold?"

He freezes. What should he say? "Yes," he utters, his heart hammering like a schoolboy in his chest, "she's paid me online."

"That's OK then," Lizzie says. And then adds, "Well goodbye," and holds out her hand. He shakes it. It is warm and firm, and he wishes he could like her, but feels that she is standing in between him and Faith, and for this reason, can't.

"Thank you," he says lamely and walks out of the shop, hearing Lizzie's voice calling out behind him.

"Dana dear," she says. "Can you clear the tables by the window, please?"

He leaves the world Faith has created and the people who now populate it and takes his long-standing grief and remorse back with him to his car and his cottage on the hill where he picks up the phone and makes a call. Then he sits in front of his easel and with a pencil starts to sketch. He holds his breath as her face begins to appear; each line is deliberate and careful. It is like he is crafting her out of glass.

I'm in the kitchen when my phone rings. I grab it from the table where it's on charge, the wire snaking up to the plug in the wall. It's Dom.

"Hello?" I say, quietly, recognising the number from yesterday.

Harvey is in the garden. He's bending over a flower bed, trowel in hand. He looks solid and uncompromising. He's got headphones on and is listening to music; I can see his head bouncing ever so slightly in time with it.

"You weren't in the shop. I took the paintings in, but you weren't there," Dom says.

"No, sorry. I forgot. It's my weekend off."

She knows he knows she's lying.

"Lizzie was there."

"Yes."

"She wasn't very friendly."

"Sorry. She can appear a bit prickly sometimes if you don't know her."

"She seems to have known you for a long time."

"Yes, we've been friends since..." I want to say since Blake was small. If I say this, then it'll be OK; talking about our families will make the kiss not matter, it will reduce it too almost nothing. Instead, I say, "... I've known her for nearly twenty years."

"You never told her about me."

It wasn't a question.

"No, there didn't seem any point."

"I see."

"No, you don't understand."

I watch Harvey straighten up and stretch, raising his hands above his head. He looks over at the window and waves. Although I doubt, he can see I'm on the phone, I snatch it away from my ear and hide it behind my back, waving at him with my other hand and then turning away from the window.

"Hello?" Dom's voice is distant and crackly.

"Sorry, must be a bad line. Reception's not great here," I say once I return the phone to my ear.

"You were saying?"

"It was just too much to tell anyone about, back then, I mean and then, as the years went by, I did try to forget. Honestly, I did. Not telling anyone else was a way of trying to."

"But you didn't manage it, did you?"

"No." My voice is small and far back in my throat.

"Can I see you again? Can you get away?"

Oh my God, I think. *This is just like before, except now it's the other way around. He's a free agent, I'm not – I definitely am not.*

Harvey is wheeling the barrow down the garden path to the compost heap, his solid legs striding out, his feet thumping on the grass, our grass in the garden of our home, where our sons played football and cried when they grazed their knees.

"OK," I say. "I'll meet you somewhere, somewhere public. Dinner maybe."

I am sure I'll be able to tell him if we're sitting in amongst other people that I can't do this, that the kiss will have to have been the first, last and only, that I am married and happy and can't start anything again with him; too much time has passed for that to be possible. I have far, far too much to lose to be able to take the risk. As it is I'm holding on with my fingertips.

We agree on a time and place, hurriedly and furtively and already I hate myself, both for the lie I will have to tell Harvey, but also for what I will have to do to Dom.

I hang up and stand staring at the screen for a moment or two. I don't hear Harvey come in.

"Faith?" His voice is achingly familiar. "Is everything OK? Not bad news?"

He assumes because I'm standing silently staring at my phone that something bad has happened to someone we love.

I turn to face him. Soil from our garden is on his shoes. He looks tired.

"No," I snap. "What makes you think that? Why would it necessarily be bad news?" Then I add, "Why am I always so watched? Why can't I just be left alone? I don't have to be accountable every minute of every day, do I?"

I know I'm being unreasonable, but it's the guilt that's making me so, guilt, regret and so many unanswered questions.

"Don't you wish," I say. "That you could have a magic mirror sometimes that you can look through and see the other path, the one you didn't take so that you can know what you're doing, where you are, who you are and who you're with, is the right choice?"

"Faith, Faith," he says my name again. "Where has all this come from? What on earth is going on?"

"Oh, it's nothing," I say, but I know I'm still snapping at him and that if I stay in the same room as him, I may say something I'll regret. So much of what I mustn't say is fizzing on my tongue, like sherbet, and so instead of trying to explain the things I can't explain, I take my phone and storm out, leaving my husband staring at the space I've left behind, leaving the phone's power cable plugged into the socket, knowing that I've upset and hurt him and that he doesn't deserve either of these things.

Thursday

They're sitting in a corner booth at a country pub about halfway between where she lives and his house. The sun is just about to set and everywhere looks like it's been bathed in rose water; the greens are soft, and the birds are chorusing joyfully, celebrating the end of the day. The other people in the pub are laughing and someone has put *Unchained Melody* on the jukebox. *It's like some kitsch movie,* Dom thinks as he pours Faith a glass of wine from the bottle on the table between them.

"Where did you say you were going?" he asks, watching her as she picks up the glass, noticing her hands are trembling slightly.

"Meeting an old school friend," she says, looking up as the waiter deposits cutlery and condiments on their table.

He's ordered steak and now wishes he hadn't; a salad would be better for him and easier to eat. "Did he mind?" he asks.

"No, he's at a late meeting in London anyway. Some networking function near St Paul's. He probably won't be home until about eleven."

"You OK with being here?" he asks, not really wanting to know the answer.

"It's so hard," she says, brushing a strand of hair out of her eyes. He watches mesmerized.

"It'll be OK."

"Well, that's just it. It won't be. I mean it's OK to meet here, to pretend that we're just having a meal, chatting over old times when, all the while, the one thing we both can't admit to is sitting here at the table with us, is it?"

"What do you mean? What thing?"

She pulls up the sleeves of her linen top, exposing her lower arms and the interlinking bangles she's wearing on each wrist knock against one another. As she moves the material stretches over her breasts and his eyes follow the soft contours of them and he remembers how they were before, wonders how differently they will feel now, now she's had children, now she's made love to the same man, a man other than him, for over twenty years.

"That you're not married, and I am, and that underneath it all, we can't change that. Can we?" she says, taking another sip of her drink.

Then suddenly, she asks him, "What do you actually want to happen, Dom? What do you want from me?"

He's surprised by the directness of her question and by how angry she sounds.

"I mean," she adds, more gently this time. "As I said, it's OK here, you and me, but I'm married, with kids. Harvey is…"

"What? What is Harvey?" He is accountably angry now, mostly because he has no idea what she's trying to tell him, but deep-down fears what it might be.

"…A good man," she says.

"I'm sure he is," he admits. "I'm a good man too, you know."

He takes her hand as he says this. He feels her slipping further away from him.

"It has to be one thing or the other," she continues, scowling slightly as the waiter puts plates of food in front of them. "It'll be fine, I'm sure it will be when it's just us, I haven't forgotten any of it, really, I haven't, but what about the bits in between? How can I go back to my real life after seeing you and pretend it doesn't matter, that I'm not doing anything wrong? I'm not the child I used to be."

He feels she's being somewhat unfair. After all, that's what she used to ask of him, wasn't it?

"We could try," he says, toying with the food in front of him. "Just see how it goes. I'll go at whatever pace you want, but…"

This is it, he tells himself. *This is when I have to say it…* "But I owe it to you," he says, "and to myself, to give it another shot. What happened before left me so…" he searches for the right word… "unfinished. I am unfinished without you, Faith."

"Don't Dom. Don't say things like that." Her voice is quiet now, almost a whisper.

"It's the truth." He takes her hand again. "Please, Faith. Don't let this chance pass us by. Lightning certainly doesn't strike more than once in a lifetime!"

He tries to laugh, but it doesn't work; it gets stuck in his throat.

It is the word 'unfinished' which does it. Suddenly I know. This is what my life's been like since him too. Harvey and the boys have been, no, still are, fundamental but there's always been a small, dark corner where unanswered questions have lurked; the 'what ifs', the bare bold longing to be sure my decision all those years ago had been the right one, a possible cure for my grief and guilt over what happened to Douggie, and there is, I know, only one way to find out. I need to hold up the magic mirror and scrutinise what is reflected there.

Smiling nervously at Dom, I pick up my knife and fork.

I tell Harvey and Lizzie I have an appointment to visit a new milk supply company in Oxford on the following Friday afternoon, which I do. We don't really need a new milk supplier, but I convince myself that it would be useful research in any case. Harvey will be in Paris again and Lizzie says she and Dana can manage the shop on their own for a few hours.

What I don't tell them is that I've also arranged to meet Dom at a hotel nearby. We will have just two hours together. I hope it will be enough for whatever may happen. I feel sick most of the time in the days leading up to Friday because I know that lying is so very easy because I am so very trusted.

Friday

It's one o'clock when I get to the hotel. My appointment is at three-thirty. Neither Lizzie nor Dana queried why I was leaving so early, but still I felt I should say something.

"Fancy grabbing a bite of lunch en route. Hope that's OK," I said to the back of Lizzie's head as I passed by the counter on her way out of the shop. Lizzie was busy getting a panini off the hot plate.

A skein of cheese had melted onto it and Lizzie was having trouble lifting the bread away from the metal. "That's fine," she said. "Go carefully and see you later."

I didn't feel too badly because only yesterday Lizzie had taken a long lunch, something about having some acupuncture for her stiff back.

Even so, pulling into the hotel car park, I am unsettled, the minutes press against my spine and, as each one passes, I can see the number Dom and I have allowed ourselves to reduce, like a stopwatch counting down. I'm also hungry.

Dom's texted the room number through to my phone; it sits there like a bullet and, as I walk across the foyer, I delete it from the cache with trembling fingers and switch the phone to silent. Looking down at the screen helps because it means I don't have to look up, meet the receptionist's gaze.

In my mind it's like I've stepped out of my real life, shed the skin of it and in a *'Sliding Doors'* moment, am living the life that could have been. Being here now seems like it always was going to be inevitable.

I push the lift's call button. The brushed metal doors glide open far too promptly. I step inside.

The lift is carpeted in thick gold, on the floor and ceiling; it's kind of womb-like. Keeping my head bowed, I daren't look in the mirrors which flank each wall. Soft music is playing. It is hot in here.

Even now I could turn back. I could press zero and return to the ground floor, walk quickly through reception and out into the mid-afternoon sun. I would put my glasses on, my car would start first time, the radio would be playing, and I would pull away, not look back at the glinting windows of the hotel, its sweeping driveway, the hot metal of the other cars, at Dom's car parked hopefully somewhere there.

But I don't. Instead, I look down at my feet in their low sandals, at my painted toenails, at the long sundress I'm wearing under my denim jacket. I remember bathing this morning, carefully shaving my legs and stretching them out so that they reached the taps and thinking of Dom's hands on me again.

Too soon I reach the fifth floor. Stepping out of the lift, I look at the signs on the walls and follow them until I'm standing outside Room 523. I knock on the door; it opens and he's there.

"Hi," he says.

"Hello."

"You, OK?"

"No."

He turns and leads the way into the room; I follow.

"I got us some tea and sandwiches."

"That was kind."

I can't eat anything though. My earlier hunger has disappeared, leaving a lead weight at the bottom of my stomach.

"Shall I pour?"

"OK."

I do what anyone would do in these circumstances and wander over to the window, lift the net curtains and look out at the view, such as it is. I can see my car, a man is wheeling a suitcase past it, a delivery lorry is reversing somewhere nearby; I can hear the beep, beep of its warning signal as it does so.

"Here you go," Dom says.

Turning, I take the cup and saucer from him and sit in one of the armchairs under the window.

"It needn't be awkward," he says, slipping behind me and pulling the curtains closed. Most of the light goes, only a framework of it shows around the window.

"I know. It's just…"

I give up on the tea, put it down and go over to where he's standing like an uncertain teenager. My other life, it seems, is nestled in amongst the pile of untouched sandwiches and, as I stand in front of him, my hands by my side, I block it out; all of it – Harvey, the boys, who haven't come back over the summer, who have left me bereft – a mother without portfolio – my house, the shop, Lizzie, Anthony, Douggie, the other secret I am keeping from everyone, everything.

It's like I've been set adrift and, for a second, I revel in the freedom, kidding myself it is some sort of atonement for Douggie's death; if my real life didn't exist Douggie may not have died.

Reaching up, I kiss Dom on the mouth. He tastes familiar, yet new. But this is no *'P.S. I Love You'* moment, not this one. This is real and not real and totally ours, not celluloid or romantic. It is necessary, selfish, cathartic, inevitable, so very wrong.

The sex, when it happens, is unexpectedly savage and urgent. In my imagination, when I'd dared think of it in the days leading up to now, if it was to happen, I'd seen it as a languorous, easily negated, gentle act, not this stripped bare, violent coupling; me wide open to him, him quick and angry. As he comes, I try to remember the other times; the guilt I felt at taking something which wasn't mine to take. Now, as he trails his lips over my breasts, to the soft flesh of my belly, I try very hard not to let the guilt at giving something which is not mine to give take over.

It doesn't quite work and, afterwards, I feel half-blessed and half-condemned. Curled up next to Dom, looking at him, listening to his breathing, waiting for him to say something, anything to ameliorate what we've just done, I wish I knew what was going to happen next, how I was going to feel when I close the hotel room door, press zero and find myself in the hotel lobby again; anonymous, unfaithful, torn, the keeper of yet another secret.

From where I am now, I fear I will never be able to accept what I've just done, never forget it, never forgive it.

It's like it's always been. After all, this isn't my only betrayal.

"Dom?" I say.

"Mmm."

"What do we do now? What happens next?"

Dom turns his head to look at her. The air is hot and heavy; a framework of fluorescent sun surrounds the hotel window. The curtains are a dark blue shot through with gold curlicues. They seem too ornate for the room and the hem of one of them is, he notices, hanging down slightly and this annoys him. It shouldn't have to be like this. They shouldn't have to be here like this.

She is lying on her side, one hand under the pillow and is watching him with those eyes, the colour of which he thought he had forgotten. But now, as he gazes into them, he realises he had never really done so; he had just been unwilling to name their colour for fear the memories would burn him.

"Dom?" she says. "What do we do now?" she asks. "What happens next?"

He kisses her hard on the mouth hoping to stop the words from reaching the wall behind his head because he fears that should they do this; they will mark it indelibly and that the irrefutable proof of them would force the two of them into deciding. She draws her head back slightly for a moment and then presses herself nearer to him. His heart quickens and he wants her again. He doesn't want to think about the consequences, not this afternoon, not now she's here and his hand is resting on her bare thigh. He moves his fingers to between her legs and she groans quietly. He has waited too long to find her again, too long to have a second chance of getting it right.

Part 5 – Summer

I'm standing with my back to the horizon where Wales used to be and in front of me is Ireland. I wish I could stay here in limbo forever. The grey-green sea stretches out before me; the line where it meets the sky blurred by mist and salt-spray and all I can feel is the rock of the boat as it ploughs its way through the foam, leaving a fan of white waves in its wake.

I still can't remember too clearly how I got away. There'd been the hotel in Oxford, and Dom, and not being able to sleep that night, or the next when Harvey came back; the knowledge of what I'd done burning the backs of my eyes like sulphur.

"Mum's invited me to visit next week," I told my husband on Sunday morning.

"Really? When did this happen?"

"I rang her late last night. Said I could do with a break, so she suggested I make the trip. What do you think?"

"I can't get away. I'm way too busy at work. There are meetings lined up for most of next week and anyway, what about the shop?" Harvey sounded petulant and his face was crumply with sleep.

"It'll just be me going," I said softly, putting my hand on his as it rested on the covers of the bed.

"I say again, what about the shop?" His voice was tetchy now. Did he guess there was an underlying reason behind this - something I wasn't telling him? How could he possibly know?

"Don't worry, I'll clear it with Lizzie. She's been saying to me for ages that I should take myself off somewhere now both boys have gone away. You know, to have a rest, a break."

"But to your *mother's*? Anyway, why now? Why at such short notice?"

I could understand why Harvey would be so incredulous, but the truth was that there was just no other place I could think of going right now, nowhere else that Dom could not follow.

189

Harvey had shuffled out of bed at that point and hadn't really questioned me too closely, for which I was grateful. He was still tired from his trip to France and his mind was full of work and diary conflicts. I knew this and was grateful for it. It took the attention away from me. I didn't, I don't bear scrutiny right now.

Lizzie had been predictably easy going, although if she'd known the real reason...

"Yeah, why not?" she'd said, when I'd called in on the way back from *Flick's* later that day. "Ben and I want to have a week away in October anyway," Lizzie had said as she and I were in the kitchen and Lizzie was taking out a load of washing from the machine, dumping it in her laundry basket. "So, this way you'll owe me! I'll sort cover out for the shop, don't you worry. Just get yourself booked on that boat and go, girl!"

As I stretched out my arms to take the end of the sheet Lizzie was in the process of folding, I saw something in my friend's eyes, a look I hadn't seen before, but if asked, would have defined it as assessing. Was there any way that Lizzie could know what I'd done, the size and scale of my betrayal, did she want to make as sure as I did that I stayed out of harm's way?

The journey across Wales had been incident-free. The car ate up the miles and as I crossed the Severn Bridge, a track called *Stuttering* by Ben's Brother came on the radio. It seemed to sum up how I felt.

So now I am on my way, I realise I'm less angry than I was before Dom came back into my life, but I'm guiltier and sadder, and am trying to stop my mind replaying the conversations I'd had with Mum, and with Dom; neither of which went well.

"So, tell me," Mum had said. "Why exactly do you want to visit? Not that it won't be lovely to see you and everything. Your father and I..." here she paused just a fraction too long, "...are always delighted to see you."

"I just fancy getting away and thought where better than your place?" I'd replied, trying to keep my voice light and transparent.

"Well, just ring when you're a couple of hours away and we'll make sure we're at the house to meet you," was all Mum had said before hanging up, calling out to someone as she did so, "No, look, I told you. Not there, here!"

Equally, Dom had been less than pleased to hear the news when I rang him on my way back from the hotel on Friday afternoon.

"Hello?" he'd said, his voice still thick with left-over love.

"I'm just ringing to say I'm going to take a small holiday next week," I'd said into the hot air inside the car. It was a comfort to talk to him hands-free, good to be at a safe distance from him when between my legs still sang from his touch.

"Oh," he said flatly. "Had you always intended to do that?"

"Yes," I lied. "It's just that I forgot to mention it. I'm sorry. Really sorry. It's a long-standing thing that I can't get out of."

"Where are you going?" he asked. "And how long will you be away?"

I pretended the line was breaking up. "Hello?" I said. "I think I'm losing you. It must be the reception. I'm sorry Dom, I'll try and call you next week sometime…"

I held on just long enough to hear him sigh; it echoed around the car, bouncing off the seats and dashboard, the words 'losing you' stamping themselves in my head like hot irons.

I hoped he wouldn't try and get in touch first; I wasn't ready to face the consequences of what I'd done, not yet maybe not ever. I also had to decide if what we'd done had now finished what had been left undone between us before, or whether we'd started something new, something dangerously new.

Whatever it is, I know that running away may appear cowardly, but it seems my only choice.

Tuesday

I'd stayed overnight at a small hotel near Fishguard and had spent a leisurely morning before catching the afternoon boat to Rosslare.

As I drive off the other end, I feel buoyed by this unexpected freedom. What if I just peel off the N25 and book myself into a B&B somewhere on the coast? I could tell Mum I'd broken down; Harvey wouldn't worry, he was too busy, and I could spend the night tucked into tight sheets, totally alone, totally unwatched. As I reach Dungarvan though, the plan begins to slip through my fingers. There's no way I can do this; I owe it to Mum to arrive when I said I would, and what if Harvey should worry? Haven't I done enough damage already?

It's evening when I reach Skibbereen and, pulling over on the bridge crossing the estuary by Inishbeg, I get out of the car and lean on its worn round stones. They are still warm. The tide is out, and the estuary flats are like wet clay; birds tiptoe cautiously across them, every now and then dipping their heads, and it looks like some giant hand has thrown the sundown in patches of golden pennies. All is quiet; just the faint cry of a curlew somewhere on the other side of the river Ilen. In the distance, St Mary's nestles in the trees; its spire is stately and sharp against a denim-blue sky fringed with ribbons of pink and purple cotton wool clouds.

I take a deep breath, smooth down the crumpled fabric of my jeans, open the car door and climb back in. As I pass the gateposts at the end of the main driveway, my heart quickens.

Dom is sitting in his studio, hand poised in mid-air. He is reaching up to peel back the red cloth cover from the portrait of Faith but finds he can't bring himself to do it. He knows that underneath the cloth most of Faith's face has been sketched lightly in; he has captured the way she tilts her head, the length of her eyelashes, and the curve of her cheek, but what he hasn't captured is her spirit, which is still roaming free, unbiddable and unknowable.

She'd called the holiday 'small', but did that mean she'd gone on her own or with Harvey? Where had she gone? Why hadn't she rung, texted, or emailed since? He feels foolish, like a boy with a crush on someone totally inappropriate and unattainable. This is not how it should be.

He thought when they'd made love again in that hotel room against a backdrop of traffic and birdsong that he had re-established some claim to her; he could not have foreseen that it would have frightened her away completely. That hadn't been the plan at all.

Finding her again was, he felt, a kind of miracle. He'd almost given up hope, given up wanting, and now? Well, now it is as though he had quenched a thirst, only for it to return stronger and more desperate than before.

He presses his hand on the covering, imagining that she is actually underneath it, soft and pliable and open to him again. Yes, she'd changed; her body was rounder, curvier and he had traced his fingers over the silver seams of her stretch marks and had tried very hard not to mind that it hadn't been his children she had borne.

His mobile rings and he grabs it from his trouser pocket. It has to be her; surely, it has to be her? He looks at the screen.

"Hi Dad," his daughter says, her voice strident and billowy.

He doesn't have the chance to say anything before she continues, "How are you?" The question is a mere matter of form, nothing more. She doesn't really want to know, and it feels as though someone has stamped on his chest and is pulling his hair out by its roots.

"I'm fine, thanks. And you?" The line crackles. "And the children?" he adds.

"We're all OK. Busy as ever. Work and that always getting in the way and there's all the kids' activities; swimming, cubs, football. You name it, they do it! You can't imagine how busy I am!"

Has she forgotten, he wonders, that he's seen it all before, done it himself, that it was her and her brother who had been the main reason he'd stayed as long as he did, why he'd never had the energy to remarry or even date much after his divorce? He'd wanted to stay available for them, as untorn as possible, but then she's probably never realised this; never needed to think about it.

"Sounds like you have your hands full," he says, in a placating voice.

"That's why I'm ringing really," she says, slightly more cautious now, her previously bullish tone replaced by one which, for her, is almost tender. It makes him remember the girl she'd once been, with her plump cheeks and flyaway hair.

"Oh." He is half-afraid of what is coming next.

"I've got the chance to go on a sales reward trip; you know it's the sort of 'perk', a thank you, pat on the back type of thing. I've doubled my sales targets in the last six months, and they've offered for me and Greg to go to LA for a week."

"LA?"

"Yes, Los Angeles. The States, Dad." She pauses and he doesn't interrupt, but he knows what's coming. "And anyway, Mum suggested that as she's going to be away too, maybe you'd like to look after the kids for us? It's only for four days, well, four days there, there's a day to travel over and a day to travel back, so that's not quite a week, is it? What do you think? I'll get friends to do a lot of the lifts and things, and the school run; it's just we need someone here, in their own home, you know. And family's best, after all, isn't it?"

"When?" he asks, hoping it'll be some really inconvenient date when he's got commitments. *But then,* he muses, as he taps the fingers of his left hand on his knee. *What commitments would I have? Maybe it would be good to get away, have something else to think about, other than Faith that is, and anyway, I should want to be with my grandchildren, shouldn't I?* He hasn't been given many opportunities over the years. And then there's Greg, her pasty-faced and not quite, but almost, useless husband. Maybe it would do them, his daughter and Greg, some good to get away too; that should be his reward as well.

"Next week," she replies, coughing slightly. He hopes it is with embarrassment. "Any chance?" she adds. "It would be a great opportunity for me, work wise and a chance to get away. What do you think, Dad? Heh?"

"It should be OK," he says. "Let me just check a few things and I'll ring you back. OK?"

194

"Fine, but it would be great to know today, if possible." She adds the last bit almost as an afterthought and already he can feel her withdrawing, her sharp, definite edges fading; the question asked, she doesn't need him so much now.

He knows he will check his empty diary, make a coffee to fill the time and then call her back and agree to do it.

And this is what he does.

He leaves the easel covered with its red cloth and walks into the kitchen.

Outside a sharp shower is tap dancing on the window as he dials his daughter's number whilst inside his head the 'if only' thought bustles in. If only he could call Faith instead and say, "Hey, let's take off. Let's go to Los Angeles. I hear it can be lovely there this time of year."

There's something about being on an island, I think, as I step from the car onto the sweeping driveway in front of my parents' house. Here no one can get to me; I am a monarch in my castle, separated by water and defences. I could, if necessary, both see and hear an invading army and then hunker down, hide or fight back.

Even though it's approaching dusk, I can see the glimmer of the estuary as it seeps out to sea and the outlines of the valley on its far side. I turn and look up at the honey-coloured render of the house and feel once again how magical it must have been to have lived in it when it was new. The Arts and Crafts movement, full of boldness and wonder, and here I am, its inheritor, I think, standing before the turret on the west wing of the house with its panoramic windows, lead flashing and weathervane perched on top. The lawns are dark, and they roll away from me to the side of the house where I can just make out the stone loveseat under the horse chestnut tree and the ghostly white shapes of the croquet hoops. I have no idea who last played the game there but like to think it was someone with young children and that there'd been laughter.

Opening the heavy front door, I walk in.

Although I'd rung ahead as instructed, I know straight away no one is home. I'd expected to be greeted by the warm smells of cooking, by my shambly father standing in the hallway, next to the grandfather clock as it dongs the half-hour sonorously. But in a way, I'm relieved that it is not like this. This way I can catch my breath and acquaint myself with my parents' lives. I've never really felt at home here; it's miles away from and a thousand lifetimes different from the small-town house I'd grown up in, and I've never been able to adjust to the people my parents became on moving here.

It was as though they had erased their past like a pencilled sketch from an artist's block and, with newly sharpened crayons, had started to draw their lives in from scratch.

Standing in the hallway, I hear the house creak around me and the crack in my heart, the one that had been there since my early days with Harvey and which widened when Douggie was born and widened further when he died and is gaping now I've met Dom again, opens like a chasm; I can feel its edges tighten and stretch, imagine the secrets pulsing beneath it like a muscle, and the word 'betrayal' hovers in the air above it.

I leave my case at the bottom of the stairs and walk through the hall, down the back corridor to the vast kitchen. There I can see evidence of some sort of meal preparation. There is a selection of pans on the stove, a bowl of mixed salad and something under a food umbrella in the centre of the kitchen table, and all around are the scatterings of Mum's diversions – clutches of empty jam jars, bamboo canes for the beans tied up in a bundle and leant up against the wall by the larder door, an open paper on the countertop, its crossword half filled in.

"Oh, there you are," I say, opening the door to the estate office in the annexe a former owner had built onto the west wing. Its floor-to-ceiling windows flank the croquet lawn and Mum is there, sitting in front of the computer in the far corner, next to the Wurlitzer jukebox Dad bought from an antique store in a mad moment, its panels sadly unlit and unloved ever since.

"Gosh, you made good time." Mum minimises what she's doing and swivels round in her chair to face me. One of the dogs struggles to its feet and pads over to me, pushing its wet nose into my hand.

"It's nearly eight," I reply, ruffling the dog's soft ears and then sitting down heavily in one of the chairs ranged around the old billiard table Mum uses as a desk in the centre of the room. The dog flops itself down again by me, its front paws just touching my shoes.

The table is covered with piles of books and paperwork and the odd dirty mug.

"Had the family from the Boat House in today," her mother says by way of explanation. "They spent nearly all day on their laptops in here. Can't imagine why they bothered to book a holiday!"

She snorts and runs her workmanlike hands through her no-nonsense hair, but I know the office is like this most days. Filing is not one of my parents' strong points.

"Still no internet in the cottages then?" I ask.

"No, we're still holding out." Mum gives me a half-smile. "But as 4G reception is so dodgy it does mean they come in here and disturb us, that's why I'm a bit behind with my paperwork today."

"I'll go and start supper then, shall I? I came through the kitchen and saw you'd done some of it."

"Oh, that would be lovely," Mum says, whirling around to face her computer screen again and I find it difficult to read the tone in her voice. Is it sarcasm or gratitude? It is so bloody hard to read Mum sometimes.

I haul myself reluctantly out of the chair, step carefully over the dog and go back into the kitchen.

"Dad'll be in soon," Mum calls out after me. "He's doing a quick delivery from Casey's to The Lodge."

I'm pleased to hear this; I'm looking forward to seeing Dad and am relieved that it's not just going to be me and Mum sitting on either side of the kitchen table wondering what on earth to talk about.

Why have I come here? I wonder as I put the heat on under the potatoes. *Why didn't I just book myself into a spa hotel; I could have hidden there just as well.*

I set the table with plates and cutlery, open the fridge to find a bottle of white wine, unscrew its lid and pour myself a glass, knowing full well why I came. It is so I can spend the time being cross with my parents for all their perceived wrongs, rather than admit to myself that I may have done something irreparable.

The potato water starts to boil, and steam rises from the vent in the saucepan lid; I watch it curl up into the extractor hood and just for a moment don't notice the tears streaming down my face.

Despite her best intentions, by Tuesday evening Lizzie is feeling a little resentful towards Faith. Yes, she'd encouraged Faith to go to stay at her mother's and yes, she'd convinced herself that the short notice wasn't alarming in any way. However, there had been something about her friend over the last few weeks which hadn't sat right with Lizzie. It wasn't anything she could put her finger on, more of a presence between them, something which was keeping them apart.

She'd done two days in the shop with just her and Dana, with Brenda coming in a little earlier, "Can't leave Stan for too long, my dear," she'd said. "He needs his tea on the table at five, not a minute before or after. It's part of who he is, the love. But I can come straight after I've cleared away. Five-thirty OK for you, dear?"

It was only half an hour earlier than usual, but it was better than nothing. At least Brenda could deal with the leftover customers while Lizzie cashed up and Dana tripped about in her usual dizzy way, taking three journeys from the shop front to the kitchen where one would have done. Even Mr Brown had grown tetchy on Monday because he'd been made to wait an extra few minutes. He'd stood before Lizzie, tapping his arthritic finger on his watch and trying to smile, but it was a thin, unconvincing smile at best.

So, by Tuesday evening when Lizzie was still trying to get some adequate cover but failing because all the agencies, they usually use seemed to have no warm bodies on their books, her back and feet are aching and, she thinks, as she eventually switches off the shop lights and sets the alarm, that she could do with a nice bath, a glass of wine and something really easy to cook for dinner. Turning away from the shop, she catches sight of the pictures the artist guy had brought in, and this makes her think about Faith again for some reason, but she can't fathom why the two of them should be as closely associated in her mind as they are. They'd worked together once it was true, but then Lizzie had worked with plenty of people in the past and if she should bump into them when out shopping or filling up the car with petrol, there wasn't that edge to the air; the feeling of something unresolved that there seemed to be whenever, now what was his name, ah yes, Nic, when he and Faith were in the same room.

Sighing, she hauls her bag strap over her shoulder and sets off for the car park, wondering as she does so what state the house will be in when she gets back, what mood Ben will be in, and Clemmie for that matter. Clemmie's hardly actually been home recently, which has been a bit of a bonus. Although she loves her daughter savagely, her grandmother's maxim keeps bouncing around in Lizzie's head, 'What the eye doesn't see, the heart doesn't grieve over', and then she rumbles around in her bag for her car keys, opens the door and slips in, resting her head briefly on the steering wheel before switching on the engine and selecting reverse.

Stepping into the hallway, the house smells stale with trapped-in air. Ben's not home yet and she can't wait to throw open the windows and taste that first cool mouthful of wine. Then from the kitchen, she can hear the tinny drone of music playing on Clemmie's phone. *Oh,* she thinks. *Well, here goes,* and reluctantly joins her daughter, feeling totally unprepared for whatever might be awaiting her.

"You're home!" Clemmie says, turning and smiling broadly at Lizzie. "I was just making some toast. Can I get you a cup of tea?"

Lizzie is stunned, firstly by the smile, secondly by the toast and thirdly by the offer of tea. This combination of things has barely ever happened during their lifetime together.

Clemmie continues, "You look knackered, Mum. Why don't you go and sit down and put your feet up? I'll bring your tea through in a minute."

In a daze, Lizzie walks to the lounge, opens the French doors and then puts her bag down on the floor by the armchair and sinks into it, convinced that she's just walked into somebody else's life. Inexplicably she feels like crying, not with relief, nor happiness, but with regret for all the years when her life could have been like this all the time. Resting her head back, she realises that she's never fully understood until now just how much energy not minding has taken.

"Here," says Clemmie, handing her a steaming mug of tea.

Lizzie takes a sip, screwing up her eyes to hide her tears, all thoughts of wine banished from her mind. *This,* she thinks, *is the best drink I've ever tasted.*

"Thanks," she says. "This is completely lovely."

"I'll go and finish my toast and then I've got some homework to do," Clemmie says, tripping out of the room.

Lizzie watches her go feeling like she's just been blessed by an angel.

As Lizzie drinks her tea in number four, Harvey lets himself into number two. His house is also hot with trapped air, but unlike Lizzie's, there are no faint sounds from its depths, no pad of Faith's slippers on the kitchen floor, no burble of the radio or the sound of running water.

He's left Ben in London at some god-awful networking thing and hopes that by now Ben has managed to slip away unnoticed and has started to make his way home too. These things are, they both know, a return to the necessary evils of pre-Covid life; evenings of standing around holding a warm beer or even warmer wine, trying to suss out who matters and who doesn't, handing out and receiving business cards to and from people who they will probably never be in touch with again but contacting them on LinkedIn just in case, while outside the traffic roars by, there are sirens and there is laughter and high up in office blocks, hard-working twenty-somethings sit in front of computer screens and the minutes tick by.

Harvey seldom has time on his own in the house, and it feels odd, like he's wearing a coat that doesn't fit. It's as though he doesn't know his role here without Faith or the boys to direct him. If Faith were here, his job would be to change into a clean t-shirt, water some plants in the back garden, open a bottle of wine and lay the table for supper. Without her here, he stands in the hall immobilised and at a loss. Maybe he'll try and ring Blake later, or Ashley, or he could even ring Ireland.

He's spoken to Faith a couple of times, and she's sounded OK, saying that she's getting on well, having a rest, taking walks, that sort of thing. With her there it means her parents can spend longer on the estate apparently, they're felling some trees, and so she's taken over the cooking and washing. *Hardly a holiday,* Harvey thought at the time, but didn't say anything, fearing that should he challenge her, she would be forced to tell him the real reason why she'd gone away.

He slips off his jacket and hangs it on the newel post, thinking that Faith had been acting strange of late and, the Saturday night after he'd got back from Paris, he'd been aware that she had been wakeful most of the night and he hadn't seen her like that since their early days together. These thoughts unsettle him.

He ambles to the kitchen, opens the back door and stands on the step breathing in the balmy summer air. Someone nearby is mowing their lawn; he can smell the sweet tang of the cuttings, and nearby some kids are out playing football, just like his used to do.

Wednesday

Anthony rings Sara from the Soho Hotel.

"Morning," he says much more brightly than he feels. He'd been out at a client dinner the night before and is both tired from lack of sleep and the effects of too much wine.

"Hello," his wife replies without enthusiasm. He doesn't blame her for this; what is there to say?

For some reason, he blurts out the first thing that comes into his head. "Heard from Faith?"

"No. Why should I?"

Why he asked that question Anthony doesn't know. Faith has never been an easy subject between them; it is like they both have a claim to her and are unwilling to share her with one another. In Anthony's mind, of course, his claim goes back further and is much more meaningful than his wife's, but even so, the women have been through a lot together and Faith has been, is – he corrects himself – a very good friend to Sara.

"Just wondered, because I haven't either," he says lamely.

"Why *should* you?" she asks him in much the same tone of voice she'd used earlier.

"Oh, never mind, just making conversation, that's all," he replies, an edge to his voice that he immediately regrets. "What are you up to today?"

This should be safer territory, but there is a risk that it won't be.

"A bit of writing, and some laundry. Just a quiet day," she says, and he can hear her tapping her manicured nails against the handset. He knows he should hang up before he says something else, he'll regret.

"Oh well, have a good one. Call me if you need to. I'm in the office all day. Meetings and stuff, but a quiet evening tonight and then back tomorrow evening as usual. OK?"

"OK."

"I'll say goodbye then."

"Goodbye, Anthony. Talk later no doubt," she adds this last bit as a conciliatory gesture, one for which he is supremely grateful.

He hangs up the phone and bends down to pick up his laptop bag. *I hate this room,* he thinks. *I hate everything about it. I wish...* He stops, wondering what he could wish for if allowed, if a genie suddenly appeared before him and granted him the standard three. Obviously, number one would be to have Douggie back and de facto his wife. Number two would be to have the balls to stuff his job, set up on his own like Harvey and Ben have done and just live in one place, rather than all this living out of a suitcase crap. And three? Number three would be to understand why Faith has suddenly taken off to visit her parents. This is because he's known her so well for so long, it's a very unusual occurrence and there must be, there just must be a reason behind it.

As he lets the bedroom door click thickly into place behind him, he wonders why, in his conversation with Sara he'd thought of Faith in the past tense and why now should remind him of before, when she'd disappeared from his life just after she started work at that, what was it? Oh yes, that quantity surveying practice.

In the cab on the way to the office, he texts Faith. 'TOY', he writes, their code word from the old days. It means 'Thinking of you'; it means he is here if she needs him.

Sara looks at her reflection in the floor-length mirror in her bedroom. Grey linen trousers and white top, with her hair piled high on her head, not much make-up and a long string of pearls, and yes, flat shoes. *Yes,* she thinks, *I look quite the part.* Her heart is drumming, and her palms are sweaty.

In her writing room, she picks up a box of books. They told her only to expect about fifteen, that's how many of the children would be able to sit and listen for long enough.

She drinks a glass of water before she sets out; it doesn't matter if she's a couple of minutes late setting out, she's given herself an extra hour an hour. Perhaps she shouldn't have.

Leaning on the draining board, she gazes at the garden, at the Judas tree Anthony planted when Douggie died. It is in full leaf. It looks obscenely healthy.

More time means a greater possibility that she will bail, not make it, run back upstairs and take off her clothes, put on her sweats and, tiptoeing past Douggie's door, ensconce herself in her writing room all day. She still has the power, the right almost, she knows she does, of putting real life on hold.

But no, she finishes her drink, and puts the glass down on the counter with a decisive 'ding'. She knows it'll leave a mark, but she'll clean it up later. Leaving now is the only option.

In the car, she switches the radio on and turns the volume up. There's a feature on the Jeremy Vine show about recluses. *How apt,* she thinks with a wry smile, busy trying not to wonder why she didn't tell Anthony the truth earlier about what she was going to do today. Maybe it was because she was afraid that she would fail to do it; fail him, again.

It's only a short journey to the day centre. Far too short. The sun is hot on the back of her neck as she steps out of the cool interior of the car and into the bright August morning.

"May we call you Hermione?" the manager asks, bearing down on Sara in reception, her hand outstretched. "I'm Gloria. We're all first names here. It's easier for the children."

Sara nods, not trusting herself to speak and move at the same time. She takes Gloria's warm plump hand and shakes it. It is a nice hand and Gloria, for all her size, has an easy, friendly face. Sara feels a little better now that she's here and this bit is over. It's good she can hide behind a made-up name; she feels safer that way.

"So, let me get our Site Controller, Evan, to carry the books in. Shall I?" Gloria asks.

Sara gives up her keys in an instant, preferring to sit in the calm of the reception than face the white, hot car park again and see the sun bouncing off the panes of glass in the windows, behind which small children are lurking; children she will have to meet and talk to. Children who may, in some way, some turn of the head, the colour of their eyes, remind her of Douggie.

The moment comes quickly. She's in a room, perched on a small chair and in front of her is a semi-circle of children, most of whom are smiling up at her eagerly. Care assistants are sprinkled amongst them, putting a restraining hand on an arm here, letting another snuggle up to them there. It is a brightly coloured moving mass of humanity, and, after her initial shock, Sara is very pleased to be here. In this she surprises herself; she had expected to hate every minute, but now she's here she has realised that this is who her books are for. Yes, they're also for Douggie, but if her stories can give pleasure to these most special of children, then it makes it all worthwhile. This is, she thinks happily, where she belongs.

She reads two short passages, shows the children some of the artist's first drawings for her some of the characters, tells them very briefly what her next book is going to be about and suddenly it's time for them to go out to play and she prepares to leave their world to go back into her own.

"That was simply marvellous," Gloria says beaming at her as Sara packs her box back up. She'd given away some books, not many, but it felt good to give copies to those children who said they wanted one. Gloria bounces alongside her as they make their way out of the classroom and down the corridor. "Did *you* enjoy that?" she asks.

"It's always great to get a first-hand reaction from some of the children I actually write for," Sara answers.

"Do you have children of your own, Hermione?" Gloria asks politely.

This is it then, Sara thinks. This is the moment she has dreaded. The question came out of the blue. It could blindside her. How should she answer? She could lie, say yes, and leave it at that, changing the subject carefully and quickly. Or she could tell the truth, brave saying it out loud at last, after all this time.

She stops by a notice board on which are pinned pictures of haphazard things, under which, neatly printed, are labels: *Joel, An Elephant, Maisy, Her House.* Gloria stops too, still smiling, but slightly hot now it would appear, a slight sheen of sweat glistening on her skin.

"I had a son," Sara says. "His name was Douggie. He died when he was five. An accident. A long time ago now. Fourteen years, actually."

She gets to the end and stops, waiting for the world to collapse around her. It doesn't.

"I'm so sorry to hear that," Gloria says. "I can understand your gift now."

"Gift?"

"Your books are your gift. Your homage. Out of something so dreadful, something good has come. Thank you so much for coming to see us today. It has meant a great deal."

"It has meant a lot to me too," Sara replies, realising with shock just how true this is.

Evan puts the half-empty box back in the car; As well as the ones Sara gave away, Gloria's bought five books as very early Christmas presents. Sara waves to the small knot of people standing outside reception as she drives by them and the windows gaze at her as she stops at the entrance. She watches them in her rear-view mirror for a moment. It is like they are smiling at her.

Pausing at the gates, she presses a button next to the handbrake. The windows of the car slide down, the boot opens and the roof above her head folds itself back into it. There is a sequence of short beeps, the windows come back up. She unpins her hair and drives off, the wind blowing it out behind her like a veil.

I'll tell Anthony when he comes home tomorrow, she thinks as she waits at a roundabout. She also wants to tell two other people; Faith and Ben, but she knows she won't.

Faith, it would seem, is hiding from something in Ireland, and Ben? Well, she just wouldn't know where to start.

Ben's pulling out when he sees Sara return, swinging into her driveway, the roof of her convertible down and her hair flowing out behind her, showing the sharp contours of her face. A memory stirs in him; her cheekbones, the small divots caused by her clavicle, the sound of her breathing...

"Oh, thank God you're here," Lizzie says sharply to him when he reaches the shop. "It's been bedlam today."

Ben doesn't want to be here. He has work that needs doing, but Lizzie has asked him to help out while Faith's away and, he thinks, as he ties an apron around his waist and says much more cheerfully than he feels, "Right, boss. Where do you want me to start?" He owes Lizzie that much. He owes Lizzie a whole lot more than this.

He stacks a tray with dirty crockery, wipes a tabletop and silently curses Faith under his breath. If she hadn't gone away, he wouldn't have to be here now and he wouldn't have seen Sara drive by him, her hair like a fan, her face lit up like he'd seen it only once before.

Dom has finally got his grandchildren to bed. It is day three of six and he's exhausted. He hasn't had time for dinner so pours himself a whisky and sits back in a chair in his daughter's lounge. *It could be thirty years ago come round again,* he thinks. *I'm kind of back where I started.*

He takes a gulp of his drink and closes his eyes. He sees Faith's face of course. Not the real one, the one he doesn't understand, but the half-finished one under its red cloth in his studio; the one over which he does have some control.

Putting his drink down on the table next to him, he tiptoes upstairs to check on the kids. One by one he bends down near them so that he can hear their steady breathing. He draws in their scent; it is of clean laundry, toothpaste and a kind of sweet, powderiness. This is what it is about, he thinks, pulling each bedroom door to and going back downstairs to his whisky, his uncooked supper and his thoughts.

Friday

Ashley tries to stretch out his legs in his single bed but can't. She's tucked up so close to him that he can't move. He's been awake for a while, listening to her breathing.

In the end, it had been so much easier and quicker than he'd ever imagined. After all the build-up and the waiting and telling himself that it would not be a good idea at all, he guesses it was instinct that took over; something primal in her that reached out and grabbed him, and his answer had been urgent and clumsy and wonderful.

She stirs next to him. "Sssh," he whispers. "Sleep now." She settles again, a small foot resting against his leg, and somehow this seems a more intimate gesture than what they've just done; it says she trusts him, that she is totally at ease with him, and he likes this. It makes a welcome change to be the good guy. He still carries the guilt of what happened to Douggie around with him; it would be good to have someone to share it with.

He thinks back to earlier in the evening and the moment when everything changed. It had just been a normal night; the band had played; he'd put his guitar back in Will's car and returned to the bar where she was waiting for him. It would, he confesses, sound corny to say that he'd had an epiphany, but there'd been a spotlight shining down on her, throwing shadows across her profile, making her eyes look huge, and suddenly his heart had done a strange gymnastic flip and he'd realised what he should have known all along; he loved her, and he always had done. All the others; Dana, the girls at uni, had been mere templates for this, the real thing.

She hadn't needed much persuading and initially, he'd been shocked to think she'd wanted this all along, and that this was why she was here, it had been the motive behind everything she'd done for the past few years.

"At last," she'd said after he kissed her properly for the first time, on the mouth, in the car park of the pub, his hands resting on the upward curve of her buttocks, feeling so gauche and huge and fearing that he might crush her. She'd seemed like a gift he'd been expecting but had no idea how to open.

He'd scrabbled about in a drawer in the room he'd rented for the summer after he got back from Prague for a condom while she was using the bathroom and, when it happened, it seemed so right, like it had been preordained and he hadn't had a moment's doubt that what he was doing was wrong or feckless or wanton.

The sex had been great, but underneath it was a joining on a much deeper level; a purging of their souls, a way of saying, *I forgive you. I forgive myself.*

Clemmie murmurs in her sleep and he reaches out a hand to touch her hair; it is soft, almost like a child's. He closes his eyes and drifts into some sort of strange half-sleep.

Saturday

The next morning, as a languid summer sun taps on the curtains, Clemmie is counting the freckles on Ashley's face, rejoicing in the fact that now she has the right to do so; she has waited a long, long time for this. She gets to twenty when he wakes and smiles lazily up at her.

"Hello you," she says.

"Hello you," he replies, kissing her.

"You, OK?"

"I'm more than OK," he says. "How are you?"

"Better now, thank you."

With one hand he cups one of her small breasts, while with the other he pushes apart her legs. *This is it;* she thinks. *This is precisely what I've waited for; me and him against the world. Now I'll have the strength to slay the demons, I know I will.* She smiles and rolls onto her back as he climbs on top of her.

"Better see if I've got another condom," he says stretching out an arm and opening up a drawer.

"Just hurry, will you?" Her insides are singing hallelujah. 'This'll show Mum and that stupid counsellor', she says to herself. '*I* was right. All along *I* was fucking right'.

"Well," Blake remembers his tutor saying. "I'd like you to take another look at your introduction. I'm not sure you've laid out your argument clearly enough. The research is good, and you've chosen some very apt quotes, but I just want you to reconsider the structure, I think…"

The man's voice droned on as Blake clicked his pen top: off, on, off, on. The sodding man was right, of course, he was, but Blake had been struggling to get his thoughts straight in his head. He knew what he wanted to say, but it felt like a brick wall had sprung up between his brain and his keyboard and, try as he might, he couldn't see over, round or through it.

And now he's waiting, waiting again. Waiting for September, for Gabs, for his mum to explain why she's taken off and gone to Ireland so suddenly. Is one of his grandparents ill or something?

Since Douggie, Blake's always been on the lookout for the consequences of what happened. He's felt under constant scrutiny, waiting for a punishment to be meted out to him, but he's never known when or in what format this punishment will arrive. *Maybe, it's here, now,* he thinks, as he checks his phone again to see if Gabs has messaged.

There are two. One's from Dad, which is, in itself unusual. He hardly ever gets in touch. 'Just checking in mate', it says. 'Call me if you have a mo'.

The other is from Gabs. It says, 'Need a fuck. c u l8r'.

He'll call Dad later when he gets back to the house but decides to deal with Gabs now. He's furious. How the fuck can she treat him this way?

'Sorry. Busy. Catch you sometime maybe', he texts back, wondering if he's making a rod for his own back in drawing yet another line under his time with her. This time though, he really believes, that this is it. He's had enough.

It's early morning and, lying in bed, I'm tempted to call Anthony. I can imagine him in his hotel room and suspect he would be glad to hear from me; it was good to get his 'TOY' text and I know that I could try and explain the thoughts jumbling around in my head to him, that he would try and understand and would, most likely, be the one person who could forgive me. It would also be useful to have the chance to marshal my mishmash of feelings before I return to Harvey, the house and the shop on Monday. But something holds me back and I don't call him, preferring after all to keep it locked up for now. *What good would it do to burden him?* I ask myself. *He can't really make the pain stop. Only I can do that, and time, of course.*

The last couple of days have, I admit, been wonderful. I've pottered around the estate, taken long walks, helped Mum in the kitchen and clipped the hedge next to the old laundry by the stable yard cottages. But now I've started to run out of things to do to keep myself occupied and stop me from thinking about Dom and the decision I need to make.

I climb out of bed and pad to the window, drawing back the heavy damask curtains and gazing at the view. The estuary is dazzling in the low sunlight and a bird is skimming the water with its wingtips.

Downstairs I can hear my parents in the hallway.

"Oh, leave it, will you, Deborah," my father is saying.

I can't quite catch what Mum says in reply, or what she'd said to elicit this response, but it is Dad's tone which dismays me.

Their footsteps shuffle on the gravel as they leave the house by the front door, and I look down on them standing by the driveway's edge as it curves around to the garages, the dogs waiting patiently at their feet. They are both gesticulating and then Mum stalks off, trug in hand, swinging it angrily out to the side, then backwards and forwards, backwards and forwards, much as a solider might swing his arms, and she marches round to the walled garden, the dogs following her. This, I know, is Mum's domain – the place where she feels completely in charge.

There is some bizarre urge in me this morning, like I'm faced with a boil that needs lancing and, after making a thermos of coffee, grabbing two mugs and wrapping up some fruit cake in tin foil, I haul on a spare pair of wellies by the back door and make my way around the other side of the house to Mum's garden.

I know from reading the history of the house that the walls of this garden are unusually low and, as I approach, I can see the top of Mum's head as it bobs up and down next to a wigwam of runner beans. The garden had been completely overgrown when they'd bought the house, but they'd moved in a couple of pigs from the farm next door and after a year the earth was ready for tilling. Mum had then created the series of raised beds running the length of the garden, hedging each one with dwarf myrtle and grading the flowers and shrubs from yellows, purples and blues at the house end, to pinks and crimsons at the other. She'd also planted ancient healing herbs and vegetables in amongst the showier flowers and trained the ancient pear trees to grow along the back wall. Next to the greenhouses was a small knot garden with an Arts and Crafts table and benches. Being there transports me back in time; it is the most perfect place.

"Hi Mum," I say, pushing at one of the double wrought iron gates which opens with a satisfying creak. The dogs lift up their heads, sniff the air and then let their noses flop onto the path once more.

"Oh, it's you," Mum replies, raising her head but not smiling. "Did you sleep well?"

"Yes, thanks. I bought coffee, and cake, for later if you fancy it."

"That's kind." There is a pause and then she says, "Thank you, dear."

Mum bends down again and keeps working, harrumphing loudly and stabbing at the soil angrily with her trowel.

"I heard you and Dad earlier," I venture. "Is everything OK?"

"Why wouldn't it be? Do you think…" Mum stands up and stares at me, shielding her eyes from the sun with her trowel-free hand, "…That because you're here we should change the way we go about things? I'm not going to tiptoe around just because you're being all moody and mysterious. If you want to know…" She rubs her back this time and flexes her shoulders. "…We were discussing the possible reasons why you might be here. You haven't said, after all, have you?"

"Well, I didn't think I actually needed to complete an application form!" I retort, trying to keep my voice light and humorous to show that I'm joking, but inside I'm not. I've known this conversation would have to happen sometime. Why not now? Maybe this is the boil that needs lancing? I shift my feet, and the silver foil around the cake crackles.

"What's wrong then?" Mum's tone is just on the wrong side of compassionate, on the edge of impatient. It reminds me of all our previous such conversations.

"It's complicated," I reply. "I…"

I pause. I what? Should I tell Mum the one thing I didn't tell her all those years ago, that I'd fallen in love with a married man and, worse than that, now that married man is back in my life and single and that I'm married to Harvey, and I love Harvey and I love Dom, and I feel I owe them both so much and probably don't deserve either of them? And should I tell her the other thing? The bigger, darker secret that rests at the heart of me? How on earth would Mum ever understand how corrosive the secrets I'm carrying are?

"Come and sit down," Mum says unexpectedly, dropping her trowel and walking briskly over to the other side of the garden in the direction of the greenhouses and seating. "Bring the coffee!" she shouts over her shoulder.

I follow dutifully, feeling about nine years old again. The dogs come too and lie at Mum's feet. They look like a bundle of carpet remnants.

We make a fuss of pouring coffee, blowing on the hot surfaces, crossing and recrossing our legs and then Mum says suddenly out of nowhere, "I had an affair. Once. When you were about twelve. He was…"

It takes me a second or two to catch up. Twelve? That would have been when Mum had started to go out all the time and Dad became quieter and the atmosphere in the house heavier. Aah, I think, perhaps it all makes sense now. Perhaps it wasn't my fault after all?

"He was what?" I ask.

"A lot younger than me. He was…" She pauses. "…Beautiful."

"How long did it go on for?"

"Three years."

"*Three* years? Did you ever think of leaving Dad? What about me?" Even to my middle-aged ears, I sound petulant, like a toddler being denied a treat.

"I thought of nothing but you and your dad."

"And him, of course?" Now I'm being unfair, I know I am, but somehow, I can't stop myself. I know what she's talking about after all.

"And him. But I didn't leave, that's the point. My life, my real life, was with your father and you. He." She pauses, sighs, then says, "He could only ever be a temporary thing."

I soften, seeing clearly and for the first time the uneasy parallels between my mother's life and my own.

"Who was he? How did you meet?"

"That's not important. Not really. It was at the time, but so much has happened since."

"Did you ever see him again?"

"Once, years later. Just before we moved here. I…" Her voice cracks now and she coughs brusquely. "…I saw him, and we chatted. He was married, of course. Had children. I was, it seemed, a whole lot older than him then. It hadn't mattered before, but that time, that last time, it suddenly did, and I realised it always would have done, and that I'd been right to make the choice I did, not just for my sake and his, but for your and your father's. It's not been easy, since. Dad hasn't let it fade as much as I had hoped he might."

"How did Dad find out?"

"I told him."

We are both silent for a moment. I take another sip of coffee. It is lukewarm by now.

"And you? Has it faded for you?" I ask.

"I can't lie and say it's gone completely because it hasn't, but yes, it has faded, and the regret and guilt have become more manageable."

The garden is very quiet around us, until somewhere up high in a neighbouring tree a crow cackles, breaking the moment like glass shattering.

Mum turns to me, takes my coffee cup from my hands and puts both our mugs on the ground. Then she takes my hands in hers. Hers are rough, her fingernails grubby and split and, for the first time in many years, I look my mother deep in the eye, and see the clear film at the back of them and know that if I could ever be as brave as her and tell the truth, not just about Dom, but about Douggie too, I too might find this type of peace, this certainty that what I'd done had been for the best, in the end.

"Whatever's going on," Mum says. "Whatever choice you make, remember it's not only you it's happening to, or who will be affected by your decision. We are like cobwebs, each of us, spinning threads out to others' lives. Nothing ever happens in a vacuum."

I think back to the afternoon with Dom; the feel of his touch and his release in me and how he'd bent his head to make me come and how I'd thought the mountains would tumble and the sky cave, and that it had been wrong, so wrong. I nod, unable to speak. Part of me wants to tell Mum everything but, I reason, as she lets my hands go and they fall into my lap suddenly cold, some things are best left unsaid. This is my battle and mine alone; it's not fair to burden Mum with it.

"Is that why you're here?" Mum asks, gazing up at the tree and the crow who's still there like the threat of something dark and difficult. "Are you trying to decide what to do, for the best, eh?"

There is an unusual trace of uncertainty in Mum's voice as she asks me this.

"Yes."

"Does Harvey know? The boys?"

"No."

"Does it hurt?"

"Oh yes, Mum, it does. It fucking does."

"Willow!" But Mum is smiling. "I know love, I really do," she says.

"Yes, you do, don't you?"

And for once I don't mind her using my first name.

It has never occurred to me before that this is the weight Mum has been carrying and how fragile a balance she's managed to keep in her life, both before they moved and since they came here to this, to all this light and space and quiet. Mum's wrongs, now I've understood their cause, like her absence on the last day of my exams could and should be understood and forgiven. I'd want the same from my own children, wouldn't I?

I'd want my friends to forgive me too, wouldn't I?

"Look. Can I give you one more bit of advice?"

"Sure, Mum," I say.

"Take your time. Don't rush it and, if you can, don't tell Harvey. Keep it to yourself; believe me, it will be better in the end." Mum stands up and, in a rare gesture, puts her hand on my shoulder. "And stay, stay here for as long as you like."

"Thanks, Mum." I find it hard to speak as the tears threaten to fall, and I watch her and her dogs walk back to the raised bed and bend over her courgette plants and wonder if I will ever be as wise as the mother, I'd once thought was hostile and feisty; ever as sure, brave, ever as healed, as generous.

Harvey doesn't like the sea, and this has a nothing to do with Douggie; he's had a strained relationship with it ever since he'd been a child and there'd been that disastrous fishing trip with his dad when they'd ended up having to be rescued by the coast guard. In later years, Harvey's often wondered whether it was his own fear, or his father's, which had been the hardest to bear. He'd never seen his dad afraid before that moment and spent many of his teenage years silently rebuking his father for not being the hero, he thought he ought to be. However, when he had sons of his own, Harvey realised that when his father had looked at him with panic-stricken eyes, it wasn't his own fate he was afraid for; it was Harvey's. This was a huge lesson for Harvey to learn and one which he had never got to talk to his dad about before he died. He regrets this a huge amount.

So, Harvey still doesn't like the sea; he's done beach holidays and the occasional ferry crossing, but has never quite been able to take his boys out to where they could become victims to deep water and unpredictable weather and, as he waits in line at passport control for the flight to Cork, he hopes that one day Blake and Ashley, maybe when they have children of their own, will understand why this is so.

He hasn't told Faith he's coming and he's not sure why, maybe it's because he thinks that should he do so, she would try and stop him. Their last few conversations have been a little odd, as though there's more than just land and sea between them.

"Can you handle the prep for next week's meetings on the shopping centre car park leaks?" he'd asked Ben on the phone on Friday evening. "I thought I'd pop over and spend the weekend with Faith."

"I think Lizzie would be pleased to have her back!" Ben replied, his tone having a slight edge to it.

Harvey decided to push on regardless. "But the prep?" he asked.

"Yeh, sure, but that's another pint you owe me." Ben's voice was lighter now, it had its familiar spark back.

"Fair enough!" Harvey said, wondering why the deep recesses of his heart were battering away with worry.

When the plane lands Harvey is struck by the lusciousness of Ireland. There's something other-worldly about the landscape; as though a giant painted it years before and the Irish have spent their lifetimes and their love touching up the colours, smoothing out the contours. He hires a car at the airport and begins the journey to Skib. He listens to the radio to stop himself from thinking because he still hasn't quite worked out why Faith suddenly took off like she did; and even though Blake did call him back, he didn't have the nerve to ask him what he thought about it either.

There is, Harvey realises, as he pulls onto the N71 following signposts to Bandon, something nagging at the back of his mind about Faith lately; a distance between them that had been there at the start when he'd first met her, but which had, over the years, gradually narrowed until he

217

couldn't see where she'd stopped and he'd begun, or so he'd thought. But now, now it is as though all that had been make-believe and that the space between them had always been there, he'd just been too busy, too certain of himself and her to have noticed it.

As he drives over the bridge to Inish Beg, Harvey doesn't stop and gaze at the view; he is tired and needs the loo. He also wants to see Faith. There is some small part of him that fears she might not be there at all.

All is quiet as he pulls up to the front door. The gravel crunches under his tyres, but then the sound of it fades away and all he can hear is the rustle of the birds in the trees and the distant breathing of the estuary.

"Hello! Anyone home?" he calls as he steps into the hallway.

Silence.

He uses the downstairs cloakroom and, feeling better, makes his way to the kitchen. There are signs that someone's around: ingredients spread over the table, a half-read magazine on the counter by the hob, a spoon resting near it, covered with tomato sauce. Then he sees Faith's jacket hanging on the back of one of the chairs and almost sinks to the floor with relief. She is here after all. He hopes he's been right to come.

"Harvey!" She walks in the back door carrying a bunch of herbs. Her face seems different, childlike almost. Her hair has curled yet more in the damp Irish air and her eyes are sparkling. She looks beautiful, so much more like the girl he met all those years ago. "What on earth are you doing here?" She's smiling at him and, putting down the herbs, crosses the kitchen to stand in front of him.

"Thought I'd just pop by!" he says nonchalantly, doing his best James Dean impression. But he knows he's fooling no one.

"It's a long way to come!" she says, leaning into him.

He wants to wrap his arms around her and pull her close so that he can taste and smell her, but he hesitates.

"You're worth it," he replies, slowly bending down his head, almost forcing himself to rest his lips in her hair. He doesn't know why he's being so cautious. This is his wife; the one person he knows best, loves best and above all others and yet, he's uneasy. Seeing her here makes him realise again that there are parts of her that he doesn't know, and maybe never has.

"Supper won't be for a while," she says, moving away from him and going over to the hob, where she stirs the sauce. "Let's go and see if we can find Mum. I think she'd like to say hello. She's probably in the walled garden again. She's spent almost the whole week there!"

The way she says 'Mum' also surprises Harvey. There's an easiness in her voice that he hasn't heard before. "You been getting on, OK? The three of you?" he asks.

"Yes, it's been fine. Really quiet, like I've said on the phone, but restful. Just what I needed."

He follows her out the back door and round to the walled garden where Deborah is bending low over a flower bed. When she hears the gate click, she stands up, rubbing the small of her back with a gloved hand. The other she raises in welcome.

"Harvey!" she exclaims.

Again, Harvey is surprised by the change in the two women; he is reminded of when he was a boy and his mother would, at last, manage to get the splinter out from under his skin. There'd still be a mark for a while, but the sharp dart of pain every time the place was touched had gone.

"You come to take her home?" Deborah asked smiling over at them, her eyes squinting in the evening sun.

"Something like that. If she wants to, that is," he replies.

"Faith's father's in the lower field. You could go and get him for me while I clear up here and Faith gets on with dinner. OK all?"

There are times when Deborah reminds Harvey of a sergeant major, and this has annoyed him greatly in the past. But now, here, in this garden surrounded by its wall of warm red bricks, with his wife someone who he'd like very much to get to know again, know better, Harvey doesn't mind, and he turns on his heels and walks out of the gate, waving back at Faith.

"Could murder a drink when I get back!" he calls out into the still evening air.

"Right," I say to Mum. "I'll crack on with dinner then."

"Faith?" Mum says quietly.

"Mmm." I stop and look at her.

"Remember what I said. Take your time. Don't rush it and don't tell him why you've been here this week. Not yet maybe not ever. Him not knowing will be difficult for you, but the truth will hurt both of you more. Believe me."

I nod, unable to speak. Not only do I feel my other decision was the right one, but this time she'd called me Faith.

Supper passes with plenty of chatter, good food and lots of wine. We talk about the farm and the estate, and the summer bookings and how parlous things had been during lockdown, and the faulty shaving point in the woodland cottage.

"They'd never even wired it in," her father says incredulously. "And what staggers me is that it's been like it for years. How come none of the other tenants noticed it I'll never know."

I let the conversations drift around me as I busy myself clearing the dishes, stepping over the dogs asleep under my parents' chairs. It's nice being here with them and my husband. There is a rightness to it and, I think, there's the wider circle too. There are our friends, Anthony and Sara, Ben and Lizzie and my sons, and there's Clemmie; all these people depend on me being here, in my rightful place, in this centre of my own making. I was right not to say anything at the time about what I saw that blackberry picking day, I was right not to since. We're OK as we are, and there is no room for the truth, nor for Dom either.

These facts hit me in the centre of my chest. We used to talk about 'The Honourable Thing'. I'd done it once before and I am, I know, going to have to do it again.

I'd deceived Harvey with Dom twice now. It may have been forgivable when I was younger, before we got married and had our children, but now? No, now it was unforgivable.

As I rinse the plates before putting them in the dishwasher, listening out with one ear to Harvey describing a leaking car park roof to Dad, I know there's no possibility of me building a small extension to my life to accommodate Dom. I will, I know, have to let him go. If I didn't it would stop me from being the person, the others think I am. The illusion is what matters. The truth? Well, the truth of what I've done and what I know, should stay buried, for everyone's sake. A kind of validation again.

"Right!" I say, turning and smiling brightly at this vital nub of my family. "Time for bed, I think!"

They make love and, as he comes, Harvey feels a jolt of surprise, like it's the first time all over again. Her climax too is different; she holds back for much longer than usual as if she is fearful of letting go, but when she does, it spirals, and he can feel it undulate through her. Afterwards, as they lay curled up near one another, not touching, but almost, he can sense she's crying.

"You, OK?" he asks.

In the gloom he can see her nod. But she isn't OK, he can tell she isn't.

"You going to let me know what's been going on? Why you came here?" he asks, very tentatively, hoping somehow that the words aren't actually being spoken out loud, that she won't be able to hear them, that she won't answer him, he won't have to know.

"There's nothing wrong. Please, don't worry," she says in a voice small and uncertain enough to tell him that there is something very wrong indeed.

He rustles the bedclothes, moves nearer her and rests his chin on the top of her head so that her face is lodged in the curve of his neck. It's nice to feel her so close, but for some reason, he doesn't want to have to look into her clear eyes. He fears he will either see the truth there or perhaps even worse, something he thought he could never see in them, a lie.

He says softly, "I thought I knew who you were, Faith. Is there something…" He can't finish the sentence because he doesn't know what he's trying to ask of her.

He tries again. "Whatever it is we can sort it out," he says. "I can't promise to make it better, but I'm here and I wish," he pauses, realising she's crying again. "I wish you could trust me enough to help you."

"It'll be OK," she says, her voice thick with tears. "I just need time, that's all."

He wants to shake her, to force the truth out of her, but he doesn't. It won't do him any good, or her for that matter. So, he says, "That's all right, yes, time. Just time, and then it'll be OK, won't it? As long as you know this is the right path, you've made the right choice, I mean your life with me. You once said you wished you had a magic mirror so you could check the life, you're leading is the right one. It is, Faith. Believe me, it is."

"Yes," she says. "I know it is, and I'll be fine. I promise."

"Night then." He reaches down, cups her chin with his hand and lifts her face so that he can now see her eyes, but still, he can't bear to look into them too deeply. He kisses her instead.

It's like trying to hold onto sunlight, he thinks as she says, "Goodnight, Harvey and…" She pulls the covers up over her shoulders and closes her eyes. "…And thank you for coming here. I'm glad you did."

"I'm glad I did too," he says, realising that they have spent years not actually telling each other what they really think. If they'd been more honest with each other, maybe she wouldn't be so sad now. What it is that's upsetting her can't be that bad, can it?

He can hear her breathing steady and deepen and knows she is asleep. Putting his hands behind his head, he lays awake for a while wondering what the thing is that has wedged itself between them, something which despite all the years he's known and loved her, seems to have oxygen enough of its own to survive. He thinks of his sons, her mother, and their friends. Whatever it is, he will have to trust her more than she trusts him. He will have to carry on believing this is the best life for both of them, that the choices they've made to be together and stay together are the only ones they could have made. He will, won't he?

This is a huge ask though, and he doesn't know if he will be able to do it. He stretches out a hand and finds the soft material of her nightdress and the mound of her hip underneath it. He rests his hand there, feels the warmth of her and, eventually, he sleeps.

Sunday

Dom is sitting in front of his easel again. He's waited over a week, and she hasn't called, and he's tried very hard not to read too much into this silence. There could be, he reckons, a hundred different reasons for it.

His daughter and her husband are home from the States, and he has reluctantly handed his grandchildren back over to their care. It has been, he thinks as he lifts up a paintbrush and runs his fingertip over its bristles, a salutary lesson for him, something he should have insisted on years ago. Just think of all he's missed out on by keeping himself at a distance from them, and that's not just the grandkids, it's his own son and daughter too. Perhaps he should look at forgiving himself for leaving them? After all, they seemed to have moved on, and whilst there's still some awkwardness and side-taking, given his ex-wife's well-known penchant for divide and rule, he should be able to raise himself above this sort of thing and move on as well. Shouldn't he?

The painting of Faith has remained untouched; he hasn't even lifted up the red cloth since he got back, and he hasn't had the energy to start anything new. Most of the pictures in *Flick's* have been sold now, but he hasn't been asked to supply anymore and that's probably just as well because he couldn't face going back there, not now.

This silence is so like the last one, the one after he'd driven away that last time and hoped in one tiny corner of his mind that she'd follow. She didn't, and it didn't look like she was going to seek him out now either, but he remembers the feel of her still, not just from this time but from all the times before, long ago when they were younger, more hopeful, far less wise.

There's no way he can disrupt the careful balance she's created, the intricate web of people and memories that support her; he can't see his way to introduce himself to her sons and say, "I was the man your mother loved once. If only…"

Is there?

No, he decides. *It is for the best.* And he lifts the picture off the easel, cover and all, and stacks it against the wall under the window, facing inwards. He stares at the view for a long time but even so, he can still feel the contours of her face burn through the paper and board, as though the pencil marks are made of mercury, not graphite.

Monday

I'm standing by the canal again. It's early on Monday morning and, having travelled back with Harvey yesterday – he'd had his hire car picked up from Mum and Dad's, and had managed the ferry crossing – just – he's never liked water – and unpacked, it seems I've never been away; the house has absorbed me like blotting paper. We have been carefully polite with one another, both anxious not to tread on the glass floor which seems to have been thrown down between us.

Another moorhen is bobbing its head in the water in front of me as if to say, "Go on. Do it."

"Dom?" I'll say.

"Yes."

"I'm sorry, so sorry."

"I know. It's OK, really it is. There was a moment when I thought it might work out differently, but now I see it's too big a thing and I understand, I really do."

"Thank you, Dom. Thank you."

"Don't say goodbye. Never say goodbye." His voice will be strained and hollow.

I am trying very hard not to cry, not to summon up his face in front of me, feel the touch of his skin and the weight of all our history and I want to run to him, I want to leave the shadows of the archway and the cold brick walls and hold his hand one last time.

I put the phone back in my bag. Maybe I'll call him later. Maybe then I'll say all the things I've practised in my head and hope his responses will be as I imagine them to be. Will he really let me go so easily this time?

I walk back up the path and onto Bartholomew Street. The sun is warm and there is the feeling that the year is turning.

There is a tightness in my throat and a hole in my heart.

Part 6 – Autumn

The days turn into a week, then another week, and yet more weeks, and it's Saturday again, another dinner party. It is, I reckon, a necessary act, one to cement everyone together, to remind myself of my place in the interlocking circles of my family and friends, my role as a paperweight. However, as I'm standing at the kitchen sink washing the customary lettuce, my hands in cold water, I falter. It's understandable, isn't it, to have moments of doubt, to wonder what it would be like to turn around now, right now, and find Dom standing in the doorway, leaning up against it, all loose-limbed and tousle-haired like he's always been, with those cobalt eyes and that smile, and feel the connection that has, despite everything, stayed with me through all the years of my marriage, through the boys' births, through Douggie's death? Maybe it's this which is the glue which holds me together, I think. Maybe that's why it wouldn't work if we did get together; he's only ever been a concept and could never be a reality. I shake the water off the salad leaves, put them in the colander and turn around. He's not there, of course, just the empty doorway, the kitchen table stacked with plates and glasses ready for later.

Harvey walks past the window on his way to the shed. He lifts an arm and waves at me.

"You look nice," he says to me later, as I study my reflection in the mirror in our bedroom. I'm wearing my black trousers, a floral tunic and flat sandals. I've tucked my hair behind my ears and threaded gold hoops through the lobes.

"Thanks," I reply, putting on the last touches of my make-up. "So do you."

It's true, he does. There's something so exquisitely familiar about him; the way his jeans rest on his hips, the shirt I ironed hanging from his shoulders like a second skin and the newly forming lines around his eyes, which are so well-known and honourably earned by all the years of care and worry. He is like a map; without him, I would truly be lost.

"Everyone coming tonight?" he asks, sitting on the edge of the bed to do up his shoelaces.

"Yep."

"Lizzie still OK with you after your impromptu holiday?"

I wonder why he would want to bring this up again now. Why couldn't he just leave it? Yes, I'd gone to Mum and Dad's unexpectedly and he'd come after me, but now I was home and, just as I hadn't called Dom, I wasn't going to explain myself to Harvey. There are, I still firmly believe, some things which are best left unsaid.

Keeping silent is the wisest course of action. It's what I did with Douggie all those years ago and that has worked, hasn't it?

"Of course, she is," I snap back. "Why wouldn't she? We're friends after all."

"OK, OK, it doesn't matter, I'm just making conversation."

He leaves the room and it's suddenly cold and empty; I hadn't realised just how much warmth he can generate, how much space he takes up.

I regret being sharp with him, but I'm edgy and feel brittle. I want tonight to centre us, centre me, but it's as though something terrible is pending. I've made my decision and, like last time, I have to live with it. I have to carry on, keep going, and not look back. I have to hold it all together.

Outside the window, I can hear the early autumn leaves rustle. It's been a glorious September day, but now the sky has purpled, as though someone has hit it hard enough to bruise it and there is the smell of fire in the air.

Harvey is setting out the wine when I get downstairs. I pass him on my way to the kitchen, but don't apologise; I know on some level I should, but somehow, it's too hard to put just how sorry I am into words.

"Did Faith have a good break?" Anthony asks as Harvey pours him a beer.

They sit on either side of the fireplace in the lounge while Sara and Faith are in the kitchen. Harvey can hear the low murmur of their wives' voices and the occasional tinkle of laughter. *Since Faith's been back from Ireland, she's been odd,* he muses, as Anthony takes his first long drink. He hopes it's going to pass, and he wishes everyone, including himself, would stop thinking of her absence and start thinking of now and tomorrow and the next day.

"Yes, thank you," he says. "I think she and her mum got some stuff sorted. They seemed a lot easier with each other than they have been in the past."

"That's good."

"Sure is."

Anthony sits back in the chair and crosses his long legs. "I'm knackered," he says.

"How *is* work?" Harvey asks.

"Same old, same old," he replies. He looks furtively at the door and lowers his voice. Harvey has an uneasy feeling and experiences a moment's impatience, both with Anthony and with the weather. He wishes it would just rain and get it over with. As the afternoon wore on, the weather had closed in, and now as dusk is falling, it seems the sky is made of bronze.

"There's talk of a transfer," Anthony is saying.

"Really? Where to?"

"Frankfurt."

"Does Sara know?"

"No, I haven't had the heart to tell her yet."

"Do you think you'll take it?"

"It's possible. It's a really good opportunity and it might force us out of this…" He pauses. "…This dead end we've been in."

Harvey decides not to say anything, but he knows exactly what Anthony means.

"It's been over fourteen years, for God's sake. Isn't it about time we put it behind us and move on?" Anthony continues. "Relocating to Europe could be the fresh start we both need. What do you think?"

"Faith'll miss you," Harvey says, knowing it to be true and, in a strange way, he'd miss Anthony too. Both he and Ben were kind of like brothers to him.

This is what Harvey believes as there's a knock at the door. "That'll be Ben and Lizzie," he says, putting his drink down and standing up, ready to answer it.

228

"Don't say anything to Faith until I've cleared it with Sara, will you?" Anthony says in a hushed voice, reaching out to touch Harvey's arm as he passes.

"Sure thing," Harvey answers and, as he goes into the hallway, he has an overwhelming sense that this evening, this meeting of the six of them, may somehow be significant. It's as though he's been walking around wearing blinkers for years, kidding himself that what he could see was the full picture, but now, Anthony has asked him to keep a secret, however small, from both Sara and Faith, a secret which years ago he may have held onto without a second thought. But things seem different now. Try as hard as he might not to, since Faith challenged him that day in the kitchen when she told him she felt watched, since she went to Ireland, he can feel a shift in the balance of things. It's like before the last dinner party they had when they won the Paradigm contract, he can sense the enormity of what they all have to lose. A shiver runs down his spine as he reaches out to open the door.

Ever since she visited the day centre, Sara has hugged the secret of her achievement to her, unsure as to why she's keeping it from Anthony and the others but is convinced it's the best thing to do for now. She doesn't want their applause or their well-meaning questions about when she might do it again. No, just for now, it's enough to have done it and to keep it inside her like a piece of warm coal. So, tonight at Faith's, she's feeling more buoyant than usual. She's swept up her hair into a chignon and is wearing jeans and a long white shirt unbuttoned just a fraction more than usual. She's also wearing heels, and for someone as small as she is, sees herself for once as almost majestic. It's probably the first time since Douggie that she's felt this way; this full of a type of invincibility she thought she'd lost.

"Here," she says after they've finished dessert. "Let me help you." And she stands to clear away some of the plates, following Faith into the kitchen.

Faith dumps the dishes she's carrying onto the table, "God, I'm exhausted," she says. "Feels like I've been on my feet all day."

"Hey, how about I sort out the coffee and cheese and you go and sit down?" Sara walks across the kitchen and puts a hand on Faith's arm.

"Would you? That would be lovely," Faith says. "I've left everything out." She points absent-mindedly to the counter by the fridge and then wearily ambles back out into the dining room saying, "Thanks ever so," over her shoulder.

Sara can hear the hum of conversation and senses movement. The others are leaving the table and settling into chairs and sofas in the lounge.

"Anyone fancy a brandy?" Harvey calls out.

There's a murmur of answers and then there's the thump of music. Sara likes being on her own; it's peaceful here and cooler than in the dining room. The air outside the house is crackling with unspent thunder. She imagines the blackberries in the woods behind the houses, their plumpness, and ripeness.

A memory stirs.

It's also nice to have some space around her, not to feel so crowded. She starts to arrange the cheese biscuits on the plate as she waits for the kettle to boil.

"I've been sent in to help with the coffees," a voice says from the doorway.

Sara turns. It's Ben. He's leaning against the frame. He's wearing chinos and a loose pale denim shirt and, like her, he's drunk quite a bit with the meal. Suddenly she is filled with the urge to laugh; laugh or touch him, she can't quite work out which. *It would be good,* she thinks. *To feel his warmth.*

As though there's a length of elastic between them being pulled taut, she finds herself drawing closer to him; she can hear her heels tap on the kitchen tiles. In her hand is a half-empty packet of biscuits.

"Ben," she says, her voice gravelly.

He's looking puzzled as if he's trying to remember something. His brown eyes are like pools, and she can see herself reflected in them. Someone's turned the music up in the lounge and the conversation gets proportionately louder.

"We never did talk about it, did we?" she asks, rustling the biscuit wrapper between her fingers. Her hands are hot, and she has no idea where the question has come from.

"About what?" Ben asks cautiously. "About Douggie?"

"Well, that as well. But I really meant about what happened with us, that time."

"Oh," he says, raising an arm and putting the flat of his hand on the side of her face. It is warm and makes the memory all the more real. He's touched her like that once before and he's as close as he was the night of the flood in her house, and whilst she thought she'd succeeded in forgetting the former, she hasn't.

Like Douggie's death, Sara's spent years pretending that afternoon with Ben didn't really happen either.

"It was so long ago," he says, not moving his hand from her face. She sees his eyes journey down her body, stopping briefly at her cleavage. Her breasts tingle. Standing here like this with him, she feels beautiful, twenty years younger, unafraid.

Then it's like someone has flicked a switch and a film reel is playing, showing flashbacks from their friendships: there's Faith and Harvey, and Lizzie, and Anthony and the children and Ben. They're whirling around like some camera obscura, waiting for her to fix on an image and say, "Stop, that's the real one; that's the real me."

Sara has waited years for this moment, and there have been times when she's thought it would never come. She places her free hand over his and feels the ridges of his veins and the loose skin over his knuckles.

"He was your son," she says. "Douggie was your son."

It takes Ben a second or two to compute what Sara has said, and when he does, it's like a huge weight lifts from him. *This,* he thinks. *This is what has been nagging at me; this is the source of the unease, my sense of guilt, and my inability to settle.* This is why he always felt he has the power to hurt Lizzie and Clemmie; why he's kept part of himself back, why he grieved so much when Douggie died, why he's always wanted to hold Sara again; not like this, but skin to skin; hoping that by doing so he can smooth away her pain, make her almost whole again.

"Are you sure?" he asks, his voice seeming inordinately loud in the hush of the kitchen. He can still hear the others in the background and from some tiny corner of his brain comes the knowledge that they're still waiting for him to return with the coffee.

231

"Yes," she answers quietly. "You just had to look at him to know. Didn't you? I mean, if you looked into his eyes, you knew. I knew, I just did."

Oh my God. Ben's mind is in turmoil. He remembers so much that it burns. He pulls her to him, smells the coconut scent of her shampoo, and bends his head until he finds her lips. He has no idea why he wants to kiss her; either to stop her from speaking or to finish what he started in that long ago time when everything seemed so simple, and consequences were the subject of history books and other people's lives.

He hasn't heard the footsteps, hasn't heard Anthony arrive, sent in search of him and Sara, the brandy glasses, the absent coffee and cheese. He doesn't see Anthony watch the aftermath of the kiss, her resting her head on his chest. He doesn't realise that Anthony has heard everything.

Part 7 – Before

Another September: one of those high-definition days that marks the turning point from summer to autumn. The lines around the leaves are almost black against the solid blue of the sky. It was a survivors' day. Ben had got through the hot days of July and August commuting to his job for a major contractor in London, and he'd been married to Lizzie for over a year. This, he thought, was some kind of achievement too. They had their lovely house on the estate and Lizzie has become good friends with Faith next door, and the four of them, including Faith's husband Harvey, had settled into a nice routine of Friday night takeaways and Sunday afternoon walks, of helping each other out with ladders and heavy lifting. But still Ben felt there was something missing. He had no idea what this something was, there was just a weight in the pit of his stomach; a feeling that there might be something else out there he should be doing.

"Shall we go blackberrying in the woods this afternoon?" Lizzie asked that Sunday morning as she hung up a tea towel in the kitchen. She waved an arm in the general direction of the back of their house to where the trees stood tall, close and majestic. Then she smiled at him, and his heart sank just a fraction. He didn't want to go. He didn't know what he wanted, but it sure as hell wasn't that.

He hesitated before replying and Lizzie said somewhat sharply, "Well, you obviously don't want to go then. I just thought it would be nice to hook up with Faith and Harvey and spend an afternoon in the woods."

She sidled up to him and wound her arms around his waist. He felt himself draw away. He didn't want to, but it was an instinctive thing, and inside he was shouting, "Let me breathe, please just let me breathe."

Lizzie continued, "It'll remind us of when we were kids, won't it?" She reached up to kiss him lightly on the lips. She tasted of toast. "Anyway, I've already rung Faith and they're up for it. They've got some friends they'd like us to meet. It'll be fun. Faith suggested a barbeque at theirs first. What do you think? Oh, it'll be fun. I'm sure it will."

233

She smiled coquettishly at him, reminding him of the look that made him fall in love with her after they'd met when his firm had to do a survey on the building in which the playgroup where she worked was housed. Then she'd seemed so sweet and charming; all lace collar, small, round face and that cute smile; he'd wanted to scoop her up there and then and take her home with him. Now, looking around the home they'd set up together, once more he felt that wave of panic rise in his chest. Trapped; he felt trapped, and the last thing he wanted to do was to spend an afternoon of inane talk with people he didn't know and then tramp through the woods pretending he was a boy again, pretending he was happy.

"Well?" she asked. "Please say yes. Faith said all we need to take is some booze; they'll provide the rest."

He was cornered. It was a done deal and there was no way he could get out of it and, he supposed, he shouldn't really want to. He should want to spend his Sunday afternoon with his wife and their friends. He should want to do this and then make love to her when they got home. "Yes," he told himself firmly. "This is what you should want to do."

Later that day, Ben found himself standing talking to Harvey next to the lit barbeque, a beer cradled in the crook of his arm. The mid-afternoon sun beat down on the back of his head and the trees rustled their leaves.

"Here they are," Faith trilled, skipping out the back door and into the garden. "Harvey, Ben," she said. "This is Anthony and Sara. They're going to be moving into number six. Anthony and I were at school together!"

She paused, looking at Anthony with an expression on her face that Ben couldn't quite read, but which he didn't feel all that comfortable with because he'd never seen it before.

She prattled on, and he heard her say, "I'll introduce you to Lizzie in a mo, she's inside with Blake, they're doing a puzzle in the lounge. Can't keep her away from kids, that wife of yours," she said, tapping Ben on the arm and winking. He wished she hadn't.

He wished she hadn't because he wanted to concentrate on the small, dark-haired woman next to Anthony. She was standing ramrod straight; she was slight, and was wearing a short denim skirt, sandals and a loose flowery top; she was also just slightly too thin, and her hair streamed down over her shoulders like a black waterfall.

She looked up at him and held out her hand. "Pleased to meet you," she said. Her voice was unsettling, intimate, and low.

"Here," he said hurriedly to Harvey. "Let's get Anthony a beer, hey? What'll you have Anthony?" He held out his hand to the small woman's husband's and clasped it.

"Bitter, if you have it," Anthony replied. Then he turned to his wife and said, "Wine for you, I suppose?"

There was a hint in this question of uneasy waters between the two of them; Ben recognised it from his own life, knowing that neither couple seemed to be able to stand up to the template of easy happiness that Faith and Harvey appeared to have achieved. *Maybe having a child was the answer?* he wondered. But then, he thought if he wasn't ready for what he'd got now, what made him think he would be ready to be a father?

He was aware of Sara nodding, and so busied himself getting their drinks while Harvey put the burgers on the grill, chatting to Anthony about work and sport and stuff. Ben heard the words, 'Arsenal', and 'defence strategy', as he went back into the house.

Peering into the lounge, he caught sight of Lizzie and Blake sitting cross-legged on the floor, a puzzle spread out between them. "Faith's guests have arrived," he said to the back of her head.

"Just coming," she answered, turning and smiling up at him. "Blakey boy and I are just finishing this, aren't we?"

Blake nodded and picked up a piece, showing it to Lizzie. "This one, where do this one go?" he said, his new teeth like tiny pearls in his mouth.

Ben left them and, as he carried the drinks out into the garden, the meaty smell from the barbeque hit his nostrils. He scanned the group huddled around Harvey for Sara, experiencing that strange unwelcome jolt when he saw her glance over her shoulder and lock eyes with him. He felt that she kept them on him just a fraction too long as he stepped across the grass and a hot and unwelcome surge of desire shot through him. It had been ages since he'd felt anything so primal.

"Stop it," he told himself. "Just stop it." He handed the drinks over and stood next to Harvey, trying to concentrate on what Faith was saying, wishing he was a hundred miles away from here, wishing he'd never come in the first place.

The afternoon wore on. Everyone except for Anthony drank too much, Blake got fractious, and the sun started to weaken.

"Oh, we haven't picked any blackberries," Lizzie suddenly exclaimed, jumping up.

Despite his best intentions not to, Ben thought her slightly ridiculous. They were adults, not kids. He was tired and nicely relaxed now he was sitting in a low deckchair, a full can of beer by his side.

Harvey had fallen asleep and so, in hushed whispers the others tried to decide what to do.

"I really need to head on home and pack," Anthony said, a look of mock sadness on his face. "Sorry to break up the party," he added, glancing over at Harvey and smiling at Faith. "Got a flight to Frankfurt in the morning. You coming, Sara?" He asked the question of his wife, but Ben had the feeling that Anthony already knew the answer.

"I quite fancy staying," she said. "If that's OK with you. I haven't picked blackberries in years, and…." She looked up at the sky, which was turning from blue to mauve. "…We've still got about an hour I would think. What do you others reckon? I could get a taxi back."

"That's fine. You stay then," Anthony said, glancing at Faith, who nodded as if giving him permission to go.

Ben couldn't read anything into Anthony's tone; it seemed easy and relaxed, but a tiny muscle was jumping at the corner of Anthony's mouth. *Odd,* thought Ben. *That's very odd.*

Anthony stood up, unrolling his long legs and, bending down, kissed his wife lightly on the head. "See you later then," he said.

Sara tipped her head back to look up at him, her hair falling backwards to reveal the smooth white skin of her throat. Again, Ben felt an uncomfortable heat seep through his bones.

Faith left to show Anthony out. Ben could hear Anthony's car pull away, up the spur until the sound of it faded.

"Why don't I help clear up while Faith puts Blake to bed?" Lizzie suggested.

"I thought *you* wanted to go blackberrying," Ben said to his wife, unable to hide a hint of impatience in his voice.

236

She stretched and yawned in reply. "Oh, it doesn't matter now. I'm actually just as happy to stay here. Frankly, I'm feeling a little worse for wear and don't think I could manage a scramble through the undergrowth. If I fell down, I probably wouldn't want to get up and I'll be lost forever and eaten by wild dogs!"

She laughed at her own joke and tried to give Ben that open-eyed, tilted head look which he'd once told her he thought made her look like a young Felicity Kendall, but it didn't quite work this time and she ended up once again looking just a little bit silly.

"That just leaves us then," Sara said, stretching across and putting the flat of her hand on Ben's knee. "Guess we're on picking duty. What do you think? Shall we risk it?"

"How many do we have to get?" Ben said, feigning unwillingness, whereas inside his heart was thumping at the thought of being alone with her. He wanted to go, and he didn't. He really had no idea what he was doing. He should stay and help Lizzie and pick blackberries another time. Yes, that's what he should do.

Faith came back out from seeing Anthony off carrying four empty plastic ice cream containers. "Do what you can with these?" she said, holding them out to Ben and Sara. "We can divide up the goodies later."

Harvey stirred in his chair and grunted in his sleep. Faith shrugged her shoulders at the others. "Once he goes, he'll be asleep for ages. Best leave him, I guess. I'll cover him up when I've got Blake to bed. He's watching TV at the moment."

She waved as she walked back into the house, her curly hair bobbing as she walked, saying, "I'll be down in a jiffy to help you clear up, Lizzie."

"Don't worry, I like this bit," Lizzie said, as she started to collect the empty beer cans and stack the plates.

"You sure you don't want to come?" Ben asked.

"I'm sure. Look you'd better scoot or you'll lose the light. Don't be long and don't let the wild dogs get you!"

"We won't!" Sara called out happily as she led Ben down the garden to the gate in the fence. "Come on then," she said cheerfully. "Let's get this over and done with."

Once in the wood Sara felt an unaccustomed sense of freedom. It had been ages since she'd done anything like this. Normally her week followed a familiar routine; there was her job at the building society in town, the housework and cooking for Anthony when he was home and the laundry. It was all so perfectly respectable, so measured.

They'd moved out of London to get some peace and quiet and were renting a place nearby while the purchase of 6 Penwood Heights went through but now, now that she had the quiet, she missed going to the theatre and out with friends; she missed the bustle and noise and unpredictability of London. It was stifling here; life with Anthony was stifling, and it was good to be traipsing through the wood with its bracken smell and the sound of the birds shouting, the leaves making tinselly sounds and Ben's footsteps behind her. She could see glimpses of the sky through the leaves, and someone somewhere was having a bonfire; wisps of smoke trailed through in the air, high up out of reach.

There was something about Ben, she thought. He wasn't like the others. There was an air of mystery, an edge to him, and she liked the way his hair curled over his collar and the brown depths of his eyes. It was, she thought, as she stopped by a bramble bush and started plucking the plump fruits, dropping them into the container and watching the juice stains grow on her fingertips, a long time since she'd felt anything so definite as this kind of an attraction. Secretly she was relieved; she'd been beginning to believe that marriage to Anthony was going to blunt her forever.

Anthony was a good man, this much she knew. He was dutiful and conscientious, and he was generous. But he was also slightly boring, and, over the past few months, there had been the odd moment when she'd wondered what her life might be like had she not agreed to see him again after they'd met at that wedding, if she hadn't slept with him, if she hadn't married him.

"How are you doing?" Ben called out from the other side of the bush.

"Not bad, you?"

"Not really my idea of heaven!" he laughed and edged round so that she could see the light material of his shirt through the undergrowth.

"Nor mine!" She was still quite woozy from the wine and her back had started to ache. Suddenly all she wanted to do was to lie down. "I'm going to take a break," she said.

"Already? But we've only been going for a few minutes."

"I know, but I don't care and anyway, no one can see me!"

She kicked off her shoes and lay down in a pile of leaves, gazing up at the canopy above her. It was like lacework, she thought. The branches stirred. It was warm and dry here on the ground and she liked the thought of the leaves in her hair. As a child she'd often wanted to parachute from an airplane, or hike the Grand Canyon and, to a certain extent, lying here abandoning her normal, boring self to the moment, was, she imagined, a bit like doing these things. She stretched her legs out, letting her skirt ride up her thighs. She sighed lazily, closing her eyes and, reaching out, picked a blackberry out of the pot at her side and slipped it into her mouth. A tiny drop of juice collected on her lip, but before she could lick it off, she felt a mouth on hers.

Her eyes flashed open. Ben was kneeling down next to her, his eyes full of a kind of loss. She wanted to mend it, she wanted to mend him. She hooked her hands behind his neck and pulled him down to her.

"You are sure you're OK with this?" he asked.

She nodded. She was more than OK. It felt like she was swimming underwater; everything had slowed, and she was surrounded by heat and darkness. There was no way she could stop now.

The thing is I saw them, Ben and Sara. I saw the rise and fall of their bodies in the leaves. I heard their low moans, their whispered words. I shouldn't have followed them, but something told me to.

I left Blake in the lounge and Harvey asleep in the garden, and calling out to Lizzie that I was going to pop a letter in the post, I slipped into the dark of the wood.

I'd seen the way Ben was looking at Anthony's wife. I'd seen the way she was looking at him. And I knew, oh God, I just knew.

And I thought I knew what I'd do with the knowledge when I had it confirmed. I was full of an intense kind of outrage on behalf of Anthony, my Anthony, and Lizzie, my dear friend Lizzie.

What I didn't know was that I was going to keep what I saw a secret, a secret that was going to consume me until it was too late to do anything about it. I was to come to realise that the damage it would do to the others was mightier, heavier, and more significant than the pain it could ever cause me.

Ben and Sara never spoke of that afternoon again. They never tried to articulate how the fabric of their lives had torn and changed them from the people they had been before they stepped into Faith's back garden, to the people who made love on a carpet of dead leaves, watched, they thought, only by the trees and tiny patches of the darkening sky. Of course, they didn't know then that the six of them would stay together in the months and years that followed; that Ashley, Clemmie and Douggie would all be born and fill their lives.

Maybe they thought they would never see one another again, that Sara wouldn't move into number six, that it was a one-day wonder, one moment of madness. How could they know that they would all eventually be bound by what was to happen five years later? How could they know that every day the lie they carried deep within them would knock against their hearts to remind them it was there?

Hastily pulling down her skirt, Sara clambered to her feet, studiously picking at the blackberry bush until her container was almost full and the sun had started to sink in earnest. She thought she'd heard footsteps in the undergrowth near her but had dismissed them. It was, she told herself, most likely a squirrel tracking through the bracken.

Just once, as they were walking back to the house, did Ben put his hand on the small of her back and she felt the warmth of his fingers, and she turned her head to look at him, imprinting the memory of the moment he'd been in her, and how she'd looked at the very back of his dark brown eyes, etched them on her heart because she knew, even if she saw him again, she just knew it would never happen again.

However, when she found out she was pregnant she also knew that the baby couldn't be Anthony's. It was Ben's. When he'd come shudderingly in her, her legs around his back, she'd felt a drawing in of the core of her that she'd never experienced with Anthony and, sitting on the edge of the bath staring at the pink dot on the tester stick, she swore, she swore that she would never tell either of them the truth.

But then Douggie's death had changed all that and she'd spent a lifetime waiting for the right moment, for the chance to say it out loud, to prove to herself that the afternoon in the woods had actually happened because although he'd so totally gone, it meant that Douggie had been real after all.

Part 8 – Autumn, Nineteen Years Later

Anthony draws back into the shadows of the hallway, leaving Ben and Sara in the kitchen. He can hear the babble of voices from the lounge, Lizzie's light laughs and the beat of the music. He feels dizzy and rests his head against the cool of the wall. What should he do? Part of him wants to creep out of the house, down the drive, against the backdrop of dry leaves rustling and the distant roll of thunder, get into his car, drive away and never come back. His mind is clear at last. Could this, he thinks, explain everything? Is this why he's never felt connected to Sara in the way he should have done, why he's never quite been able to love her completely?

How long has she known that Douggie wasn't his child? How had she let him grieve so hard for someone he actually had no right to, no real need to love so intensely? He remembers the silence which wrapped itself around them both after Douggie's death, and how hard he has fought over the years to break through it and emerge, albeit only half the man he was before, but out in the open, able to breathe at least adequately. He also remembers how Sara has chosen not to but has kept herself locked inside her loss like a willing captive, and it is this distance between them, not just the fact of her colossal betrayal, which causes him to believe that this latest damage he has suffered at her hands is not only irreparable but also a gift.

And then there's Ben. How could he have pretended all these years to be Anthony's friend when, all along, maybe once, maybe many times, he'd fucked Sara, deceiving his own wife, Faith, Harvey, and all their children? Anthony's head is throbbing. There is silence from the kitchen. Mere seconds have passed.

The responsibility of this is huge. *It is me who has the power to shatter the world the six of us have created*, he thinks. One word from me and the whole fucking edifice will tumble down, making a mockery of all we've been through together: all the meals and theatre trips and outings with the kids and the pints and pints of beer I've drunk with Harvey and Ben.

His legs are trembling as though the ground is shifting beneath his feet. Without these things will his life come adrift? Without these anchors from his past, who is he?

"You look like you've seen a ghost," Harvey says popping his head round the lounge door. "And where's that coffee? The brandy glasses. We're gagging in here!"

"No, I'm fine," Anthony lies. "Just coming," and he coughs loudly as he walks into the kitchen.

Ben and Sara are standing on either side of the room, each leaning back against the countertops, and both are looking at their feet. "Harvey's asking after the coffee," Anthony says brightly.

"On its way," Sara replies, her mouth set into a thin line, her shoulders stooping with the effort not to cry. Anthony recognises her each and every move; he's seen them thousands of times before.

Harvey disappears back into the sitting room, and Ben follows him. He doesn't look at Anthony but keeps his head lowered, as though in prayer. Sara holds the tray of coffee and cheeses out in front of her like she's making some sort of sacrifice. She casts a glance at Anthony as she passes him, but he cannot read her expression; her eyes are glittering and furtive, and now he knows the true cause.

He plucks the brandy bowls out of the cupboard by the fridge and slots them upside down in between the fingers on both hands. His arms drop to his sides as he carries them out of the kitchen.

When he joins the others, he bends down, carefully flipping the glasses upright and placing them on the low table in the middle of the lounge. Slowly he straightens his back to stand, looks at his wife as she's pouring coffee from the cafetière into the tiny porcelain cups Faith likes to use on these occasions; Anthony has drunk out of them many times before.

"So," he says. "Douggie wasn't my son after all."

In the minutes and months which follow, each of them in turn, sometimes together, sometimes separately, will wish that Anthony's words could be unspoken. Outside, rain starts to splatter on the windows. Large drops like outstretched hands stick on the glass for a while, then start to tumble. In the distance, there is thunder.

Sara stands, coffee pot in hand. Her eyes flash across the room at Ben and even those who didn't know before know now. "Ben?" she asks, her voice strangled and low.

"Oh my God," Lizzie says in barely more than a whisper. "What do you mean? What's happening?"

Anthony folds himself into a chair; it is as though someone has unpeeled his spine. He puts his head in his hands. No one speaks for a second. Then he raises his head to look at Sara. "Tell them," he says. "Tell them what I heard you tell Ben in the kitchen. How Douggie wasn't mine."

He looks at Ben, a blend of anger and despair in his eyes. The skin on his face seems to have lost all its elasticity.

"For fuck's sake," Ben says. "I never asked to know. Lizzie?"

Faith and Harvey can do nothing but watch as Lizzie rises and goes over to her husband. She puts her hands on his shoulders. "No," she says. "It's not true. Say it's not true."

"I didn't know until now. Just this minute. It was only once, I promise Lizzie, only once," he says, his shoulders twitching as though her hands are hot.

"How could you?" Lizzie turns and spits the words out to Sara, then to Anthony. "How could you?" She grabs Sara's arm. Hot coffee spills. "How could you? All these years. It beggars fucking belief. And you?" Anthony can't look up at her. "Why did you have to say anything? Why now? Oh my God, why?"

"You want to know? Do you all want to know what it's really been like all this time?" Sara stands absolutely still, her hair a black sheen, her eyes full of fury. "Then I'll tell you. Ben's right, it was just once. A mad afternoon of too much wine, being alone, picking those fucking blackberries you wanted, Lizzie, and then I found out I was pregnant and you…" She looks at Lizzie again, her expression unreadable. "You got pregnant soon after too so I vowed I wouldn't let on, let on that my baby couldn't be Anthony's, he just couldn't. All you had to do was to look at Douggie's eyes to know."

I gasp, and all eyes are suddenly on me.

"You knew?" Harvey asks. "Faith, tell me. Did you know?"

So, I tell them, tell them what I saw that afternoon, tell them I've been keeping the knowledge of this ever since. I tell them that as soon as Douggie was born I knew.

"He had Ben's eyes," I say. "Anyone could see that."

"How could you do it, Faith?" my husband asks me, his voice baffled, disappointed, still full of love.

I know we are at a liminal moment.

I don't know how to answer him.

Outside, the storm is raging now, and the September dark is total. The trees behind our houses sound furious in the wind.

Around us is devastation: coffee dripping onto the carpet, guilt and blame seeping through the walls. Our friends are watching us, and I can't believe this is it, this is the sum total of twenty years of friendship. In another part of my brain, I'm wondering how on earth we will get the coffee stains out and then, it seems, I'm gasping for breath as I realise yes, I could have stopped it from happening. If I'd spoken out when I should then we wouldn't be here now – all of us – facing this loss of what we thought we knew about each other, the loss of a child who may not have died had I done things differently.

How many of us think we know our friends, I wonder? We see each other daily, we share our hopes, and our fears; we confide and console, we trust, and we forgive each other's missteps. Are there others who, like the six of us, sit around the dinner table on Saturday nights and eat and drink together, even during lockdown when we did it on screen, thinking they are safe with one another?

I guess so, and yet, and yet, what all this has proved is that there's always that secret place in each and every heart where we hide who we truly are. I know I do.

If I'd ever thought the secret of how I'd betrayed them with Dom, both long ago and more recently in that hotel room in Oxford, was the worst thing about me, this, this is a far greater wrong.

"Harvey?" I say my husband's name as though it's a question. It is. I want his absolution. I want him to forgive me. I want him to tell me how to forgive myself, and I want it all to go away. I want us to be able to go back to the start and undo all this.

Sara carries on speaking as if what has happened in the pause hasn't. She needs to say it, say it all. She can't get her head around Faith's part in this, not yet.

"And then there was living the lie," she says. "It was…" she pauses, searching for the right word. "…Exhausting. It was just exhausting. I never knew we'd stick together, the six of us, never imagined the meals and sharing and all the conversations and I tried, I tried so hard to push it out of my mind. I really did." Her voice trembles. She shakes out her mane of hair, shifts her feet, her stiletto heels digging into the carpet pile.

"And then he died. *Your* children…" Here, with her free hand, she points at Faith and Lizzie. "*Your* children have to be to blame. They do, don't they?" No one answers her. "Without them, he would still be here. Without that bloody picnic, your son Faith, and you." She turns to her husband. "If you'd checked on them earlier…"

She trails off. Harvey springs to his feet. "You can't blame the children," he barks. "It was an accident. All the police interviews, and the evidence, it could only have been an accident. None of them was old enough to know better."

"Then why did you let them take him with them?" Sara curls the fist of one hand and smashes the coffee pot on the table with the other. A crack appears in the glass tabletop, but no one moves.

"Why did *you* let him go Sara, if you were so sure the rest of them couldn't be trusted?" Harvey is standing squarely in front of her now, every nerve end stretched. He swallows hard.

"Don't you think I've asked myself that a thousand times? A million times?" Sara asks. "But it wasn't just me. It was all of you. You and your children. Your children who are still alive, when mine, my child…" She looks over at Ben again. "…Our child," she says and Lizzie flinches as though she's been punched. "Has been so fucking dead for so fucking long."

At last, Ben moves. He goes over to Sara and, motioning for Harvey to stand aside, he comes face to face with her. "How could we have known this is how you felt? You never told us. You never said anything to me, to us." He sweeps his hand out to encompass Lizzie, Anthony, Faith and Harvey. "What gave you the *right* to deny us this? If we'd known, maybe we could have done things differently…"

246

"What things?" Sara laughs savagely. "What could *you* have done? Would you…" Again, she stops mid-sentence. "…Would you have left Lizzie and your daughter for me? Would you have taken us far away so that we wouldn't have been by that river, on that day, and he, my son, my baby, would still be alive? Would you? Would you?" She is poking at Ben's chest with a finger and each stab feels like hot metal through the fabric of his shirt.

Ben doesn't answer straight away.

"Well?" Lizzie asks in a whisper. "Would you? What would you have done, Ben? If you'd known before, would you have gone?"

"How can I answer that?" he replies.

"I think," Lizzie says. "That that you just have. You should have just said 'No', Ben. You should just have said 'No'."

"And you, Faith?" Lizzie continues. She's standing, poised to run. She is fizzing with anger, boiling with rage. "How could you? How could you keep this from me for all these years? Both of you, my husband, my best friend, *you, you* have betrayed me in the worst way possible."

She runs from the room then they hear the front door slam shut. There's a flash of lightning, closely followed by a crack of thunder.

So, this is when doors slam, footsteps run through the dark, I think. But then there is silence. It's like the night has swallowed her whole.

"I have to go after her," Ben says, grabbing his jacket.

"Ben?" The word escapes from Sara's mouth as if unbidden.

"Ben nothing," he says. "You made your choice then when you knew but didn't tell me. Both of you." He looks at me as he says this. "I can't, I just can't," he continues. "I can't do anything now to turn back the clock, undo the things that have happened. The only thing we can do is try to repair the damage. It's my responsibility to help Lizzie to heal and Clemmie too. Just think of the pain she's been carrying, all three of our children have been carrying. Have you ever thought of that? Have you?"

"Let *me* go," I say. "I have to go after her."

And now it's my turn to run. I leave the carnage in my lounge and dash through my hallway. I don't stop to look at my things, our things, mine and Harvey's, all is a blur.

As I reach the front door and step out into the storm, I call her name.

And I'm on the path and we're facing one another. The rain is falling in rods around us, and the wind is howling.

Just three small words; she says them again, "How could you?"

And I have no answer, not here, not now.

I thought I was prepared for this. I'd feared it for years, feared that I would let it happen and now it's here, and I don't know what to say.

And there's more. There's Dom. I know Mum knows I am carrying the burden of a wrong like hers, but I also know she will carry this other secret to her grave because she's all too aware of the damage the truth of such a betrayal can cause. One is more than enough.

Lizzie's still looking at me, hair plastered to her head, and then she starts walking backwards, away from me.

Say something, I tell myself. *Do something*.

At the end of the path, she turns to face her own house.

The moment is passing. *Say something*, I tell myself again.

And that's when I call out to her. "Hey," I say, lifting my voice above the noise of the weather. "What would you have done had it been the other way around? Would you have told me?"

She shrugs and I can't tell from this distance and in this darkness whether they're tears or it's rain on her face, and then she's gone, running again, this time up the path to her front door which opens and closes behind her – an oblong of yellow light – and there's nothing more for me to do than go back into my own house and face the wreckage of the friendships and marriages that awaits me there.

"It's all been make-believe then, hasn't it?" Sara says and it sounds like she's speaking from another room, it is so faint and almost as indecipherable.

The rain is dripping off my clothes as I stand before them and Ben says, "It looks like it has." And he throws his jacket over his shoulders, ready to follow Lizzie home.

Another gust of wind eddies through the trees.

"Come on," Anthony stands and goes over to Sara. He takes hold of her hand. "I'll walk you back," is all he says. Then turning to me adds, "Like Lizzie said, Faith. How could you? How could you lie to us for so long?"

The room is very strange without the rest of them, like an empty stage. I can imagine the smell of the grease paint and feel the left-over heat of the footlights. Suddenly I am very tired.

"I'll start on the clearing up," Harvey says gently. "Shall I?"

I nod, looking at the remnants. I can see the coffee cups, the uneaten cheese, the crack in the glass-topped table, the coffee stain on the carpet and I can feel the fragments of the people I thought I knew; they are jostling in the spaces between the furniture, their voices are echoes, and I know it is my fault as much as Sara's and Ben's.

I am responsible for my sons' grief and Clemmie's. I have been a coward at not facing up to it. Just as I've been a coward with Dom. If I hadn't been so hung up on *my* past, *my* marriage, and *my* children, I would have, should have, spoken out for the greater good. If I hadn't let Dom back into my life, I wouldn't have felt the need to gather everyone around me tonight to remind myself of who I am and maybe this whole thing may never have happened.

If I had challenged Ben and Sara all those years ago, then maybe Douggie would not have died.

I'd once thought that in keeping Ben and Sara's secret I was acting like a paperweight, something which stops the things I value from slipping away but maybe, all along, I've been holding on to nothing but air.

Without her need for reclamation, Sara may not have told Ben, Anthony may not have overheard and all that had happened in the last few minutes would be undone. Surely that would have been better.

But life is messy. However hard we try to keep what we want close, keep our lives on the straight and narrow, and bask in predictability, there is the chaos factor waiting in the wings ready to hurl the unexpected at us, just as it has tonight.

I lean over to the table, pick up a napkin and put it on the carpet. It turns dark as the coffee stain seeps into it, like blotting paper again. It reminds me of blood.

Then I take the napkin into the kitchen, put it down on the counter and rest my head against Harvey's back as he stands by the sink.

"I'm not sure Vanish will get that stain out," I say. "We might need to do something else." He steps aside and I get the canister out. "I'll give it a go anyway," I add.

"Were you ever going to tell me?" Harvey asks, not turning to look at me and his voice is strangely distanced.

"I don't know." I have to answer him truthfully as I tuck the spray under my arm and fold the cloth I'm carrying. As if cleaning the carpet would ever expunge the damage done. "Can't you see what an impossible situation I was in?" I say.

"Not right now, no." Again, his voice sounds like it's coming from a million miles away.

As I make for the door he says, "Faith?"

"Yes." I look at his back, at the creases in his shirt.

"Are there any other secrets you're keeping from me? Any at all? Like why you went to Ireland?" He sounds inexpressibly sad.

This time I can't be truthful. This time I need to lie to him as Mum told me I should. "No, Harvey," I say. "There aren't. I promise you. I really do."

"So not everything we thought we knew about each other is a lie then?" he says, turning to face me at last.

I toy with the lid of the Vanish.

"Not all of it," I say. "Not everything."

Saturday Night/Sunday Morning

In bed, Harvey listens as the storm fades. He imagines it over London, and wonders if there are children who are scared of it. He was right to be wary, he thinks. He was right to fear what may happen tonight; it has obviously been brewing for years, for decades. How would they ever come back from this?

Faith sighs but he knows she's not asleep. For some reason, he can't explain he can't reach out and touch her. He knows he should, but he can't and doesn't try to stop her when she slips out of bed around dawn, goes downstairs and out the back door.

At number six Anthony rests his head on Sara's writing room door. The hems of his jeans are still wet from the dash from Faith and Harvey's. They feel surprisingly cold through his socks. Inside the room, he can hear his wife's fingers typing furiously. *No,* he thinks. *Strike that.* He can hear his wife's furious fingers typing. Although why she should be so cross is a mystery to him. Maybe she's been so angry for so long that it is now a constant state of being, rather than a choice. He is inordinately tired, as though he's just finished a marathon, one he didn't know he was running, but now that it's over, he thinks back in awe and wonders at the effort it's taken, the fierceness of the competition.

He is also very, very relieved. At last, he thinks, he doesn't have to try any more. There is an end to pretence. Yes, he can still mourn the boy he thought was his; but now there is nothing holding him to this place, this woman. The sound of typing stops for a moment, then starts up again. He has no curiosity about what she is doing, even what she is thinking. The enormity of the wrong she has done him is just starting to hit him; he will, he vows never forgive, never ever forget.

Thank God for Frankfurt, he thinks as he closes his eyes, and moves away from the door, his head still spinning, a deep dull ache spreading across his shoulders.

He goes into the guest room, takes off his wet trousers and lies down on the bed but can't sleep. He stays there until just before dawn when, heart racing, he steals into his and Sara's room, pulls on his joggers, trainers and a hoodie and he goes out to the shed, picks up the axe and carries it into the garden.

Sara had not slept in their bed either. He doesn't know where she was.

In the garden, he hacks and hacks until around him is nothing but carnage.

And then there's Faith, wrapped up in a coat, her face lined with worry and exhaustion.

"What are you doing?" she asks.

"What does it look like?"

"Why?"

"Why do you think?"

He's furious: with himself, with all of them, but mostly with her.

"How could you do it?"

"What?" She has her hands thrust deep into her pockets.

"Not told me, about Ben and Sara, that's what. It's your betrayal which seems to hurt the most at the moment."

"Don't say that," her voice is quavering; he can see tears tracking down her cheeks.

"But we were friends," he adds. "*Best* friends. All those years, us as kids, when Douggie died, since then. I *trusted* you. So, I ask again, how could you do it?"

The early morning breeze stirs the wet leaves at his feet. All is still damp and sodden from the storm.

Her voice is a whisper as she says, "It wasn't my secret to tell, Anthony. Surely you can see that?"

"No, I can't see it, not like that, not right now."

"If I could go back," she's still whispering. "I would. Believe me, I would. The last thing I ever wanted was to hurt you."

"But I am hurting; I've been hurting for years."

"I know, and I'm sorry." She takes a step towards him, then another.

He wants to hold her and be held by her, but stands there, too rigid, too unforgiving. "Don't," he says. "Don't come any nearer. Just go. Leave me to this." He points the axe at the fallen branches. "And Faith?"

"Yes."

"If you've lied about this, it makes me wonder if you're keeping anything else from me. Are you?" There is a pause, a deep silence and then he says, "It feels I don't know you at all."

Her shoulders fold into themselves. "No," she says. "There's nothing else, Anthony. You have to believe me."

"Really?"

"Yes, really."

And then she turns away and goes as quietly as she arrived.

Sara had no idea where Anthony was. She thought she heard him come in, and climb the stairs, but then there was a silence, a profound silence, broken only by an indistinct shuffle, a sigh and then silence again. She drafted an email to Suzanne asking for more readings in schools, at last agreeing to do the book signings in Waterstone's that Magda has been on at her for ages to do and when the message had been sent, she clicked on Rightmove and started looking at houses: small, private, terraced houses, somewhere in west London, far away from here, from this space and from the people she has so badly betrayed, who have betrayed her.

She was beginning to understand Faith's part in this. If she'd known all along, couldn't she, shouldn't she, have done something to break the deadlock of those early days of Douggie's life? If she had, then maybe Sara and Anthony would have taken Douggie away and he wouldn't have been at that picnic that afternoon, he wouldn't have...

It was gone two in the morning when she emerged from the room. She padded along the landing, stopping at Douggie's door and going in. There she curled up on his bed and slept more deeply than she'd slept in years. If someone had come and broken down the door of the bedroom, it wouldn't have woken her.

At seven the next morning, she finds his note. He's taken some, but not all of his clothes, but his laptop's gone, together with the photograph of his parents from the sideboard in the dining room and the one of Douggie, aged two, from the lounge. The letter mentions Frankfurt and divorce, but she doesn't want to read it too carefully just now. There will be plenty of time in the weeks to come. The one thing that does really surprise her though is, looking out of the kitchen window, she sees that he has hacked down the Judas tree. Its trunk and branches are on the ground like corpses.

Ben hasn't slept and now it's morning and he sees the day stretch out before him and it makes absolutely no sense to him without Lizzie. He wonders how he could ever have thought otherwise.

When he followed her home last night, she had, he realised, gone straight upstairs, taken off her wet clothes, put on her nightdress and crept under the covers of their bed. She was resolutely facing her bedside cabinet. He sat down on the edge, his shoes damp from the rain. She didn't speak or move, so gingerly he lifted the duvet and slipped in. The bed was already warm. It smelled familiar, like a thousand other nights.

He had no idea whether she was awake or asleep and this surprised him, he thought he should have known. Now, though, he can tell she's awake. It's the small sounds she makes, the involuntary twitching of her feet. He'd woken around dawn to some noises in Sara and Anthony's garden but hadn't got up to investigate, falling back asleep easily, too easily perhaps.

"Lizzie?" His voice sounds odd in the morning quiet of the house. Thank God Clemmie's staying at a friend's overnight he thinks and, although he's whispering, the volume is that of a claxon. "Lizzie?"

She doesn't turn to face him, and this worries him, but she does reverse ever so slightly towards him, her back mirroring the curve of his body. She breathes out.

"Yes?" she says softly.

"What happens next?"

"You make me a cup of tea, that's what happens next," she says. "Like you do every Sunday."

Of all the things she could have said, this is perhaps the one he least expects. In some small corner of his mind, he wonders whether still, she might turn to him, teeth bared and snarling and say, "What the *fuck* were you thinking? How could you?" And in another corner was a tiny flicker of hope that the Lizzie he had known and loved so hard for so long would find her own way to forgive him and therefore show him how to forgive himself. It had been a moment of madness and it's led to a lifetime of regret.

Even now he can't explain it. He remembers the day, the dull thud of frustration behind his ribs, that hot bolt of desire that Sara had stirred in him, and when he'd seen her lying down in the leaves, a white noise had filled his head. It was an invitation but even so, after he'd kissed her, he asked if it was OK, he checked before going any further and she'd pulled him down, she had taken the next step, her hands behind his head. He remembers the pressure of her fingers, the fullness of her lips under his, the need in both of them, the hunger.

Yes, he should have pulled back and, in the many versions of that afternoon he's replayed since, he did.

He really wishes he had, but he also truly believed he would never see her again, that the house purchase would fall through and both she and her husband would disappear from their lives. At the time, he justified what he did with these thoughts.

And it had been wonderful: the release, the savagery of their coupling, the bliss when it was over.

The guilt didn't kick in until later and when it did it was vicious and tenacious. It seemed unable to let him go.

They never spoke of it and for this he was grateful. What he'd done, what they'd done could have unravelled them in the years that followed but they kept it hidden, buried, secret even from themselves. He really thought they'd got away with it.

Now he knows they didn't. What happened has had enormous consequences, consequences he should never be allowed to get away with. But then, but then, one of those consequences had been Douggie and how can he wish he'd never been born? Even if he had died too soon and his death had caused such destruction and heartbreak, he couldn't imagine life without that boy with the brown eyes, the same brown as his father's.

And now he must confront what he's done, seek his wife's forgiveness and do everything he can in the years he has left to make amends, if she will let him.

"Sure," he replies. "Back in a jiffy then." And he gets out of bed, stepping over his own damp and discarded clothes.

Downstairs, the lights are still on, and Lizzie's handbag is on the dresser in the hall next to the pot pigs she bought Clemmie at some school fayre. The pigs are, he notices, facing one another. How long have they been like that, he wonders, puzzled as to who turned them round and when. The thought of Clemmie pulls him up short once again. How will she ever forgive him for what he's done? How will he ever tell her?

In the kitchen, he puts the kettle on and stands and gazes at the garden. He dares not think about what is happening at Anthony and Sara's house, or Harvey and Faith's for that matter. After the tea Lizzie has asked him to make, after she gets up and showers, he has no idea what will happen next in his own home, and the thought terrifies him.

While Ben is making the tea, Lizzie sits up and clutches her knees to her chest. She is sobbing tears of rage and hurt, but also tears of relief. There is so much that could have been different, she knows this now. Instead, she's had Ben and her home and her child for all these years and these are things which she is not going to forfeit. No, she's worked too hard, and loved too long for this to undo her, undo them. She does, she realises, still love Ben and she will protect Clemmie from the truth; she'll have to. Clemmie is still too fragile to cope with anything more than Douggie's death.

How Lizzie feels about Sara is not clear. That may take longer to sort out in her mind. Her betrayal is of quite another kind.

And Faith? What should she do about Faith's part in all this?

She thinks about the question Faith asked her on the path. 'What would you have done had it been the other way around?' She doesn't know the answer to this either.

In between her sobs, she gives thanks that she and Faith had decided to throw caution to the wind and let Dana manage the shop today with the help of a couple of agency girls, at least she doesn't have to worry about the café or face Faith today.

Her crying eases and she listens to the sounds of her husband downstairs.

The noises are the same she's heard a million times before; he's moving from the kitchen to the lounge, he's drawing back the curtains, taking the security chain off the front door, and he's tidying up the scattered newspapers from yesterday. She can hear the rustle of the pages as he slots them into the recycling box in the cupboard by the sink. The bin lid opens and closes and then there are his steps on the stairs.

She finds she is really looking forward to seeing him. They will, she knows, be OK. They have to be. Lizzie has always been a fan of the path of least resistance and believes if ever there was a case for following it, it's now. There is a box into which she can put the past, both the actual past and the 'what if' past, and she has, she tells herself, the strength to close the lid firmly and lock it tight. She owes it to Ben and to Clemmie to do this; she can't face the thought of her life being anything other than it is. This may be cowardly, but it's what she wants and she's going to fight to keep it even if fighting means doing nothing. The alternative is unthinkable.

Ashley is watching Clemmie as she sits in the armchair in his university room. The summer had passed in a blur, the rented room, the gigs, that festival in Prague, more gigs, booze, sleepless nights and here he is, another year.

She's reading a magazine, one she'd borrowed from the salon where she's now working, her head is bent over it and the light from his desk lamp is illuminating her hair. It's no longer scraped back in a savage ponytail, but she's had it cut so that it frames her face and it's feathery and shiny and gold and silvery; she looks like a pixie, he thinks. Since she's had it cut, it seems her eyes have grown larger, her skin softer and, because she's smiling so much more these days, her mouth is relaxed and is able to say generous and kind things. He does, he realises, with a jolt, really love her. He loved her before, of course, but now, now he feels he has had a part in her obvious contentment, and this makes him happy beyond words. Maybe now's the time to say the unsayable?

He looks back at his desk and flicks a page of the book spread out in front of him, but he's not really concentrating. "Clemmie?" he says.

"Mmm?" she lifts her head.

"Can we talk about it?"

"About what?" She unfolds her legs from under her and stretches them. He can see a small hole in the bottom of one of his socks she's wearing.

"About the accident? About Douggie? I mean," he stumbles on, not daring now to look her in the eye. "I mean we've never really discussed it, have we?"

She is very silent, too silent and immediately he regrets saying anything. Just because he needs absolution, it doesn't mean it's fair to expect her to help him achieve it. She's probably got her own demons to fight anyway.

After a long gap, in which Clemmie carefully folds up the magazine and puts it on the floor next to the empty plate on which he'd put the sandwich he'd made her earlier, she says, "No, we haven't talked about it. Not you, not me, not Blake. I've sat in those fucking stupid counselling sessions with Mum, without Mum, fucking pigeons swaggering around the counsellor's fucking garden and the stupid posters on her walls, and not once have I been brave enough to say, 'It was my fault he died', when that's all I've ever thought, ever since. I even thought…"

"Yes?" Ashley says gently, getting up from his chair and moving across the room to sit at her feet. He leans his back up against her legs. Warmth spreads through him as the seconds tick by.

"I even thought not eating would help," she says. "I thought it would be some kind of punishment. It gave me that element of control I never seemed to have in my life, not since I'd put together the puzzle pieces of that day. It took years, didn't it?"

"What did?"

"To understand fully. To remember every tiny detail. The picnic, the heat, the water. Blake daring us like he always did in those days. Us not stopping Douggie from jumping."

"We were only five, how could we?"

"I know that with one part of my mind," she says, reaching down and weaving her fingers through the soft hairs at the back of his neck. A shiver runs through him. "But with the other part, the part that looks at it with an adult's point of view," she continues, "I can see so clearly that we should have saved him."

"Don't forget the code," Ashley says.

"What code?"

"The Mockingbird code. Remember when we did the book at school and there's that bit when Dill's trying to get Jem to go up to the Radley porch?"

"Yes," she says uncertainly.

"And it says that Jem had never declined a dare. Well, we have to remember, we were just kids. We lived by the kids' code, by the Mockingbird code."

"That makes sense, kind of," Clemmie says. "The whole Mockingbird image. Douggie never hurt anyone either."

Ashley turns around so that he's kneeling in front of her, and he cups her face in his hands. "I know what you mean," he says. "I've felt the same way for years. You know the adult's versus the child's verdict. For years, I couldn't sleep, kept seeing the scene over and over and over again whenever I closed my eyes, but now, now I'm getting better at shutting it out. It was an accident, that's what I have to keep telling myself. It could have been me, or you, who made that first jump after Blake. No one intended for Douggie to get hurt, so it has to have been an accident. Doesn't it?"

Clemmie is crying; huge dry sobs are shaking her shoulders and Ashley holds on to her tightly; it is like trying to comfort an earthquake, he thinks. Eventually he can feel her nodding. Like she is beating a rhythm to music, she is pulsing with some sort of reparation, or at least that's what Ashley hopes.

"Why didn't we talk about it years ago? Why didn't our parents?" Clemmie asks, her mouth pressed up against the wool of his sweater so that her words are indistinct and muffled.

"We weren't ready, I guess," he says into her hair. "Nor were they. Don't you think we've all been blaming ourselves and each other all along?" he asks, suddenly aware of how true this is, how much he needs to see his brother, tell him these things, tell him it doesn't matter, that where Douggie is concerned at least, grief has to be able to exist without blame.

The two of them sit there for a long time. Outside, students shuffle along the pathways outside the block of flats where Ashley has his room and there's the occasional shout and the slam of a door. A car revs its engine and there is laughter.

"Do you think we should tell them about us now?" Clemmie asks at length.

"Yes," Ashley replies. "I think it's time we did."

In Cheltenham, Blake is staring at his laptop screen. On it is his paper on William Blake. Funny how it seemed so important and now that's he passed his degree and started on his PCGE course, he's moving on again, is putting what happened to Douggie further and further behind him. And Gabs too.

It's been weeks since he's heard from her. In fact, he hasn't since that last text when he'd said, 'Sorry. Busy. Catch you sometime maybe', and because he's taken himself out of her orbit, there's been no more midnight visits, no evening fucks and, whilst he misses her, he is also relieved beyond measure. He hears of her sometimes from his friends who say things like, "Saw Gabs in a club last night. She looked OK. Had some new bloke in tow." Or "Gabs was in Tesco's on Tuesday, buying milk. She looked wrecked but said hello."

Blake would want to ask whether she'd asked after him, but never had the courage, fearing both a yes and a no. So now she's mostly gone from his life, he is concentrating hard on his course, phoning home on Sunday nights, exchanging brief texts with Ashley every so often and trying to believe that he will meet someone new, someone good, someone who will help him make sense of what happened.

He still struggles with the memories. In his head there are two versions. There's the one where he says, "Go on Douggie, jump." And the other where he doesn't. In the second version he clambers back down, crosses the stream, joins the others and all four of them scamper back to the picnic, their parents and a whole alternate universe is created where Douggie grows up, they all stay mates, and he doesn't have to live with this fucking awful weight in his chest.

Occasionally, he lets himself fantasize about this second scenario, but he's always pulled back to the first one, to the skein of blood in the water and still he struggles to forgive himself for moving Douggie's body, or for not moving it soon enough. If he hadn't done the former, might he have been saved? If he'd done the latter…

He also tries to forgive his parents for not letting him go to the funeral to say goodbye. They should have let him go, they really should.

He shuts the lid of his laptop, stands and stretches. Maybe he'll go for a run, that should clear his head. As he bends down to pick up his trainers from beside the bed, the doorbell rings. He waits for someone else in the building to get it, but no one does.

The person then knocks at the door. "OK, I'm coming," he shouts as he thunders down the stairs. This place is certainly less shitty than his previous one, but the other tenants seem just as lazy.

He opens the door. "My God," he says to Ashley. "What are you doing here? It's not Mum or Dad, is it? They're OK, aren't they?"

"No, it's not about them," Ashley says, grinning at him. "Just thought we'd swing by and see you."

"We?" Blake asks, leaning up against the doorframe.

"Hi," says Clemmie. "By we, he means him and me."

"Oh my God. You can't just swing by, it's miles from Birmingham to here! Not that it's not great to see you both. Come in. Bloody hell, come in."

Ashley steps back to let Clemmie enter and she wanders off down the corridor.

Then Ashley says, "We've come to tell you something. It's time we talked about things, about me, Clemmie, about me and Clemmie and about you and about Douggie. It's time, isn't it, Blake?"

"It sure is," Blake says, taking his brother's hand and pulling him inside. They stand there awkwardly for a second until Ashley opens his arms and Blake moves cautiously towards him, letting his head rest on his brother's shoulder. Two heads; one light, one dark. Two men; one slender, one tall and broad. In need of forgiveness.

"It's OK," Ashley says. "It's going to be OK."

There's something about the sea that always reminds Dom of his childhood. It makes him remember beach hut holidays with his parents, and Calor gas stoves, and windbreaks, and popping the bladder sacs on strings of seaweed with his small boy fingers. He remembers sand between his toes and in the bottom of his sleeping bag and swimming in the rain with his father; a man he'd never really got to know very well and who had died when Dom was nineteen. He'd already been angry about many things at the time, and his father's death just made everything so much worse. Maybe that was why he'd been so driven, had set up the practice in the 80s, had married so unwisely. Whatever the cause, the one thing he can never deny though is the fact of his children and now, even more especially, his grandchildren. Now he's more reconciled with his daughter and has had faltering conversations on the phone with his son, he actually feels more blessed than he has done in years.

In some ways, he thinks as he pats the bottom of a bucket filled with damp sand with a bright red spade and glances across at his three-year-old grandson's fierce look of concentration, this weekend in Cornwall is doing more to help him get over the fact that he's lost Faith for a second time than all of the preceding weeks of sitting in front of a blank sheet of paper and staring at the screen on his phone. Here, with a low sun on his back and the salty tang of a sea wind on his face, he can finally see his way forward.

His daughter, wrapped in a blanket, is dozing in a deckchair and her husband is chasing the wavelets at the edge of the sea with their daughter. Their joint belongings are scattered on and around spread-out towels. There are discarded shoes, gloves, and an as yet unopened picnic hamper. No one looking in from the outside would guess at the journey he's taken to be here.

"Hurry up, Gramps," his grandson says from his position squatting seriously on the other side of the moat they've already dug. "The baddies are coming, and we need our castle!"

"I'm hurrying!" Dom says, patting the bucket more emphatically. His knees are aching from kneeling on the sand and the bottoms of his trousers are fringed with water, but he doesn't care. He knows that Faith's not going to call, and he doesn't blame her; he wishes her well and he will try and come to terms with the fact that whatever she had felt for him once wasn't enough to make her leave what she's got now. Maybe now he'll even learn to let go of the 'what might have been' that have peppered his life since her and move on. Maybe he'll even meet someone else, someone who will help blur the edges of his residual pain. What had started out as no more than a fling for him had developed into something which had changed his life. But he wouldn't have had it any other way. He knows that now. Maybe he knew it all along. After all, it's what we live through that makes us who we are. He will finally really give up on the sketch of her, stop trying to mix the colour of her eyes with his paints and he'll concentrate on his family, his cottage, his roses and perhaps he'll start experimenting with oils or pastels. There's a lot more he still can try.

"There!" he says, as he turns the bucket over and starts to lift it. A perfect sandcastle appears. His grandson's laughter fills the beach and a young couple sitting on a blanket nearby look up at him and smile.

Monday

Waiting in line to check in at Terminal 4, Anthony has the mad desire to spin himself around and around, fast enough to make him dizzy, like he used to do as a child. Then he'd count how many times he could rotate before falling over. It was something he did when he felt especially giddy, when his head didn't feel attached to his body. That's pretty much how he feels now.

He spent Sunday at the Soho Hotel making calls and sending emails to fix a series of meetings in Frankfurt for the coming week. The relocation deal he's been offered is very generous and, even if he hadn't found out what Sara had done, he would have been very tempted to take it. But now it's a no-brainer.

The flight leaves at noon and he's flying business class; all he's taking is a carry-on case, the rest of his stuff can stay in the hotel storage facility until he returns on Friday and the rest of it, all the clutter of his marriage, well that can go to hell. He'll set up a Zoom call with his solicitor to start the divorce proceedings and, of course, he'll be generous. He doesn't need much to start again with; the less the better actually.

His phone buzzes. It's a text from Faith, just their three letters: 'TOY', it says. Strangely, Faith's the person he'll miss most; she's been like the ballast in his life for so long that being overseas without her will be odd, even if it feels that her betrayal is almost as bad as his wife's.

But maybe it's what he needs, this severing from his past, the things that kept him tied down. Anyway, she can visit him in time. She and Harvey can come over and stay; he can take them to the museums and galleries and restaurants. Yes, it'll be good to have them to stay. Maybe Faith'll even come over on her own, and they will be able to talk, really talk. Maybe.

The queue shuffles forward; a pretty blonde in a short black lacy dress, denim jacket and cowboy boots turns around from a few places in front of him. They lock eyes. She smiles and Anthony smiles back. Her legs are long and firm and tanned; she'd be late twenties he thinks. Something stirs in him; it's a feeling he hasn't felt for a very long time. Again, he wants to spin round very fast with his arms spread out wide and his eyes tightly shut.

Sara's really enjoying labelling the furniture; yellow stickers for the sale room, pink for the removers, green for the thrift shop. Obviously, she hasn't heard officially from Anthony's solicitor yet, but she knows the letter is coming and she knows he won't really care what she does with the stuff.

There is an immense sense of relief knowing that he doesn't care anymore; being responsible for his unhappiness was such a burden. Now all she has to worry about is herself. Yes, she'll miss Faith and Lizzie and the balance the three of them managed to maintain despite everything. But she'd always known it was a lie; knew she would be found out one day. She's also relieved that that's over and done with too. There's no need to dread its coming; it's here and she's dealing with it.

Peeling off another label, she moves from the lounge to the dining room. Already she's imagining arranging the furniture she's decided to keep in the small back room of the small house she'll most likely buy. There'll be a garden which she'll make pretty with tubs and variegated shrubs, and she'll have a wind chime by the back door and a shelf for the books she's written in the lounge next to the fireplace and maybe someone will come and visit her there, a new friend, someone who never knew Douggie, or Anthony, or the others, and they'll drink herbal tea and eat warm scones fresh from the oven. There'll be no Rachel the cleaner in her new house either. Each week she'll do the cleaning and laundry on Saturday mornings and will be much happier in a smaller house, one that's totally hers. She'll also write; each day she'll write in the mornings, take a light lunch and go out in the afternoon in a small easy-to-park car, a Mini maybe or a Fiat 500, and do readings at libraries and schools, or visit her publishers, and have meetings with her illustrator. There'll be new clothes too; clothes in shades other than black, loose flowing tops and combat trousers and she'll let her hair curl, or even get it cut and have highlights put in it, in coppers and soft browns. All this she'll do to assuage the past, to vindicate the choice she made when she decided to tell Ben the truth, knowing as she did, that Anthony was there just outside the kitchen door, listening.

She's decided not to confront Faith and daren't see Lizzie. It will be easier to let go if she does neither of these things.

What she'll do with Douggie's room, however, she's not sure. Part of her wants to move it in its entirety to the new house, to replicate the shrine. But another part of her wants to box it up, give the toys and clothes away, store just a few keepsakes and let the memories rest at last.

Sticking a pink label on the dining table, she stands with her hands resting on the back of one of the chairs and gazes out of the window at the felled Judas tree. She must get around to calling the tree surgeons and have them come and put it through their shredding machine. Maybe they'll even spread the bark chippings on the flower beds for her if she asks nicely. The large flat hand-sized leaves, she notices, are already starting to die off.

She moves on from the dining room into the kitchen and opens a cupboard door and surveys its contents. The dinner service they were given as their wedding present lurks on the shelves. Taking a yellow sticker, she presses it gently onto a teacup.

The tube is stuffy, and Harvey's forgotten to do what the posters say and bring a bottle of water with him. He's annoyed with himself for this and shifts uncomfortably from one foot to another. Only three stops to go to Canary Wharf. The Jubilee train whines and wheezes and he wonders how today's meeting will go. More than this, however, he wonders how he and Ben will be with one another. He hasn't spoken to Faith about it, but since it happened, he's been batting the thought back and forth in his mind that maybe he and Ben should dissolve the partnership and move on. Then, halfway through the night he'd awoken just knowing this would be the wrong thing to do; they'd come too far, worked too hard to give up on it now. In some ways, he thought as he stared out in the darkness listening to Faith's steady breathing, his partnership with Ben was also a bit like a marriage and he ought to fight to keep it alive.

The train lurches to a stop and he steps out onto the stainless-steel concourse. He takes the escalator up, taps his card onto the reader, and then up the other escalators under the archway and into the plaza. He's meeting Ben at a coffee shop by the clocks; it's what they'd agreed on

Friday, before Faith's dinner party, before the revelations, before the coffee stain on the carpet in their lounge which Faith has already booked a cleaning company to come and tackle.

Ben's there, nervously looking around and tapping a spoon against his coffee cup. In front of him is a laptop containing, Harvey knows, the tenders they've come to discuss with the client. It's almost as though Saturday night hadn't happened; perhaps it would be best to pretend that it hadn't?

"Watcha," he says as he approaches Ben's table.

"Hi," Ben replies, immediately looking down and moving his phone around in an effort to look preoccupied.

"Top up?" Harvey asks, signalling to a waiter.

"Sure," Ben says. "I'll take an espresso."

"Think we both need one," Harvey says grinning. "Got quite a few cobwebs to clear away this morning."

Ben glances up, shielding his eyes from the glare of the sun with the flat of his hand.

"It was some night on Saturday, wasn't it?" Harvey says, putting his document case on the table and sitting down opposite Ben.

"It sure was."

"How's Lizzie?"

"It's odd, but she's carrying on as if nothing happened. We haven't really talked about it. In a way I wish she would bring it up, but on the other hand, I'm just grateful for the chance to keep going."

This is what Harvey hoped Ben would say. When he'd thought about Ben and Lizzie as dawn had crept through the gap in the curtains that morning, he'd fervently hoped that they would find a way to work round this and that the four of them could carry on as before, like they were in the old days before Faith introduced them to Sara and Anthony. Friday nights will be different without Anthony but, being selfish, he just isn't ready for a fundamental shift in his life just now. He still feels he has so much more to do with both of them as his friends, and with Clemmie too, and with Faith and the boys. He needs to focus on Faith now too. Whatever she's done, he needs to give her space to come to terms with it.

One day perhaps it'll be as though her escape to Ireland never happened. One day enough time will have passed for her to forgive herself for keeping the knowledge of what Ben and Sara had done to herself. But then, you never really know someone until you step into their shoes, he muses as he surveys the plaza, the sun bouncing off the thousands of windows, at the bustle of people and distant hum of London and takes a sip of the bitter liquid. It burns his tongue and sends a bolt of adrenalin through him.

He is truly grateful for what he's got, wonders how he could ever have wondered whether it was enough, and vows to keep hold of it tightly, to show Faith more obviously how much he loves her, has always loved her, how much he knows she has sacrificed for him and the others, and finally how hard he knows it is for her now the boys have moved out.

"God, that's good," he says, smiling across at Ben.

"What, about Lizzie?"

"I meant the coffee, but it's good about Lizzie too!" he says, laughing a little haltingly.

"And we're OK, I mean, us, the business and everything?" Ben asks, picking up a page from in front of him and waving it in front of Harvey.

"Sure, we are, you soft sod. Now, come on, let's go through these proposals once more and check our recommendation's the right one. You know that Rob guy can be a real arse sometimes."

It feels as though a bridge has been crossed; a rickety, broken bridge made with slats of worn wood held together with pieces of string and the odd nail. But both men are safely on the other side now and, as they study spreadsheets and sip their espressos, Harvey can't help but look up now and again at what might have been on the far side of where they've just travelled from and give thanks for his and Ben's safe passage. It is, he realises, only when you risk losing something do you understand just how much it means.

"I am sorry," Ben says, as they start to clear away the paperwork as the time of the meeting approaches.

"I know," Harvey replies.

There's a flicker of a pause. Then Ben says, "He was *my* son, Harvey. *My* son."

"I know that too, mate," Harvey replies, placing a hand on Ben's shoulder. He wishes so badly that he could help heal the wound. "Come on," he says. "Let's get this bloody meeting over and done with and then perhaps we can have a pint at lunchtime."

"That sure sounds good to me." Ben smiles as he says this.

They pass under the clocks and make their way across to the other side of the square. Harvey looks up and sees a plane, silver against the intense blue of the sky. He thinks about Anthony and says to himself that he'll call him when he gets home tonight. 'Yes, that's a good idea'; he'll call him and see how he's doing, see whether this whole Germany thing's going to go ahead. A move'll probably be the best thing he can do now, won't it?

When they reach the vast rotating doors of their client's offices, Harvey lets Ben go in before him and then he follows him in. He's looking forward to this meeting, to getting the job going. The receptionist looks at both of them and smiles. Her teeth are exceptionally white, Harvey notices.

The light in the foyer is blinding and Ben stumbles as he crosses the polished floor. Harvey reaches out a hand to steady him.

He feels lighter since he'd said the words, 'He was *my* son, Harvey. *My* son'. But he also feels heavier, burdened by this new knowledge that it will take him years to assimilate, to accept. He thought he knew what grief was like, but this is a totally new kind, this grief for a boy he never knew was his.

Today, as I open up the shop I'm filled with a sense of dread. The thought of seeing Lizzie sits in my chest like an unexploded firework.

I think back to the me of before, for whom this was my favourite time of day, and almost pity me my naivety.

There's been no word from Lizzie. I waited all day yesterday, kept looking out of the lounge window hoping to see her familiar figure coming up my path, the path we'd stood on in the rain on Saturday night and said what we said to one another.

But she didn't come. I don't even know if she'll come today.

I go through the motions of setting up the shop, but I don't turn the 'Closed' sign to 'Open', not yet. It seems to be tempting fate to do so.

And then I hear the rumble of a car engine out the back and hurry through to open the service door.

And there is Lizzie's car and she's stepping out of it, and I watch as she goes to open the boot and pull out the trays of cakes and bread from the bakery.

I can't speak. I don't know what to say.

She doesn't look at me as she walks past.

We work in silence, and I dread Dana's arrival and the need to explain to her why Lizzie and I aren't talking to one another.

The minutes tick by; the air in the shop is getting heavier and heavier.

At last, I summon up the courage to say her name. "Lizzie?"

She stops what she's doing and rests her hand on the counter and, taking a deep breath, looks at me, her face ravaged with sadness.

"I love Ben," she says. "I truly do."

"I know you do," I reply.

"I'm going to stay with him."

"I'm glad."

"Are you and Harvey OK?"

I can't read her tone. You'd think I'd be able to, but right now she's an enigma to me. "Yes," I say. "We'll be all right, I think."

"I'm glad."

There is more silence, more heaviness of moments passing.

Then eventually she says, "You asked me, on Saturday night, what I'd have done if things had been the other way around. If it had been Harvey who'd betrayed, you. Would I have told you? Could I have done?"

"Yes?"

"Let me finish."

"OK, sorry."

"…Truth is, I don't know, Faith. I really don't. Part of me is furious with you for keeping this from me, but another part, the better part maybe, can understand how difficult it must have been for you. What they did was wrong, but there's no black and white here, is there? I have to forgive Ben otherwise I couldn't carry on living with him, and I need to live with him for Clemmie's sake, and my own, and his. We are a unit. We've become a unit."

"I know what you mean," I say. "I really do."

"But how can I forgive you? I don't know how I'm going to do that."

I go over to her and put my arms around her. She seems so fragile, and she is, I realise, trembling.

"We're a unit too, aren't we?" I tell her. "I did it to protect you; the last thing in the world I wanted was for anyone to get hurt. It was an impossible situation," I continue. "It still is. All I've ever wanted is to protect those I love from pain, but I failed, didn't I?"

"We've all failed in one way or another," Lizzie replies, her voice muffled against my apron. "It's a condition of being human, I guess," she says. "We all make mistakes."

And, right there, right then, I think that my dear friend can't know how true her words are.

"You're right," I say. "There have been so many wrongs in amongst so much love. Another part of being human, I guess."

I let my arms drop so I'm not holding her anymore and she turns and leans against me, still trembling, still, I believe, my friend, although I know it's going to take time and patience and so very much love for us to be at ease with one another again.

"Shall I turn the sign to 'Open'?" I ask.

She moves away from me and says, "OK. I guess you should. Another day, another dollar, eh?"

Thursday

We've been quiet with each other all week. Both Harvey and I, and myself with Lizzie and Ben. But it's been the quietness of healing, or so I hope.

Not so with Sara though. I didn't feel I could face her and knew this was cowardly, but justified my behaviour with the thought that she wouldn't want to see me either. I did, however, put a card through her door and in it I told her that I was around if she wanted to talk but would understand if she didn't. I was hugely relieved when day after day went by, and she didn't call or message.

It is a huge shame that it's ended this way, but in my more rational moments, I realise there were always going to be casualties. I guess I should be relieved we've managed to limit the damage as much as we have.

Lizzie and I are in the kitchen of the shop. In the distance is the hum of early morning customers and the peal of Dana's laughter.

"Can you cut more lettuce?" Lizzie asks.

"Happy to."

As I'm chopping the iceberg lettuce into shreds, Lizzie asks, "Heard from the boys?"

"Yes. They've both said they're planning on coming home for the weekend."

"That'll be nice."

"It will, it really will. I feel I haven't seen them in ages."

Another pause.

"How's Clemmie?" I ask. "What are you going to tell her?"

"Nothing. She's really well at the moment; she's eating and has put on a bit of weight and, as you know, she's had her hair cut. I think she's started seeing someone. She seems really happy and I daren't upset the balance right now. Maybe one day, but not now. Definitely not now. She's asked if we can have a family dinner next Saturday," Lizzie adds after a brief moment of silence. "Says she's bringing a friend and would that be all right."

"Sounds interesting."

"Does, doesn't it!"

"Actually," I say, picking up a fistful of grated cheese in my gloved hand. "Ashley said he wouldn't be in for dinner on Saturday and would that be OK. Odd that isn't it?"

We look at one another and smile tentatively, cautiously.

"It's about bloody time too," Lizzie says, grinning widely. "At last." It's the first time she's done so since Saturday. "Fancy joining us for dinner then," she adds. "You and Harvey?"

"Wild horses wouldn't keep me away," I reply.

I incline my head towards Lizzie's shoulder and Lizzie bends so that her cheek is resting against the top of my head.

"That's OK then," she says. Then, "I've come to realise something," she continues.

"What's that?"

"It wasn't your secret to tell, was it?"

Not about Ben and Sara, I think. *But about Dom? Yes, that is my secret to tell and is still my burden, still mine alone.* "No, it wasn't," I reply. "Thank you for saying that; it means a lot." And, I think, I must trust Harvey, know him better. He deserves that. He deserves a better kind of love from me too, and I resolve to give this to him. Man of mystery no longer, my husband is, I realise, the other half, the better half of me and I can't risk showing him the underbelly of need and guilt, like I did that day in the kitchen when I railed against being watched. The thing about leaving – in any form – is that at some point you have to return.

It's nearly ten-thirty and Mr Brown will be in shortly for his flapjack and coffee, so I start to wrap the sandwiches in their packaging, put my glasses on and write today's date on them.

"Shall we get that Nic guy to give us some more paintings to sell?" Lizzie asks as she sweeps a cloth over the countertop, corralling the heaps of crumbs. "They went down well before, didn't they?"

I falter and the pen slips, crashing to the floor where its plastic casing shatters.

"Sod it," I say, bending down to pick it up. Once upright, I look over at Lizzie and say, "No, I don't think so. I think I've grown out of his work. We could try someone else. How about we go to the library after the lunch rush? There's that art exhibition on. We can see if there's anyone else who we like. We could go to Oxfam too and take some of our books from the book swap shelf and see if they'll swap. What do you think?"

And, I say, pausing. "We should go to the cinema soon. We haven't been for a while, have we?"

"No, we haven't," says Lizzie. "But that all sounds like a plan and, about the art, if you're sure that is. I know he said he'd be happy to come back."

"Who did?"

"That Nic guy I was talking about."

"No, Lizzie. Let's just leave it as is, shall we? There's no point trying to go back and recreate something that's gone, is there? Nothing lasts forever after all."

"I guess not," Lizzie says.

Later, plucking my phone out of my apron pocket, I send Anthony another text. 'TOY', it says again.

Saturday

Clemmie, Ashley and Blake are sitting at the dinner table. Faith and Harvey are there but Sara and Anthony aren't. Mum's told Clemmie that Sara and Anthony are splitting up.

"They were carrying too much grief in the end," she'd said.

But Clemmie has the feeling there's more to it than that. And her mum and dad are being weird with one another too, looking at each other and then looking away, treading carefully around one another as if afraid the other might explode if touched. She's not seen them like this before.

And Faith and Harvey are on edge too. It's like there's some huge bubble of knowledge waiting to burst, but Clemmie will bide her time, all will be revealed some day she's sure and anyway, she has more important things on her mind right now.

"All we want is for you to be happy," her mum had said. "Me and your dad, that's our main priority."

Clemmie smiles at Blake, who smiles back, and then she looks at Ashley who's sitting beside her. He's telling his parents about his band's new record deal, and he reaches out and takes her under the table. His touch makes her skin fizz. *Yes,* she thinks, *I am happy. At last.*

She'll get her mum to put away those blasted pot pigs and picks up her fork with her free hand, scooping a mouthful of mashed potato and eating it with relish. She is, she realises, famished.

Part 9 – Winter

I eventually rang Dom halfway through October, when the leaves had turned, and the skies were leaden. Enough time had, I thought, gone by for us both to have some perspective over what happened that summer day in the hotel in Oxford.

I had thought I wouldn't need to call him, but as time went by, I realised I did. It wasn't fair, or nice of me not to.

"Hello, stranger," he said when he picked up.

It was then I choked and found that tears were streaming down my face.

I was standing by the water again, on my way to work, but no one paid me any mind. My own tragedy was just that, mine.

And Dom's of course.

"I'm sorry," I said after a while as the line hummed between us.

"I know you are," he replied. "And I'm sorry too, for last time, for not being who or what you needed me to be at the time."

"And now it's my turn," I said. "My turn to disappoint you."

"It's OK, it really is." Then he added, "Well, no, it's not OK, but there's nothing we can do about it, not now. Our timing always was off, wasn't it, Faith. But at least now we have closure, eh? Like in the movies…"

His voice tailed off and I had to gulp to get more air into my lungs. The tears were still falling.

"Don't cry," he said.

"I'm not."

"Yes, you are."

"Yes, I am."

There was a pause and then he said, "Take care of yourself, Faith. Always, OK?"

"And you," I replied. "And you."

And then I hung up and it was over, it was finally all over. We had said the goodbye I'd imagined we would never have to say.

And now Anthony is back in London, briefly. He will be returning to Frankfurt in the morning.

"It was my idea. I want to do something," I said. "To help us all heal."

Anthony hadn't been sure, but then he rang and told me he'd got used to the idea, that there was a kind of symmetry to it. Another form of closure, I thought. "And it'll be a chance for us to be together again," he said. "For me to see you too, Faith."

Sara had said she wouldn't come, and this didn't surprise me. In fact, I think we were all relieved. Anthony had told us she'd moved to Winchester in the end and had a new book coming out in the spring.

And so, we've gathered, the five of us, around Douggie's grave and we are each carrying a posy of snowdrops, tiny flowers for a tiny life.

It's cold, clear and cold, the sky almost translucent and the bare branches of the trees like ink against it. Around us is the purr of traffic, diesel from the buses hanging in the air. It will be dusk soon. The church is already a dark mass in the background, its windows unlit, its bells silent.

We don't talk much, there's not a lot to say. Just being there is enough. Ben cries, so does Lizzie, and Anthony stands, pale and grim-faced. I am holding Harvey's gloved hand. I feel the warmth of his body seep into mine and hope mine is doing likewise for him.

This is, I think, a necessary act. A tragic one, but one that will do us all good.

Afterwards we go our separate ways. I'd suggested a drink at the pub, but no one else had wanted to do that, so we get into our cars and drive away – a convoy like, but very different to, the one the day of the picnic all those years ago.

As we pull out of the car park, I can't resist looking back at the grave of the son who was Ben's but wasn't, who was Anthony's but wasn't, and it's then I see a slim figure step out from the shadow of a yew tree and lay her own flowers down alongside ours.

Epilogue

And then there's the version of this when, in the before, I confront Ben and Sara and they tell me it will never happen again, they promise me this.

And, in this other version, Sara comes to me when Douggie is born and says, "What should I do?"

And I say, "Leave. You must take him and Anthony away from here. You must protect them both."

And I know that by saying this I am protecting Lizzie and Ben, and Harvey, and me too. How I square away my role in deceiving Ben and Anthony as to Douggie's true parentage I don't really know. What I do know is that this is the lesser wrong. By doing this, the people I love stay safe, undamaged.

And so, they go. Sara tells Anthony she wants to go back to the city and, because he loves her, he agrees. They take Douggie away and a new family move in next door. We get to know them as passing friends; I am wary now of getting involved.

And I keep in touch with Anthony over the years and Douggie gets to know us as Aunt Faith and Uncle Harvey. We send birthday and Christmas presents. We rarely see them, and our friendship with Sara peters out.

And so, the six of us don't go for picnics in the high heat of that particular summer when Douggie is five, Blake doesn't dare him to jump, and Douggie grows up into the man he should have been, and Blake, Ashley and Clemmie live lives unblemished by guilt, as do we all.

And I see pictures of Douggie at his wedding.

I see him cradle his children.

I see all this.

And I see Clemmie's open smiling face, her girlhood curves, her huge heart – all possible because she hasn't been bowed down by grief.

And I see my sons growing into men who give themselves permission to swagger now and then, who take risks with love and life and who become the people they should have been all along.

I see my husband and Ben and Lizzie living alongside one another affably without the guillotine of the secret I was keeping hanging over us.

And when Nic Bradley comes into my shop, I am brave enough, strong enough, kind enough to let the past rest where it should. Because Douggie didn't die, I don't need the solace I believe only revisiting my past, only finishing what I thought unfinished, could provide and he, Nic/Dom, moves on, finds someone who is not me and he too is happy.

In this other version of us, what we thought we knew about each other remains as it should. We live our best lives with one another, nothing needs undoing. We do what is right and, however hard this proves to be, it is the better option, it is the only option.

And I am like a paperweight, a real one, heavy, made of something solid and, in this other version of us, I never have to ask the question what would you do if what you thought you knew about your friends was only a fragment of the truth, what would you do if you knew your best friend's husband had a child with your other best friend's wife, and that child died?

No, in this version of us, I am able hold my life in place, stop the best bits of me, of all of us, from blowing away, and there is no tiny grave for us to stand around on a chill winter day, no name etched on its headstone, no one watching the five of us from the shadow of a yew tree laying flowers on the frost-bitten ground, no one leaving her own tribute there after we've gone; the petals already curling in the sharp, cold air.